CHLOE C. PEÑARANDA is the *New [York]*
bestselling author of the *Nytefall* trilogy a[nd]
lifelong avid reader and writer, Chloe disc[overed]
in her early teens. Her stories have been
fictional characters and exploring Tolkien-like quests in made up worlds.
During her time at the University of the West of Scotland, Chloe immersed
herself in writing for short film, producing animations, and spending class
time dreaming of far off lands. In her spare time from writing in her home
in scenic Scotland, Chloe enjoys digital art, graphic design, and down time
with her three little dogs. When the real world calls . . . she rarely listens.

www.ccpenaranda.com
Instagram: @chloecpenaranda

Praise for The Nytefall Series:

'With a forbidden romance to die for, a complex world, and plot twists
galore, *The Stars Are Dying* is a gripping story about a woman learning
to trust herself and a man who can't always be trusted-and the tension
between them, which was thick enough to slice with a knife.'
Genoveva Dimova, author of *Foul Days*

'A spell-binding start to the series, The *Stars are Dying* combines
celestial magic and vampires with an unforgettable love story.
Poetic and whimsical, with characters you can't help but root for,
this is romantasy at its finest!'
Elizabeth Helen, author of *Bonded by Thorns*

'A spellbinding tale of light and darkness set in a world teetering
on the edge of collapse. Peñaranda's prose will captivate you
until the very last page.'
Rina Vasquez, author of the *Solaris and Crello* trilogy

BOOKS BY CHLOE C . PEÑARANDA

THE NYTEFALL SERIES
The Stars are Dying
The Night is Defying
The Dark is Descending

AN HEIR COMES TO RISE SERIES
An Heir Comes to Rise
A Queen Comes to Power
A Throne from the Ashes
A Clash of Three Courts
A Sword from the Embers
A Flame of the Phoenix

THE
NIGHT
IS
DEFYING

CHLOE C. PEÑARANDA

WILDFIRE

Map and page designs © 2023 by Lila Raymond
Character illustrations on p. viii and p.434 © Osmar David Valencia Damián (@damian.in.the.den)
Part title illustrations © Tristan3D/Shutterstock

First published in paperback in 2025 by Wildfire,
An imprint of Headline Publishing Group Limited

1

Cataloguing in Publication Data is available from the British Library

Paperback ISBN 978 1 0354 1537 3

Printed and bound in Great Britain by Clays Ltd, Elcograf S.p.A.

Headline's policy is to use papers that are natural, renewable and
recyclable products and made from wood grown in well-managed forests
and other controlled sources. The logging and manufacturing processes
are expected to conform to the environmental regulations
of the country of origin.

HEADLINE PUBLISHING GROUP
an Hachette UK Company
Carmelite House
50 Victoria Embankment
London EC4Y 0DZ

The authorised representative in the EEA is Hachette Ireland,
8 Castlecourt Centre, Dublin 15, D15 XTP3, Ireland
(email: info@hbgi.ie)

www.headline.co.uk
www.hachette.co.uk

For my readers, always.
Believe in yourself more than anyone
and despite everyone.

THE REALM

ARANIA

FESARIS

MISTVEL

PYXTIA

ALISUS

VESITIRE

THE UNDITH

CONSTANTS BAY

VOLANTIS

PART ONE

Nyte—Past

He watched the darkness tipping his fingers fade back to a warm tan, but what lay in his heart would never retract so easily. Nightsdeath settled like a sleeping monster within him once again, proud of the bloodshed that surrounded him.

The scent of vampire blood would always reek of decay. Especially the nightcrawlers. Plucking a cloth from his jacket pocket, Nyte wiped his face as he stepped over the bodies. He felt nothing and hardly remembered tearing through the dozen of them he'd come across in Alisus.

"Your father won't be pleased," a vampire called Ripley said from behind.

He was a soulless—the kind of vampire that consumed souls instead of blood. From Nyte's understanding, they could glimpse everything of a person through their souls and once held a close alliance with the celestials to keep peace and rid the land and stars of those who'd committed sins unworthy of redemption.

"He's never pleased," Nyte said. It would be his punishment to face, but he didn't really care.

He approached the wagon of captured fae. They all cowered, thinking they'd been saved from one fate only to be staring at something far worse. It wasn't far from the truth, if his intentions for them were anything like the slaughter they'd just witnessed.

With ease he broke the lock, tossing it away before the iron door swung open.

The fae didn't move.

This was the soul tarnishing part he had to turn off every emotion to face. They couldn't all live. For it to be a believable ambush in that most escaped, there had to be casualties on both sides. Yet, looking at every frightened life before him, it was never a choice he could make.

"Not all of you can be saved, but you get to choose who walks away," Nyte said.

It didn't matter what he did or who he saved; there would always be a villainous taint to it. Lives had to be sacrificed, and those who got to walk away were not his redemption.

Salvation didn't exist for a servant of Death.

The fae looked over each other, forming guards, protecting themselves and their young. Nyte stepped away from the carriage and watched them exit. Five males, three females, four young.

"Decide now which of you will die. Better yet, kill them yourselves, and you can walk away with a lifetime of wealth."

Nyte stood calm and still. His mind reached into each of theirs. Waiting.

They'd made their choice before they got the chance to act on it.

Nyte reacted to their unspoken intentions, snapping the neck of one male who planned to lunge for the female next to him to save himself. Then Nyte twisted, reaching a hand into the chest of another who was about to turn on his friend. Finally, the last male succumbed to the hand Nyte wrapped around his throat, for the target he'd made of the young in his company. Nyte tossed him aside, not looking as Ripley caught the fae, and his silent cries didn't last long as his soul was devoured.

The blood on Nyte's hand disappeared in wisps of smoke as he turned to the remaining fae.

"Run south and don't look back," he said to them, devoid of any emotion.

It took them a moment to decide Nyte wasn't going to turn on them as they tried to escape. They were right to be cautious, and he could only hope their fear of him, and other vampires that could come after them again, would keep their wits sharp.

The females guided the young, but one male turned back. One with short deep green hair and small horns that curved away from themselves.

"W-why did you help us?" he asked.

Nyte didn't know what to do with such a question. It wasn't one he'd faced before, and this group was particularly slow at retreating from him when the door of opportunity opened.

He didn't have an answer to give. Instead, Nyte said, "Your hair could pass as a Starlight Matter enhancement. Your horns and ears will always single you out to them as fae." He cringed at the implication. "If you want a chance at a normal life, or to stay alive and fight back . . ."

"I understand," the male said. "Thank you."

The gratitude didn't sit right.

"There's a human called Lucinda Havesten. Go to Delven Inn at the edge of Alisus. She'll help you."

The fae male nodded. "I won't forget the debt we owe you."

Before Nyte could say that he didn't want any favors, the fae took off after his group.

"My lord," a new vampire interrupted. A young shadowless named Lionel. "You shouldn't be here—"

"They have the star-maiden."

Nyte's eyes targeted the guard at once, causing him to stiffen.

"If that's true—"

"It is. They have her captive in the tower back in Astrinus."

Cold, cruel laughter erupted inside him, but he didn't release it.

"They don't have the star-maiden," Nyte said with mocking calm, but a thrill began to rise in his chest. "She has them."

She had her back to him. Lengths of unique silver hair spilled behind her with strands catching an iridescent sheen from the moonlight she stared at.

Nyte dismissed all the guards before entering the cell.

This moment was his. To face her once and for all. He wanted to relish it all to himself.

He kept back, cloaked in shadow, and her lack of reaction had him questioning her highly admired senses and wit.

Until she began to turn.

Only a flicker of silver-blue caught his sight before he was slammed by a force as shackling as death and as condemning as hell.

Nyte slipped into her mind out of instinct, erasing the sight of him. The shadow cover was not enough to hide from it.

This impossibility.

It *was* fucking impossible.

A wicked trick, yet he couldn't figure out how she was convincing a part of his being that they belonged together. That she was his to bond and protect and strengthen.

No. She was his to weaken, destroy, and eradicate.

She was a cunning yet absolutely stunning little thing.

Fury rose in him at her utter audacity in trying her celestial bewitchment on him. Her silver eyes searched the cell and Nyte eased a fraction knowing she wasn't immune to his ability to bend minds.

Astraea.

The Daughter of Dusk and Dawn. The beloved ruler of all Solanis. The star-maiden.

A magnificent and undeniably powerful creature.

The pull to her became gravity-defying while he stood rooted.

He had to get out of here and took two steps before her voice did something no other had before: it silenced every beast of his mind.

"Why do you hide?"

Her voice.

He fought a strong urge to expel it from his mind, losing to the rapture of wanting to hear it again.

"Why do you pretend to be captured?" He couldn't resist the answer he eased into her mind.

She heard it with a shallow gasp. Drawing his gaze to pink full lips now parted faintly and—*fuck, he should kill her and be done with it.*

Nyte hadn't come armed when her death by his hands alone would be most gratifying. Now, there was a demon in his mind that would sooner tear at his own flesh than lay on her with malicious intent.

Astraea would die. He would make sure of it.

The heavy chains clanged as she examined her bonds.

"They certainly feel real," she said. "Though I can't say the same for you."

He wanted to melt the iron circling her wrists and strangle the guard who was responsible for equipping them with the chain between them.

Stars above, he wanted to—

"You must be the one they call Nightsdeath," she drawled.

The name wasn't right. Not from her. Yet that evil within him peeked out with sinful glee toward his greatest enemy.

Starlight.

It marked her. The scent, like lavender and honey, pulled Nyte inches closer to take a full inhale. Intoxicating. Another step. She was a drug, and he was oh too curious to sample knowing he could cut out the affliction like any plague. *Just indulge a little more.*

"Where do you get that impression?" he sent back in answer.

He'd faced countless threats. Seen bloodshed of every color. Yet danger of the most lethal kind was always the most beautiful. And Astraea . . . she was such a mesmerizing, taunting, and beautiful thing that it didn't seem fair to the rest of the world to compare her to anything else in it. In the shadow of what she was.

The brightest star.

"I've heard of your mind talents," she said plainly, so unimpressed, *unafraid.* Her indifference toward him flared wildly in him.

When her face lifted fully, the impact of her eyes locking on his was like his next step slammed straight into the stone wall.

It was right then, against his will, he pledged to her: No one would harm her. No one would touch her. No one except him.

So when he found the mark scoring across her cheek, freshly scabbed and still flushing rose against her pale complexion, Nyte almost lost his whole fucking composure.

He wouldn't ask her. No. Something about the hidden gleam in her eye told him she would use any words as a craft. The impression that he cared about a mark on her was sure to strike back like a blade in his chest.

Yet even more perplexing was how easily she found Nyte's stare when he was sure his image was still blocked from her mind by his compulsion.

"I've faced monsters before," she taunted, easing closer to the bars. He became fascinated with her. "You won't scare me if you show yourself."

For once he didn't fight the curl of his mouth. Her daring nature was plucking long dormant threads within him, and he was thrilled to test how far this creature was able to bend before he broke her.

Nyte resisted the urge to join her boldness and erase more of the space between them. The scent of her blood still lingered from her wound and the sharp teeth appearing in his mouth snapped his awareness.

He slipped from her mind, releasing it fully.

Astraea blinked as if she knew. Felt it. She searched for him even though she'd already had him pinned.

It wasn't in cowardice that he kept himself semi-hidden in the shadows of the room; he couldn't be sure exactly what was truth or myth about the star-maiden. He had to be cautious.

"Trading one method of hiding for another doesn't count," she said.

"I'm right here," he answered. "I've always been right here."

Nyte didn't know what to make of her reaction when she finally distinguished his form from the darkness. She stared and stared without a single word, and it was damn infuriating. Itching his skin so badly he wanted to snap her neck to be rid of the attention.

As quick as the thought came, he imagined holding her fragile lifeless body, wondering if she would wake again or if she wasn't like him at all. Not a true immortal. It didn't seem right that the daughter of two primordials would be anything less.

The movement in his chest was foreign, and he didn't know what to make of it. A faster beat like the adrenaline of war, then a skip that felt like regret.

Nyte had taken a step out of his shadow cover without even realizing. Her chin tipped back a fraction to keep those cool eyes on his.

Fire against ice. *What destruction they could commit.* It hummed between them like a dare, just waiting for one side to announce war so the battle could begin.

"Astraea," he said. Only to taste her name, and *fuck,* did it flare something possessive within him that took claim of it that instant.

"Nightsdeath."

Again, he didn't like the sound of it from her. Especially in the way she *toyed* with it. A name that brought vicious beings to their knees; she used it like she found a thrill in provoking a dangerous beast.

"Just Nyte," he corrected her.

He wanted to retract the token he extended to her as soon as it left his lips. It was better to have her keep testing the name that was priming the monster inside him to *devour her*. Nightsdeath would want her to push and push until Nyte had no choice but to give over to it completely and there would be no hope for her then.

"You are not what I expected," she observed.

The slow trail of her eyes over him grated on him like knives. Everything she did was so purposeful . . . attentive. Nyte had to figure her out before she could him and when their eyes met again it was like the race had begun.

She wasn't captured. Of course not. Nyte had tried that himself, and if some other had managed what he couldn't, he would damn well hand them a sword and lay his neck at their mercy. There was some foolish bastard, perhaps several, who were gloating about how they'd caught the star-maiden. And Nyte couldn't wait to hunt them down.

He wondered, "Dare I ask what assumptions you had about me?"

Her mouth twitched as though the stories she'd been told amused her.

"Older, for one," she started. Those silver eyes roved over him and *stars;* the disruption in him was unwelcome to their impression each time. "Like far older. With a beard and maybe carrying a scepter."

"A scepter?"

She shrugged. "No one knows how your magick works. I figured the mind manipulation might be some kind of rare artifact."

Nyte couldn't fight the amusement curving his mouth. Such a strange feeling he wasn't sure how to suppress it.

"Like your key?"

Astraea looked away. The legendary weapon of the star-maiden was feared by all, and he was fascinated to see it.

"It's many things, but it cannot trick minds."

"If it's in the void, you know I could find it."

"Which is why it isn't. You think I don't know of your capabilities, *Nyte?*" She approached the bars again, slipping her pale hands around them and leaning her forehead to the cold metal. "I know how many times you've sought me out. I know that it's been your father's highest goal."

"You've been watching me?"

"Of course."

"I know a lot about you too, Astraea." She liked hearing her name from him. He could tell by the way her eyes creased a near undetectable fraction each time he'd said it. "Do your guardians know you're here?"

The fall of her face was all the answer he needed.

The star-maiden had been raised by six of them in mortal flesh, divinely chosen by the God of Dusk and Goddess of Dawn to raise the one true leader that would usher in the Golden Age. They were three Bonded pairs and a mix of all species to demonstrate and instill peace in the star-maiden. Once she came of mature age, they gave up their millennium-old mortal forms to rest, leaving their Bonded spirits, known now as the legendary Serpent, Panther, and Raven, to continue to guide her.

"They've long been of the opinion the best way to deal with you is to never acknowledge you."

"I'm wounded."

"I doubt that."

"So why did you come?"

Astraea looked to be contemplating. Deciding if her guardians were right or if she should trust her own intuition.

"What do you know of the quakes?"

It wasn't what he expected her to have risked her life to come here for.

"Now why would I give you any information?" Nyte decided to play with her. This was the most fun he'd had in decades.

"Because this affects you too."

"Does it?"

Her eyes narrowed, trying to read him. It was adorable to watch her try.

"The stars are dying," she said, giving away her first note of fear. "Plummeting this world into darkness would create a catastrophic imbalance."

"I quite like the dark."

"So I've gathered."

A smile played on his lips. "Are you asking for my help?"

"You might think the disruption to solar magick only affects the celestials and humans, but you're wrong. Vampires would become uncontrollable. Nightcrawlers would roam freely and ravage, this world is not ready. Your *father* is not prepared to handle something that will quickly spread beyond his control like a bloodthirsty plague."

"If I'm not mistaken, one of your guardians was a nightcrawler."

She pursed her lips, deliberating how much she was willing to share with him.

"He would not have wished their freedom in the daylight. It is the only way a lot of them keep their control. Them aside, the celestials would become powerless eventually, and before you think that triumphing over them would be enough reason to leave the quakes be, you should know that you don't understand what that would truly mean. Souls would never cycle to the stars; the soulless would become another insatiable force and their greed would them instead. Starlight Matter would no longer be a trade substance. Without the sun, nothing would grow. The humans would die out too. Then, with them gone, the fae would be the last to come under attack in the vampires' desperation. So yes, a vampire reign would be achieved, but it would be a world only of monsters. With this course, there would be no governing them, no order.

Only pure chaos and bloodshed. If your father wants to overthrow me to rule a nation, whatever is shaking our balance must be stopped."

Nyte thought for a long moment. She came for an alliance. The idea was as fascinating as it was ludicrous. He wouldn't expose his intrigue so easily. Wouldn't tell her he believed she was right and had been unsettled by the discovery of the imbalance that had grown worse. The quakes were at least a century old. Nyte didn't remember a time without them. But they were becoming more frequent in recent decades, and for the star-maiden to have come to him, the effect of them on the celestials must be edging on dire.

"Why did you not speak to my father?"

"Because I have been watching you," she reminded. "And I think we both know who really has the power to do something here."

Nyte wouldn't admit the unexpected lift of relief that she hadn't voiced any of this to his father. He wouldn't see her reasoning. There was a delusion to his thoughts that would disregard any warning and use this knowledge to gain his advantage no matter the cost. As her enemy, Nyte couldn't deny it would be smart if done right.

Yet how could she not see the betrayal in coming to him?

He could discover what was causing the quakes, end the star-maiden, and take reign over the celestials. Then stop whatever was causing the disruption himself.

"You're cold," he diverted. Deciding he needed time to calculate exactly what he would be getting himself into.

Nyte's observation earned a shiver from her that seemed like she'd been stifling it the whole time. To not show weakness.

"You'll have to tell your guards it'll take more than a few freezing nights in here to kill me," she said, pacing the cell now.

Her deep-purple gown had sheer sleeves to show off magnificent metallic-silver tattoos. The constellation over her chest was that of the star-maiden. An exquisite thing. Though for the dead of winter, her attire was not adequate.

"They took things from you," he said, surprised by the darkness leaking into his tone.

He couldn't help it. Imagining hands on her surged a need to rip them from the bodies of those who'd thought it appropriate to touch her without his knowledge.

"There's a particular brute with a scar over his lip who was *thorough* in his search for weapons," she said. Unfazed by the handling she'd been subjected to. "Make sure they don't damage my dagger, will you? I'm rather fond of it."

Seeing no place for her to equip herself with weapons, his sight targeted her thigh, catching the flicker of black leather when she stepped from the cut of her gown. Cold murderous rage overcame him quicker than he could suppress it.

"Are they supposed to scare me?" Her voice snapped him from a reel of deplorable thoughts.

Nyte followed her attention, examining the ripples of shadow that had spilled into her cell. They circled her, and he knew the nightmares they could inflict when they made a target out of someone. His allegiance with them was a match made in hell's most sinister depths.

The beat in Nyte's chest quickened, readying him to intervene, but the shadows weren't interested in attacking. They reacted to his curiosity about her, and he had to wonder if it was misplaced courage or stupidity that had her reaching out a hand to touch the animated darkness.

Nyte's fist clamped and whatever emotions expelled from him to give the shadows form dissipated, and it fell like black smoke, disappearing into nothing.

"If you're serious, find me again," he said, leaving without another word.

He marched down the dark halls of the keep they'd taken over a few years ago in Astrinus, not really knowing any direction, only driving against the force not to turn *back*.

"We have the elusive star-maiden?"

Drystan's approach didn't come as a surprise when he'd all but skipped up in his eagerness. Nyte's younger half brother was starting to join in with their father's never-ending plans and strategies in a war he often scaled higher than it was because of his own paranoia about the celestials. Overthrowing them was no easy feat, and while Nyte entertained his orders, nothing short of the maiden's death would get him what he sought.

"She'll be gone by morning," Nyte said stiffly.

He could practically feel the frown Drystan wore.

"She's in a cell, chained in steel laced with Nebulora."

Nyte hadn't failed to notice the burning around Astraea's wrists from the cosmic plant harmful to her kind. It wasn't enough to incapacitate her.

"She'll figure it out."

"Father has tripled the guard detail around the fortress."

He stopped walking, turning to Drystan when he was certain no one lingered around to overhear.

"Never underestimate your enemy when they still have resources to best you. For Astraea, breathing is enough."

Drystan quirked a brow as if waiting for a joke.

"You've never given an enemy that much credit," he said, folding his arms.

His apprehension of Nyte's judgment grated a nerve, but his younger brother had a lot to learn about how to rank his enemies.

"I've never met my match. But don't be concerned for me, brother. A word of advice though—don't be around when father hears of her escape."

2

Astraea–Present

I held a dagger to my heart, knowing he would come. This bargain, our bond, would summon him from the risk to my life.

"There are more enticing ways to get my attention, Starlight."

I wanted to deny the silk of his silvery voice caressing my skin in pleasure. I wished the rage I harbored would translate it to disgust.

"If what you said is true, this shouldn't kill me," I challenged.

Maybe I was losing my sanity, but being held captive between stone and iron, even for the single day he'd locked me here, had grown my resentment beyond caring.

"No. But it would hurt. A lot." His hand curled around the bar as his golden irises danced. The bastard was enjoying this. "And there is only one place I wish to hear your screams—where I can own them."

My hand poised with my stormstone blade fell as I pinned him with a heated glare.

"You own nothing of me," I seethed.

I made the dagger vanish through the Starlight Void. I paced, trying to focus, focus, *focus*. While I had become accustomed to retrieving that one item, I had yet to figure out how to *move* through it like Nyte could.

My fists flexed as I paced, as though imagining them around his neck would spur enough determination to succeed.

"Astraea." His voice dropped low and my eyes scrunched to it, hating the low tone of a plea. "Just one more day."

I gave a bitter laugh.

"I hope it was worth it," I said. My teeth clenched to the ache of my heart. "Gaining their loyalty at my expense."

"That's not what this is."

"Then what the fuck is it?"

My eyes burned but I wouldn't shed a single tear for him.

"Protection."

"Control," I corrected in a cold calm. "That's what you told them. You *forced* me to retrieve the key to display your power over me. You should kill me with it, for the second you let me free I will find a way to kill you."

He'd taken the key and somehow blocked my ability to retrieve it. Maybe I was glad when this captivity made me volatile, and I couldn't be sure what my untrained *power* could be capable of.

"You are absolutely stunning."

My resentment took an ugly turn.

"I called you here because I want you to tell me about my Bonded. The one Drystan mentioned," I said, enjoying how it wiped the smile from his face.

"You had a lot to process as it was; Drystan had no right to throw that at you when he did," Nyte snarled.

"I'm glad he did," I taunted. "Maybe I'll find this other person more tolerable than you."

Shadow touched me before his skin did. A featherlight caress of his fingers mimicked the darkness, trailing up my arm.

"Why won't you wear the things I brought you?"

"I don't want *things;* I want to get the hell out of here."

I didn't look to the change of clothing on the bed. It was tempting and beautiful. Something like a gown but there were also leather pants and high boots. My pettiness made me not want to take anything from him.

"It wasn't safe."

"It'll never be *safe.* You have a court of vampires above us that all want me dead."

"Wrong. They want you alive, now that they understand that so long as I live too you being alive keeps the celestials weak."

The reminder of our doomed existence crushed me every time.

"Controlled, then."

"More like it, yes. You would make their greatest ally."

"You would force me."

"I could."

Nyte loved this game between us. I wanted it to burn.

He tipped my chin slowly and I kept my eyes cold.

Nyte murmured, "I want you to belong with me."

The next beat of my heart traitorously stumbled.

"Possession," I stated.

"Alliance," he corrected.

"It is only *your* desire."

"Are you sure?"

"*Other* Bonded," I said to divert his attention. That key word of Drystan's had played a tormenting loop.

"Surely you understand by now why you followed me so easily, even though I wasn't truly there. When you were frozen on that lake in Alisus you yearned for me. Through your trials you called for me. Your soul . . . I wish I could say I hate to tell you this, but I don't—I'm your Bonded, Starlight."

I thought a part of me had always known, when the confirmation didn't come as a shock. Instead, my stomach fluttered. A reaction I wished I wouldn't have when the words repeated over and over in my mind.

"We can't be. Our mere existence together is collapsing the stars."

His lips inched closer to blow warmth against mine.

"I tried to be selfless for a moment in coaxing you toward the veil instead of coming to Vesitire for the Libertatem, but the moment you were right before me there was no letting you go."

We shared breath, and I was torn between wanting to kiss him and wanting to stab him again.

"You didn't try hard enough."

"I assure you, that small push toward the arms of another tore apart every fiber of my being."

His lips slanted against mine and I was a damned fool for letting my anger melt under the heat of him even just for a moment. He pressed his body to mine, not against the wall but rather with an arm around my back, eager to feel how my body curved effortlessly into him.

I pulled out of the kiss abruptly, remembering my irritation with him. I pushed his chest to gain space.

"How can I have two Bonded?"

"A trick of fate. A loophole, if you will," he said. "Every person has a Bonded. Same sex or opposite. I am not from this realm. We never should have met, and it is cruel yet punishing that two souls from separate worlds came to a perfect collision. Hence, you have two of them."

Stars above. The rarity of us—it was as magnificent as it was tragic.

"What does it mean?" I whispered. "To be my Bonded?"

It flared a light inside me I tried desperately to snuff out.

"Nothing, should you wish."

Hearing it thrown away by him unsettled me. I tried to distinguish if it was how he really felt about this *thing* that ran between us. A bond that could tie us to each other.

"A bond has no heart. You told me it didn't require love."

"You misunderstand," he said carefully. "I never claimed there was no heart to a bond. It is a life partnership. You vow to protect and strengthen each other. You bond your soul to another."

"What happens if one dies?"

A plummet in my stomach accompanied the cold touch of expanding shadows around him.

"A pair that have claimed the Bond? One heart becomes a burden to keep beating without the other."

The way he said it answered a question about us I wasn't ready to hear out loud yet.

"You knew all this time . . ."

"Of course."

"Everything you feel for me—"

"Has nothing to do with it. There was a time I *wanted* to kill you. You were my enemy in more ways than one. I was my father's son—it's all I knew how to be—and you were something that would always be in his way of getting what he wanted. To be the ruler of Solanis."

"You didn't follow through on your father's order . . ."

"No."

"Why?"

"You made me believe that maybe monsters aren't born, they're made. I was never a son, only a ruthless soldier. Even when you were gone, I still couldn't figure out why you cared. You approached a villain everyone would sooner run from as the star-maiden, but over time, you showed me Astraea. Just you, no title. It was then I understood there was a light I could not just tolerate but crave."

I would never deny Nyte was capable of monstrous things, but he was not a *monster*. Then I had to wonder if my own feelings could be betraying me to think that. I felt his care and it was deep. He came for me, stayed with me, guided me. But how could I be certain it wasn't all for his own gain in a way I've yet to discover?

"Me being alive keeps the celestials weak . . ." I muttered. Pacing to the wall, I leaned a hand to the stone, needing to feel something solid when my world was as fragile as glass. "How can I be sure you're not keeping me here for that too?"

"I took no pleasure in overpowering you on the rooftop," he said darkly. My skin tightened at the growing presence of him at my back. A shiver broke me from the wrap of shadows, hands made of them that turned me around by my waist before his real body caged me against the wall. "You have *every* power over me. Tell me you know that."

It couldn't be true. How someone as influential and dominating as Nyte could be under my power.

"Release me from your bargain," I said.

His jaw worked. "It's to protect you from doing foolish things."

"Like saving your damned life?"

He tried to force me away through our blood bargain when he was in trouble and the pain to defy it was like nothing else.

"Exactly like that when it could have ended a hundred different ways that would have gotten *you* killed."

"A regrettable decision now."

"But look at what fun we're having."

"I hate you."

"Hmm." Nyte refused to keep personal space around me. The slither of air breezing between us became static. "Try saying that again; see what happens."

The dare in his tone was enticing. A dormant language I felt awakening between us.

"I—"

Pausing, the suspense rose from the tips of my toes. It flared a passionate light gold in his irises.

"Yes?" he coaxed.

A challenge. I shouldn't provoke him, but shit, I wanted to.

"Hate you."

I gasped at the sudden, familiar pull of the void. Sharp air surrounded me, and I had no choice but to wrap my arms around Nyte's neck when all I saw around us was clouds. My incredulity was stolen for a few seconds by the beauty of the moonlit landscape, and above us, I treasured the map of the stars.

"One more time," Nyte said.

My sight snapped back to him, and my irritation returned. He carried me in a position where he could easily drop me. His large, midnight feathered wings beat the night air around us.

"I have wings too."

"Do you? Let's see."

He let me go.

My stomach flipped and tumbled with the rapid descent and there was no grace to my flailing form.

Nyte was a twisted, infuriating *bastard*.

He dove after me. I could just about make out the dark form of him through my blurry sight with the slicing wind and cold stinging my eyes.

"I hate you! I hate you! I hate you!" I screamed in my mind.

I wasn't sure if that's what made him dive faster until he reached me, slipping a hand around my back and our fall lessening, slower and slower. Until my body felt tugged up against gravity.

Then stillness. A jarring, confusing stillness and warmth soothed the sharp cold nipping my face. I had to blink a few times to reorient. He'd taken us through the void again and I now lay on a bed with Nyte and his magnificent wings towering over me. His body pressed into me lightly and I was too stunned and dizzy to do anything.

"I love it when you hate me," he purred over my jaw. "Don't you find it thrilling? It's one of your brightest forms of passion."

"My hate is going to find something sharp and drive it through your heart."

"You remember where to aim this time, good girl."

He was positioned between my legs, and I couldn't deny my hate wanted to unleash in other traitorous ways right now.

"Release me from the bargain," I repeated.

"Astraea, I release you from your blood bargain to me."

My lips parted with the faint tug within me, and I knew it was done. Relief that he didn't fight or elude me on it relaxed me into the mattress. Nyte's wings disappeared in a wave of shimmer like stardust. He shifted to lie propped up on his side next to me and it was only then that I started to take in more details of the room and knew we were in the one I was assigned for the Libertatem.

"Why didn't you make me retrieve the key sooner, when you could have commanded it?"

"You were healing."

"Your father had the deadliest weapon he'd been after for centuries."

"You were *healing*," he repeated. "Even attempting to call it in the state you were in could have killed you, and there's nothing I wouldn't let burn to the ground if it meant your safety."

I wanted to push him away but instead this tether to him wound tighter beyond my control. Only to make the impact that much sharper when he left. How could I forget that he planned to leave this realm?

Leave me.

"What did your father do with it?"

Nyte eased away, sitting with his back to me on the edge of the bed as I pushed up on my forearms.

"He managed to get inside the temple, but I don't think they granted his wish. The doors were open, but something wasn't right."

"You have the key?"

"It's in the Starlight Void. The key is a powerful weapon, but it is most lethal in your hands. You have unparalleled power without it; at least I have to believe you still have it in this life and can get it back. The key is an amplifier for you. To anyone else, it's a volatile catastrophe waiting to happen. It will corrupt the mind of anyone who tries to wield it when it was only intended for you. In turn, it weakens the magick you harbor in punishment for allowing it to slip out of your possession."

"But I was able to call it back even when your father had taken it."

"This time, yes. But you can be blocked from that; my father just didn't figure that out."

"You did." My gut twisted with betrayal. Then realization. "You've done it to me before. In the past."

He didn't deny it.

"I want to help you. Do you believe that?"

Nyte's gentleness would never fail to bring out the fool in me. The pining heart that *wanted* to trust him.

I shook my head. "You haven't given me much reason to."

"Bond with me."

Each word struck like a knife. Widening my eyes on him to search for the joke.

"You can't be serious."

"You are half my soul. Whether you choose to bind yourself to me or not, that will never change. But this gives them what they want. The vampires are restless; they'll stop looking to you as a threat with our powers merged."

"I am a threat," I hissed. "I will become everything they fear before I give them the satisfaction of thinking you or they *own* me."

Nyte's mouth curled, suppressing his approval.

"Sometimes the key to winning is letting your opponent think they're in the lead."

Nyte stood and I was compelled to slip off the bed too. We were like two resisting magnets. My irritation kept my feet planted, but Nyte gave in more times than I thought he realized. He approached and my hands subconsciously curved back around the bedpost to him, erasing the space between us.

"Bond with me," he repeated in a low murmur that skittered over my skin. My head leaned fractions to the side, to the brush of my hair he spilled over my shoulder to expose my neck. "Power and loneliness corrupts. We are infinite together."

My breaths came shallow at the light press of his body. My blood ignited at the thought of his teeth in me again.

"You can't ask that of me."

"Why not?"

"You have a knowledge of my past that I don't have of yours."

"Yet."

Nyte's lips pressed to my throat. The seduction was a distraction to scatter the rational thinking I was grappling to keep hold of. He was addicting in ways that felt timeless, endless. That made me prey in his hold and tuned out the voice of reservation.

How much could I trust myself, my instincts? Or perhaps that was what led to my fall in the past and I had to be wary not to repeat history.

So in the arms of the one who was once my enemy, and perhaps could be even now, I had to craft a plan. One that might tear my soul. But what were wounds to the heart became armor to the mind.

Over the last day, I couldn't stop picturing the veil. Imagining the winged celestials beyond it.

My people.

The concept riddled me with as much exhilaration as it did terror when I didn't know if I was worthy of being what they thought I was. What I *once* was.

"I will bond with you," I said.

His face pulled back and those beautiful golden irises searched me in surprise at my agreement, but I gave him nothing else. My emotionless answer seemed to affect him.

"Good," he said, equally as cold.

Nyte turned from me and headed for the door.

"No more cages?" I said.

I walked to him this time. A muscle in his jaw worked.

"If you ever find yourself in one again you're going to have the means to break it."

"How can you be sure?"

"I know what's hiding within you."

It was hiding *from* me too.

"The vampires?"

"Won't touch you. I've ordered most of them away. Only Tarran and a few others linger as part of our agreement."

"What agreement?"

"Once we are Bonded, you are one of us. In alliance, of course; it will not change anything about your celestial heritage."

I had so many questions on what *would* change. How this tie between us would affect me and if it meant I could never escape him. Not alive.

"How am I supposed to discover what my heritage means and what I can do when I can't go to the celestials in Althenia?"

"I'm going to train you."

That took me by surprise. "Why?"

"To get your power back. I have to say it's for them—to show them you are still powerful, and this bond is a great advantage. But they know nothing of my plan to leave. This is for you. To get back what has been suppressed against your will. Your magick and your wings; it is for you we do this, so you stand the best chance to end this war when I'm gone. Do you believe that?"

In the hours he'd left me in that cell I had been practicing one retrieval. One maneuver.

My hand thrust to his chest, slamming him back against the door as he was caught completely unawares. My other hand reached through the void and my fingers gripped the cold and twisted handle of my stormstone dagger.

My heart thundered but my hold didn't tremble with the point of the wavy purple blade under his chin.

"You ever lock me in a cage again, this goes through your heart. Only for me to watch you wake and do it a second time."

Nyte smiled, a stark warm contrast to my icy glare. His hand reached up, and though his teeth gritted with the added pressure of my dagger, he tucked a loose strand of hair behind my ear.

"Welcome back, Starlight."

3

Nyte

Balancing on the stone rail of Astraea's balcony while she slept inside unawares might be considered immoral. Wrong. I didn't give a fuck.

My wings shielded me from the worst of the bitter winter air but I didn't plan to stay long. I'd come here with the intention of soothing the need to see her. Even though I had been with her a few hours ago.

I couldn't sleep. Not with the torment that made me believe if I did I could awaken back in that wretched cave below the library. Demons plaguing my mind turned the sight of her to a vision, the feel of her to a torturous whisper. I had to come here for the reminder that I didn't need to look up and search the sky anymore, only forward to where my fallen star lay.

I'd thought just seeing her sleeping peacefully, safely, would be enough.

It wasn't.

Shadows crept toward the lock as I dropped soundlessly onto the balcony. I opened her door. I didn't bother to conceal my wings as I welcomed myself in; I really wouldn't be here long and she wouldn't know I'd come.

Astraea was still angry with me, rightfully so, and it was sadistic of me to find thrill in it. Every dark and dangerous thing living inside her I wanted unleashed on me. Then together, on our enemies.

Circling around her bed, she was a goddess against the moonlight that glittered her silver hair. Fucking exquisite.

Mine.

I was obsessed. Incapable of letting her go even when death and time joined forces to try separate us. It wasn't enough. Nothing ever would be.

The dark and withered thing in my chest came to life in her presence. It became terrifying yet beautiful—a vulnerable reminder every day of what was at stake. I couldn't lose her again. I wouldn't. My search for the one who'd taken her from me for three hundred years began the second the light faded in her silver-blue eyes.

Pain clenched like a fist around my heart and I had to block out the past. She was here. Right here. Impulse won with the need to feel her.

Astraea slept on her side, hands tucked under her cheek. My fingers brushed the hair at her temple, and the way it eased centuries of torment from my mind, even if just for a second, was bliss.

Her eyes flickered with a deeper inhale. Lips parting sleepily, she said, "Nyte?"

Fuck, I wanted to get on my knees for that quiet murmur that asked for me.

"Starlight," I whispered.

The hint of blue in her irises came out more in the shadows. They trailed high over my shoulders before following the curve of my wing.

"They're . . . beautiful," she said, her consciousness not fully there.

I couldn't help myself. Leaning down, I pressed my mouth to hers. The soft sigh she gave invoked peace in me, pulling at a yearning to be lying beside her.

"Sleep, love."

Astraea attempted to shake her head but I'd already lulled her mind and her lids slipped closed. She wouldn't wake to remember this as real. A flicker of a dream, maybe.

It took everything in me to straighten away from her when I should be holding the only reminder of why I wanted to live. Astraea was born unafraid of monsters and when the worst of them came to her, she bent my will to hers without even knowing it.

There was only one thing keeping this world safe from me.

Her.

I would find her killer, and for every year they took from us, I would make them suffer to stretch a day as a month, a year as a century. They wouldn't remember their existence without pain.

When because of them, torture and terror only had one meaning to me now: being without her again.

I crouched by her. "Another truth for you, Astraea. Letting you go . . . I'm not capable of it. You offered your hand to walk through worlds with me and I haven't been able to suppress the most selfish thoughts. It makes me no better than my parents when I want our time in this realm to expire, only to walk with you to the next and condemn it too eventually. I wouldn't care about the destruction we left in our wake, and I don't know what that makes me. If you would be horrified by what I would do to keep you." Before I could stop myself, I leaned in, pressing lips to her head and breathing in the only scent that could bring peace to restless darkness. "There are many treasures across many lands, but you're mine."

4

Astraea

A tug within pulled me out of a peaceful rest but the trickle of familiarity dulled my initial alarm. Sitting up, I rubbed my eyes of the thickness of sleep, squinting through the dark like I would find someone. Only the moon highlighted silhouettes of the furniture occupying the room with me.

I couldn't shake the feeling I wasn't truly alone.

I slipped out of bed and grabbed a cotton robe as an unexplainable gravity pulled me toward the balcony. My bare feet nipped against the icy floor, but I unlocked the doors regardless. My eyes fixed on the distance. I stepped out, my body tensed, but I became numb to the biting temperature as my sight trained on the roof of the oval library, searching through the dark.

An angel was watching me.

Their silver wings couldn't hide even in the darkest night, but they were careful, keeping close to a tall piece of the structure, and as long as they didn't move, no one would suspect the celestial.

My chest beat with wonder.

Bracing hands on the stone rail, I tried not to blink, as though they could disappear.

I wanted them to come closer. If I was dressed, maybe I would have been reckless enough to venture out in the hopes they would reveal themselves to me.

Voices outside my door drew my attention away from the silhouette, but those in the hall passed. When I looked back, the angel had disappeared.

The tension in my body relaxed with disappointment and the cold broke a sharp tremor as I hugged myself. Without the rush of adrenaline, the wind wrapped me tight and I shivered, teeth bashing together now. I quickly shuffled back inside but just as I met the door, I gasped, heart leaping up my throat with the fright that locked me utterly still.

The reflection of a crouched hooded figure and towering silver wings was as breathtaking as it was daunting. My pulse slammed, but my mind threw a block on anything that could reach Nyte, who would arrive to scare them off if he felt my fluctuating emotions.

"Who are you?" I breathed when my throat became tight.

I was too afraid to turn around. My magick hummed and though I didn't know much of how to use it yet, I was confident I could defend myself long enough to call for help.

"It's really you," he said. A deep, low voice that tried to pull a reaction from me. Familiar, maybe?

"Depends who you're expecting me to be."

Finally, I squared my shoulders before turning. His hood shadowed a lot of his face but his jaw was lined with short hair and I could just make out his eyes to be a dark brown. I thought I'd seen the likes of his clothing before: leathers with notes of purple and a long blade sheathed at his side.

"Astraea." The way he said my name once again sparked something dormant in me. I should know who this man was.

He leaped gently off the railing to stand on my balcony, reaching up for his hood. His brown hair was cut to his shoulders, half tied back in a knot but some strands framed his face. He was beautiful. Yet I backed up a step when he advanced forward and I didn't know where my bubble of unease rose from.

He stopped, assessing me carefully as if one wrong move would cause me to scream.

"I've waited so long for you. I can't believe you're finally right in front of me and yet . . . this is not the happy reunion I dreamed we'd have."

That stumbled in my chest and tightened in my stomach. My hand braced in the frame from the dizzy sweep as I processed who he was, but why was I also calculating how fast I could get inside and lock him out?

"Auster," I acknowledged.

He gave a single nod and the world didn't feel so firm anymore. This man was my other Bonded.

"You shouldn't be here," I said. "If he finds you—"

"I'm not afraid of him. And I won't leave you for him to further poison your mind any longer than I already have."

"He hasn't." I realized how naive my defense would sound to him.

Nyte was his greatest enemy, and I was a cause for battle waiting to erupt between them.

"Why did you come?" I asked instead.

"For you, of course. I've been looking everywhere for you. For five years since you came back."

"But why tonight? I can't just run off with you."

"Why not?"

Auster took a step closer and my body tensed. He seemed to notice, and I almost felt guilty for the disappointment in his eyes. I couldn't help but compare this with how I'd felt the first time I saw Nyte. Had he offered to run away with me after my dance at Goldfell Manor, would I have gone with him? I didn't think so, but not for lack of desire, only in terror of Goldfell's retaliation. Then I shook my head because I knew so much more about myself and the world now, my reservation about Auster despite the safety he should offer was natural. Wasn't it?

"I don't expect you to run away with me in the night," he said. Auster gave a soft but saddened smile. "I just had to see you and hope you would want to see me again."

I eased at the assurance he wasn't about to grab me and fly away, or keep pushing to persuade me to go with him. He had memories of us I didn't harbor anymore but I was trying to listen to my instincts. They were what made Nyte feel safe before I knew who he truly was. When I'd heard about Auster, I couldn't deny I was daunted by the idea of meeting him. Perhaps I was glad he came unexpectedly when I might have otherwise avoided an invitation in my cowardice.

"You wrote to Nyte," I said, recalling Nyte's simmering irritation before he turned the note to smoke. "What did you say?"

Auster's eyes narrowed a fraction. The feeling toward Nyte was clearly more than mutual.

"Of course he wouldn't tell you," he said bitterly. "I asked to see you and he ignored the request. So I came tonight and I hope you won't speak of it."

"Why not?"

"If he kept my request a secret from you, he'll find a way to keep *you* from seeing me again."

"A lot happened in the last week; he didn't want to overwhelm me."

Auster gave me the type of look that made my body flush in embarrassment. As if I was too sheltered and manipulated to believe Nyte had my best intentions in mind. He didn't need to say anything and I felt the sting in that silence because maybe I didn't know if I could trust my judgment either.

I was so exhausted and confused.

"Astraea, will you see me again? There's so much you need to learn when we didn't anticipate you'd return without your memories. Find a way to meet me without his knowledge. I lost you once to him; I can't let him hurt you like that again."

Auster had drifted close enough to touch. He reached up, and it took everything in me not to recoil as he brushed his fingers along my neck, hooking a strand of my hair. I placed it to guilt. That Nyte was somewhere inside and though I didn't know what was between us and I was still somewhat angry with him, having another man on my balcony felt wrong.

My eyes were attracted to a glint at his side; my sight fell to discover his left hand was still and made of solid silver. I didn't know why my brow pulled together and my heart sped faster, like I should know how it happened and the memory was something so dark and terrible.

His fingers tipping my chin up to meet his eyes snapped me out of my reeling thoughts. My nerves tried to calm when his brown eyes were soft and pained.

"I have missed you dearly," Auster mumbled.

I couldn't reciprocate, only stand there like a clueless fool, and I was beginning to grow uncomfortable with his closeness.

"Where will I meet you?" I said, more as a distraction when his eyes searched my face and he was seeing someone I wasn't.

"There's a woodland just outside the city. Can you meet me there in three nights, time? I'll find you."

"I can't promise. I don't know when I'll have an opportunity without him finding out."

"Then use your key. Five flares to the sky and I'll come for you. We'll always be looking for your signal."

Inside me was an entanglement of nerves, rebellion, and excitement. I nodded in agreement, wondering if I was being reckless. No, this was taking back control and learning to trust myself.

Held by his brown stare I began to appreciate the flecks of hazel in them. They pulled at something inside me.

"Where will you take me?"

"Home, of course. To Althenia."

My mind brightened with the name. This was my chance to go to the one place Nyte couldn't take me. Beyond the celestial veil. He'd coaxed me to go there before I ever entered the Libertatem, and now my chest was squeezing with that selflessness that would have condemned him to his prison.

"I don't have wings yet," I admitted.

Auster smiled; he wasn't horrified or judging my lack of progress. I had no reason to be nervous around him, so I trained my body to relax.

"Perhaps being back on celestial land might help you gain them back. You'll always be held back here."

Excitement rose in me. This is what I needed. Though I was grateful for all Nyte was trying to do, he had a vampire army to tame. One that planned to claim me before I even had the chance to reclaim myself. I knew what I had to do then, and for the first time I was racing with a new drive of purpose.

My eyes trailed over Auster's shoulders, and I tried to imagine my own wings. What it would feel like to soar the skies myself. They were made of beautiful silver-toned feathers, but I couldn't help comparing them to Nyte's dark wings that allured me more.

"Thank you for coming," I said.

Auster's hand lifted again but he seemed to catch himself, realizing it was a habit from the past.

"It's already killing me to leave you, to not whisk you away right now. But I can be patient."

My face creased in gratitude. It was all I had. I didn't know if my memories would return or when, but for now I had to try to rekindle what I could and trust in my intuition that felt pulled from the past.

"I'll find a way to come as soon as I can," I said in consolation.

He nodded with a kind smile. "Don't let him know," Auster reminded me as he climbed the railing. "We might have recovered from our loss in the war centuries ago, but we can't risk him sparking it again too soon."

I didn't like the way Auster made it sound like Nyte was the cause of all that had gone wrong and ended with my fall. Maybe it was my heart he'd managed to capture in this life before Auster could, and that terrified me more than anything.

"Goodbye for now, Astraea," he said.

Then he stepped off the balcony, and I watched with a beat of awe as he shot skyward before the night clouds stole him away.

Inside, I locked the door and stood in a trance. Only when my body gave a violent shiver at the cold did I snap back into myself. It felt like a dream, so I replayed the short meeting over and over. Pacing my room, for I was sure I wouldn't fall asleep again tonight.

I was skipping with giddiness at the thought of getting to see more celestials and beyond the veil that was once a fable to me. It made me think of Cassia with a swell in my chest. My vision blurred but I was smiling—she would be so excited. We would have kept this secret together and she would have snuck away in the night with me, without a doubt or fear in the world.

I wanted to tell Rose about the forbidden, maybe even dangerous, quest. Though my excitement wasn't without a note of guilt over deceiving Nyte.

The Libertatem had come to an end, but I felt like my trials had only just begun.

5

Astraea

I paced in front of my enchanted map on the dining table adjoining my bedroom. It displayed the whole of Solanis now at my request.

No longer was I confined to a single city or kingdom; the expanse of Solanis became a trove of secrets and places to help me uncover how to be the star-maiden. More dauntingly now I knew magick was beginning to fail again; with my being back, Nyte and I had to resume a past quest to find a way without death for either of us to stop it. I couldn't accept that him leaving was the only option. He might have called this my world, but I didn't want to claim it without him, even in times I was mad at him.

My sight lingered on Althenia across the veil. It had peace and safety while the other kingdoms to the west fought for survival against the vampires. It became harder to excuse the celestials for hiding all this time. They could come and go; the veil only kept us out. No—not me.

Every time I remembered I was one of them, my stomach tightened and my skin prickled. The sheer sleeves of my black gown showed my silver tattoos adorning my arms. The low dipping neck proudly showed more of them, with my constellation over my chest. My skirt was cut at both sides right up to my hips. With so much flesh exposed, I'd never felt more free, like I'd regained something of myself that had been forced to hide all this time.

Reaching over the table, I dragged the overlay I'd gotten from the Crocotta during the Libertatem. It was useless now as it only had the marker destinations of my trials, but I couldn't stop my attention from shifting back to it, as if it might magically change to provide a new constellation and show me where I had to go to start figuring things out.

What things? I couldn't be certain and might go mad in my spinning thoughts toward that first step: direction.

It made me consider Auster, who could provide a new source of information now that I'd met him and became curious. He wanted to show me a land that was once a fable in my quiet corner of the world in Alisus. I was giddy with thoughts of that adventure even if I was nervous about the company.

The other puzzle my eyes slipped to now was the celestial dragon egg. I often found myself hypnotized by the black shell and swirling silver etchings.

My fingers traced the silver swirls delicately, and our markings glowed and my skin warmed touching it. I had a stack of books on the celestial dragons but none had turned up anything about how to hatch the egg, or even attempt it, and my gut sank at the thought of it being long past survival.

Some of the dragons were depicted with leathery wings, while others, I was fascinated to discover, had breathtaking feathered wings. I fantasized about what could be within the black and silver shell. If it hatched, I pictured what colors, or wings, or certain spikes, or feathers the dragon could have.

With a sigh of wistful longing and frustration, I folded and pocketed my map. Drystan had given me the enchanted map that aided me in the Libertatem, and I kept it close to me with a sharp edge of wariness about how he might come to collect it back when I still couldn't figure out why he'd given me the life-saving advantage.

I needed air.

On the stretch of rooftop where Nyte had first shown me his wings, I stood searching the night sky. It didn't take me long to find the stars shining brightest to me.

Cassia wasn't just a single flare, she was a small constellation. For a sorrowful pause I wondered if I was mistaken or desperate, until it blinked three times. It was likely undetectable to anyone else, but I captured it in my heart.

"Hey, Cass," I whispered.

"There you are." I startled at that interruption of my quiet moment.

My mood lightened at Rosalind's voice and my eyes fell down to her. Twisting, I didn't realize how on edge I'd been to see her until I spied the pink hair bouncing toward me over her black fur-lined winter cloak. She scanned me from head to toe, then gripped my upper arms in her hands and examined me closer. I didn't think she would give in to a hug, but a sigh of relief left me when she pulled me in.

"This is all a mess," I said quietly, careful with my words when I couldn't be certain who was listening. Watching. While I stood as the prime weapon and hostage to the vampires of this castle.

"We're going to get out of here," Rose said with determination despite the damning odds.

I'd hoped she would say that. Anticipated it. I was bursting to tell her about last night with Auster but I had to find out what I'd missed first.

"What happened to you after everything?" I asked when she pulled away.

Rose warily surveyed of our surroundings, seeming to deliberate how much she could voice openly too. Looping my arm, she walked me to the rooftop perimeter.

"Nightsdeath declared me the winner of the Libertatem—Pyxtia is safe from vampire attack for now. For all the world beyond this castle knows, the cycle continues."

It felt odd to hear her address Nyte by his notorious name, but I couldn't blame her for seeing him as the monster he was portrayed to be. She did so with resentment that unsettled me with conflict.

I wanted to hate him as much as Rose did. He'd come into my life as what I'd thought was a cure only to be revealed as the cause of the curse. Yet the traitorous thing in my chest wanted to fight against the twist of fate we faced.

"Zathrian?" I asked.

"He's been trying to explain why he's an ally to Nightsdeath and what happens now that he's freed and the Libertatem is over with the king missing. Everyone is acting as if things are normal; it's irritating. Zath's wounds healed far faster than I expected. He was stabbed and I can't quite wrap my head around the fact that he's up and around as if nothing happened. I knew the healers would help along with magick, but . . ." Rose shook her head, dropping that train of thought. She stopped walking, turning to face me. "All we need to focus on now is taking Nightsdeath down. I've been thinking—at first I thought we should escape, but to what end? He wins that way. We need to find out how to kill him."

"There is no way," I said. Rose opened her mouth to argue but I explained, "He's something not from our realm. And too similar to what I am; it's our clashing existence that is failing magick. He can't be killed, but I can."

"No—you can't," she said firmly.

It's exactly what Cassia would say. Exactly the hard determination she would have worn on her fighter's face. I didn't expect this fierce protection from Rosalind and I think we both knew it was Cassia's legacy, her spirit we carried between us, that made the bond growing between us something worth guarding.

With a long breath, I embraced the confidence of both of them. This was my realm, and I had to start believing my death, my failure, could not be an option if we were to win.

"I have to tell you something that happened last night," I whispered to her.

We found a small pavilion to sit in and kept our voices low. I explained Auster's visit and who he was to me. I knew Rose would be eager for a reason to leave the city, even if just for a while, but I didn't expect how enthused she would be at the notion.

"This is great!" she said, taking my hands. The comfort and joy was kind of jarring.

"We don't know that yet. It could be a trap."

"It's your people!" She gushed. "Another bonded; this is wonderful."

Then I understood. Rose saw this as a way out. That I wasn't wholly con-demned to Nyte if I chose Auster instead.

"That doesn't mean anything to me," I said.

Her face relaxed. "It will. You have to give him a chance to show you. For all we know, Nightsdeath has been manipulating your feelings all this time. With his mind ability, how can you trust any of it?"

My skin was beginning to prick with ire but I didn't expect her to under-stand. To everyone on the outside, Nyte was a monster known to kill without mercy and manipulate for his gain. It wasn't a matter of truth but perception.

Rose asked, "Will you tell Zath?"

"I want to," I admitted. "Do you think I can trust him?"

"As much as it pains me to give him any credit, yes, I do. He might have come to you by Nightsdeath's request, but his love for you is undeniable. I don't think he would betray your trust."

"He already has—in keeping Nyte a secret from me all that time."

It made sense now. How easy it had been to get him to follow Rose in the Libertatem instead because he knew Nyte was with me. I was never alone, whereas Rose had no one.

"What would you have done if he had told you? It would have distracted you when there was already so much to figure out in that game."

She was right, and it was unexpected for Rose to be the voice of reason. I liked the layers of her that were peeling back one by one.

"I guess there's no reason not to tell him then. Maybe he can help make sure Nyte is distracted or come with us. I'm hoping to learn more about the celestials and see where it will lead me."

"I never believed in them, if I'm honest. Cassia found them fascinating even if they did turn out to be a fable. She promised that after the Libertatem we'd go to the veil, close enough to touch it."

Rose leaned her arms on the side of the pavilion and rested her cheek on her hands to look up. I did the same, and for a moment that stole me away, it was like the three of us were together.

"She got to see it first," I said bittersweetly. "The whole world."

"It was her dream."

"I miss her." My voice reduced to a whisper. "So much that I wonder if it'll ever get easier."

Rose's hazel eyes were bright in the moonlight, her gaze falling from the sky to me, and she smiled sorrowfully.

"I hope it never does," she said.

I'd come to learn grief was not something to heal but embrace. Every time it came back strong enough to take the light and pull me to my knees, I would thank it and treasure the days I had to carry on for both of us.

"Can we make a promise?" I asked quietly.

Rose nodded and our friendship pulled fractions closer.

"If we find ourselves overwhelmed or unsure how to move forward, we'll look up at the sky, and the brightest star will guide us back."

Rose reached for my hand, a binding of our promise that settled securely in my chest.

"Stray." Zath's voice carried as gentle as the wind and we both straightened.

As he headed toward us across the roof, his face bore so much concern scanning every inch of me.

Over the last two days, I'd been wondering how I would feel to see him again. After all he'd confessed, I wasn't sure how to process. But now he was here, and I stood from the pavilion as he stepped up. I walked into his arms as naturally as breathing air.

My brow crumpled in his strong, familiar embrace. There were very few places in the world I felt this kind of safety, and despite everything, I was glad to find that never changed.

"I'm still mad at you," I mumbled into his chest.

"I know," he said, like a breath of relief.

"Has Nyte asked anything more of you?"

I dreaded the answer as I pulled back, still wanting to cling to the belief that Zath was still mine. My friend, my ally. Not Nyte's spy.

"I'm here for you. Not him. Please believe me."

I nodded, choosing to be grateful he was here at all.

Rose remained silent, but her hard stare on Zath spoke enough hostility.

"One sheds thorns while the other grows new ones daily," he muttered.

Her scowl only deepened, but the twitch of his mouth before she stood told me he riled her on purpose. That was a tangle of vines I didn't want to find myself in the middle of.

We headed inside and ended up intercepted by Davina, who fussed over me. I'd longed to see her again, despite the fact that she also had a secret alliance with Nyte and posed as my human handmaiden during the Libertatem when she was really a skilled fae warrior. She held my arms, scrutinizing every inch of me and scolding Nyte for putting me behind bars even for a day. I was glad to not be alone in my ire about it.

"He means well but his methods aren't always right," she said, looping my arm as we walked. "We need a plan to get back at him."

My mouth quirked at the thought. It was twisted of me to find a thrill in provoking Nyte.

Inside the castle, the free-roaming vampires set me on edge. There was a hierarchy among them that had become clearer; now that I was around more of them, with time to observe my fear of them lessening. I had to admit I found it intriguing to learn more about the vampires.

The soulless were seen as the most elite. I noticed how they dressed in finer wears and carried themselves with a certain arrogance. The shadowless were like commanders to their generals. Then the nightcrawlers were the foot soldiers. Their tall leathery wings and piercing red eyes only stalked around when the sun fell, but the nights were stretching longer. Giving more hours to the creatures cursed to darkness.

Davina led us to the banquet hall where a long spread of food was laid out on two benched tables. It was a common dining area and we tried not to pay attention to the vampires littered around. It was odd to see them eating and drinking wine—or was it blood in those chalices? I shuddered at the notion. Oddly, I didn't expect them to be so . . . ordinary.

Their stares made my skin crawl. Most only regarded us with a passing glance. Others glared a little longer. I swore a shadowless licked his lips as we passed and I wanted to suggest we dine elsewhere.

I had to get used to this. Coexistence. It was a struggle to let go of the stories I had eavesdropped upon from the rafters of my old manor and the tales Goldfell told that made the world seem too vast and full of terrors. That there was no mercy and nothing worth leaving his safety for. They weren't full lies, but he'd warped my mind to make every small fear a monster too big to face.

Now, I had to become their monster. There was a time of peace and if they wouldn't follow me in amity, then fear it would have to be. There was a power inside me I hadn't truly touched yet, and I didn't know what it made me to be itching for it.

To never be powerless again.

So I let them stalk their hungry stares on me so I could know which ones to starve out first.

We sat at the end of a bench and I filled my plate with fruits and a few cuts of meat. I barely got a few mouthfuls before a dark and familiar awareness stroked my senses. My head turned enough to watch Nyte stroll into the hall. He pinned his attention on me the whole way, as if I was the only person in the room.

I couldn't explain the language in his eyes every time he stalked me with them. It was personal, always daring, and enticing. Noise muted around us the longer we locked defiantly. He slipped onto the bench beside me, and the breaking of our stare felt like something physical.

"Glad to see you are all surviving your first meal without becoming one," Nyte said pleasantly. A suspicion in itself, but he merely smiled at me.

Rose glared at him from across the table while Zath shifted a nervous look around the vampires.

"He's being an ass," Davina muttered. "He wouldn't have let us come here if there was a real threat."

"Oh, there is," Nyte countered. "I'm just confident I could intervene before a vampire could finish the course."

"Why are we here?" Rose grumbled. "I'd rather eat in my rooms."

Nyte was turned to me, one hand braced behind me on the bench, the other casually lifting food to his mouth from my plate as if he didn't have an empty one to fill right in front of him. He even started adding things absent-mindedly to mine, like the little cinnamon rolls I couldn't reach.

"We have to show a united front," he explained.

"You don't have control over shit then," Rose said.

Nyte found entertainment with Rose, and it was like she enjoyed prodding him for weakness.

"I see you want a demonstration. There's a few targets on my list right now anyway."

Nyte stood and the room darkened with the shift in him. The first cry to echo through the hall came from the vampire I'd seen walking in here who tracked me as if I was meal. Nyte moved so flawlessly through shadow that I only blinked and he'd gone from standing in front of me to across the room, hand retracting from the vampire's back with a bleeding heart in his palm.

The food in my stomach threatened to come back up when he placed it onto the plate next to the vampire's head. The blood on his hand wiped away in shadow.

"Let that be a warning to anyone else who thinks about tasting Astraea's blood. I will hear you, then drain yours," Nyte announced.

He sauntered back to us with a calm smile.

"That was an overreaction," I muttered as he sat back beside me.

"Really? Then I won't tell you the other thoughts that crossed my mind before tearing his heart out."

He reached for a square of cheese from my plate but I grabbed his wrist.

"You're not touching my food with a hand that was in a man's chest a minute ago."

Nyte's mouth curved in amusement. "I like it when you're firm with me."

I shoved his hand away. Deviant bastard.

"What is the plan now?" I asked, changing the subject.

"I've never been one for plans. I find they end up unfolding in every which way but the course that was expected."

"So we do nothing?"

"Of course not. I'm looking forward to seeing your magick alive again."

"What about the bond? You made it sound urgent we . . . *bind it.*"

"There's nothing I want more," he said so close to my ear that I breathed consciously to force down the sparks of desire. "I only needed your agreement to it. I'll tide the eager vampires over about it until you're ready. They'll be happy you're making progress with your abilities; after all, that's what they want on their side for this alliance."

I didn't like how this made me feel like a pawn to gain and move.

"I won't yield to you," I said, turning my head to lock our eyes close.

"Good. One day, every person in this world will kneel for *you.*"

"I'll give it to you," Rose said. "Your manipulation is pretty."

I tensed at the gibe at Nyte and while he would usually play along with her, this time she struck a nerve.

"This is the only time I warn you," he said with deceiving calm. "Insult me, attack me, think whatever you want of me. But never question my intentions toward Astraea again."

"Burn in hell, Nightsdeath."

Nyte reached for his cup of wine. "When you come looking for me down there, I'll be the one burning brightest for once."

"Anything new about your father?" I asked carefully.

It was an attempt to sway the conversation but the mention of his father might have made him more volatile.

"He can't hide for long. Once he comes out, I'll be waiting."

"You're not concerned about what power he might have gained from the opening of the temple with my key?"

"I'm not concerned about what I can't control. It is done, and I'll be ready for him no matter what he's planning."

I didn't think it was the whole truth. His composure was masterful, but underneath, I could feel his tension brewing but I didn't know how to soothe it.

"I wasn't expecting Drystan to be at the front line with the most notorious vampires behind his father's back. I didn't even know the prince was your brother; how could you keep that from me?" Zathrian complained.

Nyte leaned an elbow on the table like the topic tired him.

"Would you really have helped me if you knew I was the son of the king you despised?"

Zathrian took only a second to contemplate. "I still don't understand why he would make an enemy out of not only his son, but someone as powerful as you."

"He hoped to have Astraea as leverage against me and tried to use Drystan to do it." Nyte's eyes shifted to me. "It's how Drystan was the first to find you—my father sent him on the hunt for you the moment we all felt you had returned—but he let you go."

"Sounds like the better brother," Rose said.

"You'll have to find something I *don't* agree with to wound me."

"We need to find him," I said. "We can't let him kill himself."

"Agreed," Nyte said, plucking a grape from my plate before I could scold him. "Only because I can't risk him coming back as a more prominent thorn in my side."

I couldn't read how much he meant that, but it hurt in my heart to think of the hate between them. I resented their father, believing he had to be the knife that split them apart, but then I remembered what Drystan had accused Nyte of in the tower . . .

My sight slipped to him and his expression turned guarded, as if he knew what I had recalled: Was he capable of killing Drystan's mother?

"Where would he have gone?" Zath asked, breaking me from that grim thought.

"I'm not entirely sure," Nyte drawled. Then he spoke to me. "He's my concern. Right now, you have to focus on awakening the magick within you."

My skin pricked at the notion. "I'm ready."

His smile of pride made a beat in my chest strike harder. "Yes you are."

Just then something caught Nyte's attention at the far double doors. I followed his sight to find Elliot standing next to a blonde woman with a cold, steely expression that contrasted the warmth of Elliot's.

"If you'll excuse me," Nyte said. He stood and I yearned to ask where he was going, but I had to accept that Nyte had a life out here. A duty. I wanted to trust he wouldn't keep things from me anymore and that if something was important he would tell me.

"When does training start?" I asked before he stepped away.

"Tomorrow," he said, leaning into me with a hand on the table. He spilled my silver hair over my shoulder like he forgot the room of people around us. "Make sure you stay out of trouble for my sanity, please." The warmth of his breath lingered across my cheek before he straightened and headed toward Elliot. To my thoughts he added, *"Think of me, or long for me and I'll come sooner."*

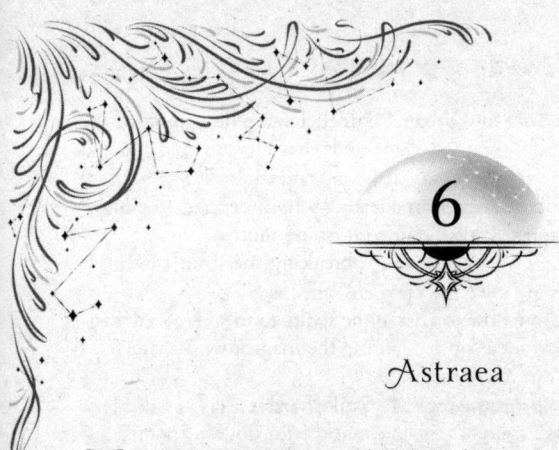

6

Astraea

I loved heights, but I couldn't deny the turning of my stomach as I stood on a small flat plane at the highest point of the castle. It wasn't from the lack of any barrier that would prevent a fall, nor the shortage of space; it was the way Nyte kept eyes on me like a predator and I couldn't be certain what his next move would be.

He wouldn't push me off the ledge . . .

Would he?

I couldn't stop admiring his towering midnight feathered wings. The silver celestial feathers were ethereal, but Nyte's would always lure me with their peaceful darkness. It trickled thoughts of Auster with the reminder I had to find a day that Nyte might be away long enough for me to leave. Guilt over the secret I harbored from him unsettled me, but it felt necessary for now, and hopefully forgivable later.

At least Nyte had the confidence to be up here while the bitter temperature made it even more precarious. I couldn't take a step without shuffling my boot to test if there was hidden ice when I didn't have wings like him to catch me if I fell.

"Why are we up here?" I asked, but he hadn't answered me the first two times I'd asked.

"Show me again," he said, folding his arms.

Part of me wanted to refuse, but I had to believe there was some method to it when he said he would help me learn my magick. My hands came together, building a tingling heat that spread out over every silver marking I wore like they were beacons of the magickal force coming to life inside me.

A glow formed—a breathtaking sphere of glittering silver and violet.

"You haven't told me what I can do with it," I said.

"You're learning how to summon it with less and less conscious effort," he explained. "It should come as easily as breathing soon."

He was right. At first I had trembled with it, maybe even feared it, but now

I was excited to feel its presence and it came lighter. I wanted to build on it, use it.

"Now, we need you to be able to handle this," he said carefully.

My eyes fell on what he held at the same time my body reacted to a magnetic force so strong my magick winked out from my panic.

The key.

"You said it's volatile for my untrained power," I hedged.

"So long as you don't know how to control it. I'm here to stop you if you get out of control with it."

"How will you do that?"

Nyte shrugged. "It will hurt immensely. Please don't take that as a motivator to make me."

I rolled my eyes. "Tempting."

He fought a smile as he held the key out to me.

As I reached for it a loud grunt followed by a thump from a few levels below and across the rooftops caught my attention. Zath was peeling himself off the ground while Rose stood, cross-armed and triumphant.

"There was ice!" Zath protested.

"You're a horrible loser," Rose gibed.

It was as close to getting along as I'd seen them since everything happened. Taking their frustrations out on each other became a language I could somewhat understand.

Nyte said, "I'm going to order them inside—"

"Don't." I reached to stop him. "They'll suffocate each other indoors. The open air makes them seem less prone to explosion."

"You need to focus."

"I am."

I thrust my hand out for the key. He handed it over and I breathed against the pulses of energy reaching inside me like it wanted to merge.

"You are the key," Nyte said, beginning to pace the small space in front of me. "It is very powerful, but it answers to *you*, not the other way around. Even when you don't realize it. Like what you did in the throne room."

I shivered at the recollection, not certain how I had commanded such power from it then when I was driven by reckless desperation with the eruption of battle that day.

Nyte reached a hand into starry shadow, retracting from it a black blade.

"Why am I not surprised?" I muttered. The glistening sword was both repelling and alluring.

"This is obsidian; it's particularly harmful to celestials." He flipped the blade in his palm, and my mouth parted in surprise at the purple side. "The celestials have stormstone, a material first created from the House of Nova which is lethal to the vampires."

My arm dropped with the key. His sword was artistic. Crafted to harm both celestials and vampires as if he chose no side or could decide to eradicate both. I wanted to get closer to take in the details of the hilt that seemed to hold a crescent moon in the center of the cross guard.

"Aren't you . . . part celestial?"

"Not exactly. The wings are more like a brand."

I traced them with my eyes again, greedily capturing every detail of the wings that shone as iridescently as raven feathers in the daytime.

"When you met the God of Death?" I realized.

"Celestial wings are tones of silver," he explained. "Black is an omen of Death Angels to them. It's His mark. To your people, I'm a mockery and an abomination."

He added the last part with a wicked smirk but I wondered if it shadowed some part of him that was affected by the notion. An angel of death seemed a fitting way to describe Nyte, though not in the way he spoke of it. Like being cursed. Shunned. I thought him beautiful. Then there was the term *my people* that didn't settle right when it felt like a divide between us.

"When I . . . stabbed you,"—I winced—"What happened to you?"

"You killed me, essentially. I've died many times; I'm pretty good at it."

The casual way he spoke it disturbed me deeply. Just like how he spoke of his torture in the cave. Nyte had long since given up believing it wasn't normal . . . that no person should live through the suffering he had lived through.

"You're looking at me like that again," he said, so stiff and ready to raise a guard against me.

"Like I want to drive a blade through your chest?"

Just like that, his tension dissolved and a cunning thrill upturned his face. What had grown sorrow within me didn't ease; however, I could pretend for him when it was clear he didn't want to be vulnerable with me. Suddenly the thought of him leaving and never having the chance to see under every layer that formed around him seized me with despair. That he would forever wear them and believe his burdens mattered to no one but him.

"Make the key a blade," he instructed.

I wasn't in the mood to engage in combat.

"How many celestial houses are there?" I asked instead.

Nyte propped himself in a slight side lean with his blade against the ground. I fought against a scowl.

"I don't like swords," I complained.

"Because the one you wield as the key is not like steel or any other material. It's featherlight and can inflict far more than a cut when you channel magick through it."

I remembered. The way an unfathomable sheet of light magick had expelled from the key to kill the guards who had held Nyte on his knees in the cave. Then again to shatter the veil.

As I thought of that moment, my palm tingled, and when I looked down I marveled at the shape-shifted weapon.

"Very good," Nyte said with genuine excitement. "There are four celestial houses: Nova, Sera, Luna, Aura. They govern Althenia."

The knowledge in exchange for practice seemed fair. Though for every piece of the world he shared I strained with a hundred questions. I would visit Althenia soon, but it was helpful to gain a little insight to not be a complete clueless fool to Auster.

I don't know why I cared about his opinion of me, but it had been riddling me with anxiety since I met him.

I lifted my arm to admire the lightness of the key. He was right—it wasn't like any sword I'd tried before and swiftly gave up on. It glowed beautifully and with a near shimmer. The cross guard was like metal filigree. Beautifully delicate with an ethereal touch. The amethyst crystal of the key shone in the center above the silver blade and in the pommel.

"You can also make it a bow," he said. "With light arrows that never run out because they're crafted entirely of your magick."

It didn't feel like that could be possible. That *I* could be capable of that but still I became exhilarated by the prospect.

"One thing at a time though. Each method of using the key drains you differently and we have to start slow. You are powerful but not unstoppable. No matter what you feel, never forget that."

"The houses; which do I belong to?"

"None of them. You are the ruler of Solanis—raised by the Guardians from all species to be fair and unbiased even though you come from celestial blood as the only heritage that could sustain what you are."

It seemed inconceivable. That this fable he spoke of, the star-maiden, wasn't such after all.

She was me. I was her.

I took a long breath trying to absorb what he was saying. Denial wouldn't help me in this.

"Are you ready to try combat with your magick?"

I nodded vacantly.

"Good."

It was the tone of that single word that stroked my instincts like a declaration of battle, lashing my other hand to grip the hilt of the key and bring it up in the nick of time against Nyte's attack.

I met his wicked gleam, glowing from the key, with incredulity.

"No warning?" I choked out.

"I didn't think you'd need it."

He moved again, and I yelped, slipping with clumsy footing. My heels went over the edge and seconds from gravity's claim—

My flailing arm was caught and both my hands wrapped Nyte's forearm as I leaned off the fatally high ledge, my soles close to losing their purchase on the roof. Nyte's hold was the only thing preventing me from falling back completely.

"We need to work on that," he commented. "You are very agile; you shouldn't be this clumsy."

"Nyte." He didn't pull me back up and my rapid breaths clouded the frosty air.

"You're thinking too much. You have an acute instinct to defend yourself; I've seen it. Past life aside."

"Rainyte!"

His eyes snapped to mine, not in warning but with devilish challenge.

That bastard.

"You know, it kind of turns me on when you use my full name like that."

How he stood like stone holding the weight of me from falling was against all laws of gravity.

"Don't you dare let me go."

That was the wrong thing to say.

"Since you've made it a dare—"

"Nyte—!"

Too late.

My stomach flipped when he let go. My utter disbelief didn't get the chance to dominate when fear gripped my free fall. I caught the fading shouts of Zath and Rose before air roared in my ears and the sharpness of the cold cut across my cheeks and lobes.

"You have wings. Use them," he spoke to my mind.

Nyte was absolutely insane. Completely mad. Utterly twisted.

If I didn't die, I was going to fucking kill him.

I closed my eyes, feeling for *something*. An essence of magick I couldn't fully grasp.

"Fly, Starlight."

"I can't."

Too many emotions cut through any belief I was trying to gather. That I could do it. Fly. The possibility felt almost tangible and I wanted it more than anything. Until my mind rebelled, chanting that I deserved to fall, and suddenly it was like the ground grew vines to reach up to ensnare me. Making wings impossible to form in their tangled clutches. Pulling me faster and faster so I would shatter when it ended.

An arm wrapped my middle and on instinct I clung to the safety. My legs wrapped around Nyte's waist, arms clamping his neck, and I couldn't help the sob that broke from me as the rapid decline turned to a gentle floating.

When Nyte met the ground I unhooked myself from him, unable to stop the barrel of rage that flattened my palms to his chest, and pushed hard.

"You're an ass!" I hissed.

He remained unyielding to my outburst and that only fueled my hatred more. The hum in my palm reminded me of the tight grip I still had on the key.

I attacked.

It was Nyte's turn to respond with only seconds to spare as he reached into the void to call his blade. Every time our swords clashed it didn't emit the clang of steel I was used to hearing but instead they sang to each other in a hymn that soothed my senses. No longer was it my anger driving my movements but a song I was sure I'd heard before.

A memory started flooding into my present.

The trees we'd landed around began to fade away.

The daylight slowly darkened to night and the air wasn't as cold anymore. It was smoke-clogged and warm.

Nyte wasn't clean and well dressed, he was battle-worn and tired.

So much heartache stretched between us like every attack and defense we made against one another was tight with regret but somehow necessary.

I stopped, panting hard, and the daylight returned like a lashing back to our current surroundings.

The key dropped from my hand and Nyte only stared back, assessing my every flicker of reaction.

I fell to my knees, touching the frosted grass with gloved fingers while my mind reeled with the memory that had filtered its way into my present.

"We were really enemies," I recalled through a labored breath.

What I'd seen was another piece of the day I'd given him the scar he wore from his right temple and over his cheekbone.

"Yes," he said.

"Why did you never heal that scar?"

Nyte's knees entered my vision in front. When I couldn't look up he took my chin. I could hardly stand to look at my mark on him.

"Because it's a piece of you."

"It's proof you narrowly escaped my attempt to kill you."

"Your determination and anger are two of my favorite things."

"How—" I shook my head trying to make sense of it. Us. "How did we look past what we are? Everything that makes us wrong together."

"We realized that what made us *wrong* was in favor of the world, and for a while . . . we got the chance to choose selfishness."

"That didn't work out in our favor either," I whispered. Words that were daggers in my chest.

He didn't try to soothe the truth. "No."

I nodded, sniffing against the emotions that were threatening to spill.

"Just as well we don't have to worry about it again," I said coldly, pushing up, I marched past him toward the castle. I would not break. "You'll be gone soon anyway."

7

Nyte

Astraea truly thought I would leave her, and my mind had been punishing itself since our training session. I enjoyed the heat of her anger, but I couldn't stand the twist of her resentment.

It was better this way. If I was *good,* I would let her continue to believe I was leaving and that I would not care. That I wouldn't look back.

Truth was, I would never look forward if I had to leave her behind. I would choose darkness because within that depth of nothingness my denial could thrive.

"Vampire," Elliot muttered.

Not to me. He'd made a game with Zeik, Kerrah, and Sorleen—the rest of the Golden Guard—trying to guess if every new person who walked into the establishment we sat in was human or a transitioned vampire.

The Guard were loyal to me and had fine skills as the most highly trained I'd overseen personally. I knew them better than I thought they knew themselves. Every weakness and flaw, habit and desire. I could break them as easily as I made them, yet that never crossed my mind. Never once had I wanted them gone, even when they tested my patience to the very edge.

We'd come to a bordello at the edge of Vesitire where there'd been a number of reports of missing persons. This new strain of vampires had rounded ears, not pointed. They were masterful at blending in, whereas the soulless and shadowless were born with an immortal grace and stillness that also set them apart.

"Not a vampire," I countered, taking a drink. The human wine was doing nothing to curb my sharp edges from being away from Astraea.

"We've been tracking them longer than you," Elliot challenged. "We know the tells."

"We *are* them," Kerrah added. She sat lazily, elbow propped on the table, playing with a strand of her brown hair.

"Exactly!" Elliot said.

"What are these *tells* you look for?" I asked.

It was Zeik who replied, "Without getting close enough for scent, it's always in the arrogance. He comes in here like he could kill everyone to get what he wants."

"Arrogance is human nature and it feeds on the rich. He *could* kill everyone to get what he wants; he doesn't need fangs for it."

The transitioned were difficult to distinguish from the humans. Even their changed scent was faint and required me to get too close for casual conversation. They were the ultimate weapon in disguise, which became clear when I'd witnessed how fast they could tear through a room with insatiable bloodlust. It was a threat I needed to get under my control.

"Now we need to find out," Kerrah said. Her palm slapped the middle of the table. "Not me."

Zeik mirrored her movement and echoed her words, his strength far greater because of his broad build; I swore I heard the table splinter. Elliot quickly followed. Sorleen was slower, not speaking but joining her hand with theirs. She was the most recent Golden Guard. It had been a hundred years since she triumphed in her Libertatem, but her past was haunted and I'd heard her game was particularly brutal, that she'd had to kill her competitors at the end to gain their key pieces. She'd then learned her whole family, who she'd been determined to protect by competing in the Libertatem, had been slaughtered by blood vampires right before she'd won safety from them for her kingdom.

"You act like children," I grumbled, finishing off my drink.

"You act like you have a stick up your ass," Kerrah countered.

I wouldn't break double figures counting how many people would dare speak to me that way.

I stood, heading over to the brown haired man who looked to be past his forties. He leaned one arm on the bar and with the other hooked the waist of a woman working as she passed. She startled to it, uncomfortable with his arm tugging her closer when she tried to keep a little space.

He was making this too easy for me.

When his eyes landed on me all the false confidence fell from his face and that conceited mouth finally stopped spilling self-importance to fill the void left by what others wouldn't give him. The woman read my signal and scooted off before I dropped a hand to the man's shoulder.

I was about to be proven right.

Nightsdeath surfaced as the thing that had a craving for human blood, the vampire kin part of me. I was born fae, made a vampire, and had the wings of an outcasted celestial. An accursed trifecta.

My teeth pierced the flesh of his neck before a sound could escape his mouth. Screams from onlookers filled in for his silent horror as I drank from him. His blood had a bitter note and certainly wasn't anything to indulge in. Human blood was like wine: there were far sweeter to be sampled and some could be simply sour. It had been so long since I'd tasted it at all that a dark hunger was overcoming me regardless, and if I didn't stop I would kill him.

I even found myself reaching into his mind, crushing the fear to make him weak and susceptible in my trap. He had no family and had inherited his money from a rich uncle who died just this year. No—he'd killed him for the money. No woman to love. No children to bear it either. He'd spent this time gambling away riches he didn't know what to do with other than drink and take.

I could kill him.

The world wouldn't miss him. No one would care.

Just a little more.

If I let him go he would continue to waste away, gamble his fortune, end up dying by some idiotic means anyway.

In all my deliberation I'd passed the point of no return. I drank the final measure that thumped one last deep beat in his chest before it had nothing left to circulate.

Well, shit.

The body dropped from my grip when my teeth released him, and I braced a hand on the damp wooden bar. I hadn't intended to kill him when I'd come over here to prove he wasn't a transitioned—their blood was foul to another vampire—and even now I wish I could say I felt guilty about it.

"Damn, I was sure of that one," Elliot muttered behind me.

I was gathering my breath, reeling so much from the trance the blood pulled me into that I'd long forgotten the euphoria of. It was racing within me now, like a surge of energy that could kill everyone in this room before one person could finish screaming. I had control of myself but I couldn't deny I'd missed the exhilarating high of a feed.

"Hunting vampires, are you?" A seductive feminine voice spoke.

The establishment had mostly cleared out. Some women workers clutched each other in the corners, observing us with both fear and curiosity. There was a time vampires were alluring to the humans. Feeding on them could be a mutually pleasurable experience.

My eyes dragged to the woman who spoke. She sat cross-legged on a table, leaning her hands on either side of her as she watched us with a wickedly intrigued smile. Her deep wine-red hair was pulled back high with several braids.

"Did you take bets on me?" she asked.

"You gave her a pass," Zeik grunted, pushing Elliot.

"In my defense, she came in looking a sad, lost puppy."

Her mouth only quirked to that. "You're lacking a mind with a deeper sense of perception," she said to me.

It wasn't often I was gripped by intrigue about someone. The others, however, took offense, now pinning her with cutting looks of disdain.

"I trust my own just fine," I said; reaching down to pluck the dead man's pocket square, I wiped the blood cornering my mouth.

"A lone wolf never survives."

"When it can't be killed, it'll take its chances."

"Then why do you keep these brainless fools around you?"

"Do you know who we are?" Zeik said, folding his arms, and making his build even more intimidating.

"The *esteemed* Golden Guard," she gushed, mocking them with a straightening pose and bat of her lashes. Then her face fell, unfazed.

"Then you know what it took to get here," he snapped.

"How you got here is well known, and I'll admit, the Libertatem sounds like hell. But many of us play a game of survival just by *living* and don't get a damn title for it."

"She has a point," Kerrah muttered. The hand she laid on Zeik's arm relaxed him. "But I was leaning more on Nyte's side with him *not* being a vampire."

They all regarded the dead human. Darkness spilled from my fingers to engulf the body, sweeping his existence away. It had been a reckless, dangerous risk to drink after so long in sobriety when it became a struggle to subdue the beast inside me wanting to seek out more. That tuned acutely to the pulse of the women across the room and made my mouth salivate with the thought of how much more delectable their blood would be.

It was a line I would not cross. Except for those who'd given themselves willingly, I'd never harmed a woman.

The others were chatting but I had to focus on my control. I needed an outlet for this rush of adrenaline and I couldn't decide if I wanted to wreak havoc or expend it in a wild heated passion. My mind flooded with the image of glittering silver hair and seductive light blue eyes. My obsession for Astraea clawed its way to the surface and every fiber of my being longed for her. I had to get this over with. Then I would find her.

"What do you want?" I asked, straightening and turning to the red-haired beauty.

"I heard you're looking for Drystan."

"What do you know of him?"

"From what I gather, more than his own brother."

"Don't play with me. It won't end well for you."

"I haven't started playing with you, and I'll take my chances."

I kind of admired her quick wit and boldness. I also wanted to snap her neck for it.

"Where is he?"

"For that, I want something in return."

"I don't bargain with rogues."

"Then let me join your little tribe of nightmares."

"My—what?"

She gestured around at Elliot and the others. "This band of *rogues*."

"We did not come out on top of our Libertatem games to be likened to strays like you," Zeik said.

"Of course, the prized Golden Guard of the king, except . . . there is no king now, is there? Looks like you're all just rogues like the rest of us."

"What is your name?" I asked.

"Nadia."

"Do you work for my brother?"

"I thought we established I'm a rogue."

"Bored of that, are you?" Zeik chimed in, studying her with crossed arms.

"You could say that. I know where your brother is; I know a lot of things about the transitioned vampire army he's been building."

"What's in it for you by sharing that with us?" Elliot asked.

"I want to join you."

"I don't know what you think it is we do," Kerrah said, leaning against a table.

Nadia shrugged. "I'm intrigued to find out what the Band of Nightmares gets up to with their time."

"I quite like the name," Zeik commented.

She wouldn't be my problem if I agreed, and I wouldn't care if the others decided to dispose of her at any point.

"Fine," I said. The others all snapped their gazes to me. "She'll get us the information we need faster. Kill her if she becomes an annoyance, or—" I targeted a look of warning on her, one that had dropped men to their knees; she wisely straightened with her first sign of unease. "If you find her to be a spy for my brother, or anyone for that matter, her death is mine. And let me tell you, little rogue, it will not be merciful."

"You're as charming as I expected, Nightsdeath," she sang.

"Expect what you want of a monster; it'll still find ways to terrorize you."

Nadia hopped off the table. "I am at your service," she said with mock bow. "Then talk."

"His highness is where he's always been—overseeing the transitioned vampires. Those who are deemed *sane* enough eventually get to leave the mountain they're trained in. A series of caves carved high in a deserted pocket of Vesitire. His—*your*—father wanted it to be of the utmost discretion. As far as I know, the other vampires don't know of the creations other than the golden guard. They have no knowledge of the scale to which the army has been built."

Elliot frowned deeply. "We know there's far more than us, but an army?"

Nadia nodded. Her green eyes shifted to me. "To prove my loyalty I'll give you the first piece of insight."

I had a bad fucking feeling, but nothing about the many storms clashing in this war would be pleasant.

"Go on," I prompted.

"It takes dying with the blood of a shadowless in the human system to return as a transitioned. Have you ever wondered what the consequences are?"

"Bloodlust isn't enough?" Sorleen muttered. They were the first words she'd spoken from her quiet observance.

Nadia regarded her as if just noting her presence. "You think you're all loyal to Nyte. But your creator can demand you turn against him at any moment."

"Our creator?" Zeik echoed.

"The transition creates a blood bond," Nadia clarified.

"How do you know this?" Elliot asked.

"I made it my business to. When you have nowhere to go and no one to see, time without purpose can drive you to madness. I never wanted to return to that mountain once I was free, but I also felt like I had to gain something back. I watched a transitioned who was out of control and Drystan stopped him with mere words. The vampire tried to resist, insatiable in his bloodlust that had torn through a dozen humans, but he couldn't fight the prince who just stood there, commanding him to stop. It dawned on me then, the power Drystan had over anyone who was turned by his blood."

My bad feeling manifested as something cold and dark and ugly, I came to a realization before she could even confirm the turn this was about to take.

"You were turned by Drystan's blood," I concluded. Her silence was answer enough.

"So if you kill your creator . . . ?" Zeik hedged.

"We won't be able to be commanded against our will," Nadia confirmed.

"Shit," Elliot muttered. "How do we know who our creator is?"

"You'd feel it if you were close to them—the submission. It's like a compulsion to please them even if you despise them."

Everyone was staring at me.

"Your attachment to me is entirely of your own foolish volition," I grumbled at the unspoken accusation.

"Attachment is a strong word," Elliot said.

"You haven't attempted to kill Drystan yet?" I asked Nadia. My fist clamped tight against my trembles of anger.

"I haven't liked my odds. He's smart, elusive."

Yes he was. I didn't credit him enough for his intelligence; I didn't think he needed it. Until now, if he truly planned to risk his life based on a fable to reach Death's realm.

I didn't tell her the problem might be solved soon enough.

"So you've come to me for an alliance?"

"I watched you on the rooftops not long after the Libertatem. I was curious about you when I heard you were back. It looked like both of you were ready to kill the other up there."

I could think about killing my brother a million times, but hearing someone else talk of it—*plan* for it—was itching at something highly defensive in me. Drystan was many things, but he was my problem to deal with.

"No one approaches him without my knowledge or presence," I warned everyone.

"We're not going now?" Nadia said, crossing her arms with an impatient frown.

It was the last thing I wanted to do right now. The night was falling, and I had been away from my Starlight too long.

"Keep her in your sights," I told Elliot.

"I didn't come to be a pet on a leash," Nadia snapped.

"Go after Drystan without my knowledge, little rogue, and you'll understand what it feels like to crave death."

"Where are you going?" she asked with an edge of bitterness.

"None of your concern. We'll visit my little brother tomorrow."

Drystan was prone to saying things that provoked the shit out of me and I was too on edge with my high from the blood to deal with him tonight. Human blood drove a certain kind of frenzy I needed an outlet for. I was trying not to kill senselessly, so instead of venturing to unleash my heightened emotions in violence, I craved to turn my impulses toward my Starlight. Astraea could taunt and test me to the very edge too, but unlike anyone else, whether in rage or passion, I desired every piece of her.

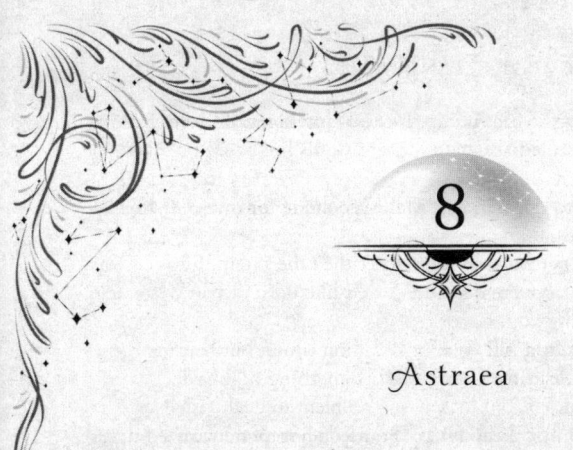

8

Astraea

For the whole climb to the tower I'd been trying to rehearse what I would say to Calix. After all he confessed in the throne room, setting me up for some anonymous hit in exchange for a way to save Cassia— a plan that got her killed anyway—I wasn't sure if I would be able to face him again. I'd made Nyte spare his life, and now I had to find out why my heart couldn't just let him die.

Nyte didn't know I'd come. He'd left this morning to meet with Elliot and the others of the Golden Guard who'd been tracking vampire activity in the other kingdoms since the end of the Libertatem. I wanted to go with him when he asked, but even more so I needed this time alone to face the betrayal in my heart.

Calix sat curled into himself in the back corner of the cell and my chest tightened. He had some hay and a blanket, barely adequate for the winter that came through the small high window above his head.

My lips parted but no words would form. He didn't even look up, though he had to know someone was here from the sound of my boots. He just didn't seem to care.

"Calix," I said quietly.

His brown eyes peeked out from the huddle of his arms. So hauntingly detached from the man I thought I knew.

"Has he ordered my death yet?" he asked, his voice barely a croak, like he hadn't used it in weeks.

"Several times. It's been tempting to let him."

"You don't have to spare me for your conscience."

"I'm not," I said. "I'm sparing you for Cassia."

Calix's eyes closed with that.

"Don't bother; she would likely kill me if she was here anyway. If she could tell you to do it, she would."

"We both know that's not true."

"I betrayed her in trying to set you up. I knew that at the time yet I did it anyway. Instead I got her killed."

"You wanted to save her."

"What are you trying to do, Astraea? Make me atone for my soul? Just let me be damned."

"She would tell you to get yourself together."

Calix huffed, a hollow humorless sound.

"Go away. You're wasting your time."

"You would rather I let him kill you?"

"Does it look like I'm pleading for my life?"

"You're a pitiful coward."

Calix didn't respond to that. I thought of going on but then I realized that's what he wanted. Validation to rot in his pitiful heap.

Unclasping my cloak, I threw it into the cell. It landed over him, and for a second I thought he might disregard it with the sour look he cast me. But he folded into the warmth of it and his body relaxed a little.

"What do you want from me?" he asked, tipping his head back.

"For you to climb out of your self-pity."

"If I pitied myself, it would mean I thought I deserved better."

"I tried to be your friend but you were always an asshole. You said you came after me, to Vesitire, to help. Was that bullshit too?"

"No," he said. Then his eyes dropped to add, "And yes."

My temper flared.

"I spared you from Nyte because I meant what I said in the maze. I forgive you. For Cass. She would have wanted us to be friends."

"That was before you knew the truth of what I'd done."

"Yet I'm still here."

"In the maze," he said distantly, "I said I'd come to say I forgive you. But you did nothing wrong. You always did right by her, protected her, more than I could."

"Stop it," I said. "You don't get to give me that credit, and I'm not going to give you merit and convince you that you were her shining knight either. You fucked up, Calix. But now you have a chance to change that. Cassia loved *life*. To see you disregard yours so easily, meaninglessly, would be the biggest betrayal you could make against her memory."

He met my eyes and for a second I pitied the plea in them. Calix only knew two things. His love, and his duty. He'd lost one and become estranged from the other.

"Take me with you," he said.

"Where?"

He shrugged. "Wherever you're going next. If I still have purpose; being a guard is all I know and I don't think I can go back to Alisus Keep. Not to live there every day when she won't ever return."

I nodded in understanding.

"Nyte can hardly stand you breathing, never mind being close to me. You can't be my guard. And no offense, but I think I could put you on your ass soon."

Calix tried to chuckle, but it was short and hardly there.

"Magick is a cheat."

"It's a helpful advancement."

"If I can't stay with you, maybe you can get me to another kingdom; I'll start again there."

That seemed like a more plausible plan.

"You made terrible mistakes. It doesn't make you a monster."

I turned from him, with a weight off my shoulders now that I had a plan with him.

"Guard your forgiveness, Astraea," he called at my back. "I'm grateful for it, but not everyone deserves it from you no matter who you are."

After visiting Calix, I was looking for Zath or Rose, or both, to suggest we get out of the castle for a while. When I turned the next corner, my steps almost faltered at the sight of the red hair advancing toward me. I shouldn't have taken this route; it was quiet, dark.

I kept my chin high to not give Tarran the satisfaction of rattling me despite his slow, predatory smile. Of course I knew he wouldn't let me pass without engaging.

"Maiden. We haven't had the pleasure of any time together since the end of the Libertatem. What a show Nightsdeath put on, and still he wins your heart."

We faced each other, and I put all my effort into maintaining a front.

"I can't say you've been on my mind as I have been yours."

"You wound me. I hoped we'd get to become acquainted now that we're going to be allies, after all. Accept my apology for any wrongdoings of the past."

"Like I said, I haven't thought about you. Not your life, nor your death."

Tarran took a long inhale, and I wondered if it was to take in more of my scent. I had my answer when it compelled him to step forward. My retreat met the wall and raced my adrenaline.

"Did he tell you what I am?"

"An arrogant son of a bitch."

That earned a wider smile, revealing his sharp teeth, and I shuddered with the glance he couldn't refrain from directing at my neck.

"I'm one of the oldest soul vampires alive, maiden. I was here long before him. Long before you. I was here when the guardians came together and created

Vesitire as the central to rule the surrounding five kingdoms. Althenia has always remained independent. I watched you from the moment of creation and as you came into the star-maiden you were. A creature so magnificent and fair and powerful, the likes of which the land had never been blessed with before. They called your reign the golden age. There was peace among all species."

"Why are you telling me this?"

"Because even the most pure and perfectly crafted things are drawn to darkness. You were no different. Everything you'd built came crashing down all for one. Heart. And now here we are, and I might get to bear witness to what should have happened all that time ago. The fall of eternal darkness because you can't let each other go. It will be an honor to witness."

I couldn't fathom how old Tarran was. It made me blanch like I was nothing more than a child in comparison. He didn't need magick when his power was built from time and patience. Crafting a reputation and an influence that was a prized currency itself. It made sense now that Nyte was being careful, strategic with someone like Tarran.

"This is what you want then—my union with Nyte."

"Of course. Once I found out what was causing the quakes and what would happen if they continued, it was to our best advantage not to hunt you, but to ally with you. But by then it was too late."

"The king wanted me dead. It could have been him who finally got the job done."

"Perhaps. No one has ever really believed he had any power and I couldn't understand why Nightsdeath would cater to his father when he held all the influence. He made the entire continent fear him. I'll admit I'm curious as to how you see though all the blood that coats him. Every sin he's committed against all you stand for."

It wasn't all the truth.

"Like you said, I was made to see the good in people. To be fair."

His head canted curiously. "Even to me?"

"I'd give you the grace of a trial."

His smile was all sly amusement—a mockery that didn't believe I had any authority over him so he would never fear my judgment.

Tarran came inches closer and my heart sped, bracing with the need to defend myself if he tried to harm me. He merely leaned in like I was prey to play with, dropping his tone so low my hearing turned acute.

"One of them is going to betray you. One of them already has."

He pulled back but I was still held tightly by that chilling statement.

"Who?" I choked, suffocating.

"The only thing you have two of. In this life and the last."

"You don't know anything."

Tarran merely smiled. Then his head tilted as if something I couldn't hear caught his attention.

"You know, Bonded is just a title really. I would be a fool not to offer you a way out of either choice. I have the might of all the vampire armies; I would treat you like the queen you are."

He couldn't be serious. Not even the slightest spark of intrigue formed over his outlandish proposal. He seemed to find his answer in my blank expression but it didn't deter the wild flare in his brown eyes.

"I look forward to the ceremony, Astraea."

He left me standing there. I couldn't move. He was just trying to scare me with that riddle. Spiral my mind between Nyte and Auster or maybe warn me to choose neither.

"There she is." Zath's loud voice bounding through the hall caused me to jump out of my skin.

I turned to find him and Rose heading toward me. His bright grin began to fall, and he scanned me head to toe.

"What's wrong? You look like you've seen a ghost."

"Nothing," I said, not convincingly enough, but my head wouldn't stop spinning. "I need to get out of here."

"Where are you going?" Rose asked, jogging to fall into step after I marched past.

"Just into the city. I need a distraction. Perhaps a drink."

"Rose and I were just heading there actually. We came to ask if you wanted to join."

My nerves were already beginning to calm.

"Why were you planning to go out there?" I asked.

"We've been meaning to revisit a particular hat shop," Zath said. I peered up at him just as he exchanged a look with Rose.

I curved a brow. "A hat shop?"

"From the trials," Rose explained in a grumble.

I thought to probe further but figured it would only bring on a headache.

Outside, I breathed the cool air steadily and let my mind empty of vampires and celestials and Nyte for a while. Well, maybe not Nyte, since I hadn't seen him all day and the absence was notable in my mood.

"I went to see Calix," I told Zath.

"How did that go?" he asked tentatively.

Zath wasn't as . . . *merciless* as Nyte to want him dead, but he wouldn't object to letting Nyte have his way either.

"He harmless and doesn't deserve to die for stupidity."

"Good luck reasoning that with Nyte."

I found pleasure in the challenge and that felt wrong to admit. He'd listened to me in the throne room, and if he killed Calix against my wishes I don't think I could forgive him for it.

The city was winding down for the fall of twilight and I pulled my hood up to hide the blaring beacon my silver hair had become to identify me. I didn't get drunk often, the last time was with Cassia. I almost backtracked on my decision but before my world cleaved in two, I remembered it had also been one of the most joyous and carefree nights we'd ever spent together.

In the corner of my eye I caught movement jumping off a crate before dipping into a dark alley. Curiosity got the better of me and I followed after the black cat.

"We were so close," Zath groaned when I diverted from the path to the inn.

I didn't respond. Reaching the end of the alley, I only just caught the flicker of a black tail disappearing down back alley stairs and chased after it.

"I thought we were looking for wine and whiskey, not watered down ale," Rose commented.

They followed my impulse anyway and we came to one of the most run-down parts of the lower city level. The street had an odor mixing damp stone and body sweat that I tried not to inhale too deeply. Some humans gathered outside various shops and taverns, and none of them hid their blatant head-to-toe assessments of us, like they were wondering what they could steal.

After a few more minutes I couldn't find the black cat again and my skin was starting to crawl. I stopped for one last look.

"Are you following me?"

All of us jumped at the sudden voice right behind us, too close for a stranger's comfort. The moment I turned to meet Davina, I relaxed. Her brown eyes blinked, curiously patient, and her black hair was in a long braid that climbed over her head and fell to her ribs.

"I knew it was you," I said in triumph.

She hooked a teasing brow. "It's about time I switch up my form of preference, I think."

"What are you doing down here?" Rose asked. She stood firm and cross-armed like Zath. I didn't think they realized how alike they were sometimes. The two of them guarded our backs and tracked subtle eyes on suspicious persons around us.

"I shouldn't really tell you. We've never had outsiders before," she said, contemplating.

I gave her my best pleading eyes. "I'm not just anyone though." May as well use the star-maiden as a token for my gain too.

"Very well, but keep to the back and stay quiet. Nyte didn't want to overwhelm you all at once, but you followed me, so I can't take the blame."

She looped my arm and I turned eagerly, anxious to find out where we were going. We went down another set of alley stairs, deeper into the under city, and while I was prickling with unease, Davina was nearly skipping along, so unfazed and cheerful.

We came to a deserted corner of shops with only a scary lone man sitting on a crate, peeling an apple with his knife. He was burly and intimidating but Davina flashed a pleasant smile at him.

"You're late," he grumbled.

"Impossible," Davina sang.

He eased a smile and I realized then he was guarding who went in and out of the seemingly abandoned building Davina led us into.

She unhooked my arm, dipping into her pocket and producing a brass pin she placed on her chest.

"What is that?" I asked.

"The resistance seal," she said.

I noted the change in her as we headed deeper into this establishment that seemed long neglected. She became focused and firm. Authoritative. We stopped walking when she did, turning to us. I glanced at the sigil she wore, but I couldn't quite decipher what it was, with arrows like a compass, an upward facing moon, and lines that crossed and fell down from it.

"Keep your hoods up. Stay at the back until it's finished."

We nodded, and Davina didn't look back nor falter a step as she pulled back the curtain and headed straight down the space between the rows of benches in the large, run-down hall I discovered with awe to be an abandoned theater.

Rose, Zath, and I slipped into the back and stayed standing with some others. The hall was packed full and the chatter began to quieten as Davina reached the low stage where four other fae were standing already.

I'd only read about this kind of place—seen it in words that painted the pictures in my mind. The theater was missing its vibrancy with the red curtains hanging torn and dust coated. The people on the stage stood to talk about terrible things and the audience were not eager for the performance. This was a place that once held laugher and cheer but now melancholy swept in leaving only the ghost of joy I'd felt from the depictions on a page.

When Davina finished speaking to the other fae, she turned to the crowd and I hardly recognized my friend. She stood with shoulders squared and hands clasped behind her, so serious but magnificent, with an air of leadership that canceled all sound in the room without a word.

"As you've heard, the Libertatem has come to an end once again," she said. It broke a murmur of disgruntled sounds and curses toward the king. Until Davina added, "What I'm thrilled to tell you is that the rumors are true—it is the last. The star-maiden has indeed returned, and Nightsdeath is freed."

A burst of excitement and uncertainty buzzed through the room. My skin pricked with the reaction of the fae in attendance.

"Is it true she has no power?" someone called from the crowd.

"No," Davina said, shifting a subtle look to me as she paced across the stage. "But she will need our help and patience."

"Patience?" a fae male scoffed, standing at the side. "She wrecked our world, then abandoned it. Why should we care about her return at all?"

My cheeks heated and Zath leaned in to me. "I think it was a mistake to come."

"No," I said. "I need to hear it."

"You can't forget the age of peace and unity she created and will restore. We've been waiting for centuries."

"We've been doing just fine without her," a female added. "She serves as nothing more than an entity with too much power that could destroy all we've rebuilt."

Agreement was passed between peers in quiet talk. I didn't know how to feel. These people were hurting and they were right. They'd been building this resistance for centuries without me and I understood their concern that I might step in and pretend to know what they've been through.

"They're ungrateful," Rose muttered bitterly.

"They're afraid," I countered.

Davina tried to reason with the crowd. "Astraea is on our side. Soon, the celestials will come to our aid now that their maiden is back."

"They hid away and abandoned us too!" someone cried out.

"We can't trust any of them," another added.

"We can't do it alone," Davina said firmly, loud enough to silence everyone. They listened to her. Respected her.

"We haven't attacked or fought back because we've been biding our time. We've lost friends and family and this is our time to focus and avenge them, not lose sight of it under resentment. Alone we are not enough and at the end of this war we want our peace again, not a divide with the celestials."

"End to the vampires!" someone called. More joined in a rowdy agreement and my skin chilled.

I knew the vampires were rising up to conquer, but I couldn't imagine a world without them entirely. I thought of Drystan. He once had a heart that cared and loved. What if there were many vampires just like him—no different to the fae, or celestials, or humans? What if there could be those who seemed corrupt and evil that wanted peace just like the rest of us?

Annihilation of an entire species was not the way.

"There was once coexistence," I said.

My voice was loud enough that some turned to me with scowls, some with accusation. How dare I stand here as the oppressed and defend the enemy?

I pulled my hood down and that seemed to trigger recognition. Looking over the faces that pierced me with looks of disgust, awe, uncertainty, hope. So many conflicting emotions but I had to weather all of it. I headed up the aisle toward Davina, who watched me with surprise and concern.

It's the Maiden, they whispered.

I quelled my nerves under the interrogation of many eyes. I might be a celestial, but these were my people too.

"Is it true you have no memory?" a timid voice echoed through the silence. I found a younger female tucking a strand of honey hair behind her pointed ear. With the way she looked at me, I felt the weight of responsibility I had to these people. They were counting on me.

"Not entirely," I said. "I don't remember all in images but I feel it. More so every day. Like right now. I feel all of you because I know we're in this together and we always have been. I stand for you and I fight for you, but . . ." my throat dried because there was no easy way to get people to understand what I've seen and what I believe. "People are not born cruel. We have to break the cycle of violence."

"She's not with us," a male shouted but I didn't see him. "Anyone who sees mercy for the vampires is against us."

As they broke out in chatter again, I felt Davina close by my side.

"They're not going to believe in you in a night," she said quietly to me.

"I know." I didn't need them to.

It would take action to prove I was on their side and I was going to help. It would take an example to show them peace could be made and once again I thought of one person, with a distant yearning in my heart.

Drystan. Not just a blood vampire but the son of the king that had wronged them so truly. If he could show he was on our side it could change everything. But the prince was hurting just as much as everyone here and pain turned people cold and hopeless.

Right now he hated me and despised Nyte.

"You'll betray us again," someone said.

"She shouldn't be here."

I couldn't see who was shouting anymore. It all blended together but I knew none of it was encouragement or faith.

"I bet she isn't even powerful."

That was the comment to prompt a reaction in me. It spurred a need to prove I wasn't powerless. Never again. The key was in my hand before I knew what I was doing and the magick within me bonded to it instantly, pulsing a violet flare through the room when the staff tapped to the ground.

"You might look at this and see power. Feel it. But you can be just as powerful. With your words or your actions in silence. I'm not enough to fight this alone even when I get my full magick back. I need you as much as you need me. So I'm asking if you'll fight with me for the life of freedom and equality you've been denied far too long."

"The world will drown in starlight," someone called out. She was young, clutching the hand of an older fae. But she was so brave, looking up at me as if wishing upon a star, and I wanted to fall to my knees to grant it.

Then another echoed her words. Until the tension from the silence was shaken completely by the crowd's humming, and now smiles started to crack the tired and dire faces of the gathered fae.

"Not bad," Davina said, nudging my side while the crowd's attention was scattered.

I took a deep breath. "It's going to take a lot more than one speech, but it's a start."

Davina gave me a sad but prideful smile, squeezing my arm.

I stepped off the stage as she called the room's attention to her again, starting to fill them in on all that had happened since the Libertatem.

"You stepped out of your cage long ago," Zath said, slinging his arm around my shoulders as we left. "But I think you just shattered it."

I needed a drink to take the edge off more than before after the secret fae resistance meeting. I couldn't tell if it was nerves or my high from positive adrenaline that turned one wine to two then three. Now I was losing count. Either way, I figured I would be suffering tomorrow.

We found a bustling inn on the lower level of the city. Humble and mostly full of humans. I kept my eyes on the few pointed ears that were regarded like royalty in here. One shadowless sank his teeth into a young man but I'd been tracking the man's mannerisms, which appeared content, flirtatious even. I dragged my sight away from the affair that turned too boldly passionate for public spectacle.

I kept my hood up, hair tucked away, not wanting to attract any unnecessary attention while we unwound away from the suffocating castle.

"You never told us you were that influential in all of this," I said to Davina, who'd joined us a while later.

She hooked a brow observing my fifth—or was it my seventh?—cup of wine.

"There's a leader of the resistance in each kingdom. Those meetings keep us all connected and in the know: how many round ups are happening in each place, numbers. We've been building this for a long time."

Zath whistled low. "So you're a resistance leader too? Never would have guessed."

Her head tipped to the side. "Why?" she challenged.

I sipped my wine, observing them over the rim with a growing tension.

"You just look so . . . delicate and breakable. You were posing as a handmaid, can you blame me?" He struggled to defend himself.

"You never know what the quietest are capable of," she said.

Rose added, "She could take you and I would love to watch it."

Zath opened his mouth to argue, but at the deceivingly innocent look in Davina's eye that invited him to try, he wisely chose silence.

At the back wall, the establishment burst into applause, and my attention was pulled back to the game they played that I'd kept casual interest in. It was knife throwing—taking turns at hitting a board with targets with points allocated depending on where they hit. A man marked a little shy of dead center, but it was the closest anyone had gotten all night.

I'd wanted to join in, but the moment I sat down and indulged, well, I might have overdone it too much to be competent now. My liquid confidence from the alcohol made me too arrogant, however, and I stood before I had the chance to talk myself out of it.

"I don't think that's a good idea," Zath sang, but his amusement was prompting me to try.

My vision was a little blurry. The ground wasn't straight. Still, I was slipping through the small gathered crowed with all the giddiness in the world until I made it to the front.

"What's the winner's prize?" I asked, not knowing who to direct it to.

The liveliness around the game hushed as more eyes fell on me.

A slightly rotund older man with a graying short beard who leaned an elbow on a nearby table, flipping a coin absentmindedly, was the one who answered.

"You name yours; I'll name mine."

"Are you the one competing?"

"No. You can face my champion."

His chin jerked toward a tall man with tousled brown hair and a wicked scar along his lower left jaw. The one who'd come close to the center. He looked at me with a side smile that didn't regard me as even remote competition.

"Drinks for my friends," I said. I didn't really need anything; their dumbfounded reactions would provide enough taste of victory.

"One night with you," he countered.

Disgust rolled in me. Of course he could think of nothing better than a temporary sense of hollow gratification. I was confident I would win, and if I didn't, well, what's one lie?

"Deal."

"I don't think so." The low menacing voice trembled down every notch of my spine. I thought the threat in those four words trembled across the floor, and the corners of the room darkened to it.

Nyte's proximity crept closer to my back and people retreated from me with fast unease. I didn't turn around, letting his body melt into mine and my eyes almost flutter to it. He pulled my hood down and my loose silver hair spilled free.

"Are you in the habit of gambling with what's mine?" he purred across my ear. "You're ruining my fun."

A thrill erupted in me with the hand he slipped around my abdomen, claiming tighter possession of me.

"On the contrary; I arrived just in time to give you a real challenge."

"You want to compete with me?"

"We both know that target would become splinters before either of us won that way."

"Then go sit with the others and let me play."

Nyte spun me in his hold, so quickly that paired with the alcohol, it took a moment longer than it usually would to find anchor in his bright amber eyes. They were near glowing right now, like liquid metal swirled around his pupils. His magick hummed around me too, and I wondered what had made him this . . . *alive.*

"You're not playing with anyone but me tonight."

"You're a killjoy."

"Are you still willing to bet a night with you?"

Need gathered between my legs and scattered over my skin. He didn't need a game for that, but there was something daring and exciting about his desire to gain it.

"What would I get for winning?"

"Absolutely anything you desire."

"Arrogant of you to wager that high."

"I never enter into a deal I can't win."

I had to admit I found his confidence right now highly attractive, but I kept my displeasure regardless.

"How was your meeting with Elliot and the others?"

I leaned into him, trailing my fingers up the seams and over the black embroidery on his chest.

"Terribly tedious and I've been suffering a dangerous desire to get back to you." Nyte held out a hand and someone quickly approached him with five throwing daggers. "Now, I want to claim my prize and get out of here—if you will."

He let me go, offering me the knives, which I took with apprehension. Before I could ask anything he was walking toward the target with one hand in his pocket. At the end, he turned back to face me with a wicked hint of a smile.

"If you so much as graze me with one of those, you win."

My eyes narrowed. "No moving through the void."

"Of course."

If I wasn't intoxicated, I would have matched him with arrogance and my sheer stubborn will to wipe his confidence would have given me better odds. Right now, I was doubting, but I couldn't go back on it.

So I braced my stance, shook my head as if that would expel any of the cups of wine from my mind, and zoned my full focus on him. Nyte's eyes became the only color in room. I didn't have acute senses like the fae or vampires but somehow I thought I found his heartbeat that canceled the rest of the sounds in the room. I imagined each dagger I held lodging in his chest to spur my determination.

Then I threw.

The second was leaving my hand before the first speared into the wall, which he avoided with an easy side step toward me. He twisted to the opposite side of my next knife. Ducked under my third. The target of him was larger with each fraction of closed distance but he glided left of my fourth, then somehow fucking *caught* my fifth by the handle.

Then it was over when he reached me with a hand grabbing my jaw.

"Mine."

Nyte kissed me despite my frustration. I took the irritation of my loss out on him. When his arm curved tightly around me, I lifted weightlessly into his arms, my legs circling his waist.

The pull of the void surrounded us but our mouths never broke apart. Icy air whipped across my cheeks but my skin was still heating with the wrap of his body and the tight press of him with my back now against a wall.

I think I moaned his name, so lost in the scent and taste of him I might have been begging for something inappropriate for where we were. He wanted me too. His hips jerked against my core, making every stitch of my pants torturous to the friction of his hard cock.

"Aren't you going to take us somewhere to claim your reward?" I said breathily when he kissed hungrily down my neck.

"Not tonight. I just needed a moment with you when I was close to tearing out the eyes of every man that was watching you in there."

"Overreacting as always."

"There's a man in there who asked for a night with you and is still breathing; I'd consider myself very merciful right now."

In the haze of my lust I didn't care for the cold or the fact we were outside where anyone could stumble upon us. My hand reached between us, hooking the waistline of his pants. Before I could do anything he was pulling us through the void again and the alcohol made everything spin so much faster.

My back pressed against something far softer and warmer, and only Nyte's hair tipping over his forehead and leaning over me made me aware that I was lying down now.

"This isn't as exciting," I said, hooking my knees around his hips and reaching between us again.

He took my wrists this time, pinning them by my head as he groaned, leaning in to plant a kiss to my neck.

"You're sweet torture, Starlight."

His voice was thick, wanting, and I couldn't understand why he was holding back.

"Stop treating me like glass."

"I'm not above breaking you if you were. But intoxication is a line I won't cross."

"I'm telling you I want it."

"Your lust-clouded, alcohol-infused thoughts are telling me that. If you wake up tomorrow and ask again, I'll happily oblige."

"Fine," I said.

The bastard drew back with twinkling amused eyes.

"Dress for bed," he ordered, slipping off me.

We were in my rooms, and he knew where everything was as he reached a dresser, picked a black satin nightgown, and brought it to me.

"I think I'll sleep naked."

The arm he extended to me fell and he looked skyward as if for a plea of sanity.

He laid the gown on the bed regardless, then leaned in to kiss me once. "My sweet torture," he murmured against my lips.

He moved to leave but what Tarran had said earlier had been taunting my thoughts all day and the insecurity tumbled out of me.

"Nyte?"

"Starlight."

"Have you ever . . . betrayed me?"

He searched my eyes thoughtfully, tucking a strand of hair behind my ear.

"I think it depends on who you ask."

"You always have a way of avoiding direct answers." I huffed, sinking down on the pillows. Nyte sat on the edge of the bed.

"No. I just don't often think there's the whole truth in a single one. But what is always true is that betrayal never comes from your enemies."

"You're my enemy."

"Is that what you feel?"

"No . . . but I think I feel guilt for it, like I should say yes."

"It's your past coming back in feelings rather than images. This is good."

"Has—" I studied him with my next question, growing nervous to mention him. "Has Auster ever betrayed me?"

Nyte's eyes narrowed for a second.

"Why are you asking this?"

"I'm trying to figure out who I can trust."

"My word to your half drunk mind isn't going to help you with that," he said, but it was with an edge of apology like he wished he could. "You'll get the chance to figure that out for yourself. Though I try not to think about you with him at all."

My guilt came in such a crashing wave that I could barely look at him. Was it betrayal to have met Auster and not have told Nyte? Even more so to be planning to meet with him again away from here. I couldn't risk Nyte stopping me.

"I'll be away from the castle tomorrow," he said. "I found out where Drystan has been hiding and I have to deal with him. We're going to find out how the transitioned vampire numbers are growing. I'd take you with me, but you might want the day to recover."

This was the opportunity I'd been waiting for. I could have met with Auster today but my conscience couldn't settle without seeing Calix. So tomorrow would be my next chance, as much as I wanted to agree to go with Nyte, especially with the mention of Drystan.

I rubbed my temples. The strings of this war were starting to pull my wants and focus in different directions.

"Probably best I stay and rest," I agreed with no small amount of ache for the lie.

Nyte nodded, looking at me with such soft eyes I treasured these quiet moments he bore to me without even realizing.

"You know how to call for me. Anytime, any distance."

"Yes," I whispered.

He gave a barely-there smile before smoke and stars stole him away. My hand reached out to the ghost of his impression on the bed.

Sitting up, I began to undress. But before I took my shirt off my eyes cast outside and my skin broke a shiver, as I wondered if Auster could be watching again. I couldn't see any pale flicker that would indicate wings.

I was never shy about my nakedness. It only became sexually empowering when there was someone I wanted to crave me; otherwise it was just flesh. So I changed, uncaring if there could be ten celestials watching. I admired my silver markings in the mirror, thinking of the fae resistance. My magick glowed faintly, wanting to join their rebellion. It was a spark of purpose I needed to see.

No longer was the war something that was a fable when it couldn't be seen. Nor an idle threat when it couldn't be felt. I had to want to see it. And I had to want to face it.

9

Astraea

The beauty of the forest around me soothed my sharp anticipation. I watched the final violet flare of the key diffuse the sky through the frost tipped leaves. Birds chirped quietly in the early hour, and the sun glittered on the snow.

Having Rose with me helped calm my nerves. I was glad she'd been eager to agree to accompany me. Auster had only warned me not to tell Nyte.

"You really don't look so well," Rose fussed again.

I'd definitely had a little too much to drink last night. In all the excitement, I hadn't eaten well either.

"I'll be fine; I just need a drink," I brushed off. "Maybe something to eat."

"I wonder if they eat and drink the same as us," Rose said.

That inspired some amusement in me. "I don't think they're much different."

"I've been picturing purple mushrooms and blue wine."

"And pixies that pick them from yellow grass meadows," I added.

"Pink waterfalls that can get you drunk."

"Talking trees of wisdom."

We both burst into soft giggles with the conjurings that kept getting more ridiculous.

"I prefer the yellow mushrooms, and celestial wine is in fact tinted light blue." A deep, new voice broke our idle waiting.

A branch cracked, indicating an advancing footfall. My head whipped with a spike of adrenaline heating my skin, tingling my fingertips with magick like it was trying to remind me we were never helpless. Never powerless. If only I gave my trust to it. I had the key at my hip and my dagger at my thigh, but I didn't reach for either when my tension diffused at the sight of Auster.

He was more beautiful in the daylight. No hood, and his smile for me fluttered in my stomach. His wings glittered faintly against the sunlight. Auster wasn't alone either, and it wasn't him who spoke. When I caught sight of the handsome dark skinned man beside him . . .

"You," I breathed in disbelief.

I blinked with the flash of memory. His hands on me. How he'd seemed to recognize me that day he'd saved me.

"I thought you . . . I heard you—"

"You doubted my combat against three amateur vampires?" he mused with a stunning smile that creased around his green eyes.

He'd saved me from them in the woodland next to Goldfell Manor before I ever knew I'd be heading to the Central. I'd heard his cry and believed he'd died for me. I became overwhelmed with relief that wasn't true.

"Thank you," I said through a breath of disbelief. "And I'm sorry that I didn't know who you were or what or—"

"It's no matter." He chuckled at my flustering. "I was clueless about your lost memories, so that apology is mine. I must have frightened you."

I huffed a laugh too, because at the time it had been terrifying to that lost, scared woman of the manor.

"This is Rosalind," I introduced as she'd been waiting patiently by me. Her face was quietly studying our company. "I hope you don't mind, but I trust her."

"A pleasure to meet you. Any friend of Astraea's is one of ours, of course," Auster said. He was so polite and elegant. Everything I expected of the celestials.

"My name is Zadkiel."

I reached for the hand he extended to me, and now that I wasn't out of my wits in fear after a near vampire attack, I felt his touch differently. Safe.

"Did I know you?" I asked. My thoughts tunneled away while we shook hands, as if trying to find some pictures for the familiarity he bore.

"I was a lot younger back then, but yes."

That enlightened me to my first idea I hadn't considered about the celestials. The vampires had long lifespans: I knew the fae did too.

Rose seemed to have the same thought as she asked, "How old are you?"

Zadkiel smiled at her, and there was something in it that had me looking to Rose for her reaction. I'd never seen her shy from attention before.

"Our lifespans can reach a millennium. We measure in decades. I'm thirty-three."

Such a number was far easier to comprehend than over three hundred years old.

Auster met my curious gaze, suppressing an amused quirk of his mouth.

"Forty-eight." He answered my unspoken question. "You would be forty-three this decade."

That's where the illusion it could translate to human aging was broken. Auster didn't appear a day older than his early thirties. His eyes were young, his skin glowed with a heathy tan, and even the few wrinkles around his forehead and eyes seemed caused more by the responsibility of being a High Celestial than from aging. Zadkiel had a youthful, carefree charm about him, and his dark skin was smooth and burdenless. I found him comfortable to be around, while Auster certainly had more of an air of authority that touched me in his presence.

I was beginning to lean more into my gut feelings, knowing some of them were pulling at threads from long ago. I was learning to trust myself, and it was empowering me more and more each day I crushed my self-doubt.

"Shall we go?" Auster said, holding a hand out to me.

I tracked the wings expanding over his shoulders and my throat dried.

"We're flying?" I asked.

"We could use the void, but I'm afraid I can only carry one person through at a time and Zadkiel doesn't have the ability. Besides, you must be missing it—flying. I hope we'll find your wings soon."

My stomach was twisting so tight. I loved heights. When Nyte had taken me high through the night I'd been yearning deeply to fly again. But staring at Auster's invitation in an upturned right palm, I wasn't thrilled with the idea of being in an intimate hold with him instead.

It's just transport. Nothing more.

I looked to Rose, because if she wasn't comfortable with it, I would insist we take turns going with him through the void. She gave me a small nod, however, and stepped closer to Zadkiel. I watched them first, and Rose let him take her into his arms while hers hooked around his neck. I almost felt the need to glance away from the look they shared.

Taking a deep breath, I slipped my hand into Auster's, and it might have been childish of me to be glad we both wore gloves. Zadkiel took off with Rose and my stomach tumbled when my legs were swept from under me, and I had no choice but to press tightly to Auster.

His scent trickled over me—a hint of honey and some kind of spice. I couldn't unlock my body. My heart was thundering fast, and I tried to tame it.

"Relax," he said gently. His brown eyes were closer than ever, and in the daylight, I was hypnotized. Locked on them, though if I let them keep pulling me, I would discover answers I wasn't sure I was ready for, with the way my skin slicked under my dress.

"Do you need a moment?" he asked.

Pull yourself together. I shook my head, swallowing through my dry throat.

"I'm okay."

"Good."

My arms tightened as he crouched, then shot skyward with long, powerful beats of his wings. To distract from the broad, muscular body I was clutching for dear life, I lost myself in the tiered cityscape of Vesitire. Auster flew higher until we were engulfed by clouds and the mist of them dampened my hair. The view up here was breathtaking. The clouds invited me to let Auster go and let them catch me in their fluffy embrace instead. A beautiful but deadly illusion of comfort.

"Is this your first time flying since you've been back?" Auster asked.

Guilt riddled me. His warm breath fanned my ear, and I was so conflicted with the closeness of him.

"No," I said honestly. "But the first in the daytime."

I dared to look at him. Auster was a dream up here, as stunning as any fable of a guardian angel. It made me anxious to discover what I might have felt for him in the past and why he hadn't been enough for my heart to let go of the one person who was catastrophic for me and the world. Perhaps I would learn that it was all me. My wrongs. My twistedness and selfishness. What if I despised the person I had been? Someone who had been close to condemning a world for the villain that terrorized it.

Auster's expression was pinched in thought as he stared ahead. The sun kissed his skin and I resisted the urge to reach for his face and trace the shadow line of his jaw. When I realized that impulse, I looked away quickly, hoping we didn't have much longer in the sky.

"I'm sorry we didn't get to you before he did. Before you ended up in that game too. But at least something good came of your triumph in it—you found your key."

"I haven't mastered the use of that either. Nyte is going to help me with my magick."

I knew I shouldn't have mentioned Nyte because it locked Auster's jaw and his arms tightened around me as if he thought of flying farther than Althenia, beyond where Nyte could find me again. I knew that was futile. Somehow, I believed Nyte would always find me against all odds.

"We're here. You might feel the veil awakening your magick."

Gravity flipped my stomach as we dropped, falling out of the cloud bank. I gawked, blinking at the sudden change of luminosity as we headed toward a bright starry infusion like the light battled the dark. I wasn't afraid of it, I was pulled toward it with a gravity so strong my hold slackened on Auster.

When the veil engulfed us, I wasn't in his arms anymore. I felt Nyte. This veil was like a full embrace of him I wanted to stay suspended in. My magick flared in tendrils of silver that found a home in here. I searched through it like I would find the only dawn that could defy the night. His eyes. I wanted to search endlessly for them but too soon I was pulled from my peace.

I could have whimpered with the lashing I felt within after leaving the veil behind and I watched it over Auster's shoulder for a while as we flew away from it. When I turned, my attention was quickly stolen by the most ethereal sight I'd ever seen.

Of all the tales and wonders, maps and drawings, nothing could come close to depicting the true impact of the otherworldly expanse that was Althenia. The land of the celestials.

High above, it appeared just as I'd seen on paper. There was a center island surrounded by four land masses that were divided by water. The illusion of the river paths was like a six point star with two extra river paths forming smaller lakes on the largest side where the veil ran across.

As we descended toward a glass castle on the central island, I couldn't stop my wandering awe. When my feet finally met ground, I stared over the city, so vibrant with color, from a grand balcony with no rail to prevent a fall.

"Welcome home," Auster said, quietly, as though he had filled with emotion too.

His two words wove in me with promise and security. I embraced that feeling—this *was* home. It just wasn't the only one I knew.

"I didn't live here, though," I concluded. When the castle of Vesitire was also so familiar.

"You chose to govern in Vesitire as it was central on the continent," he confirmed.

"You didn't stay there with me?"

"I did for a while. When I thought we might . . ." he trailed off, catching himself against the wound of the past but I knew what he was going to say.

At some point in our past, I had to have contemplated a life with him. It would have been favorable to the land, the people. It seemed utterly outlandish I wouldn't choose him.

Auster said carefully, "What happened to you these past five years? When you fell, we almost had you—" he slipped a look at me and if I didn't know any better, I would have thought he appeared *nervous*. "We failed you. The trace we had disappeared, and we have never been able to pick it up again. Then our spies were certain they'd seen you in Vesitire, in that wretched game, of all things. We learned Nightsdeath was back, and he had you."

"I don't know where to begin," I said honestly.

Auster stood with clasped hands behind his back where his towering silver wings displayed proudly. I could see the coat of authority he wore well, fit to rule the people.

My attention was once again caught on a glint of silver at his side.

"What happened?" I asked, transfixed on his metal left hand.

Auster faced me so I couldn't keep staring. My cheeks warmed. I couldn't help it when it was as if my mind reached for a cloudy memory like the first time I saw it. Trying to remember how he'd lost his hand, as if I should know.

"It happened in battle," he said somberly. "Close to the end."

My brow knitted together in the cloud of sorrow we shared.

A familiar laugh turned my body to the doors behind us. Rose appeared so soft and relaxed in Zadkiel's company that it was unexpected but a joy to witness. They joined us outside and when she found me, her eyes lit up.

"Isn't this place incredible?" she gushed.

"Yes," I agreed.

It meant so much to me that she was enamored with these lands. It was as if all past burdens and transgressions didn't follow her here and showed a new bright layer under Rose's usual guarded exterior.

"This has been and always will be your home too, no matter where you settle to govern," Auster said, having edged closer to me, his soft eyes angled down at me now.

My chest tightened. I didn't want to give the impression of anything other than learning the ways and land here. I wasn't ready to face anything of . . . *us* yet.

"Can we go down there?" I asked, glancing over the magnificent spectacle of Althenia.

In the distance, I thought I could make out other glass buildings as grand as this one across the wide river that encompassed us.

"I would love to show you my lands of the House of Nova. We occupy the center island of Althenia."

I was gripped in fascination, and from the twinkle in Auster's eye, he knew I would follow eagerly as he turned, heading inside. Zadkiel and Rose walked with me.

"When you see the other islands governed by each of my brothers, you'll find there's a distinction in our wears and a few of our customs are different. But where a celestial is born doesn't prevent them from ever changing location. It's not as simple as moving at will. There is an assessment for migration to keep the populations sustainable."

The tall entrance doors opened at our approach without any physical influence. This place was made of magick. It hummed in the air and as we stepped out I realized something I should have realized sooner.

"Does the veil distort the weather on this side?" I questioned. While it was cold, there was no snow on this island.

"Not exactly; it is my magick that influences the temperature. I am known to some as the God of South Wind. My magick is crafted of storms and it charges through my lands. It's why some celestials move. They find themselves drawn to another High Celestial's power, which is a certain call to them in itself."

I found that fascinating. Maybe that's why I felt charged by it—from being his bonded. Perhaps the Nova province called to me most.

"Look to the North; you can see the snow capping the mountains of the Luna province. My brother Zephyr is the God of North Wind. He's most powerful in the winter."

"And the most good-looking always," a new voice interrupted behind us.

When I spun I was met with a striking blond man. His hair was short, sleeked back with a circlet like Auster's over his head. While Auster wore notes of blue, this High Celestial, whom I assumed was Zephyr, wore tones of green that matched his mossy-green irises. As he came to stand with Auster, I saw they matched in height and strong build.

"You didn't mention you were visiting," Auster said. If I didn't know any better I might have said he wasn't thrilled about it.

"You thought I wouldn't come greet our maiden the moment she's back on our lands?" he said, not taking his bright eyes off me.

My body decided it was relaxed around him, which was odd considering my nerves to come here waiting for Auster. Did I know him well in the past? I wanted to ask, but it didn't feel right with an audience.

"You don't remember me, do you?" Zephyr said, his mouth curving. My sheepish look was answer enough for him. His hand lay over his heart. "Here I had hoped our friendship was strong enough to break through the cracks of your blocked mind. No matter; I'm sure it'll come to you as one of the firsts."

"As I was saying," Auster drawled. "To your left is the Sera Province of my brother Aquilo—he thrives in spring as the God of West Wind. And finally, behind us, the Aura Province of my brother Notus—he favors fall as the God of East Wind."

Zephyr said, "Though don't expect a greeting from them. You're not their favorite person; but don't worry, the feeling was mutual."

I slipped a look at him, appreciating his honesty, but no one liked to hear they weren't thought of fondly—more so when they couldn't remember a damn thing of what could have caused the hostility. Shit, what did I do? What did *they* do? I might not be at fault here.

It was odd to realize there were things I could have done in the past to affect me now that I had no recollection of. I couldn't decide if ignorance was bliss or if I wanted to know so I could direct the same energy back when I inevitably faced them.

Auster steered me back to his lesson after cutting Zephyr with a warning look for the interruptions. "The humans have likely forgotten the feel of our winds as the veil has stopped them from passing through. Before, our magick would expel from our lands from time to time and kept a certain balance throughout the seasons. Now, their winters are too cold, their summers too hot. You see, there is so much to be restored."

"You expect one person to be responsible for that?" Rose asked, voicing the incredulity I couldn't.

"Not alone. You have us, of course," Zephyr said, giving me a small look of assurance.

Auster said, "You're the people's hope more than anything. Physically, we're here to fight for you."

I didn't want that. To be excluded from the fighting. Nyte wanted to train my power; he was adamant to awaken it. Auster seemed content to be gentle and take on that role for me. I had to show him I was more than that. I wouldn't be another trophy in a case.

"I'm going to get my power back," I said.

"Then let me help you."

"I'd rather my time here helped me learn about my heritage."

I didn't mention I thought Nyte had to be the one to bring out my power. It awakened at his touch, and it often felt like our magick was kin. Opposite sides of the same coin. With Auster, he could teach me the ways of the celestials and all that happened when I was gone.

Auster stopped walking, regarding me with a look of excitement and pride I didn't know what I'd done to invoke.

"I'm looking forward to having time with you. It brings me the most joy I've felt in the vacant centuries you've been gone that you want to return to me here. If you say the word, you have the might of all four High Celestials and their houses against the wrath of Nightsdeath, should you want to stay with us. Until then, you must keep it from him, to not risk a war sooner than we're ready."

Zephyr interjected with, "Nyte may have quite the bloody reputation but he's strategic. Always has been. I've been trying to tell Auster the most telling him you're here would do is rile him with jealousy—you would rejoice in that, brother."

"He's savage and unpredictable," Auster snapped.

I grew tense and unwell with how they debated Nyte's nature and crimes. Conflict wracked me. I didn't want to believe that Nyte would start the war he was trying to prevent if he found out I was meeting with the celestials. But Auster's concern was enough to make me doubt. Althenia was thriving and peaceful, like they existed in their own realm. I couldn't put them in jeopardy if there was even a small chance Nyte could react against them.

"Perhaps I could come here once a week for now," I offered. That shouldn't be too hard—eluding Nyte for one day. He seemed to have a lot to occupy himself with regaining control of the vampires, and I would use that to my advantage.

Auster nodded. "Use your key, and I'll come for you. We'll always be watching for it."

This was it—how I would begin to collect the scattered pieces of my history and figure out which were truth and if any were lies?

Rose never looked at me with as much hopefulness as she did now. But I couldn't ignore the sinking feeling in my gut that any path away from Nyte would be favorable to her. Perhaps Zath would agree too, but I didn't know if I could trust him with this secret when he'd worked for Nyte before.

My happiness about these lands and what I could discover became tangled in a web of lies I had to keep secret for now. Nobody wanted to believe there was good in Nyte, but I did, and I hoped my greatest betrayal wouldn't come from my own heart.

Astraea

Nyte was my enemy.

It had never been clearer than right now, locked in a stance of a battle I couldn't remember starting. The conflict between us tore through me with heartbreak and anguish so powerful I thought it could kill me. Both of us held the key, the glow between us hummed otherworldly energy that we shared.

We were two hearts, one soul.

This is what fire on fire felt like and we could break the world in half. His eyes glowed bright with the amber diffusing from them while my vision saw the world through a white film. While we seemed to pause in our war, the pain in his stare mirrored everything breaking me apart, that I couldn't fathom how we got here.

His face bled. A crimson trail from his temple over his right cheek.

I'd inflicted it moments before.

This attack was mine.

My body moved of its own accord, pushing off his hold on my weapon, only answering a scorching drive that coursed through my veins like betrayal. Only I couldn't remember why I wanted him dead. And though he defended himself, my rage didn't make sense to me, considering the agony and confusion painted across his beautiful, battle worn face.

How long had we fought?

My chest heaved with exertion. Striking him down wasn't a want. No—everything in my heart cried against it. But in my mind, it was a *need*.

To make him bleed like I was hurting and so I lunged for him—

"*Astraea.*"

His lips didn't move and my vision doubled. The scene turned to blurs of darkness and it wasn't him who fell, it was me. Plummeting faster and faster until I crashed into reality.

My breath drew sharp, then began to stab my chest when I couldn't gather it fast enough. I blinked hard against the darkness and in my panic, with a weight pressing over me, I latched onto the only thing of color to grapple what was happening.

A few locks of black hair curled over golden eyes that held me, flooding me with both dread and relief when I knew we weren't on any battlefield. The ground registered hard against my back. We were on the floor, Nyte pinning my hands by my head and the horror of my nightmare flooding back slowly.

"Welcome back," Nyte said, sounding almost *panicked*.

He released me gently, easing off the straddled position he'd held me in.

"Did I attack you?" I choked, pushing myself up and almost collapsing to the wobble of my elbows.

"Unless you were dreaming of me with affection."

Nyte ran a hand through his messy dark locks, sitting back against a tall bed, and only then did I realize he only wore sleep pants. No shirt. No shoes. And I became too aware of the dainty piece of silk I wore.

Scanning the room, I realized I was in his when I hadn't fallen asleep here. I got to my feet on weak knees, the air breezed to chill over my sweat-slicked skin.

"Sorry," I mumbled, staring off with my drifting thoughts.

Recalling the dream, it began to settle in my mind as much more. My hand vacantly rubbed my chest with the ache growing even in my awareness.

"It wasn't a dream," I whispered. I was sure of it.

Standing in the same room as someone I'd clearly wanted dead at some point in our history, I couldn't be sure if I wanted to flee or confront it fully.

"The battle again?" he asked carefully.

A loud rattle jolted me. It was merely the winter wind battering the balcony doors, and the coldness of the room started to wrap around me now that my adrenaline was dwindling.

The second thing to startle me a second later was a weight over my shoulders. I eased into the warmth and scent of mint and sandalwood far too easily. Nyte's hands lingered at my arms after placing the black blanket over me.

"Why is it always that I'm ready to move on from the obvious?"

Nyte only passed a few seconds of silence with the knives of the past come to open their wounds.

"I have a theory," he admitted.

Nyte steered me around the bed, which I noticed with a twinge of guilt was disturbed. I'd pulled him from rest.

"It can wait—"

"No, it can't."

I watched him bend by the fire, and something so mundane as lighting it had felt like witnessing some precious part of him. Nothing powerful. Just Nyte.

When amber licked across the dark space I gravitated toward it. Kneeling where he crouched, my palms splayed toward the flames with a soft sigh when the warmth rippled over me. To his silence, my head turned a fraction, knowing he was watching me. What I didn't expect was how soft he would appear. In times like this it was easy to imagine that anything beyond our sphere didn't exist, but our reality was that we were destined to destroy each other, or the world, if I didn't resist this pull to him.

"Your theory?" I prompted.

Nyte sat back, getting comfortable with one knee bent, so close to touch.

"I should have realized sooner. I think your parents are trying to give back the worst of your memories involving me before you might remember anything . . . *good*."

It was a certain type of anger to be resentful toward gods when no confronting them would help.

"They're not fond of me," Nyte mused.

I couldn't help my short laugh. "I can't imagine why."

"There were many times you wanted to hurt me. We were enemies, Astraea. Born to be. For a while, I think both of us acted true to that, until we tempted that fate. Crossed a line that was never meant to be."

"Were we . . . Bonded? Like *fully*."

His eyes met mine and though he didn't speak, they gave me the answer, which erupted within me.

"The battle you keep seeing . . . it was the repercussions of it."

That stole any excitement from the prospect. "Was it against my will?"

He didn't answer right away, leaving seconds for dread to pool—

"You chose me," he said. Distantly, as if he wished it wasn't true. "But the Bond . . . it only happened because I had no choice. You were dying, and I didn't know how else to save you than to bind you to me. I think it was the first attempt against your life. To this day, it is my greatest failure and torment never to have discovered who finally succeeded, but I haven't stopped looking and when I find them, I plan to kill them a thousand times. Even then it won't be enough for the thousand more I died from losing you."

I tried to process, but all I became was cold. So cold. I didn't want to hear what was going to shake me further but I needed to know.

The impression of Nyte tucking in behind me slipped my eyes closed. I shouldn't want it. Yet even if these moments of accepting his comfort would bleed out of me later, part of me thought it was worth it.

"Why did I attack you back then?" I whispered.

"Before I tell you, I need you to reserve your judgment. As much as I want to kill him, but for far more selfish reasons, he protected you for a long time. You trusted him."

I didn't want to accept this next truth, but I couldn't run from it.

"Auster?"

Nyte's hand slipped over my thigh like the name triggered something in him. As though it could make me leave to go in search of it when I didn't have to. He'd found me.

"He made you believe I only Bonded you to merge with your power. That it was a vampire who attacked you with the key by my order and that it killed him to do so. Your key is highly protective of you, as the only thing that can kill you. Unless you give your blessing to it willingly, anyone who tried to wield it without will face punishment. I guess the severity depends on what power or resilience to it they might have."

If there was even a possibility it was true, I could be sitting in the embrace of my killer. Not by his hand but his orchestration.

"How can I be certain you didn't order it?"

He pressed closer, and I became hyperaware of his hand trailing higher on my leg while I still knelt.

"Do you believe answers can be found in the heart?"

"You think I'd believe you because of heated touches and romantic notions? It's a manipulation of the highest form."

Somehow I could *feel* his smile. It always shifted a playful energy that shivered my skin and I was daunted by how in tune to him I was becoming.

"I don't mean in your feelings for me. You've always had a very acute intuition. Listen to yourself."

It wasn't that easy, not when I couldn't be sure my feelings wouldn't betray me just as easily.

Nyte's hands hooked the blanket at my shoulders. He moved so slowly, ready to stop at the slightest rejection if not from my voice then from my body. Yet I remained utterly relaxed, wanting him to slip it from me and replace the heat of it with his skin instead. My lips parted at the feel of him. It was a craving I didn't think I would ever be able to fight.

"I must have believed Auster came after you back then," I said.

"I can't blame you. He's one of your people, someone you were close to for far longer than you knew me. You grew up together."

"Why didn't I Bond with him?"

Nyte's lips hovered between my shoulder blades. "I can't answer that for you."

"Please."

"I can't answer because it's not fair to expect you to take my word for it. All I have is what you expressed to me in the past but you might feel differently in this life. I can't plant words that could influence you as you figure out your wants."

"Is that why you wanted me to go to the veil . . . before the Libertatem?"

"Yes."

"It would have condemned you."

"But it might have given you a chance to find the feelings for him that you couldn't before."

"You would wish that?"

"No, of course not. I would have gone mad in jealousy. But he is safer for you."

I couldn't believe that. Not when, despite all he was, never had I felt safer than when Nyte was near. Not even as much as when I was with Zath. It wasn't just his power either.

"Would you let me go to him?" I asked quietly.

Nyte's breath blew across my skin, then he pulled away.

"I would lose the vampire trust if they knew you'd gone to Althenia and I allowed it."

Part of me anticipated that answer, but I hated that it felt like he was denying me a right. I pushed up on my knees, turning to pin my heated stare down on him.

"So I'm your prisoner."

Nyte's golden gaze stared up at me but he didn't react to my anger. Instead, he wore awe in those beautiful eyes.

"You're my eternal torture," he said with a low gravel.

My breath drew sharp when he reached for my sides and pulled me to him. I had no choice but to brace myself on his shoulders for balance but my hand slipped into the back of his hair, gripping tightly enough to angle his head back in warning. The bastard grinned up at me, so slow and devious. It ignited a challenge of passion infused with anguish.

"This isn't because I've forgiven you for everything."

"Of course not."

"In fact, this is because I hate you."

Nyte squeezed under the curves of my ass and I bit back my whimper.

"Then hate me. Lower those hips and feel what it does to me."

It was tempting, but I wasn't ready to give him what he wanted. My thumb reached around, tracing his facial scar carefully. Then my fingers dropped, finding the one among many on his chest.

"Do any more of them belong to me?" I asked.

"No."

I began to chart the map of cruelty on his skin. Pausing on the next.

"My father," he answered. Nyte became so still that I hesitated moving again, but all he did was watch me, and I couldn't explain the permission in those amber irises. How they tried to tell me what he couldn't voice.

I paused over the next one, a serrated longer scar along his bicep.

"Battle."

The next.

"Father."

Over his chest again.

"Father."

I took in a few more until I couldn't stand to hear that word again with what was boiling inside me.

"Where is he?" I said, in a dark tone that was new to me with the need for vengeance crawling inside me.

"I don't know."

"Don't you want your revenge for what he did?"

"Yes. Eventually. But right now, all I want is you. They're very old wounds, Starlight. I feel nothing for them anymore."

"The act doesn't erase," I said sharply, surprised by my own anger. "You killed Hektor for me. For a while I wanted to hate you for it but . . . I don't think I could have done it. Not again. But I want to kill the king for you."

Nyte tucked my hair behind my ear. The pinch of his brow a mix of heart-ache and pride.

"I don't wish that. In fact, I'd do whatever it takes to make sure you never cross his path again."

"You can't be me shield from everything."

"No, not everything, but whatever I can. I will be your shield, your shadow, your weapon. I will be whatever you ask of me. There's no denying I'm the villain they whisper me to be, but since you, I'm at peace with what I am. Because now I do it all for you. To see you rise to everything you were created to be."

"Anything I asked?"

"Yes."

"If I asked you to stay? Stay in this realm with me?"

My heart thundered at the fear of rejection.

"I'd only ask one thing back . . . would you be willing to condemn your world for it? Because I would. I would lie with you and watch every star plummet to land," he said in a gravelly whisper, leaning in until his breath teased my throat. "This world would fall to darkness and I would spend everyday content never to see the daylight, because I have this. You. My brightest star."

It wasn't fair. To have this choice that balanced my heart and a duty the world depended on at opposite ends of a scale.

"I don't think I want to choose," I said.

"Astraea—"

"Don't tell me it's impossible. Not after all we've been through."

No one could be certain of the future to come, but right now I broke for him.

My lips met his with an urge to release all that had been building between us since he'd betrayed me for Tarran on the rooftops. I understood why he'd done it, and maybe I wasn't truly angry at him for it. I was furious that it was necessary. So beyond frustrated to be a pawn in this war when somewhere within was the locked potential to be the game master.

I took it out on Nyte—let out the fire of our ages-long war with feelings and blood that was so far from over.

He groaned into my mouth as I pulled his hair tighter, then pushed him back to straddle him.

"There's a perfectly good bed right there," he muttered huskily.

As I traced up the contours of his abdomen to his chest, the bed was the last thing on my damned mind.

"Why did I choose you back then?" I asked. Even though the responses of my body over him thought it to be the most ridiculous question.

"I can't answer that either," he murmured, trailing hands up the backs of my bare thighs, and it was like I melded into him with that touch, sinking myself lower.

Frustration angled my nails to drag over his chest. His teeth clenched against a hiss but those molten eyes swam with desire.

"Then show me," I pleaded. "I need more of us."

"Say you trust me. Because I can also plant lies and manipulations. I'm very good at it and you would never know the difference. It was my father's second favorite thing to use me for."

"I trust you." It was the truth. And I was becoming desperate when my *parents* were determined to meddle and give me only the worst of him against me.

Nyte's eyes flexed, as if he warred with himself over that response.

I said, "Why do you try to push me away yet you won't let me go?"

His palm slipped around my nape, pulling our heads closer until I could feel the warmth of his breath across my lips.

"Because I am incapable of it. Because I selfishly want you to choose me despite the stars we collapse and the war we incite."

"And if I don't choose you?"

"Don't provoke me, Starlight," he muttered huskily. "Don't make me show you why you can't stop this anymore than I could."

My legs wanted to close with the heat gathering between them, pooling a slickness he was bound to feel if he—

With a palm to my lower back, Nyte erased the few fractions of space I left hovering in his lap. A small gasp escaped me, then all reason scattered far to the rush of desire meeting his hard cock beneath me.

"Or do you want to run . . . ?" he said, the vibrations of it shallow against my lips. "So we can both meet after the thrill of the chase? Because there is no where you can go that I won't find you."

"Is that a threat?" I breathed.

"It's a damned promise bound until the end of time."

His lips crashed to mine and I answered in a moan he took as an opening to deepen the kiss. Hungrily. We clashed lips and teeth and tongues in a raw passion that beat in my chest like a war drum.

Nyte broke from my lips to trail down my throat, and in the haze of my pleasure I barely registered movement until my ass touched cold wood and the last licks of starry shadow dissipated when my eyes opened. He kicked the legs of a chair out his way, with his lips never leaving my body. I sighed his name, tightening hands in his midnight locks while it seemed he planned to feast on me right on this solid black dining table adjoining his bedroom.

"May I?" He asked thickly.

I didn't realize he'd paused with fingers hooking my nightgown. For some reason, his tender care even in the heat of passion warmed in my chest.

"Yes," I said through a labored breath.

As Nyte slid the silk material over my head, his golden eyes began a slow trail of my body. He'd seen it before but it was like he savored every inch for the first time in that short pause. I had never been shy of my naked body but never before had I felt like the skin I wore was made of shining armor. The admiration in Nyte's expression made me feel *powerful*.

"There is no star in the sky that shines as bright as you."

I combed fingers through the locks tipping over his eyes.

"There is no darkness that defies the night like you."

His eyes flickered with awed surprise. Then he met my lips again with a new ferocity that exploded through me. A large palm cupped my breast and I moaned into his mouth, close to begging for *something, anything,* at my core that had me hooking legs around his hips to draw him closer.

"Greedy," he murmured wickedly.

"I need you," I said, shamelessly trying to chase my pleasure against him.

"How do you want me?"

The answer came in such a scatter of urges that I couldn't form a coherent sequence of words. His hands, his mouth, his cock—I couldn't decide what I wanted where because I *was* greedy to have it all at once.

"Here—?" he muttered in a low growl. My hands planted behind me, tipping my head back with a moan when his fingers ran down my center. Only once. My eyes locked on his just as he brought his thumb to my lips, pressing down gently. "Or here?"

My tongue flicked out on instinct, and I delighted in the wildness it evoked in his eyes as he watched.

Feeling bold, my fingers hooked into the material slung low on his hips. My gaze trailed over the deep contours of his pelvic bones dipping under it. My hand followed, earning a hiss from him when I palmed the length of his cock, which raced a thrill in my blood. I squeezed on my next pass, keeping my eyes locked on his face to consume every flex of muscle from what I was doing to him.

There was something empowering and triumphant in owning Nyte's pleasure. Knowing the torment I could cause if I stopped, and the utter bliss I could give if I wanted. To have Nightsdeath at my mercy.

"Take them off," I ordered with a seductive edge that was new to me. "And sit on the chair."

The flare in his eyes spoke of feral thrill. He obeyed.

Slipping off the table, I fed on the lust clouding his irises as he leaned back, trying to anticipate my movements as I approached.

"You don't have to—"

Dropping to my knees I took hold of his cock, earning a white knuckled grip on the arm of the chair.

"Astraea," he groaned my name, which sparked my confidence.

He was big. Intimidatingly so, which I hadn't fully conceived of the last time. I didn't know what I was doing but tried not to let the seed of uncertainty cause my focus to waver. I drove his pleasure with slow strokes at first, adding pressure until I discovered the right amount that had him refraining from thrusting into my hand.

Then I took the head of him into my mouth. Tasting him slipped a moan up my throat and Nyte's hand slipped through my hair, tightening.

"Fuck—Astraea," he groaned, like anything else but my name eluded him, and that brought me satisfaction.

My cheeks hollowed, sucking in harder when I wanted him to come undone for me. My hand worked his base in tandem and I tried to take him deeper into my throat but panic rose when the tip hit the back and I realized how much my palm still covered.

"That's it," he said in a strained voice. "That pretty little throat is as perfect for me as the rest of you."

I hummed, and that seemed to heighten his pleasure. His hips moved with me, hand in my hair guiding me, and I wondered if he was holding back.

"Stop," he rasped sharply.

My lips unwrapped from him to peer up. Nyte was a breathtaking sight to behold. Chest heaving with his scarred, golden tattooed skin beginning to sheen against the dull light.

"Bend over that table for me, love."

My core ached at those words. I did as he asked, leaning until my breasts met the cool bite of the wood. My palms splayed by my head, and the anticipation tightening in my stomach pooled between my legs and down my thighs.

I expected his cock at my entrance, so when glorious heat lapped over my core instead, I cried out shamelessly.

"Spread your legs wider," he instructed. I shuffled, nearly boneless already. "Good girl."

His tongue alternating between dipping inside me and curving over my apex elicited unchecked sounds from me that I was far too consumed in the pleasure to feel shameful about. My hips wriggled, desperate and greedy for *more* but not knowing what to beg for. Nyte groaned against me, then his hand curled around my knee, lifting my leg sideward gently until I understood what he wanted me to do. My flexibility eased the extension of my leg until it was across the table and my body angled. It splayed me completely to him, pressed tighter to the table.

Nyte devoured without mercy. Though I clenched around emptiness as a warmth pooled in my lower belly, beginning to tingle over my trembling thighs.

"Give it to me," Nyte ordered. He sucked hard, spreading me for his tongue to dip inside deeper than I thought possible.

"Oh gods," I rasped. So close and unexpected. "Yes."

"I could spend my fucking life on my knees behind you," he growled. "So long as you call out for *me,* Astraea. Let me hear it." His teeth dragged sharply over my ass.

"Nyte!"

My nails scratched into the table with the force of a climax when his mouth returned to my core. The quick shift from pain to pleasure detonated every internal piece of me. I shook with the instinct to slip my leg off the table and make him stop but he held me still, continuing his assault that stretched my climax on and on until my vision began to pepper around the edges.

Nyte finally pulled away and I panted hard against the table, willing my consciousness to hold on after the most shattering bliss of my life.

"You are incredible," he murmured, leaning over to press a kiss to my shoulder.

I whimpered at the gentle press of him at my entrance. "Are you okay to take me?"

Stars, yes. I was boneless and still blinking back my vision but I needed him. "Please," I said.

"You never have to beg for what is already yours."

Nyte eased into me slowly. My nails clawed into the wood, lips parted on a silent cry.

"I am yours, Starlight. Do you believe that?"

I could hardly hear him through the pleasure roaring in my ears, so the response came and went in such a blur that I didn't think it left my lips.

"Astraea," he growled, sinking deeper.

"Yes!" I cried out.

"I want to hear you say it."

Another inch stretched me so full. *Shit*, I didn't remember him being this much.

"You're mine," I said, claiming him with my body and my soul.

No matter what was to come, I didn't think that would ever change. I could attempt to live on without him, but the lies it would take would be like applying balm to my chest when it could never touch the wound that carved deep under my skin.

"And?" he prompted, giving my hips a squeeze but not moving again.

He was wicked in his torture.

"I'm yours," I said, bringing my head back to lock with his eyes.

"Eternally mine," he growled, then thrust forward suddenly.

Finally seated fully, he stilled for a few seconds to let my body adjust. Then he let go, driving into me over and over, and there was nothing tender left in the way he claimed me back.

The friction of the table against my apex heightened my pleasure with his hard thrusts while causing a whimpering frustration that it wasn't enough. My breasts crushed into the wood so I could hardly grapple for stability.

Nyte groaned with his next punishing plunge into me and he stopped, leaning over my back, and I shivered with the radiating warmth of him over my sweat-slicked skin.

"You have to see what I do," he said, voice thick as he pressed his lips over my shoulder blades.

I couldn't ask what he meant. Only let him guide my leg down from the table and take most of my weight as he carried me through shadows.

Then I stared at my naked body in the washroom mirror, which stretched the length of the entire wall. There was a counter before me.

"Hold onto it," he said thickly. "Tight."

My hands reached to brace against the wood. His hands guided my hips out and my legs farther apart.

"I hope you know I'll never get enough of you," he said, running his large hand over my ribs to cup my breast. "Not even when I have you every day of our eternity."

"Presumptuous of you."

"No, Starlight. There's only one way we end and that's if the world ends with us. Even then, I'll find you in the next and happily collapse that too if that's to be our never-ending fate. I'd choose destruction every time if it meant having you."

Nyte entered me again and my face pinched with the shot of pleasure. His skin glowed, the gold markings flaring to life and only then did I realize we matched. Our magick awakened as if it reached to bind too.

"I'm so close, but I need to you to come with me," he rasped against my neck. His thrusts were slow and deep. Savoring.

I wanted to shake my head, I didn't think I could handle another climax as intense as what he'd given me but that control was slipping further away from my exhausted mind. His hand curved around, circling my apex, and I cried in utter bliss and torture combined.

"There you go," he growled when I tightened around him, so fearing the eruption of what was about to unleash that I couldn't even muster sound anymore.

When it hit me, the sound that came from me was between a scream and a cry. My eyes clapped shut and my back curved up against Nyte, whose hand slipped around my neck. He kept fucking me though my orgasm, which felt endless. Waves and waves of pleasure rocked through every piece of me.

Nyte picked up the pace before he slammed into me one last time with a powerful groan, burying his forehead into my neck while his body jerked against mine with his end, gripping me so tight it was claiming. The only thing keeping me upright was him.

We remained like that for a stretch of silence to collect ourselves, our sweat-slicked skin against each other and our breaths fighting to steady.

Nyte pulled out of me, and I whimpered, bracing against the counter again.

I couldn't move. I focused on collecting breath and staying standing, listening to Nyte run water and then return. I couldn't say anything to the warm cloth he ran up my thighs and between my legs.

"I've made a mess of you," he said with quiet admiration. "So beautiful."

Letting Nyte guide me around, he took my legs from under me, carrying me into the bedroom.

He lay me down in his bed, and I nestled into his scent that wrapped me. Nyte slipped in and I tucked into him comfortably.

It was always when I felt most content with him that my fear of losing him crept in.

"What if we're always destined to end up there . . . on opposite sides of a battlefield?" I asked quietly.

Nyte's lips pressed to the top of my head. "Then my vow is to never give up trying to rewrite the stars."

11

Nyte

I didn't want to be here, so far from my Starlight, but I needed to see for myself what my little brother had been doing in my absence. Following the red-headed rogue Nadia brought us deep into the mountains. The cold was sharper this high up, but it was a hidden spot, perfect to conduct the sinister project of transitioning humans to vampires.

"You know they say the blood vampires first came into creation from humans?" Nadia said. She sat on a rock she'd dusted the snow from, swinging her legs.

"Then how come we have shadows?" Elliot pondered.

She answered, "Because the original blood vampires were a consequence of mortals having their shadows stolen by a cursed god that terrorized the realm. Then they procreated, of course."

Kerrah huffed, tucking a flying whisp of brown hair away. "That's a ridiculous claim."

Zeik was peeling an apple with his small knife. He joined in the discussion with a full mouth. "Don't they also say some of the Maiden's guardians were cursed gods?"

Their eyes started to target me as if I would have more knowledge about Astraea and her guardians. In truth, I didn't get the chance to learn as much as I wanted to with her in our past life.

"Doesn't matter," I said. "This is not the same. You were among the lucky ones who faced this dark magick to transition humans and kept your sane minds."

"Lucky," Sorleen echoed my word with cold detachment.

Elliot lingered by her as he usually did, casting her a saddened look.

"There is luck even in misfortunes but that doesn't cancel out a fraction of your burden," I said.

Sorleen didn't look at me; I was growing used to her vacancy and Elliot seemed to be the only one who stayed close by her regardless of the silence.

When I first found out about my father's plan to bring back the making of vampires . . . it took a lot to horrify me and that was exactly the thing to do it. He'd made the discovery in a book of long outlawed and forbidden magick. It was barbaric and unpredictable to create such a species that caused periods of such carnage in our history that the celestials had no choice but to have all of them hunted and slaughtered to stop the procreation. Even though some transitioned could be as civil as the Born. It was too much of a risk to mankind.

I would never forget my father's first successful leap to repeat history. Elliot's terror was something that threaded through his charisma even to this day when I looked at him. He'd survived, and mercifully after his first feed, he didn't become something uncontrollable with thirst that I would have had to have put down. It wasn't often that I cared, but something about him made me curious.

"How many?" I asked Nadia.

"Twenty thousand, give or take."

Shit. It was far more than I'd expected. Exceeding the recorded number of creations our history had ever reached. If those were the survivors . . . the number of humans dead as a result would be even higher over the past century.

"How many roam through the kingdoms?"

"At least half. The others are either too savage, kept in cages within these mountains and fed enough to keep them alive, or still undergoing training before they can be let go to join civility."

Training was a cruel word for taking someone's humanity and forcing them to learn to live with the monster they'd become. Or they would die.

The transitioned vampires had one ability to help them to remain untraceable. They could compel the mind of someone whose blood they'd drank, and their saliva healed any puncture wounds in flesh. The humans would never know the sinister change in some of those they'd taken in as neighbors and friends. The transitioned vampires were the ultimate predators of the species they once were, and that was the cruelest twist of fate.

"Some of them are insufferable little beasties," Kerrah muttered.

"Like snapping nymphs," Zeik added, bashing his teeth to depict it.

We watched the cave entrance far below us as a new wagon pulled up and I could hear the frightened cries of the humans within. When I saw who was being escorted out—

"Children?" I seethed, standing from my crouch.

"The king's order," Nadia said, low and resentful. "When I was there, they would often disappear, and I'd never see them again. I always assumed they'd died in the attempt to change them."

These humans couldn't be much past their first decade.

"How long ago did he start bringing them in so young?" Elliot asked her.

"Around eighty years ago."

"I'm going in," I said. Rage was already coursing through me and perhaps I would get to release some of it.

"The wings aren't fair," Zeik grumbled.

"You won't be too far behind," I said, stepping off the high ledge.

Dropping down in front of the carriage, my fist tightened at the soulless whose hand connected with a crying boy's face.

The soulless straightened immediately at the sight of me, his contorted face of ugly anger blanked to terror.

"That wasn't very nice," I said calmly.

My words caused him to shudder more and take a step back, as if he could deny doing what I saw.

"M-My lord," he stuttered, giving a short bow of his head. "Their cries—they won't stop."

My eyes fell on the boy, then across the ghostly faces of those in the carriage cage.

"Look away and cover your ears," I said to them.

They didn't hesitate.

Zeik and Kerrah caught up first, bickering over who would take the reins of the carriage. Elliot stayed back with Sorleen, who kept stoic. Nadia stood closest to me. It looked like I wasn't doing a good enough job of repelling her from me. I'd have to work on that.

"Terror does that to a person," I said to the shuddering soulless. The vampire cried out when his knees slammed to the ground without a trace of physical force. "What's worse than the cries of frightened children are the wails of cowardly men."

The shadows that climbed his body began to seep into his ears, his mouth, his nose, then his eyes. They robbed all his senses to induce the most silent and lonely kind of physical suffering. It had taken some time to learn everything the shadows were—what they could do. The dark could be crafted and learned and they answered me like kin.

The soulless wasn't worth any more effort than the snapped neck I commanded through his mind without touching him. The darkness spilled like smoke from his body when it fell.

"Get them out of here," I said, not looking at any of the Guard in particular.

Many years with them led me to anticipate that Zeik and Kerrah would take the wagon, while Elliot and Sorleen followed behind me along with the rogue.

The scent of damp stone was lined with a faint copper tang of blood. Despite the cold, there was a certain humidity that began to choke the air the deeper into the cave we ventured.

My focus was wrapped around myself, however. Calling to the beast that lived inside me already clawing the confines I kept it in. Nightsdeath had become a reputation, but it was a harrowing essence inside of me. The kind of pure darkness that repelled any kind of light. It was something I could be in control of, though it had taken decades of torture and discipline not to let the power become *me*.

"We weren't expecting you," a woman, soulless, spoke when we entered a wider expanse of the cave.

"If you were, you'd already be dead," I answered.

"Of course, my lord." She dipped her head, avoiding my sight as if that would stop me seizing her mind.

At first, the eyes were the door—a necessary to breach the mind. That was an obstacle I'd torn down centuries ago.

"Your arrival doesn't surprise me, brother." I inwardly groaned at the sound of Drystan's tone of amusement. He really was hell-bent on testing the limits of my mercy toward him. "Though I am disappointed at how long it took you."

Easing out from the cloak of shadow, he approached with a swagger that was far too comfortable in this place of evil. So much had changed in this last century, and I still had catching up to do before this new version of him would settle in my mind without conflict. Before he had always been innocent, curious. His thoughts were filled with wanderlust and untouched by darkness. Now, I could hardly stand to look at the mirror image of *me* he was becoming.

This is who he was now. Not the naive young prince that was eager for my company. Not the enthusiastic male that once lived in his own world spared from the malevolent corners of reality.

"So in my stead, father placed you as the overseer of this?" I commented dryly.

"You could say that."

Drystan spared a look at my company, and the faint twitch of his brow landing his attention back on me tightened my fists. He didn't need to say it, nor did I need his thoughts for it: he questioned Astraea's absence.

The tension between us grew, grating even more against my skin with the small audience we had.

"A word alone, brother?" I ground out.

To my relief, he obliged, leading us off down an open passage. Only a single look at Elliot was needed, and he knew to stay and stand guard with Sorleen. Nadia took a step to follow me.

"You stay with them," I ordered.

"You wouldn't be here without me," she protested.

"I won't risk you doing something reckless facing the one person you want dead the most."

"I'm not some reckless, unhinged thing or I would have attempted it long ago."

I couldn't believe I was entertaining this conversation as long as I was.

"You can bring your new pet, it makes no difference to me," Drystan said.

Her green eyes blazed at him then and that's all the confirmation I needed that she was too much of a temper risk.

"Stay. Here."

Elliot came up to her, putting a hand on her shoulder, but she shrugged out of it, storming back toward the entrance.

"Stars help us," Elliot muttered.

I followed Drystan down a narrow dark hall until we came to an office, elaborate and finely decorated. So many items and tones made it easy to tell this room belonged to Drystan and had for some time. Several maps hung on walls, some with pins and strings that likely calculated a hundred ventures he would never see. There were books and compasses and telescopes. He always had a fascination with the wonders of the world.

"It was a convincing show you put on for Tarran on the rooftop after the Libertatem, I will say. Even if it was all wasted breath to grapple the reins of control you've lost with the vampires. But I haven't," Drystan said, wandering around the walnut desk littered with papers.

"You've grown in confidence; I can admire that. Even if it's of pure delusion."

"You've always underestimated me. It means nothing to me now. In fact, it only makes this all the more gratifying in the end."

"This only kills you in the end," I snarled.

"Careful. It almost sounds like you still care for me."

I wished I didn't, but I wouldn't abandon my responsibility for him as my brother, no matter what he did to me. I was condemned as his enemy in his eyes, but I would be damned if that's what I truly became.

"Do you know where our cowardly father is hiding?" I asked.

"Actually, no. I figured you would by now and I planned to ask you that. Are you losing your touch?"

"A hundred years behind a veil seems to have slowed me a little."

Drystan waved a nonchalant hand. "It's only been a few weeks. I won't hold it over you."

I studied him hovering around his desk, shifting some papers around absentmindedly. It was jarring to watch, when there were moments I wanted to deny anything had changed at all in him. Between us.

"Your new recruit is . . . feisty," he settled on his word choice.

"She wants you dead."

Drystan's caramel eyes flicked up in mild surprise.

"Have I personally offended her?"

"Taking her life against her will?"

His sight dropped and he straightened. I wanted to know what he was thinking. He'd become so masterful at hiding his emotions, but the silence was filled with his unspoken thoughts.

"Is this how it feels then? Shouldering all the blame for something far larger?"

"You've been providing your blood for some of the transitions. Did you know it created a blood bond?"

"Of course."

"Then you are to blame."

His eyes turned sharp and resentful on me.

"Forget it. As if you could ever understand anything but your own self," he said bitterly.

"Nadia wants you dead to break the bond. Do you know how many enemies you'll make if all the others you've transitioned find out?" I snapped.

He turned, bracing his hands on the table, and I didn't recognize the threatening demeanor that fell over him.

"Then best kill the rogue before she starts talking. Better yet, hand her over to me."

"You're no killer, Drystan."

Yet as I said the words they seemed laughable in the cold irises he pinned me with.

"If she figured it out, others will too. Killing her doesn't eliminate the many deadly threats you've made against yourself."

"They're only deadly to someone who can be killed."

My jaw clenched tight in anger infused irritation. "Death is not a god that can be summoned and grant you fucking wishes. They don't give dark power to those with ambition, or father would be the one with the beast inside him. Is he making you do this?"

Drystan straightened, and I knew I'd struck a nerve.

"I wanted the key to never touch his hands as much as you did," he said.

"Why?"

"Those who crave power as savagely as he does are the ones who should never come close to it—you taught me that."

It disturbed something in me that he would recall anything I said to him. There were few regrets I harbored in a long existence crafted of many vicious deeds, but what I'd done to him in taking his mother would always be one of them.

"I know you don't trust me. But neither of us want our father gaining more than he already has. We could find him together."

Drystan huffed, a bitter sound.

"You're right, I don't trust you. It's best we keep our endeavors separate. How about a race though? First to find our father gets the reward of killing him."

"What is your endeavor?"

"You were always masterful at keeping me out of yours; why would I tell you mine?"

"That's not true and you know it. I told you everything I could."

"You and Astraea had secrets."

I wouldn't deny that. We'd included Drystan as much as we could. It wasn't that I didn't trust him back then, there was just so much at stake.

It was getting exhausting to reason with him.

"Did you really come here just to interrogate me and think I would spill everything to you after all this time?"

"They're children," I snarled.

That wiped his expression to indifference.

"You know age is no barrier to cruelty to our father."

"Then why are you doing this?"

"Because I was tired of being a pawn in everyone's game."

"You're better than this."

Better than me. I spent my life trying to stop him from falling into the same villainy I had and now looking at Drystan was like seeing a horrifying reflection I wanted to shatter.

"We're all born better," Drystan said, his voice stripped of anything familiar. "At some point the pain behind us makes us turn around, and the person we find holding the knife in our back makes us realize being *better* is what made it a shock. Becoming worse is how we never give another that power again."

I couldn't believe how much he'd changed. How guarded he'd become. Somehow I always thought him to be the most resilient person I knew, but the spirit he once harbored had been broken, and I would always shoulder the guilt of it.

"I want to meet with Astraea," he requested. "Alone."

He might as well have tried to strike me considering the rush of rage and defense that tightened my skin.

"No," I growled low.

"Then good luck finding father on your own."

The anger simmering under my skin strained the tethers of my control on the magick that could incinerate everything in this room with a thought.

"What do you want with her?"

"What part of *alone* didn't convey that it's none of your business?"

My teeth ground. There was no one else who could rile me to the point I had to hold back my impulses like Drystan could. In some ways, it had trained me to maintain control in a way that I suppose I should be somewhat grateful for.

"She's not coming alone. I'll be outside wherever it is."

"Our old gambling establishment," he said. "One week's time."

"I won't force her."

"You won't have to."

I didn't think so either, but it was soothing to think of her refusal for a second.

Suddenly, my world silenced to a distant lance of pain within me and I trained on it, forgetting the presence of Drystan. It was an echo I knew from far and long ago. Even as a small, negligible tug, it was worse than any physical torture I'd endured on my own flesh—because it was a signal to Astraea's pain.

I left without a word, with Nightsdeath already a straining, deadly force priming at the surface to discover what caused her harm.

12

Astraea

The years I'd spent keeping hidden at my old manor served me now to be able to elude the vampires crawling the castle ground and cross the courtyard to the library. I couldn't enter through the main doors without Drystan—or I supposed Nyte would be able to open the ward, but he wasn't in the castle.

After returning from Althenia, Nyte was still away and to occupy myself I thought to retrieve more books. I had no other choice but to make my way down the familiar hatch. My skin prickled through the damp, dark passages that gave off a chilling reflection of memory.

In the cave, I had to pause with the slam of the vision I'd last seen in this place. The dark blood of the vampires I'd killed restraining Nyte still coated the ground, but their bodies were gone. My swallow dragged painfully down my throat.

I planned to head straight up to the library, my first thought to begin finding out more about the celestials and the war. I was bursting with excitement to learn anything I could before I went back to Althenia.

It all dulled as I stared at the open shackles attached to the thick iron chains. I was overcome with the gravitational pull to them. At the point where the veil had separated us, my hand reached out as if it could have returned. My fingers passed through the air but not without a phantom break of energy that pulsed through my body.

I wasn't sure why I felt compelled to reach down for one of the bindings. My brow pulled together at the heavy weight of just *one* of them. There was a space that led to somewhere dark and depthless. I shouldn't venture further, but something in me wanted to know exactly what Nyte had lived through for a century. Each step tightened my chest. This kind of darkness felt lonely and burdensome.

My heart rate picked up with each echo of the steel chiming through the passage. I'd brought the shackle with me, only to know how far Nyte could reach when he was bound in them. I would only be in here a moment, but Nyte's time would have felt like an eternity with no sure indication he would ever taste freedom again.

I couldn't explain the tether within pulling me farther into the cave, like I knew I would discover something I needed. The tightening, ominous passage tingled my skin with a warning I should abandon this venture, but breath came easier when light broke ahead, and what opened before me . . .

My eyes couldn't take it in fast enough.

The pool of turquoise water reflected throughout the cave like I stood in a kaleidoscope. Crystals littered the space, growing from the walls, the ground . . . it was unlike any place I could have imagined existing in this world I'd known mostly in monochrome. From humble homes in towns to the pristine of the black castle, the marvelous beauty of this hidden space was a treasure.

Crouching by the edge, as soon as my fingers dipped against the ethereal waters, I gasped at the pulse of energy shooting up over my arm. Before I could find a reason why undressing to dip in fully was a bad idea I was already out of my cloak and boots. The exhilaration at bathing fully was unexplainable.

The water had a current, slowly enveloping my body like tiny threads of magick wound around me. Glancing down at my arms, I marveled at the gentle glow of my silver markings. I was learning to bond with my magick. Listen to it, not cower from it.

As I fully submerged, a new determination balled at my core. I wanted to let it out. This thing that felt like a bottled scream that had been suppressed for so long was a part of me that feared what it could unleash.

Still holding the shackle, I thought there was a gap in the stone beneath the turquoise water. Could it be a way out? I clutched the stone edge, wanting so badly to let go and dive down toward it, but I didn't know how to swim. I hadn't before—unless by some chance I'd known how to in the past and it could unlock from my mind if I tried. I wasn't so foolish as to attempt it alone when I could drown easily.

I thought of asking Nyte to bring me back, but I couldn't make him revisit a prison he'd just escaped from.

A hauntingly beautiful echo of a song filled the small cave. I looked around but couldn't find the owner of such a melodic voice. It conflicted me with a desire to feel peace and an urgency to get out of the water.

Until a sleek head of black hair emerged above the surface. She looked human, but from the dark movement under the water I knew she didn't have legs. Though beautiful, there was something deadly enticing about her depthless black eyes.

"You must be his star," she said, confirming that the voice that had sung belonged to her.

I felt a strangely entranced by her, content to let her float closer.

"They talk so much about you. The maiden. The savior. They talk of how delicious your blood must be even deep in our seas."

That struck an alarm in me, but I didn't want to move. I kind of wanted to sleep.

"Who are you?" I asked, my words heavy on my tongue.

"My name is Fedora," she said, canting her head at me curiously. "Your Night owes me something."

"My—my, uh," I couldn't get the words out as the song began to weave around us again, slowly lapping me with sleepy comfort.

I shook my head and the moment I had a clear thought I reached for my magick to combat the spell that was pulling me under. It snapped me awake with a gasp, clutching the shackle I held tighter.

Fedora giggled, swimming across the pool, and I watched her black tail chase after her in fascination. I had an uneasy feeling about this creature.

"You know him?" I asked.

"I visited him a few times over the decades. What a sad, lonely fate he fell to."

I traced my fingers over his shackle with a tightening in my chest.

"I didn't know he had company," I said.

"He wasn't very good at it," she pouted, still drifting back and forth across the water. "Being company."

"Yet you kept coming back."

"I found his stories . . . fascinating," she said, shooting over to me suddenly. "The night and his star. The star and her night. They sing songs about you. Such tragic poetry."

"Are they all . . . tragic?"

That tilted her eyes to me, like she knew she had a toy to play with against me and she was a creature of games and tricks.

"It depends on your perception. Would it really be so bad to have night fall eternal?"

"Yes. It would throw the whole world out of balance."

"It seems rather obvious what you have to do," she sang, floating so close that our bare chests almost touched. "What is the one thing Nightsdeath can't stand?"

"The light."

Her smile revealed sharp, serrated teeth.

"You have to become so bright that not even Nightsdeath can defy it. That is the only way to kill him."

"I can't," I breathed.

Fedora cupped my cheek and my heart raced in anticipation. I didn't know what she was capable of or could do to me. She spoke in alluring songs and taunting riddles. She spoke of my blood and those teeth could tear my flesh to shreds.

"Meet Death not with your life but another's this time," she whispered, inching her lips closer to mine. "Only one villain can win, Lightsdeath."

She kissed me, and I was so stunned by it I could do nothing but allow it. Fedora pulled back with a sweet smile, running a hand down my hair.

"Lightsdeath?"

The name trembled through me with something so dark and foreboding.

She nodded, lost in thought. "Silver only suits your hair, don't you think?"

My head was beginning to throb, trying to solve something I had no whole pieces for. Her words only served to torment me about my dire fate with Nyte.

I couldn't kill him. Even if I found a way. Everything in me was tearing apart at the thought and if that's what it took, then I was no savior. Perhaps that was Fedora's warning.

Only one villain can win.

"He knows I'm not a very patient person," she said, but I could hardly process anything else. "I'm hoping this will remind him I'm still waiting."

"What are you—?"

My scream turned to a gurgle when she dove under the water in a mere blink, gripping my leg and yanking me down with her too fast for me to react. I flailed against the strong resistance, trying to blink through the blur and sting of my eyes. Water filled my mouth, and I lost precious air with a silent yelp, scrambling to keep my tight clutch on the shackle that was all that kept Fedora from pulling me under any further.

Pain lanced up my leg with the sensation of sharp talons tearing through my flesh. My screams bubbled in the water and my struggle was futile.

I was going to die here.

No—that couldn't happen. Not when I hadn't had the chance to *live* yet.

Determination to have that life awakened something inside me, and perhaps whatever magickal essence that touched this pool aided me in my fight. The warmth around my body became hot. I blinked the sting away and started to focus my sight under water too. It was like I was looking through lenses of bright light that flared at the edges. My tattoos glowed, and as I looked down I suddenly wished I couldn't see at all when I found the beautifully vicious creature staring back at me. All pointed, snapping teeth and claws, her face shedding any mask of kindness.

The hold on me began to slacken; maybe she would let me go before I drowned, but I attacked, shooting a bright gale toward her from my palm. When I was free I didn't wait to find out if it had killed her. Fire was spreading rapidly in my chest and up my throat.

No more air.

No more time.

The surface seemed too far away. Too impossibly far and I wouldn't break it in time.

I stopped swimming up and gave into an instinct that told me to slip my eyes closed. Trust. Don't panic. Unleash. My arms were moving as I focused my mind to *feel* the magic that could save me. A current formed around me, and before I could comprehend anything, air rushed down my throat but I breathed steadily. The power that consumed me soothed the threatening hysteria. All was so beautiful and light and I was floating in it.

Then falling.

And falling.

But the impact was gentle to my knees and my hands caught my balance against the stone when gravity weighed on me again.

I came around slowly, trying to grapple the thread of reality. Pain returned to my senses; a hot line of fire shot up my leg and I found three deep gashes the length of my calf. I winced as I stood, limping to my clothing. The euphoria of the magick dulled, returning my senses with a punishing force. I needed help.

Dressing quickly, I whimpered at the material of my dress rubbing the wound that was bleeding too much. Was Nyte too far away to feel me? I had to make it out myself.

My vision swayed me through the passage and climbing the ladder seemed like an impossible feat with the drowsiness pulling me under.

Keep going.

It wasn't my own voice that came to me. Like before, I whimpered that it was Cassia's that became my strength in dire moments.

"I don't know if I can," I panted, but I reached for the ladder.

Don't give up now, you're just getting started.

I gritted my teeth, getting to the top, pushing the hatch, and tumbling out of it.

On my hands and knees, I didn't want to get up. I couldn't. Darkness was claiming me. Not the kind I craved but the kind I feared more than anything when it would leave me unaware and vulnerable.

"We can't," a voice hissed.

Terror shot through me.

"Just a little, no one has to know," another argued back.

Oh stars. I was about to become a vampire's meal and that had me pitifully crawling a few paces across the stones as if it would achieve anything.

You need to survive.

A glow broke past my cuffs, and I breathed in the slow waves of calm, not sure how I was doing it. But it dulled the pain enough to allow me to straighten and cleared my dizziness enough to stand.

I turned but barely caught full sight of the vampire before hands caught me by my upper arms.

"You don't want to do this," I rasped, rallying bravery to push back the fear overtaking me, locking on feral red eyes within the vampire's hold. His taloned, membranous wings towered high.

It was like he couldn't hear me, and there would be no reasoning with him when he could scent my blood. Another shadow closed in from his right, then his left. The one who held me bared his teeth, preparing to lunge for my throat—

Smoke wrapped his neck—no . . . it *sliced* through it. My hand covered my mouth at the gruesome sight of his body falling as his head rolled away from his shoulders.

I didn't get the chance to react when choking and high pitched cries struck the night. I could hardly keep track of the form that blinked through starry shadow. Snapping the neck of another. Then tearing the wings from the final nightcrawler only to draw out his agony before his body slumped to the ground without his heart.

When the air fell silent, my pulse drummed in my ears.

Nyte stood with his back to me, shoulders rising and falling steadily like he was collecting himself. A golden glow broke the cuffs of his jacket, but my attention caught on his blackened fingertips dripping with blood that began to turn to smoke as he flexed them several times.

"Nyte," I said, testing his name with caution.

I took a step to him—

"Stop," he ordered. His voice was a low baritone I'd heard before.

He battled with Nightsdeath.

"I'm not afraid of you."

I stepped again but a gasp caught in my throat when it caused Nyte to move so fast I couldn't react. Pressed to the wall, I watched the sun diffuse from his irises. His hand wrapped around my neck but not with any pressure as his arm shook with restraint.

"You're too bright right now," he said with a controlled calm. "And I'm still too volatile to being able to control this."

It had only been a few short weeks since he'd been free, but he was trying. Black veins crawled his neck and the tips of his ears matched his fingers. Shadows circled around him like snakes priming for their moment of command.

I nodded and Nyte let me go. Slipping out from the cage of his body, he remained facing the wall, hands braced against it, trying to reel himself back.

"Go back to the castle."

I stood still against his order. I couldn't leave him like this.

"*Leave!*"

Wincing at the demand, I stayed defiant.

"I can't."

His bowed head shook. "Please."

I couldn't resist the pull toward him no matter how lethal he was.

"I can't." I placed my head tentatively against his back, which turned taut against my touch. "The brightest star needs the darkest night, remember?"

Heart speeding in my chest, I slipped my arms around him until my front pressed to his back. I gave a violent shiver, so instantly greedy for his warmth that I clutched him dangerously tighter, now treasuring his heartbeat under my palm as my cheek lay on his spine.

His pulse was just as desperate as mine, speeding to the ache and fear.

My drowsiness returned but I tried to hold on. My eyes slipped shut, so content against him that I thought I might fall asleep right here.

Nyte's hand slipped over mine on his chest. It caused him to straighten immediately, turning, and my protest faltered when his arm around my waist became the only thing that stopped my buckled knees from collapsing me.

"Shit, you're freezing. And why is your hair wet?"

"I—uh—was—" *What did he ask?*

I was falling without the consciousness to catch myself. I didn't need to when his glorious heat enveloped me again and I nestled into it as best I could in Nyte's arms.

"Oh, Starlight," Nyte sighed. "I might not be able to truly die but you're certainly making sure I never forget what it feels like."

13

Astraea

The bitter air stopped nipping my skin. I tried to blink so my vision would focus, and I was placed down on something soft. The heat I craved was drifting away and I clutched it with a weak fist.

Nyte's soft chuckle gave a similar warmth within. He took my hand. Then he was sliding in behind me and I relaxed.

"I'm bleeding," I said sleepily. "Quite badly I think."

"I know," he answered. "I would get a healer, but it would take too long. Do you trust me?"

"Do I have a choice?"

Nyte didn't answer, and the next thing I knew his arm was lifting to my mouth; my hazy sight caught the gleam of crimson. I tried to jerk my head back, only to be restricted by his solid chest.

"Shh," he soothed. "It won't do anything but heal you."

I was too tired and in pain to refuse. The alarm in me dulled with his gentle approach, waiting for me to accept. I closed the distance, and the first hit of metallic liquid on my tongue drew my brow together.

I was drinking Nyte's blood.

Soon, the copper tang turned to something sweet. Addicting. I clutched his forearm like some starved creature that couldn't drink fast enough.

"Easy," he warned, but it was distant from the roar in my ears craving more. More. *More.*

Nyte smoothed back my hair before that spare hand slipped around my waist. A low vibration against my back tightened my core painfully, and I needed him to relieve it. Frustratingly, his hand didn't dip to where I wanted but rather circled me, trying to restrain my movements against him.

His lips pressed to my neck and I whimpered. Sparks shot through every nerve cell and I came so close to a climax I was near feral. Desperate. He continued to tease down my sensitive throat, and I wanted him to bite so badly I could have begged for it.

"That's enough," he said, his tone thick with lust.

It wasn't enough for either of us, and I couldn't understand why he was denying it.

I could only speak or act on the desire overtaking me if I let go of his arm from my mouth and tight clutch. But I wanted his blood so much at the same time that it became maddening.

Finally, I let go when I couldn't inhale enough air through my nose, alone with the exhilaration sharpening my breaths.

"Good girl," he growled over my collar. My head tipped back against his shoulder while he continued with his kisses along the base of my throat.

"Nyte," I panted, not sure what I wanted to follow with, and then my mind became hazy.

"Starlight," he murmured. So relaxed, calm. When I felt the complete opposite. Wanting to take over the world hand in hand with him right this moment or wage a war in these black sheets.

"Did you find Drystan?" I asked, trying to grapple anything to ground me while I was soaring.

"Yes."

"Is he a danger?"

Nyte pushed the hair over my temple in relaxing strokes.

"I don't think you really want to talk about him right now."

No, I didn't.

My blood was racing too hot, scrambling anything else but the feel of him. Desire crawled my skin and I wanted the clothes between us gone.

"I feel like I need you," I breathed.

"It's a natural effect of drinking from a Bonded," he explained. "You are absolutely stunning."

His compliment drew my attention to my arms—the silver markings that were glowing.

"Did we—"

"No, we are not Bonded fully from it. It requires a blood exchange and spoken words."

I nodded, not sure what was stronger, my relief or—

Stars, I didn't want to acknowledge it fought with *disappointment*.

Between my legs still grew so warm that I could hardly keep still.

"I need—"

"I know."

Instead of helping me the way I hoped, he slipped out from behind me too fast for me to voice my dismay. He couldn't just *leave* me like this.

My scowl up at him was met with a knowing smirk.

"Undress for me," he said, leaning down to press a kiss to my head, and I was too pent up with lust to admire his tenderness.

He stalked into the washroom and the irritation didn't leave me as I heard the water running. Fuck, it crossed my mind to reach my own hand between my legs and finish what he hadn't.

"Go ahead." Two words of pure enticing gravel. My sight flicked up to find Nyte, cross-armed, leaning sideways in the door frame. "I won't stop you."

It felt like a dare. Would he break or I? Perhaps his blood, the unexplainable surges of magick I'd endured both in the cave and with him, had clouded all sense and reasoning.

"Get out of my head."

When I stood, my knees took a moment to feel like they would hold me before I walked to him, never breaking eye contact.

"I'm not in your head," he said, irises melting to a liquid gold as they watched me, like he was trying to anticipate my every move. "Your body is my favorite language."

I turned when I reached him.

Nyte made a noise of faint amusement. "Not in the mood to stretch today?"

The high was beginning to fight with my returning fatigue, but the need between my thighs kept me wide awake.

My gown dropped after Nyte untied the back, leaving only my undergarments. Nyte took my hand, guiding me with backward steps into the washroom. He braced hands on my waist; reading what he wanted to do I gripped the counter behind as he helped me atop it.

The basin beside it was full of warm water while the bath was still filling. He dipped a cloth inside, then dropped to his knee, taking my calf tenderly.

"Every wound on your flesh inflicts a new one in me," he said in a voice of shadowy confession.

"You shouldn't allow it to. I can be quite accident-prone."

"Too late."

I didn't know what to say to that. How was I going to be able to sever this tie I had to him?

"It won't matter when you're gone," I said quietly.

Or if I was gone.

His golden eyes flicked up and I could barely withstand the misery in them. "It will *always* matter."

I couldn't bear the determination in his gaze.

"You had company . . ." I diverted. "In the cave?"

He huffed a humorless laugh. "I would rather I hadn't." Then his eyes flexed as he asked, "The nymph that hurt you, are they still alive?"

Certain he could incinerate all life within mile-long stretch of pool if I gave the wrong answer, I was wary of being honest.

"She said you owe her something."

"What happened?"

I became distracted by the way he moved. Standing to dip the cloth in the basin, the water turning deeper shades of pink each time. His jacket removed and sleeves rolled to his elbows showed every contour of his golden tattooed forearms and all I could think about was how I wished they weren't flexing to wring out the water but rather working with his fingers in *me*.

The next time he stood he dropped the cloth and did not retrieve it. Instead my breath caught on an inhale as his hands trapped me on either side and he leaned in close.

"Fuck," he growled, slamming his lips to mine, and the surprise of it drew a moan from my throat. "I can hardly think, hardly breathe, with the scent of your arousal driving me wild."

"I want you," I said, drunk on the assault of his mouth on mine, my jaw, my neck. I wanted him to bite.

"You have me," he said in a low, gravelly murmur. "For every call. Every whim. Every minor inconvenience, I am yours."

I gasped when his fingers slipped into the low neckline of my cotton corset and he tore the material down the front. It felt so carnally possessive that I shivered at the dark look he trailed over my silver marked skin.

"I could have taken it off in a minute."

"A minute too long."

Nyte dropped to his knee, dragging my underwear down my legs to expose me to him fully. Desire pooled out of me from the mere anticipation as he lifted my knee over his shoulder and shifted me to the edge of the counter.

"Look at you," he marveled, running his hand over my navel before dipping fingers through my core. "So ready for me already."

He sank a finger in and my head tipped back with a cry, my fingers threaded through his hair in a silent demand.

Nyte smiled sinfully, kissing slowly up my thigh while his finger worked in and out of me. It was utter wicked torture and he knew what he was doing.

"Nyte, please."

"That's it, sing for me."

He added a second finger and my hips tried to meet his strokes. Needing deeper, faster, *something,* when the slow teasing was making me so hot and needy it was maddening.

His mouth finally met my center and my back curved to the pure bliss of his tongue pressing and licking and devouring me in every way that made my thighs shudder around his neck. This was my favorite thing, I decided. Nyte and his perfect talent between my legs with his mouth. He read every small reaction I gave and adjusted his assault, sucking on the sensitive bud, curving his fingers slow then faster.

"You're going to come so soon for me, aren't you?" he hummed against me.

I didn't have words. Something of a mewl and a cry came from me in confirmation, and Nyte growled, the vibrations teetering me to the edge—

Nyte pulled his fingers from me suddenly and his lips stopped sucking. I moaned, shuddering from the denial of my release that was right. There.

I barely managed to drag my head up and open my eyes when Nyte gripped my hips and his cock replaced his fingers, sinking into me deeply. I gasped at the fullness, reaching for his nape for purchase as he groaned, and we both watched him thrusting in and out of me in a fast, deliciously brutal pace.

"I haven't stopped seeing this every time I close my fucking eyes," he ground out. "The sight of you wrapped so tightly around my cock."

I wanted to feel it, reaching my other hand between us and parting my fingers where he fucked me.

Nyte swore, leaning his forehead to mine and slowing his pace for a second to marvel at us.

"You're a stunning creature," he whispered. Nyte leaned his mouth to my ear; his tongue flicked my lobe before his sharp teeth dragged down my neck.

I must have squeezed him like my hand did in his hair as he stilled with a groan with his next deep plunge into me.

He was still fully clothed, and I found it wildly attractive. How he'd snapped his restraint so fast that he didn't take the time to undress.

I rubbed myself to chase my orgasm faster, and Nyte's eyes closed like he was on the brink of losing sanity. He kissed me hard once, then his hand planted behind me, the other gripped my hip, and his pace raced both of us to the edge.

"Good girl, keep touching yourself and come with me," he rasped.

He hit a spot inside me that tightened my skin with each thrust; my own movements climbed my pleasure so high that I tensed for the fall.

My thighs clamped around him tightly as I came, clawing the skin of his neck with the intensity wrecking through every internal piece of me. Nyte groaned loudly as he reached his release, spending himself inside me in slow, deep plunges until we were a panting, entangled heap.

"You have destroyed me, Astraea," he said, kissing me tenderly. "In every life, that is your power over me."

I wanted to say it wasn't power since I felt at his mercy too. My attempts to keep distance would always be feeble. If my past was at work in ways I never knew, I thought we were doomed. We were cursed with this cycle of destruction, and I didn't know if we could break it. If we were strong enough to defy it. And that became my greatest fear.

Nyte pulled out of me, and I shivered with the cold lick of air across my center and my slicked skin. He cleaned himself off before fastening his pants. I hadn't moved. He came over and lifted me easily from the counter and over to the bath where I let go, moaning softly with the gentle lapping of hot water I sank into.

"What happened under the library?" Nyte asked, pulling over a stool to sit by the bath.

"I truly intended just to go for books," I started. Flashbacks of where he'd been locked for so long threatened to spill sympathy on my face that I knew he would hate. So I looked away. "Without you I had to go the only other way in, and then I . . . I only wanted to know what you'd endured all that time."

"You found out it wasn't as dire as it seemed? That I had a luxury bathing room and delightful company."

"No," I whispered. "I found out that not even the most beautiful place should be anyone's prison."

I sank down to my collar with the wave of peace lapping within me. "But in that cave . . . what is it? It awakened my magick."

He held out a palm, which I slipped my hand into without hesitation. "There are certain magicks that call to one another."

His skin and mine both glowed and within me pulsed a precious life awakening. A demonstration. Magick, I was discovering, was something to join with inside myself. It was a language waiting to be learned and only I stood in my way of using it.

"That cave used to be for the celestial dragons; it's imbued with their magick even after all this time. That's why it calls to you. It leads out to the Great Lake surrounding the city and so from time to time a wandering water creature might find itself inside."

"They don't seem friendly."

"They can be," he said. "I'm so sorry, Astraea. I don't think Fedora would have killed you, but I owe her a debt and she used you to prompt me along."

"You bargained with a—" I searched for the word he'd used.

"A nymph. And yes, she did something for me a while ago."

"What?"

"She left your dagger in Goldfell Manor for you to find."

My lips parted with the shock.

"It was you?"

"I hoped it might spark a memory or at least give you some sense of the power you had."

I didn't know what to say. That dagger had meant the world to me—the one treasure I had that was a secret rebellion and made me feel safe.

"No memories, but it did more for me than that," I said, hushed from the emotions flooding me.

Nyte's fingers laced through mine and I had no willpower to stop what was going to make the end of this hurt so much worse.

"You'd better give her what she wants before you leave this realm for good," I said, trying to make it humorous but my heart cracking deeper with the impending departure. "I'll find you only to kill you myself if she starts plotting her vengeance on me instead with you gone."

Nyte smiled sadly, his lips pressed to my knuckles.

"What did you find out from Drystan?" I asked.

"Not much yet. He's being very . . . difficult."

I huffed. "I expect it's on purpose, even for amusement."

Nyte groaned, swirling fingers over the surface of the bathwater.

"I'm trying to be nice."

"Your version of nice doesn't typically align with others'."

"I'm nice to you."

I couldn't deny that. There was a softness that calmed the darkness in him and curved his sharp edges when we were alone. He'd done some things that turned me sour but there was always a reason.

There were so many versions of the person beside me that lingered in the minds of men. No one knew the real one. Not even me. But I was committed to him and if he was as committed to me—knowing who I am in this life—he would forgive me for wanting to figure out Auster too.

My wet hand cupped his face and I leaned in, kissing him softly.

"What was that for?" he asked.

I kissed him again, more needy this time because I didn't want that to ever be a question again. As if he thought anything kind or warm had to come with a reason other than that I cared for him. No matter our differences or what was to come, I didn't think that would ever change.

"We need Drystan," I said quietly. "The fae want a vampire annihilation because they've never seen anything good in them. He's the son of the king that wronged them—a blood vampire. On our side, he could help change the tide of this war."

Nyte groaned, reaching for a bottle of purple soap and pouring some onto his hands. I dipped my head under the water and let him lather it into my hair when I came back up.

"He's not going to be easy to convince. Once we eliminate my father, he'll want my death to follow. He might bargain his allegiance to you if you find a way to do it."

"I don't believe that. He wouldn't truly wish you dead."

My eyes slipped closed with the pure bliss of his fingers massaging my scalp. He took his time, giving my hair his utmost care and attention.

"You're severely underestimating his vendetta against me."

"Or you're too stubborn in your self-conviction that you want him to be hell-bent on condemning you."

"Is that so?"

"Just try," I said, barely a sigh from my lips when all I could focus on were his hands.

They slipped down my neck, kneading my shoulders, and I did moan then. It was a different kind of arousal and between his glorious massaging and the hot water my existence was melting away.

"For you," he murmured under the shell of my ear. "I will."

His lips pressed to my neck and I was needy for him again, resisting the urge to touch myself under the water.

"Did I ever have these kinds of feelings for Auster?" The question slipped from me before I could stop it, as if his touches relaxed me far too much to think clearly.

Nyte's hands stopped moving against me and the pause of silence became charged.

"What kind of feelings are we talking about?" he asked enticingly, pressing fingers into my skin again. I knew it disturbed him that I asked about Auster, but I thought this was his way of quelling the insecurity.

"You know what kind."

"I like to hear it. Your body might bend for me but you often deny me your words."

I guarded them because I was afraid. When they felt like fragile tokens of me voiced to a world that could break me with them.

"What if I don't have the words to do it justice?"

"You just gave me everything I needed to hear."

Nyte retrieved a bowl, gathering water and rinsing the bubbles from my hair. His care was bliss and agony.

"I want to try something," Nyte said gently. "I've been thinking about how to help your memories. That if you're beginning to trust your intuition then maybe some images can help, even if they're not in your . . . perspective."

My stomach erupted with a giddy thrill. I craved anything that could help me gain the pain to move forward in this present.

"You want to give me yours?" I thought.

Of course, how could I not have considered the possibility before considering his ability to reach into minds?

"I want you to understand how we got here. That it wasn't easy then and it never will be."

It felt like he was trying to warn me, but I wasn't afraid of what I could see.

"Thank you," I said, overwhelmed by the trust he was extending to me.

"Please don't," he said, pained.

Standing and retrieving a towel as I got out of the bath, he handed it to me and I hated the guarded expression he wore. My kindness repelled him, like he was always braced for me to suddenly look at him and see the villain everyone wanted me to.

"How do we do it?" I asked carefully, scared he might take back the suggestion.

"Come," he said, guiding me into the bedroom.

"When you wake, you'll have it," he agreed. I was giddy, anxious, but ready to see what would meet me in my dreams filled by him.

"How does it work?" I asked curiously. "Why do I need to be asleep?"

"We both do. Where I'm from, my father called it Nightwalking. The subconscious mind is most susceptible to having thoughts and feelings and images woven in, masked as being of your own creation."

It was both a daunting and fascinating concept.

He picked a violet nightgown as I finished drying off. I lifted my arms and he slipped the material over my head, neither of us really conscious of our movements anymore.

He took my hand, guiding me to the fire instead of the bed. Sitting in the tall chair, he pulled me onto his lap where I sat sideways. Between the comfort of him and the gentle heat of the flames, I was already fighting sleep and my hair had to dry. I thought this must be why he chose here, when watching the flames flicker in an amber tango, I became hypnotized.

Then Nyte spoke, his voice a gentle murmur vibrating softly in his chest.

"Once upon a time, the brightest star met the darkest night . . ."

PART
TWO

14

Nyte–Past

Nyte idly twisted the stormstone blade into the game table. His thoughts drifted from the fan of cards he held, watching the intricate black wings of Astraea's dagger turning, spinning threads about her in his mind that carried too many questions. It was an interesting design, considering how the wings of her people were shades of silver, and the dark touch was considered profane.

He would know, since his own black wings branded him an evil mockery to the celestials. Most of the time he kept them hidden.

Smoke choked the air of the elite gambling hall he sat in. Nyte wasn't here out of want or leisure but as a regular player. He couldn't give the vampires here the impression he'd rather be anywhere else.

Nyte hadn't gone looking for the star-maiden after her escape two weeks ago. His father thought that was what occupied his time away: tracking her down, following his outrage.

When Nyte became old enough to know his capabilities, his father's short temper stopped being inflicted on him physically. He pitied whatever boy likely took his place as the outlet now, but at least it wasn't Drystan.

His brother's heart might never have felt love from their father, but Drystan had his mother to warm the coldness their father left. Under her protection and Nyte's, he was safe from the king's cruel ways, but not oblivious.

Nyte's eyes flicked up with the thought, finding Drystan with a victorious grin aimed toward a scowling blood vampire at his table. He was winning. Suppressing his smirk, Nyte flipped the dagger before laying it on the table. The two soulless and three shadowless eyed the deep purple blade warily. It was made of the one material that could kill them instantly if plunged into their hearts.

The star-maiden had his thoughts starved for things he didn't need to be able to kill her. But he couldn't stop swaying from that goal. Couldn't turn off the curiosities about her that were driving him to a very dangerous and irritable edge.

He had patience, however, and didn't need to expend energy seeking her out when he knew she would come back. Her return to him this time grated on his ire. They weren't any closer to discovering who would go down in the fire growing between them when their task was over, but worst of all, in the silence without her he'd discovered something that may very well test the limits of his patience: Astraea liked games.

Nyte chose the moment he felt her descending on the staircase to pretend he needed to hold his fan of cards. Placing his turn, he didn't look up from them as the star-maiden sauntered into the room. Her confidence was a statement in this room full of those who might kill her despite the king's order. A shame her brazenness was going to go unappreciated.

His inward smile didn't mirror on his face.

"The quakes don't seem all that important to you if it's taken you this long to come back to me," he spoke to her mind, keeping the table oblivious.

"Sounds like you've missed me."

Nyte flicked a glance up, greedy for any reaction from her spectrum when he was too damn eager to sample them all. Perhaps he shouldn't have torn his sight from the cards, because his full attention became hers in an instant. Observing the room, she was quick to realize what was happening since she still stood without disturbing a single person's attention except Nyte's. And he relished that satisfaction. She was *his*.

"None of them can see me?" she concluded. He didn't need to confirm.

The headache that formed was too dull to erase her presence from the whole room. Even a splitting migraine would be worth it.

Astraea walked around the circular table and Nyte stalked her like a vulture eyeing its prey. Not to kill, not yet, but she was utterly fascinating. He wondered why the color black was what she preferred. Her attire was almost a dress but split high on either side to reveal her leathers beneath.

She stopped at his table, bracing hands on the back of the seat of the male opposite him. "How was your father's reaction to my escape? I wish I could have witnessed it."

Astraea flicked her cool blue eyes up from studying the male's cards. Something in him stirred at that look. Something long dead given life with the challenge she stoked.

"What are you up to, Maiden?"

"You didn't earn the reputation you have with such poor interrogation, *Nightsdeath*."

"My lord," the soul vampire to his left prompted him to take his turn.

"You're going to lose," Astraea said.

"If I wanted to cheat I could do that easily myself."

"They just trust you not to?"

"Believe it or not, my reputation is outstanding for more than just killing."

Nyte's attention returned to the table. Astraea didn't know what cards he had, but she'd let slip the advantage that whatever she'd glimpsed in the other hands gave them high odds. Nyte found himself no longer studying the cards but a much more enticing game. Astraea wore a ghost of a smile.

Was she misleading him?

The thrill erupting in him wasn't welcome, but he could admit he'd never felt such excitement before in this gambling hall, or anywhere for that matter.

She said, "I'm flattered for the protection, even if it's unnecessary."

He couldn't decide if her confidence despite being alone in a room full of vampires was admirable or foolish.

"Actually, I'm about to win a very large sum of money and you erupting chaos would jeopardize it."

Astraea fought the curl of her mouth, continuing her stalk around the table, eyeing the players' cards.

"So your father sends his most notorious leader to gamble for the funds for his armies?"

"If you've come to talk about my father, you can leave before I release the glamour on you instead."

"Touchy subject."

Nyte's jaw clenched. *"You've come for my help, Starlight. Don't provoke me."*

Her cool eyes lingered on him, but whatever she thought of disappeared before she spoke it.

The player she stopped behind reached for a card. As Astraea reached with him, Nyte's whole damn body tensed as he fought the impulse to jerk when she touched him. He could hide her from sight, but he couldn't erase her fucking existence. The soulless felt her guiding his hand to another card instead. His brow twitched, as he likely believed that intuition, a mere gut instinct, changed his mind. He lay down Astraea's choice.

Astraea met Nyte's warning look with a twinkling challenge. Briefly, he caught Drystan's eye across the room. His brother's brow furrowed, suspicious of Nyte's behavior. When Astraea's hand slipped over the chest of the soulless, Nyte slammed his cards to the table before he knew what he was doing.

The room hushed at his disruption. Astraea made him look like a damned fool for reacting to seemingly nothing. If she wanted to play, fine.

Nyte released the glamour on her, and in an instant, every set of vampire eyes pinned on the star-maiden, who wisely backed up a few paces to the wall, straightening her stance, ready to retrieve the key strapped at her waist.

At the first snarls through the room, purple light flared from the weapon she drew as she shifted it to a staff.

"Nobody takes one fucking step toward her," Nyte said with calm but deadly authority as he rose slowly.

It became a challenge to keep track of so many vampires holding their dangerous restraint against lunging for her. Both the soulless and the shadowless wouldn't pass on the opportunity to indulge on celestial blood. Unlike human blood, there was a far more compelling and powerful property to it.

One taste of Astraea and he knew none of them would have the will to leave a single drop.

Nyte's head snapped with a vicious glare at the first movement. Drystan held up his hands, edging closer cautiously, and Nyte had to take a few moments to push back the darkness of Nightsdeath that was clawing inside him.

"Perhaps we should take this elsewhere," Drystan hedged.

"I know who you are," Astraea said to him.

Drystan's face relaxed, even seemed pleased, though it wasn't said in friendship. His brother had been eager to hear more about the star-maiden since the last time they saw her, and Nyte had been reluctant to give away that he thought of her at all.

Storming to her, Nyte hooked her elbow, leading her to the exit.

"You have no idea what you're doing," he hissed in her ear.

Outside, she ripped her arm from his hold, matching his stare.

"I didn't need you in there. One step toward me and they would have been dust," she snarled.

Drystan had followed them out; he whistled low as if to cut the tension. Astraea made a target of him, her key flaring at her command, and Nyte felt the rise of Nightsdeath beginning to blacken his fingertips and darken his sight.

She took in the changing features carefully, then his neck, his ears. So slowly but not with the fear he anticipated. Instead it seemed to distract her, fascinate her. So much so her key winked out its light.

"What are you?" she asked, more a slipped thought than as if she expected any real answer.

"Why did you seek me here?" Nyte bit out.

"You told me to."

"You could have done so more privately rather than cause another rage from the king when he hears of your mockery around his territory."

"Your father has no territory," she snapped. "Don't forget for one second that it doesn't matter where you hide or try to settle, you are in *my* realm."

"We'll see about that."

Drystan cut in, "Does one of you want to tell me what this is about?"

"Why is he here?" Astraea grumbled.

"Why are *you* here, Maiden?" Nyte countered.

A muscle in her jaw worked. "Follow me."

She wasted no breath before starry shadow began to encase her. Nyte only had seconds to grapple her projection to follow.

Before Drystan could voice his protest, Nyte said, "I'll tell you later, promise.

Try to do damage control in the hall before father loses his mind hearing out-landish versions of it. "

His younger brother groaned, Nyte clapped a hand to his shoulder in fare-well before following Astraea's trace through the void.

When the smoke cleared, he surveyed his surroundings. Unimpressed, he wondered why an out-of-commission bell tower was her location of choice. Spying the last flicker of silver hair before she turned a corner, Nyte followed across a narrow, precarious rafter.

He didn't expect to find a room laid out for living. With a grand bed dec-orated darkly like the tone of everything else but the brightness from outside the several open archway windows gave it beauty.

Astraea leaned against one overlooking the city. Nyte discovered then they were in the heart of Vesitire. The grand castle reflected proudly in the near distance.

"Why here?" he asked, feeling a strange sense of peace so high and hidden.

"It's away from possible trespassing."

Nyte studied the contents of the room with more attention. A few personal items sat on the dresser. There was a tub for washing and the scent so promi-nent here . . .

"You come here often," he stated.

"Expectations are heavy on the ground," she said distantly, pushing away from the window. "Up here, they don't exist."

Nyte could relate. He didn't want to find common ground when he could feel an attachment to her threatening to wind around him. They might share a common goal for now, but he wouldn't forget his enemy.

"Your mission was to find out about the quakes—where do you suggest we start?" he diverted.

Astraea sat on the bed, leaning back on her hands. "I've been making in-quiries around the High Celestials in Althenia. Everyone is at a loss. I thought it might be worth trying to see if you knew anything, or if there could be someone among the vampires who knows. Like your father."

"He's never mentioned it."

"Why would he?" she countered. Pushing up, she leaned on her thighs, observing him curiously.

"You didn't come to me for an alliance," he said darkly. "You think I have something to do with it."

"It would be foolish of me not to have considered it. If I kill you, I'll have my answer."

"Try it."

"You have no other suggestions to explore before I do?"

Nyte turned to view the city, but he felt her try to use that as an opportunity to stab him in the back. He spun to catch Astraea's wrist, the sharp tip of her stormstone blade hovered inches from his heart. The instinct in response to the threat forced all his darkness to the front at once, and she became a bright, insufferable source of light.

Her silver-blue eyes widened, but he was lost in something sinister that needed to snuff out the light. As Nyte held her, twisting her around, Astraea gasped as he pushed her and she was forced to lean out the low window with only his hold on her arm keeping her from falling out.

"You don't want to contend with me," he said, taming the beast inside him that wanted to kill her so badly it pained him.

"Let me go."

"Fine."

Releasing her, Astraea fell from the high height. Nyte stepped up to the short ledge, taking a few long breaths of the calm air that helped to subdue Nightsdeath. His eyes opened in time to watch her magnificent wings come out from hiding, splaying wide to stop her rapid fall before beating strong to shoot her high.

He spared a few seconds to admire the most magnificent thing he'd ever seen. Her wings were light silver but uniquely touched by a faint purple hue around the edges of the outer feathers.

Nyte dropped into the air in pursuit.

It wasn't often he flew in the daytime. He preferred to blend into the darkness with his black wings.

Astraea soared high past the cloud bank, and when Nyte broke through he came to a hovering stop a few meters away.

He felt the energy of her magick before he saw it. What formed from her was like pale glittering stardust, and it blasted toward him to meet his starry darkness. The collision was exhilirating, like nothing he'd experienced before, and it took all his effort and focus to push back.

Light against dark.

An utterly mesmerizing and catastrophic rage of forces.

Both of them withdrew their magick, and he was left panting with the exertion, having never been tested like that before. The clouds had cleared around them, showing the specs of the city buildings far below. On the ground, their power battle could be devastating.

The star-maiden was unpredictable, volatile. But what stunned him with sudden conflicting feelings was how he'd become so addicted to her that he wanted to collide with her again.

He needed to be away from her. Out of the line of that look she pinned on him while chasing her breath. Nyte was as desperate for her thoughts in that moment as he was terrified of them.

Terrified.

He didn't think anything frightened him anymore. Yet there it was, adrenaline that raced through his veins and exploded in his chest like it could end him, or complete him. She became a new beacon of terror.

"I'll see what I can find out," he said to her mind. *"Don't come to me in that place again. I won't intervene if you do."*

Nyte took off before she could give a response.

He flew, hard and fast. His shoulders protested but he pushed and pushed. As if the thin air would force him to focus on his breathing or the pain in his body would flood his mind. Anything to drown out the revelation that wouldn't stop blaring.

He'd felt it the moment he met her but believed it to be a celestial bewitchment. Yet now that he'd felt her magick it was so undeniable.

She was his Bonded.

A primal, dangerous urge was taking over him, and he kept flying as if he could reach the end of the world and his denial would reverse that curse.

He kept flying against everything that wanted—no, *needed*—to go back to her the moment he left her.

15

Astraea

Twilight was falling as I stood in the bell tower. The last time I was here I'd felt the same wrap of comfort. Home. Only now I knew why and I wanted to spend days here, the only place on the land that felt out of the reach of any burden.

"How are you feeling?" Nyte asked gently from behind.

He'd been gone when I woke this morning and I lay recalling the memory he'd given me while we slept.

"Good," I said, barely a whisper when I was so calm and lost in thought with the view of Vesitire.

It looked much the same as it had back then, except the view far beyond. The veil that became a separation between the world and the celestials.

I ran my hand along the metal of the telescope while my skin prickled at the awareness of Nyte's slow approach.

"This wasn't here before," I said.

"I had it made after you left. To see you."

My heart clenched. Looking up at a sky diffused with hues of navy welcoming the early nightfall, it was hard to imagine myself up there. Though maybe some part of me yearned for it again—to be with Cassia.

"You still came here often?" I asked, though I knew the answer.

This place had been kept up well, not left to become dusty and neglected.

"You showed me what true peace felt like in this place. It became agonizing in your absence, but the strongest, most authentic pieces of you remained right here."

"Why couldn't you let me go?" I whispered, finally turning to him. My chest was swelling too much. "Everything would be so much easier if we both just let go then . . . and now."

Getting pieces of our past . . . it was both exciting and gut-wrenching. I watched myself through his memory and wanted to tell that version of me not to fall, knowing the catastrophic events that were about to unfold.

It should have been enough to repel me from him now, but those golden eyes stole me every time I found them and I didn't think I would ever stop bleeding inside if they were lost forever.

"Is that what you want?" he asked.

"No."

"Then I don't choose easy. Nothing I've faced has ever been granted *easily,* and you . . . you're something I'd trek through hell and back to have."

My forehead had fallen to his chest when he'd come close enough. It was an entirely selfish way of thinking but Nyte didn't care. I knew he would condemn the world for this but I couldn't.

"You said we tried . . . that you were leaving to go back to your realm because it's hopeless. As hopeless as it was back then."

I wanted more of our story but I didn't know if my heart was going to survive it when I was still denying that it was either him or me in this world . . . not both.

"It was never going to be forever," he confessed. "I'm incapable of letting you go."

"But you said—"

"When I said I had to leave this realm it wasn't me giving up. I'm determined to find another way to rewrite our ending. Over and over. Through time and space, finding you in every story and living the agony until I find the one where we were triumphant. I refuse to give up on us. I refuse to accept that there is no having you. You're mine, Astraea."

I didn't realize it was something I'd been waiting to hear. An insecurity that had been festering inside me since he said he was leaving. I should have been horrified to hear it—his leaving would have been heroic for our world, selfless, and I don't know what it made me to be glad he was no hero.

"Maybe we could go together," I said, looking up at his face, the beautiful streaks of fleeting sunlight glowing in his amber eyes. "If we can stop the vampire war, then we'll deal with our curse. Together."

Nyte's palm cupped my cheek as he kissed my forehead.

"I want that more than anything."

Peace soothed the anxiety that had been building in me. I wanted more of our memories together, and now they might be bearable despite the end to our story back then. No—it was just a pause before a new parting. I didn't know how many of them we would need to write before we reached the true end, but there was hope threading around us as we stood there, defiant against the fate that tried to write it for us.

"What's on the agenda for today's training?" I asked, with my spirit lifted.

"Since you've seen a glimpse of the fae resistance, how would you feel about seeing another side to it?"

A thrill broke out in me. I was more than ready to act rather than just learning idly and remotely.

"Will Davina be there?"

"Of course. She's hosting a smaller meeting in the woodland with a certain group of vampire hunters."

"Hunters?"

There were so many stems of this war. Subtle roots and rebellion I was engrossed to learn about when all I'd known was submission. Believing the humans were silent and compliant, and the fae had long ago been sent into hiding or wiped out.

Nyte's arm circled me and I braced for the pull of the void he took us through.

"Davina might argue she deserves the credit for recruiting fae and humans as hunters for the resistance, but it was my suggestion, even if she was the one to implement it. People wouldn't trust it coming from me—likely believing that I'd set it up as some gain or control for my father."

My heart felt for Nyte, how everything he did was in his father's evil shadow. He spoke of it like he didn't mind, like he didn't do it for *credit*. Then why did he?

When we stilled and my boots met ground, I looked down to find sticks and moss beneath my feet. The thick tree canopies snuffed out the last of the daylight.

I thought back to what I knew of my short, sheltered existence. The few things I'd heard about Nightsdeath. He took my hand to walk through the woodland, and the simple gesture warmed in my chest.

"Cassia told me Nightsdeath was the one that kept the vampires under control and prevented them from savaging the lands and wiping out the humans," I recalled. "Is this how? You would hunt them?"

"In some ways, yes. Even my father was struggling to hold the vampires in check. He was slipping his authority over them when they started to grow restless. He promised them a vampire reign but so far it reaped little reward for them."

"The vampires are wealthy and known as the elite. What else were they hoping for?"

"In Vesitire, perhaps. But they were promised all the reigning lords would be replaced with vampires. That the humans would lose their rights and become servants to the vampires. My father liked the control he had over the reigning lords; if he'd let the vampire reign happen, they could easily band together and overthrow him as the king."

"So you kept them afraid. Instead of removing him from power and taking over all the kingdoms anyway," I concluded.

Nyte drew a long inhale. "It was rather taxing, but yes."

I shuddered at the ominous power he had. How frightening he was to keep an entire species afraid of his wrath if they went against him.

A glow broke the darkness ahead and through the timber bodies, smaller silhouettes moved faintly around the campfire in the clearing.

"We're late," I whispered.

They all bore attention on Davina who paced at one side, lost in whatever she was saying to them with a serious frown disturbing her expression.

"We're just observing, not participating," he answered.

We stopped at the tree line and Nyte leaned back against a tall trunk. I stood in awe of the many uniformed fae in attendance. Their wears were subtle enough. All black that blended them into the night like wraiths. On the back of their jackets, they all wore the resistance seal embroidered between their shoulders.

Nyte's hands slipped over my waist, and in my trance I lost all sense of gravity as his gentle pull leaned me back against his front as we watched.

"The vampires are evil," a fae male sitting on a log by the fire said. It attracted murmurs of agreement. "There have been two savage attacks in the last week between the outskirt towns. They killed a human child among others."

Davina answered, "Then we need to form groups again and assign them to each town. They're taking advantage while there's been rumors the king is no longer in power."

Nyte idly played with a strand of my hair. "How did you meet Davina?" I asked quietly. We were far enough away that I didn't think they would hear me while their meeting seemed to be growing intense with the topics they discussed.

"She's from Astrinus. I found her after stopping a vampire attack that wrecked her whole town. Her parents and sister were murdered. She was fairly young but old enough that I had to ask if she wanted to fight back one day. I planned to hand her over to the resistance in Astrinus, but she didn't want to stay there."

"You don't seem the type to take on apprentices."

"Davina was very spirited and made her case pretty convincingly."

"You mean she was defiant and irritated you enough that you had no choice?"

He huffed a short laugh. "Something like that. I brought her back to Vesitire and she worked her way up in status with the resistance here all on her own. She was mentored by the previous leader, cropped her ears in full dedication to the cause, and when the last leader was killed over a hundred years ago, there was no one better to take their place."

My heart broke for my friend. All the losses she'd suffered, and my pride in her resilience was immeasurable. I looked at her with awe, inspired by what she'd become for herself and her people. She hadn't let the past break her, and I found a light in that.

Just then her brown eyes flicked up to us briefly, like she knew we'd been here all along.

"Drystan wants to meet with you," Nyte said with a taste of bitterness.

That sparked my nerves and intrigue. "Did he say what for?"

"Of course not. And I'm not allowed to be there with you."

My stomach knot tightened.

"Do you think he'd join our side again?" I asked.

"Truthfully, I don't know. I thought I knew my brother as well as I know myself but so much has changed in him and I've neglected to keep up."

I felt his sorrow and regret like a cold, haunting aura. It wasn't just him who had failed Drystan. That burden had to be mine too.

"We should be glad he's willing to hear either of us out."

Nyte's hand on my hip circled around me absentmindedly.

"I don't know why yet, that's the uncertain part. Before, it would have been out of the kindness of his heart but . . . I don't think he harbors that anymore. I just can't figure out what he's trying to gain other than to overthrow me in the end. But even that seems too broad of an ambition for him."

"I want to meet with him."

Nyte sighed; his head leaning down as he breathed in the scent of my hair.

"I had a feeling you would be willing."

"Look at them," I said, observing the angry faces of the fae in conversation with Davina. "They think the only way to end this is to kill all the vampires. Drystan could be our only chance to start changing their minds."

"I'm not hopeful he'll be on our side, Starlight. You shouldn't be either. No matter what you see from the past, he is not that person anymore."

I didn't believe that. I thought rights and wrongs could shape but never erase what lied in the heart before.

"Shit," Nyte muttered. I turned utterly still. "I'm rather comfortable and hoped for a relaxing evening."

He reached across my hip and pulled out my key. I took it at his prompting.

"I hope you won't need it, but maybe a live threat will help trigger your memory with it. Hone your instincts, love."

Nyte straightened with me and rolled back his shoulders. My heart raced, his words jarring against how lax he was. The fae started to become alert too, standing from the logs, and Davina retrieved her weaponized fan.

Then it all happened so fast.

Nightcrawlers came out of the darkness with snarls and vicious expressions. The key warmed in my hand and I flipped it, grabbing it again as it shifted to its stunning iridescent blade form.

Nyte watched me with a small smile of pride despite the fighting that erupted around us. Then his eyes darkened on something behind me, and it was the fastest I'd seen Nightsdeath change his appearance before he blinked out of my sight. I turned around in time to watch him rip the wing off a nightcrawler like it was made of paper. The shrill cry pierced my ears and I winced, but a hiss to my right drew my attention and I gasped, reacting out of instinct.

My blade swiped through air, not to make impact with the key. A slice of light projected from the angle I cut and for a second I thought I'd missed as the nightcrawler stopped running but stood in front of me, staring with wide eyes.

Then the top half of his body fell away from his lower half.

"You still have your touch," Nyte admired.

I was still so stunned by what I'd done that I didn't register the other attack that was just a few feet from reaching me before Nyte intercepted, stopping their advance with the hand he plunged through their chest. Retracting, he didn't take his eyes from me as the heart slipped from his lazy fingers and the blood coating his hand wisped away in shadow.

"Your focus could use work. On your right."

I gasped, whirling, and my palm cast out, fingers posed to the ground that cracked like lightning stroked beneath it, then I pushed that force of magick up, and the nightcrawler cried out as he was launched into the sky from the exploding path under his feet.

"I don't think I've seen you do that before," Nyte mused.

A second later he shot to the sky, grabbing the flailing nightcrawler who tried to catch himself with his wings while Nyte tore them from his back. I winced and wailed agonizingly but it was silenced when Nyte's shadows smothered him as his body plummeted to the ground.

"You seem to have a habit of doing that," I said, subconsciously rolling my shoulders.

Nyte landed gracefully.

"The wings? It's the most pain they can endure."

I figured.

There's at least a few dozen more around," he informed.

Nyte blinked away again and I honed my senses to help end this vicious, blindsided attack.

My pulse blocked my throat as I spun, and instead of the key I formed light in my hand, pushing it toward the nightcrawler who screamed when it slammed into his chest. Then the light seeped into his screaming mouth, his ears, and eyes. I felt the warmth but it would be nothing to the magick setting him on fire from the inside out and he couldn't make a sound. His body burst into flames and though I should have been repulsed by the death and fighting, I was too in awe of the magick that was answering me. Methods of attack filtered through me like lost threads and I came alive with the action.

I would never be weak or helpless again.

All this time I'd been made to feel like I needed someone to protect me. I'd been manipulated to believe I couldn't survive out here.

Goldfell was right. This world is vast and full of monsters but fear is a choice. What I let it do to me was *my choice.*

I would never let it own me again.

I wouldn't fear trying. Or failing. Or myself.

Tears pricked my eyes and my adrenaline coursed proud and determined.

Running into the clearing, I targeted the skies. My only frustration came from the fact I couldn't chase the nightcrawlers in flight. I threw the key from my right hand as it transformed, catching it in my left as a bow and conjuring magick to craft an arrow with three heads.

I aimed skyward, waiting for the attention of all three nightcrawlers that were closing in. Awareness that one was racing toward me on the ground pricked my skin but I shifted my legs, keeping my stance braced.

Almost.

Two of them dove for me, but the third was a little too far away.

Terror pounded in my chest but I used it to craft my focus.

The enemy on the ground was moments from pummeling into me and then . . .

I let my arrow soar, not getting a chance to watch if it'd separated to strike all three like I'd attempted, certain I'd achieved it before.

The key became a blade in a breath, and the nightcrawler's snapping teeth came inches from my face as he ran straight through my blade. The weight of him made me drop it completely.

Then I was standing face to face with a pleasantly surprised Nyte.

"I'll admit, I doubted you for a second there."

I scanned the clearing, and got to witness the last of my triumph when I found three light arrows fading like burned-out matchsticks from three bodies.

The stillness came down chillingly and exhilaratingly. The ground was now covered in bodies but to my relief I didn't see any fallen fae in a quick scan.

"There you are," Nyte said. I'd never heard such awe in his voice.

"I don't . . ." I panted, the exertion only just now touching me at all. "I don't know how I did any of that."

Nyte scanned my face with sparks of pleasure dancing in his eyes.

"I do," he said, tipping my chin to him. "You've just been hiding for a little while. But you are breathtaking."

He kissed me, hard and only once.

Then he pulled back and reached down, yanking my key blade free from the nightcrawler's gut. Darkness spilled down the key and the light magick hissed, but it only lasted a few seconds before Nyte's magick erased the blood from it.

Nyte held the key out to me.

"Thanks for the help," Davina said, wiping the blood off one of her blades and returning it to her fan.

Making her way over to us, she stopped to pluck another from the neck of a fallen nightcrawler.

"Are all of them like this?" I asked, looking around the gruesome display of death.

"They are the more untrained and savage of the vampires, but not all," Nyte said.

"Was one of your guardians not a nightcrawler?" Davina inquired, folding her fan and fitting it to her thigh.

Nyte had mentioned them before, and I was beginning to sense that it was important I backtrack to them. As if it could unveil something necessary.

"Alisus," I muttered. "There has to be a reason why I fell to Alisus."

"Of course," Davina said as if just remembering that fact. "The Guardian Temple. You should go there."

Inspiration erupted in me. Every time I felt myself clutching a new thread to help me learn my path I became giddy with anticipation.

"They might have more to say than your parents," Nyte agreed.

"I need to visit there first," I said. The temple in Vesitire I'd come to at the end of the Libertatem.

I could have opened the temple then and I'll never know what that choice could have granted me instead. But I'd chosen Nyte.

"Are you heading out with us?" Davina asked. "The night is young and this has only warmed us up for some vampire hunting tonight. The attacks in the towns are getting out of hand."

Nyte looked to me to decide. "As much as I'd love nothing more than to persuade you to come back to the castle with me, the choice is yours."

I was hoping to meet with Auster tomorrow, and the thought of that coiled such guilt in me that my eyes dropped.

"I think I've had enough for tonight. Best not push my luck with whatever is coming back to me," I said.

Nyte nodded with no judgment and Davina squeezed my arm.

"It gave them hope to see you; you should be proud," she said.

I hadn't thought about the other fae. They fought just as valiantly and were now scattered throughout the clearing, beginning to gather the bodies into a pile.

"I hope to join you again, though."

"Anytime."

Nyte circled my waist and I exchanged a smile with Davina before he took us through the void. My rooms expanded around us when the starry smoke cleared and my heart now weighed heavy.

"I told Rose I would go with her into the city tomorrow. She has a few errands to run." It was a pitiful lie, and I was anxious with the thought that he knew it.

"So you're saying I need to occupy myself in the meantime?"

"Are you saying you have a shortage of things to do?"

"That would be a blessing. But things are far more tolerable when you're by my side."

Stars, he was making it difficult to keep up this secret. Or to even want to go to Althenia without him at all.

For a moment I imagined him there with me instead. That he wouldn't be shunned or feared, that he would get to enjoy the wonders of those lands just like any other. That was a future that seemed so precious yet impossible.

I didn't think Auster would ever welcome Nyte on his land.

"Can we go to Drystan in the evening though?" I asked.

"Probably best we don't delay that, yes."

I nodded, and when Nyte made to leave me for sleep, I couldn't stop the request that tumbled from me.

"Can you stay?"

Maybe it was my guilt that made me think keeping him close would compensate for the secret about Auster I was harboring. Or maybe I was only trying to soothe the wicked demons in my mind that were taunting that I could come to find an attachment in my heart to someone else.

Nyte's expression turned so soft and yearning. It was moments like this that he was merely a person and so was I. We had an attraction without curse, and feelings without burdens. The pretend might be the only thing that kept the spirit of our bond alive.

"Those might be my favorite three words you've ever said to me."

He tucked in tight behind me in bed. His shirtless chest against my back and how his warmth enveloped me made it impossible to believe I could feel this from anyone else. My hand slipped over his knuckles at my chest and our fingers entwined.

"You're particularly nice to me today," he murmured, pressing lips to my shoulder. "Should I be concerned?"

"Don't get used to it," I answered lightheartedly.

He huffed softly. "I wouldn't dream of it."

16

Astraea

When Auster brought me to Althenia for the second time, he assigned handmaidens to help me change before we ventured into the city.

Unease at the elaborate wears that took a lot of pleading to get me into crept over me. The gown was pure white and silver and it was like a waterfall of crystals fell from a train at my shoulders. It was elegant, but a statement.

My hair was braided so many times before it was pinned into a gathering at the back of my head. Then what I wouldn't cave to was the diadem they were insistent I wear.

I didn't want the attention, but Auster wasn't content with me covering up under a black hooded coat. They looked at me and tried to hide their horror when I asked if they had any gowns of black or even a dark purple instead. I couldn't explain why the pale color didn't appeal to me, like it weighed purity and expectation on me.

"Now that is a star-maiden," Rose's voice said in appreciation as she entered the room.

She agreed to change too, but her pink gown was far less elaborate. With the spectacle they made of my appearance, I may as well have walked out onto the balcony and screamed my title.

"It's too much," I groaned.

Rose tried to hold down her amusement. "It's . . . a lot," she agreed. "But what do I know of your Maiden customs."

About as much as me, I thought.

"You look magnificent," Auster interrupted.

I turned to find him in the archway into the room. He was a sight to behold too. No longer clad in his black and navy leathers, he wore an impeccable embroidered jacket of deep blue and white. A silver circlet laid naturally on his head now. The perfect depiction of ethereal royalty.

"It feels like it will draw a lot of attention," I said, nervously picking at the crystals on the bodice and glancing back to the mirror.

"I hope so," Auster said, trailing his gaze over me as he stalked closer. "The people have been wishing for your return for centuries, Astraea. Let them feel the hope and joy to have you back."

I didn't argue. It felt too much too soon when I wanted to discover all that it meant to be the star-maiden before I felt the weight of the full expectations of what it meant to be her.

I caught Zadkiel joining us behind Auster, and he exchanged a pleasant smile with Rose.

"Will Zephyr be joining us too?" I asked eagerly. Even though we'd only gotten to meet briefly last time, I'd thought about him since and wanted to explore his easy company more.

"Not this time," Auster said.

My shoulders fell a little.

Auster's hand grazed the small of my back and I drew a sharp inhale. The shock of the touch stole him from the reflection and erased the room around me.

In this vision he stood in front of me, far younger now. The room we were in was dark, glowing with warm firelight. His hand on my back pulled me closer—too intimately close—and my protest pushed him away with a hand to his chest before he could kiss me.

I snapped back to the bright daylight of the dressing room with a single stumble back from that unexpected flash of memory. Auster's hand circled my waist now as if to catch me. Steady me. My heart was thundering and my whole body turned stiff in his hold.

"Are you all right?" he asked; concern pinched his brow.

"Yes," I said, shaking my head to clear it. "Can we go to the city now?"

"I know just where to begin," Zadkiel said with a bright grin.

Outside I was once again marveling that I only needed a light coat here when across the veil was bitterly ice cold in a long winter. The streets were made of pristine white and beige stones. Many of the buildings were white with dark wooden supports, doors, and signages. It wasn't as bustling as Vesitire's tiered city, but what constantly caught my attention with awe was the many sets of wings.

I stared after each set in admiration, until the celestials started staring back. Stopping their walks and whispering with one another. That's when I started noticing people following, watching, gawking. I caught faint murmurs of "Maiden" and my skin began to crawl; my posture straightened too unnaturally from the attention. As if I was an impostor in the skin they doted on. That I hadn't the chance to become the hope they thought I was and I wished I'd fought against the proud icon they'd made of me.

Auster's hand gravitated to my back again, but it inspired the opposite of the comfort I thought he was trying to give.

Instead, I focused on what I could control. My breathing. My thoughts. I let my sight drift further up to try to forget the gathering crowds and the volume of voices that grew. I found beautiful purple banners hanging above our heads between some of the buildings. They glowed like magick infused them and my hand raised to my chest, recognizing the same constellation adorned them that also marked my skin. On the banners it shone over a simplified version of the key as a staff between silver wings.

"What are they for?" I asked, finding more things with that sigil, such as posters and other types of banners.

"It's Star-Maiden Day next month," he explained, admiring them with me. My cheeks warmed to that.

"Why would there be such a day?"

"It's the anniversary of your creation. Your birthday, so to speak. It is the biggest celebration of the year and used to be across the whole continent. They might have let your existence become a fable across the veil, but everyone here remembers. This will always be your true home."

"What happens on Star-Maiden Day?"

"It's a day of unity and complete peace in your name. Between noon and twilight everyone visits their nearest temple to pray to the Maiden. Families come together, those without are always welcomed in. People will feast and laugh and enjoy company. In the past you would have been here, visiting people and spreading your love that was always endearing and infectious. You touched one person with your words or just your presence and they carried it through masses."

It all sounded wonderful, like a fairytale I wished to be part of and hoped to gain back. That tale lifted my spirit here and I smiled back at some of the celestials in passing.

Zadkiel led us to a massive round building and the moment we stepped inside, my pace slowed to the most incredible, huge, and wondrous invention I'd ever seen. It was both daunting and exhilarating, though I had no idea what I stared up at that took up the entirety of the domed hall.

"Welcome to one of my personal favorite spots, the Solar Sphere," Zadkiel announced proudly, his voice echoing beautifully in this place.

"What is it?" Rose said, as awestruck as I felt trying to take in what looked like a sculpture of spheres and stars and the moon, but it *moved*.

"It tracks the position of planets and stars beyond us. The universe is vast and full of the unknown," Auster explained.

"It helps us know when solar magick is strongest. Look," Zadkiel said excitedly. I walked closer to him and followed his gaze up to a gold carving of the sun and moon. "We're actually close to the opposite. A solar eclipse that unfortunately is predicted to fall on Star-Maiden Day this time. There are a couple of astronomers who say that it won't, and those who are predicting that are trying to scare people into believing it's a bad omen to be wary of."

"That's a bad thing?" Rose wondered up at the sun and moon that moved, barely detectably, toward each other.

"For as long as I can remember there's been an old superstition that when an eclipse falls on Star-Maiden Day, the wrath of the gods will rain," Auster said.

My throat turned dry and I swallowed hard as my sight fell from the metal structure to Auster. He merely smiled like it was a scary story he had never entertained a true belief in, but I was haunted by the notion.

"Will you celebrate with us on Maiden day? It would mean everything to those who could see you here. Our lands are vast, but even staying in the Nova province would be the greatest gift," Auster said, so kind and encouraging it was becoming hard to think of anything but keeping his hope from draining every time he looked at me with those soft brown eyes.

"I would like to," I said, and I meant it.

It was a month away. That would be enough time to tell Nyte I'd been coming here. And if he opposed . . . I didn't want to think about that right now. I knew he couldn't pass the veil, and though it hurt deeper than in my chest to imagine defying or somehow hurting him, I had to come here.

"He never told you about Star-Maiden day, did he?" Auster asked.

"Not yet," I said quietly.

"He likely never would have if he could help it."

"That's not true."

"You don't remember the decades he hunted you. When you were aware and elusive toward him, never letting him find you, while you watched him. Waiting for your chance and figuring out his weaknesses. None of us could have predicted you'd become his biggest one."

My heart skipped at that sudden enlightenment. It was something I already knew, but it hit me differently hearing it for the first time from someone on the outside. I didn't want to ask when I didn't know Auster too well yet—but I wondered when he had discovered that my hunt for Nyte had turned into something else. I didn't want to believe I would have led Auster on if I was gaining feelings for Nyte . . . but once again I was back to being sickeningly overwhelmed by the idea I could hate the person I was.

"Dragons," Rose said in a breath of wonder that traveled to us from the echoing hall.

I held Auster's stare for a moment longer and his expression seemed to war pity with yearning, then I dragged my sight to Rose.

"Celestial dragons," Zadkiel corrected.

"What's the difference?" she asked, tracing over the carvings into stone.

I approached her with piqued interest. My lips parted in stunned admiration of the depictions.

"They say the celestial dragons were like royalty among the species during the age they filled these lands. Their wings are feathered, which sets them apart. Legend has it that they're not all truly gone. That they're still here, on our land, waiting to be awakened. That they were only forced into hiding to prevent annihilation around seven hundred years ago, before your first reign."

My head whipped to Zadkiel. "Is it true?"

He shrugged, folding his arms. "It would take one of their direct kin to do it. So unless one survived I don't think so."

I thought about the dragon egg I'd gotten in the maze. For a second magick hummed in me, but I fought the urge to reach through the void and retrieve the egg. I didn't know where the rush of doubt came from, like it could be taken from me if I showed it to Auster and maybe he'd say it belonged here in Althenia even if it was just to be a prized artifact the people could come to gawk at.

"Do you have a library?" I asked, when I hadn't discovered what it took to hatch an egg but perhaps I might find it here.

"We can go there next time," Auster said warmly.

I sulked a little at that.

"I don't know when the next time will be," I admitted. "Not without telling Nyte."

The mention of him fell the kindness from Auster's face. It rattled an internal chill to watch how fast his mood could switch.

"Then stay with us," he said, stepping closer and dropping his tone so soft and pleading. "Stay with me, here. This is where you belong."

He took my hand and the contact scattered pin pricks up my arm. Conflict began to drum in my chest like I wanted to feel the same yearning he had in this touch but instead I was trying not to rip my hand away.

"I still have much to learn on the mainland. You said you weren't ready for war and me leaving him could incite one."

"We'll be safe behind the veil for a while. As long as it takes to get your wings and full power back and ready our armies. We've been preparing for a long time, just waiting for our final piece—you."

I shook my head. "I've been getting some memories back—"

"From him?"

The dark tone in that accusation unsettled me. I pulled my hand free then.

"He's the only one who can give me some insight to begin threading the past together."

Auster huffed, giving me a look over as if I was a naive child and my cheeks flamed.

"He is your *enemy,* Astraea," Auster snapped. "How can you look at him, trust him to plant thoughts in your head, when all your people have suffered because of him."

"It's not just him."

"You're right. It's *you.*"

That struck like a searing pain through my abdomen. Enough that it felt so tangible when my hand hovered there. Then I reached for my key with a trembling hand. It was still at my thigh but my mind was mocking me with the illusion that it was piecing my flesh instead.

"I'm sorry," Auster said. His hands on me caused me to jerk away from him. "I didn't mean to be so harsh."

My heart raced and raced and I couldn't tame it.

"I want to leave now," I said.

I needed to be away. From him. Here. I needed a moment to reel back from the unexplainable pain that made my throat too tight to breathe and the air too hot to withstand. I was *dying.* Slowly and with the ache of something dark and terrible crying in my soul.

"Astraea."

It was Rose calling my name, but she sounded too far away. I leaned on someone but I couldn't make out faces, or objects, or anything.

All I could think about was how Nyte would never know something. I called to him but it was like we were separated by a thick wall of impenetrable darkness. Death itself. He couldn't hear me, and I would never get to say goodbye.

Then I realized what had overcome me was a flicker of the most haunting memory I would ever get back. My death. I didn't gain pictures of what happened that day but the dreadful, helpless feeling collapsed my knees.

I didn't fall, I floated. Higher and higher but it didn't matter if I was pulled up to the heavens or dragged down to hell, either way it was too far from the only person I wanted to stay right here in a mortal body for . . .

I woke with a sharp spear of air piercing my throat, not remembering falling asleep.

"Shit, you scared me." Rose's voice came around clearer as I tried to figure out where I was.

I didn't recognize the room of blue with white floral decorations along the walls and elegant gold and white furniture. I propped myself up in a plush bed with blue satin sheets.

"You're all right, dear," an older voice said at my other side.

I jerked at her proximity and she leaned back with a patient smile. When I relaxed, she brought the cloth to my head again.

"As I understand it, you have a shortage in your blood," she said.

"Yes," I said, then rubbed my throat because of how awful I sounded.

"Here," Rose said, holding a glass out to me. She helped me drink, and I felt miserable in my state.

"I think the events of the day took a toll on you. You haven't taken any medicinal herbs or tonics before?"

"No," I said, not elaborating my wariness of substances because of Goldfell.

I was glad to awake to Rose's presence instead of Auster's. Recalling what happened in the Solar Sphere, I didn't want to explain why the worst of my past dragged forth at the most embarrassing, inconvenient moments sometimes. I lay back down when my head pounded to imagine what he must think.

Weak maiden. How was I to rule like I once did? I had a lot to prove and show here.

"What time is it?" I asked, suddenly panicked that I had to make it back to Vesitire before nightfall.

"Almost dinner hour."

"We need to go," I said, pushing myself up.

"Not so fast, young lady," the older woman scolded, laying a frail hand on my shoulder. "You've been holding yourself back all this time. If you don't get your health in check, you can't possibly hope to recover your power or memories, dear."

I hadn't thought about them being connected. With a sheepish smile, I propped myself back against the headboard.

"I haven't been great with pills," I admitted.

Rose shared a look of understanding with me.

"How about a tonic then?" the woman said cheerfully.

I watched in fascination as she took a white pill and dropped it into a small bottle. Her hand waved over it to turn it into a silver liquid that looked like Starlight Matter.

"What is it?" I asked apprehensively when she held it out to me.

"It will compensate for the missing levels in your blood, that is all. If you remember to take it once a week, your health will greatly improve."

It sounded nice, almost too good to be true when I'd lived a life of waking with fevers and dealing with prolonged headaches.

"Thank you," I said, but I didn't take the dose.

Her aged face pinched in understanding. She reached for a cork, and left it on the side table.

"My name is Agetha. I'm the court healer and at your call for anything, Astraea."

I gave a grateful smile as she left.

"Why won't you consider staying here?" Rose asked tentatively. "Is it just because of Nyte?"

It was the softest she'd ever spoken of him—even using his preferred name. So I knew she was trying to be gentle in the way she thought me a fool for not considering Auster's offer.

"We don't know Auster yet. I haven't even met the other High Celestials besides Zephyr. It doesn't feel right to abandon everyone and hide on this side of the veil. Zath is reluctant to come here, and what about Davina and the resistance?"

That dropped Rose's gaze like she hadn't considered everyone I'd be abandoning.

I watched her stand and gravitate closer to the long windows. The sun was beginning to set and we had to get back to the castle in Vesitire before Nyte did. But for a moment I was lost in the vulnerable sight of Rosalind. She hugged herself and stared out at the Nova province, lost in thought. It was then that I realized she wasn't just talking about me abandoning everyone—she wanted to stay here too.

My legs swung gently off the bed.

"You've never spoken about your history," I said carefully, like she might raise her steel guard any moment. "How you came to be in the Libertatem— your family."

"There's nothing to tell," she said distantly.

"Living here won't help you run away from whatever it is back home."

"You can't give me advice on running away," she scoffed.

"What is that supposed to mean?"

"That you're hardly giving Auster a chance."

"You hate Nyte, I get it. But you don't know a thing about either of them."

"Look at the world Auster wants to give you," she gushed over the lands beyond the glass.

I didn't have to look, because it didn't matter to me. Nothing of land or beauty or things could replace Nyte so easily.

He was the home my soul chose.

"I know you don't trust him, and I'm not going to convince you to like him. But he wouldn't hurt me or you, nor would he let harm come to me."

Rose's hard expression targeted me. "He's responsible for the death of thousands—perhaps millions," she argued. "He is the villain in this war. The leader of the vampires."

"It's not as simple as that."

"They own this world, Astraea. Stop being so naive just because the most wicked of them all decided you were *his*."

That hurt. Deeply.

I pushed off of the bed, taking a second on my feet for balance. Reaching for my coat, I didn't want to argue with Rose when I didn't think it would end well for either of us.

"I'm sorry—"

"I'm not going to convince you what Nyte is or isn't," I snapped when I whirled around. "There are two kinds of belonging: possession and alliance. You're right, I am his. Because I chose to take the hand that wanted to help me, not own me. I'm not naive. And I wish everyone would stop fucking treating me like I am."

I made to leave.

"What Nightsdeath said . . ." Rose started. I stopped with my back to her. "How I wasn't supposed to be in the game—it's true."

"You don't have to call him that."

"It's what he is to me," she said coldly. My teeth gritted at the hostility between us but I forced myself to hear her out. "I came to Vesitire to kill him, like Cassia said we would. I didn't win Pyxtia's trials to become the Selected for the Libertatem, but I couldn't let Cass go there alone when I knew she would try to carry out our plan herself. So I . . . I had no choice. I switched the information about Pyxtia's Selected for the Libertatem before it left for Vesitire."

I watched her tell the story with so many twisting emotions I couldn't place. Fear, regret. There was something else to it she'd left out, but it was enough of a struggle for her to tell this, so I didn't push for now.

I didn't know what to do, how to console her when a tear fell down her cheek. She swiped it quickly, sniffing hard as if it would halt the others gathering.

"I'm sorry you never got to meet Cassia in the end."

"Me too," Rose said, her head bowing.

"You should hate me," I said. "When you saw me in her place. Why didn't you hate me for being here instead?"

"I did," she admitted. "Or at least I wanted to but . . . then I saw why Cassia loved you. Not because of so many explainable attributes when you seemed so opposite to her. It was something about your company. Being around you has some kind of energy that made me want to stop *thinking*. Thoughts of resentment for Cassia not being here. Anger at myself for what I'd done. Every time I was around you the present became more important and I wanted to learn what you are."

I didn't know what I'd done to make her feel that way, but I was grateful to have found a friendship I now treasured. As prickly and stubborn as she could be.

"You look better." Auster's voice cut our tension.

My spine straightened and I stood as he entered.

"We need to go," I said to him. "I'm sorry I wasn't well enough to enjoy my full time here."

"It's no matter, we'll make sure the next visit isn't so long away."

I kept my mouth closed to that.

"May I have a moment alone with Astraea before you leave?" Auster asked Rose.

She nodded, casting me a look in case I objected, but I didn't. Zadkiel waited by the door; she headed toward him.

"Are you sure you're well enough? If you need more rest, we can deal with—"

"I'm fine. It was just a lot to take in for one day. The dress, the thought of Star-Maiden Day. I'll be more prepared next time," I assured.

That seemed to satisfy him. The promise of my near return.

Auster approached me and I let him. I was trying to be receptive to his advances. He moved to me like Nyte did sometimes—as if it was a natural habit and no time had passed at all. The only difference was me, my openness to Nyte in comparison to my reserve with Auster.

His hand raised, slow and ready to retreat if I reacted wrong. I did nothing but hold his brown eyes, trying to find a tether in them, something that would assure me had been something between us in the past that could spark again. His warm, tan skin across my cheek sped my pulse and this time I tried to pretend it was with the same yearning he doted on me.

"Have you visited the temple of your parents yet? In Vesitire," he asked.

"No."

His brow twitched to a near frown.

"I'm not trying to turn you against him, only trying to make you see why you did in the past. You should see the Gods of Dusk and Dawn and hear what they have to say."

"They're the ones who took my memories."

In truth, I'd been too afraid of their disappointment in me. Their daughter, or perhaps I was just their creation, had fallen into dark hands once more. They pulled my memories to prevent it, and how was I to face them when they would regard me as their greatest failure before I'd even begun my life again?

"It's not too late, Astraea. For you to choose right, and do right by your people."

The avalanche of responsibility from that statement alone buried me to the point I struggled to breathe.

I nodded but it felt like a lie. As if I knew I wouldn't be the hero he wanted me to be. What shook the fragile pillars of my existence was wondering if the villain was never Nyte . . . but me.

17

Astraea

Back in Vesitire, I changed quickly and couldn't bear the restless waiting for Nyte to retrieve me to seek out Drystan. So I used the void to travel to Nyte, wondering if it was his blood or something deeper that ran between us and manifested stronger each day, making it easier to track Drystan to this mountain top.

He didn't sense me right away, and I didn't make myself known when the sight of him stunned me still. Nyte *laughed*. Not as hard as the others in the golden guard, and I didn't know what they found funny, but he didn't hold back that flicker of enjoyment even if it was fleeting.

A red-haired woman dusted snow off her shoulders with a scowl while a broad, dark-haired man dipped down to gather more in his gloveless hands. She knew it was about to be aimed for her again and tried to get away, narrowly dodging the incredibly fast throw of it. I was taken back by a childish normalcy I didn't expect from the transitioned vampires. The woman gathered her own snow, throwing it with the same velocity, but the man twisted to avoid it, and it hurled straight for Nyte instead.

I inhaled a euphoric breath at the ripples of his dark power that created a veil of shadow and starlight as a shield with the wave of his hand. The moment the snow made impact it fell as shimmering dust once more, and his magick pulled away on a breath of wind.

I'd known the Guard respected Nyte and looked to him for leadership, but he hadn't been forthcoming about how much they meant to him. Not a leader and his generals. These were friends, though I didn't think Nyte would ever admit that.

When he spotted me with a casual slip of his gaze, his eyes locked on me and the expression that relaxed his face stole me away for a second. He was moving toward me in an instant.

"Astraea," he said, stunned to see me here and scanning me over for harm. "How did you find me?"

"I'm not entirely sure."

"You're getting too good at the void."

"Is there such a thing as *too good?*"

"When you're beginning to contend with me, yes. But then again, I do love competition with you."

I pushed his chest at his playful smirk, and my sight fell to the four golden guards behind him and someone new I didn't recognize.

"You know Elliot," Nyte turned to them with me. "This is Zeik, Kerrah, Sorleen, and Nadia—the bold rogue we can't seem to shake."

Sorleen was the most standoffish, not even breaking a smile, and her eyes were distant. Nadia gave a sweetly prideful smile at Nyte's comment and I had her pinned as someone cunning, perhaps deadly, already.

"So we're all going to see Drystan?" I asked.

"No. His order was for you to go alone," Nyte said.

My brow lifted at that; I didn't think Nyte would agree.

"I'll be right outside," he said to my unspoken thought.

Why Drystan would want me alone riddled me with unease.

"Take me to him," I said.

Though I was nervous to confront the prince after all that happened, I had to know if there was any hope of salvation in him. If what Nyte said was true, we had once had a friendship, and I hoped I wasn't a fool to believe there could still be something there after all this time.

I knew this place which Drystan had requested to meet me. I'd seen it in the memory Nyte gave me. I'd *been* here before. It was the first time something in a vision unfolded as real before me, and I had to take a moment in the archway entrance leading to the elite underground gambling den. Sweat began to slick my skin. My heart raced. It was all true—what Nyte had shown me. I knew this, yet it still broke me in that moment. Nyte trusted me enough to open himself to absolute vulnerability and give me every thought and feeling in his memories.

"I knew you would come," Drystan drawled from across the room. He sat in the empty space by a chess board with no opponent. "You would never let go of a spark of curiosity."

I thought about the version of him I'd seen from the past, only a glimpse, but in Nyte's memory his brother was so light spirited and *happy*. Who I saw now had lived through the kind of tragedy and suffering that ice-touched anything warm within. He'd become distant, untrusting, and that saddened me.

"Why did you want to see me?"

"Join me," he said, nodding to the empty seat.

The establishment was fully vacant as far as I could sense. I couldn't even feel Nyte though I'd parted with him just above the entrance.

Drystan smiled to himself as he spun the board to give me the white pieces. "Your move first."

Was this just to mock me? My teeth ground as I looked over the game. I picked up one of the front row pieces, moving it one square up out of nothing more than guesswork.

Drystan huffed a laugh. "You know far better openings than that."

My cheeks heated. "You know I don't."

"Because you're not trying to remember."

"You don't know anything."

Drystan moved one of his front pieces two leaps forward.

"The pawns can only go forward. Two squares at first movement, then only one."

"I didn't come here to play a game," I ground out irritably.

"Sure you did. You love games and puzzles."

He was taunting me. Trying to prod at my vulnerability to see what I would react to.

"If you wanted me . . . you could have told your father who I was right away when I arrived."

"I'm not a fool, Astraea, despite what you and my brother always believed."

"We didn't."

"I thought you don't remember?"

"Nyte is showing me."

"And you trust it all to be the truth? Memories from the realm's most notorious villain."

"Why would he lie?"

"To keep you on his side."

"He was prepared to leave the realm for me."

Drystan's jaw shifted, like that hurt him to hear.

"Then why is he still here?"

"I'm not ready."

He regarded me with a pitiful look.

"Take your turn," he said.

I took a breath to calm my irritation. Drystan leaned back casually in his chair, his expression bored and distant.

Looking over the pieces, I didn't know how any of the others could move and it seemed hopeless. Out of nothing more than a faint pull of gravity, I reached for the horse. Picking it up was like a shock of energy. I didn't have images flood my mind but somehow . . . I knew exactly where I wanted to place the piece. Still, I did so hesitantly in case Drystan scolded me it was wrong.

He didn't. When I dared to look up, he was staring at the horse piece like it had taken his thoughts elsewhere for a second. His eyes glazed with ice the moment they were back on me.

"How do you think you can throw daggers with such expert precision despite seeming to have little training? You're adept with a bow. How do you think you solved the puzzles in the Libertatem so easily?"

My chest pounded as he recalled the unnerving things for me.

"How long have you been watching me?"

Drystan dropped his gaze to take his turn.

"You've not been engaging in the things that you did often before. Perhaps if you do, you'll find yourself again somehow."

Nothing about his reception was kind. He didn't appear to want me here at all. Yet why did it feel like that was a small nudge to helping me? I thought back to the night in the woods with the fae resistance. When we were under attack, it was like I knew what to do. How to fight back. Right now I had a similar instinctual feeling toward Drystan. That no matter what, I couldn't give up trying to reach him to help us both.

"I'm sorry," I said. It slipped from me before I could brace for the daggers it would earn from him, like I'd insulted him instead.

"What for?"

"We were friends . . . and I abandoned you."

Drystan searched my eyes, until his narrowed and a bitter smile stole any vulnerability.

"Did he tell you what to say? That poor little Drystan is wounded and all he needs is a hollow apology?"

"He didn't tell me anything."

"Maybe not directly. But his manipulation will always hold you."

"Why did you want to keep us apart?" I asked, recalling how he kept trying to steer me away from Nyte—painting him as a monster.

"Because he was never going to leave this realm if you kept giving him a reason to stay."

"You really want him gone that badly?"

"Our father is going to kill him."

That silenced the world around me.

"It's impossible."

"That way of thinking is exactly what will make it very possible."

I moved another pawn and Drystan mirrored. Then my knight crossed one square and I almost lost myself to the game as my concentration started to sharpen like we'd played this exact strategy before.

I was winning.

"You still care for him," I said quietly, like a single wrong word would shatter the glass we walked on.

"I feel nothing for him. Nor you. I just have to live in this world when you two are finished destroying it and I would rather you took down my father with you."

"What happened to us?" I asked sadly. "We were friends, weren't we?"

"It doesn't matter anymore. You can stop looking at me like something to save."

"Why did you want to see me then?" I ground out irritably.

Drystan assessed me, scanning to the entrance and back.

"I can't trust my brother isn't eavesdropping this very moment. In your mind or outside close enough to hear."

"I can't trust you don't have spies somewhere either."

I moved my final chess piece, and somehow I knew . . .

"Checkmate," I said.

Drystan looked over the game board but not in surprise. He studied it like it was an answer he had been waiting for.

His chin tipped a fraction when he seemed to decide something.

"Trust your intuition, Astraea. If it's all you have, it's enough."

Drystan leaned forward. "There's a particular memory I'm waiting for him to show you. You'll know which one. And then you'll come to see me again. A hint—it involves something you've been holding onto since the maze."

My mind flared with hope and giddy intrigue.

"The celestial dragon egg?"

His eyes spoke all the confirmation I needed, twinkling with the same fascination I harbored.

"What do you know of it?"

"Find me when you have the memory."

"That might take too long," I protested in ire.

"Everything has an order, maiden."

The unfriendly way he addressed me stung.

"I trusted you," I said as he made to leave. Drystan stopped with his back to me. "In the Libertatem. I shouldn't have, but I did."

"Then maybe your intuition can lead you astray too, and you need to take caution with what you felt in the past and what is true now."

"You helped me. You gave me the map that helped me find my trials faster."

"Yet you still kept getting distracted by my brother," he said sourly. "I wanted you to get it over with and find the damned key. Then you let it fall into the hands of my father, something we were all trying to prevent, and you have no idea what it's done."

I was taken aback by the snap of his tone. Rising, I was near trembling with foreboding.

"You know what he gained?"

Drystan's lips pursed tight.

"Tell me," I pleaded.

"I owe you nothing."

"Please."

He contemplated, like he too battled with the echoes of the friendship we once had, but the wounds of loss and betrayal still bled between us.

"All I can say is if you truly cared for him, you'd make him leave."

I shook my head. "That can't be the only way."

Drystan didn't answer, only dropped his eyes, and it was the second time today I was hit by the notion that I was the cause of devastation in my selfishness.

"Did everything fall because of me?" I asked him, so quiet in case Nyte could hear.

I knew Nyte would tell me no. That I was never the cause and he would blame himself.

I added, "Was everything better without me?"

For the first time Drystan looked at me not with disappointment or resentment, but pure tragedy.

"You're the reason," he said gently. "But it doesn't make you the blame."

My lip wobbled but I didn't want to break in front of him. I turned around, trying to grapple with the threads of my composure, but I was so tired.

Of trying to figure out who I was.

What I should be.

Who I wanted to be.

Everything would have been better if I'd never come back.

His hand weighed on my shoulder and my brow pulled together tightly. My chest felt so tight that I was going to collapse. I was torn with the strong desire to turn around and embrace Drystan, but it was only the echo of an instinct from long ago. Now, our broken friendship was only cutting deeper the more time I spent around him.

His hand squeezed once, then let me go.

I waited until his footsteps turned lighter and disappeared. Then I broke. I couldn't hold back the sob that wrecked me, then the emotions that drowned me.

My hands braced on the chess table and I could barely make out the blurry pieces. My past was right in front of me in the way I'd won that game but it was merely a mockery. She was never coming back. Maybe I didn't want her to.

With a cry of anguish I scattered the board and all its pieces, which crashed around the room. That was merely the lid bursting free off of a bottle of rage that had strained too long.

The table I gripped flew across the room next, breaking against the wall. The chair Drystan sat on was in my grip one second, then in splinters around me the next. The impact of it slamming against the wall that shuddered through my body was merely fuel for the emotions that were pouring out of me now.

"Astraea."

I felt Nyte's presence before I heard the soft echo of my name, which so contrasted the scene he'd walked into. I didn't—couldn't—stop. I picked up glasses, throwing them against anything that would shatter them.

Everything I was inside started to mirror around me and that only drove my anguish harder. *More broken pieces. More destruction. More nothingness.*

Then my skin was glowing and prickling and I didn't feel weak anymore. I felt dangerous. On the verge of burying us both under the rubble I would make of this place.

Nyte approached me and I wasn't thinking when my hand cast out. A flare of silver shot for him but it was engulfed in darkness. When it cleared he was gone.

He appeared fast out of darkness right in front of me and I braced both hands charged with magick against his chest.

He'd pulled us through the void before my strike sent him flying back from me. The impact threw me off balance too, landing on my back to watch Nyte's wings catch him in the night sky. I felt the cold, wet grass beneath my fingers and snow was falling heavily now.

"Get up," he ordered in a vicious snarl.

He hovered above me like an angel of death and my teeth clenched tight with a rush of frustration because I couldn't reach him up there. I should have been able to and I was a pathetic celestial, a laughable maiden, to still be without them.

Nyte dropped to the ground, slamming into it with an impact that vibrated under me.

"You're not done yet. Get. Up."

He pushed on my defiance and anger as I rose from the icy ground and tracked him through the dark and the snow. He blended in so hauntingly, with only bright gold eyes to split the night.

I slipped the key out of the holster at my hip and it formed a beautiful glowing staff as I twisted, lunged, and sent a streak of pure power toward him. I anticipated his easy deflection, so I struck again and again, lost in a dance of memory and passion.

Then Nyte stared to attack.

Darkness collided with light and the trees around the clearing bent with the velocity of our merging power. I'd never felt more alive. My blood roared, my heart sped, but I felt unstoppable.

When our collision broke, I was panting, facing off with Nightsdeath.

"You're going to keep moving forward," he called. "Even if it kills me and you and the fucking world. You're not allowed to give up."

I rolled my shoulders back.

"I'm just getting fucking started."

His smile was all wicked delight. Then I struck first.

Our power battle continued. A push and pull of darkness against light. The snow hindered my movements, but I didn't have any option other than to keep my focus no matter what because Nyte wasn't going easy.

It made me push through the fire in my lungs. It drove out a will and defiance to contend with him. But he was undoubtedly still stronger right now. It didn't slow my drive.

He'd forced me into the tree line with his onslaught of attacks. His darkness dissipated against my blocks with the key that spun from hand to hand and around my body as I moved, at one with the weapon.

Doubt started to creep over me when I was still on the defensive, still retreating through the trees that were splintering with the explosions of our magick.

Out of the trees again, I managed one sideways glance to discover with a trickle of trepidation that we were coming to a cliff's edge.

That didn't seem to concern Nyte and I wondered if I'd lost him to Nightsdeath. If he would keep going until he achieved what he wanted, which was always to cancel the light. I couldn't tame my magick right now, not before he might end me.

Our blasts ceased and I panted hard with ice battling fire in my throat. Nightsdeath stalked to me still with glowing, terrifying gold eyes and black vines crawling his neck and jaw.

"I can't go on anymore," I wheezed.

"You should never start what you can't finish," he said in a low chilling growl.

I met the edge of the cliff, my heels almost slipping off.

Nyte stopped walking. He was so beautiful, and horrifying, and I was mesmerized by his wings. We locked stares and our heartbeats thundered in the silence.

Then I let myself fall.

18

Astraea

Falling at the complete mercy of gravity was the true test of one's state of mind. The first time I'd been here, I was terrified, but also liberated. I'd wanted to hit the ground and have every burden silenced in the impact. At that time it had felt like winning, when the world would no longer be able to hurt me anymore.

Freedom had a different meaning to me now. It was accepting that life was going to hit me down time and time again, but I wanted to get back up. It was full of challenges and choices and I would make many mistakes, I would be selfish, but nothing worth anything was without strain on the heart, soul, or mind.

So long as I kept wanting to get back up, it was not the end.

I caught myself.

The wings that expanded from my shoulder blades arched my back, and I was not afraid anymore.

They spread wide and I twisted, defying gravity's claim, and I could almost reach down to touch the snow before I swept high.

I was flying.

The exhilaration made me beat my wings harder, faster, uncaring of the burn and the strain it took to keep climbing. Bursting through the cloud bank expanded the stars above me and I became awestruck, floating in their palace.

I gasped when an arm hooked around me, pulling me a little higher and my back curved at his touch. The dark angel catching the light.

"You are absolutely exquisite," Nyte said, barely a whisper. "There will still be days that you fall, but it can't be forever so long as your will to stand, to fly, is greater than your demons."

Pulling me, it felt like floating and our lips met with a burst of freedom and longing up here. I kissed him harder. More desperately. The air was sharp and icy and my hair had turned damp. My legs almost circled his waist until a blast of lightning struck from nowhere, tearing us apart. A second strike of blue illuminated the sky and pain scorched through me.

Not mine. Nyte's.

I watched in horror as he fell, swallowed so fast by clouds that my heart tore from my chest. I followed my instinct to dive after him. It wasn't fast enough to catch him. My wings beat harder and faster, closing the distance, but now we were both plummeting at a speed that would shatter us on the ground. But I was desperate to reach him despite the ground closing in.

My relief at hooking my arms under his was short lived when I tried with all my might to slow us. A cry ripped from my throat at the powerful strain on my wings, but i didn't stop trying to prevent our plummet.

Nyte came around enough so that his arm circled around me. Then his dark wings closed around us, tucking mine in tightly, and I wanted to scream at his submission to take the impact of the fall I was trying to stop. We both knew I wasn't strong enough. His magick grew around us next and all I could do was hug him tightly.

The impact came like the world exploded around a sphere that kept us safe. At least from broken bones but the moment we landed it was like Nyte used the last dregs of his strength. His wings fell away, opening our cloak of darkness, and he was so still under me.

So deathly still.

My face pulled back from where I had buried it in his neck and I straddled him. He was still breathing but it was faint. I laid my palms over his chest and they glowed. My eyes slipped closed and I didn't know what I was doing, only that I reached for him and I felt him more deeply than I ever had before.

His pain and anger and heartache. My eyes pricked being wrapped by so much loss and loneliness from within him which I tried to heal with parts of me. Filling myself into the voids, the splits in his soul, but it wasn't enough. Without Bonding it would never be enough to heal the fractures inside him but for now I could soothe some of the pain.

Nyte's heart came back stronger each minute my magick infused him. The darkness was tamed by the light until we were an entanglement of peace.

"Nyte," I whispered, utterly terrified by the silence. "Please wake up."

"Astraea!" A voice called down to me.

I looked up, blinking my blurry vision to find Elliot at the top of the crater. Then several more forms—the Golden Guard—were around us too.

"He's still not moving," I sobbed.

"He'll be okay," Kerrah said, trying to be assuring.

"Are you injured too?" Zeik asked.

"No."

At least I didn't think so. I could hardly feel anything in my rush of panic.

"What the fuck happened?" Nadia asked.

"There was lightning and it—it happened so fast." I sniffed. *Pull yourself together.*

"Well how are we supposed to pull him out?" Zeik grumbled.

"It's steep. None of us can," Elliot said.

None of them had wings. I did but Nyte was too heavy.

I thought of the void but I'd never tried going through it with another person by my command.

When I felt a weak squeeze on my thigh my sight snapped down, finding a flicker of gold through fluttering, tired eyes.

Relief washed over me to see it.

"Thank fuck," Zeik muttered.

"Are you hurt?" Nyte asked, barely a croak.

He was the one lying against the cold ground, dark wings splayed but I hoped they weren't broken. He'd been the one who had been struck twice by lightning and had taken the worse of our impact.

"I'm fine," I said, brushing a lock of hair from his eyes. "I don't know how the weather turned so fast."

Nyte's eyes cast to the sky, but he didn't voice his thoughts. He looked so tired—it was frightening to see him like this.

"I don't know if I can take us through the void. Are you strong enough?"

Nyte took a long inhale, but it was slow enough that I knew he was trying to mask his pain from me. He sat up and I helped with a hand around his nape.

"I think so," he whispered.

"We'll head back to the castle after we scope the area," Elliot informed.

Nyte held my other hand at his chest. "Can you do that again?" he asked.

"What?"

"Give your magick to me."

I didn't realize that was what I'd done, but when I remembered how it felt to reach into the depths of his being, my palm warmed with a violet glow, and Nyte sighed like it offered him some reprieve.

Then I shifted closer, tighter, as he pulled us through the Starlight Void.

Beneath my knees was cushioned now and I looked over the black silk sheets. I didn't know this room, but the fact that he'd brought us here made me think that it had to be his bedroom. Nyte's wings fell over the side of the bed and I'd used the void to alleviate mine for now. The broken feathers pinched my brow.

"Does it hurt?" I asked quietly.

"I'll be all right."

"Take my blood."

"No."

"Nyte—"

"Can you just lie with me, please?"

How was I to resist that weak and vulnerable plea? Shifting, I tucked into his side and monitored the rise and fall of his chest, riddled with the anxiety of it stopping still.

"What did my brother say to you?" Nyte asked.

"Not a lot," I said honestly. "He showed me how my past skills can come back—I beat him at chess."

In the small pause of silence, it was like I could feel Nyte's smile. His hand idly traced up and down my arm.

"Then why the anger?"

"I just needed . . . to let it out."

"You did so beautifully," he said in quiet admiration. "But do you want to talk about it?"

"I feel like I'm being torn apart," I admitted. The confession tightened my throat. "Between who I am and who people expect me to be. Even back then. The hero would have let you go . . . but I didn't."

"The hero would have left this realm . . . but I couldn't."

"So we're both villains, then?"

"I don't know," he said. "If you ask me, there are no heroes. For everyone's wrong deeds are justified by their own means. I don't care what you are, how you came to be here; you are a person, Astraea. One who loves deeply and as much as you try to give it to the world, your heart deserves to be selfish just like everyone else's."

I absorbed his words in the silence, fighting my mind that wanted to rebel against what felt like *permission*.

"This world will try to make you. What I do know is it can take many good things to make them believe in you, but only one bad one to make them condemn you. That's why there is no single version of you that can exist. What matters are the ones you have that live in your mind with everyday."

I leaned my chin on my hands over his chest. "Is that how you accepted what people made you out to be?" I whispered. "You stopped trying to change their minds?"

"I wanted to be better once. Seen as *good*," he admitted. "When I thought there was some hope we might break the curse, I didn't want you to live with being shunned by your people for choosing me when I was only a monster in their eyes. It's all I knew how to portray and I didn't care before. For you, I did."

"They never would have let you be good," I said quietly.

"I don't think so. I've done cruel and heinous things in my life and I don't ever want you to forget that part of me exists. In my past, and my capabilities now."

"It's in my capabilities too, isn't it?" I asked carefully.

Nyte tucked a strand of my hair, his expression thoughtful.

"Yes. But you wouldn't harm someone without great reason. You are fair, and just, and precious. So very precious, love."

He weaved a lock of silver between his fingers, watching it while he seemed lost in his own mind.

"You were a child of war, Rainyte," I said gently.

That brought his amber gaze to me with a twitch of his brow.

I added, "You were given a dark power without a choice so young, and made into a soldier without ever knowing what it meant to be just a son."

"Don't excuse what I am. All I've done. It's in your nature to do so but every innocent life I've taken I knew what I was doing, I just didn't care. About anything. I looked around and I saw life after life in cycles of love, violence, greed, anger . . . so much anger in every mind and it made me resent carrying my own existence yet I was cursed to eternity here. So all I could do to make *some* of the demons clawing my mind apart relent was to inflict this pain on others. My father ordered me, but I can't say I put up much resistance for a very long time. That is why they call me Nightsdeath. That is why there is no amount of *good* that could atone for all I've done. It was a delusional dream to believe otherwise."

"I still believe," I whispered. All he told tore me apart, but I didn't know what it made me to be mourning for him above all.

"Your heart is the only one I've come across in my long and torturous existence that allowed me to come close enough to touch it. It's possibly the most dangerous thing you've ever done."

I pushed up on one hand, my mouth curving in challenge. "You don't scare me, Nightsdeath."

That broke a tired smile on his face. "I never have. It's been my life's torment."

My fingers traced over the burned material where the lightning had struck his chest, close to his heart. I began to undo the buttons of his jacket.

"You don't have to—"

"Just let me. If you're not going to take my blood I'll have to patch you up the mundane way. Can you sit up?"

I pushed off him, letting him take off his jacket and shirt as I went to collect what I needed in the washroom. Coming back with a basin of cold water some cloths, and a salve I found, I felt my chest ache as I watched him shift on the bed with gritted teeth.

"Shouldn't you be healing faster?"

When I got closer, the wound was far worse than I thought. I thought only the second strike had hit him, but that was the one to make him fall after the first hit him to break us apart.

"I should be," he said with a disgruntled huff.

"You didn't warn me flying could be dangerous with unpredictable weather," I said lightheartedly, sitting on the bed. I couldn't help reaching my hand out to his feathered wings. Nyte's eyes closed with a soft sigh to my touch.

"There's a lot to learn about flying," he said. "But you'll pick it up naturally."

I laid the first cold cloth to his burnt skin and Nyte hissed.

"I didn't expect you to be so . . . fussy," I mused.

"This isn't a typical wound," he grumbled in defense.

I fought amusement even though I hated the pain he was in.

"I need to go to the temple in Vesitire—the one I almost opened until . . ."

"Until you chose me. Your first incriminating act of villainy if you ask the gods you wish to see."

That shook me with dread. Perhaps I shouldn't see them if all I would face was their wrath and disappointment, but Auster had made me believe it was important.

Nyte's eyes slipped open lazily at my silence as I wrung out the next cold cloth.

"I can't keep cowering away from it," I muttered.

As I laid the wet material on the rest of the scorch mark on his chest, the veins in Nyte's neck protruded with the sting but he didn't make a sound this time.

"You're not. You're taking steps as you need to for *you*. They can wait their turn."

"The only reason you're a bad influence on me is because of how easy you let me off with everything."

"Did I go too easy in the woods?" He lifted a brow. "I'll have to do better next time."

No—he hadn't. At one point I feared he would keep attacking until he struck me down. But it was what I needed, and what ultimately made me take that chance to find my wings.

I scooted deeper on the bed and leaned over him. My fingers gathered some of the salve for the smaller wound across his side. Then I couldn't help tracing fingers along his scars, near lost in a trance over his skin.

"We can go to the temple tomorrow," he said gently.

My eyes flicked up to his. "When do we need to make the Bond?"

"When you're ready."

"They must be getting impatient—Tarran and the vampires."

"I can handle them."

Somehow I didn't think that was true, but he didn't want to concern me. Telling Nyte about my small interaction with Tarran would only serve to make him angry, so I kept it to myself. It had just been hollow words to scare me, and in some delusional part of his mind, plant the ludicrous idea I'd ever side with him over Nyte and Auster.

I wasn't siding with anyone. Not before I had the chance to ally with myself.

"Can I have a memory?" I asked.

"I don't think I have the strength tonight."

Disappointment dropped in my stomach though I understood. I couldn't stop thinking about gaining whatever it was Drystan was anticipating I would see, and I didn't know how much longer before it came in the story Nyte was writing.

"Feeling your magick tonight, bold and unleashed, was the most fun I've had in centuries," he mumbled sleepily.

I laid down again gently, mindful of his wing. "Fun? I guess *I* need to do better."

He huffed, a barely there sound of amusement. "No. You are progressing exactly as you should be. Faster than I expected, in fact."

Hearing that lightened me, when it felt like the world was spinning so fast and I was too slow to keep up.

"I'll be able to best you soon."

"I'm counting on it."

I smiled, laying my cheek on his shoulder and tuning into his heartbeat. It filled me with serenity. And fear, I realized, when today it had become so shallow right under my palm and I didn't want it to ever come close to that again.

19

Astraea

The doors to the temple were open. I'd expected it to be bright within, but the slither of dark space wasn't as inviting as I'd hoped.

"You don't need to go inside," Nyte said gently, waiting patiently a little behind me.

He wouldn't follow me in. It wasn't a welcome place for him. Yet he wouldn't leave me alone and I didn't want him to.

"I do," I said.

I'd waited over five years for this moment. I knew I was the Daughter of Dusk and Dawn, and I needed to learn what that meant even if I would come to find I never had doting parents. Not like what I'd yearned for witnessing Cassia with her father Reihan. I wasn't born, I was made.

Taking a long breath of courage, Nyte's presence stroked my senses within one last time before I slipped into the temple.

Only a strip of light from outside cut down the middle and I used the key clutched tightly in my hand to expand more luminance. The sound of grating stone made me whirl around, and my throat tightened in panic watching the doors finish sealing behind me.

All was silent. So eerily silent. I didn't know what I had expected but something felt . . . *wrong.*

I walked tentatively, using the key as a torch to examine the interior. Two giant sculptures towered at the far end and a long stone bench stood before it.

My hand reached up on instinct, and the moment I touched the bench a vision exploded in my mind. Nothing whole or certain. I could only see blurs of color and several spheres that moved. People. My heartbeat suddenly felt so small and precious. I tried to count how many could be surrounding me but I lost track at four, entranced by the murmurs of voices I wanted desperately to hear in full clarity when they tugged at something safe and familiar within me.

This is where I first came into the world as an infant.

"My child," a feminine voice said. This was far more clear in my mind,

sucking me back to the present time in this temple. It was too close, as if spoken to my mind.

I was about to search for her, but when I looked up at the ethereal stone face of the Goddess of Dawn, the voice attached itself to her in my mind.

"I—I don't know if I am," I said honestly.

"Who you are doesn't change in a new beginning."

"I came for my memories," I said, trying to rally my bravery. "I can't do what you need without them."

"You bargained them to us for your return."

"Why would you want them? It doesn't make any sense and I'm so lost."

My throat tightened in pain as I tried not to cry like the frightened child I felt reduced to here. In front of something I couldn't see and could barely feel but if these were my parents I was crumbing with that notion when they were nothing I could hold, not people who would try to comfort me like Reihan did for Cassia.

"To give you the chance to do right this time. Yet you allowed darkness to claim you again."

"Nyte?"

She didn't answer. All I could feel was coldness and disappointment.

When I looked down from the goddess I gasped in fright, turning and turning to meet a hundred reflections of my own horrified expression.

Then screaming rattled my bones and I whirled to the noise, finding a scene relaying through a mirror I headed toward with vacant steps. I'd seen flashes of this day. *Felt* the anger and heartache and pain from it as I stood on a battlefield.

"We will always be enemies." Nyte's voice tore me away from the mirror.

He stood behind me and I blinked in confusion at his anger toward me.

"We don't have to be," I breathed.

He was wholly Nightsdeath with no warmth in those glowing amber eyes. Only hate and cruelty and his black-tipped fingers lashed out around my throat.

"Please," I choked. His fingers only clamped harder, closer to crushing my throat.

I clawed at his vise grip as the frightening, merciless image of him turned blurry and my soul snapped in two.

Then he let me go with a careless push.

I fell backward but I didn't meet the ground. Instead I kept falling down a well and those golden eyes watched me with such icy loathing I felt like I was *dying* inside. Closing my eyes, I succumbed to the misery.

"Astraea."

I blinked, disorientated when I didn't remember the impact after the fall nor how I stood again, watching my reflections and the approach behind me.

Auster was shirtless. His body was broad and toned and he was a stunning craft to behold. His front pressed to my back and his breath caressed my ear. My blood roared with a want to step away but I was stunned utterly still. Helpless to do anything but watch as his lips pressed to my neck.

"We are perfect together," he said. "Made for each other."

I knew it was true.

For the world. To the gods. To the celestials.

Not to me.

"No," I choked out in a whisper.

He stopped his gentle touches, and his face firmed with a frightening wrath. As he spun me in his hold, he gripped my arms and I whimpered.

This wasn't real.

"Stop," I cried to the goddess.

"You keep choosing wrong," he snarled.

Then he pushed me and I fell again, wondering if this was to be my existence.

Always falling.

Always choosing wrong.

Always failing everyone.

I sank into a pool of freezing water that shocked through my entire body then floated me in the embrace of a numb oblivion.

There was a time I had been drowning and I didn't want to be saved. Yet Nyte had come for me. He'd defied the laws of magick just to reach me.

Through my blurry vision it was like someone stood above the ice this time, watching me drown.

This time, I reached for him.

I wanted to breathe again.

To live.

To fight.

I wanted *him*.

Agony sliced my skin and my lungs burned but I swam hard. Reaching the ice, I tried with everything I had to break it but I was running out of air. I wanted to get back to Nyte. Yet it seemed the more I wanted him the weaker I became. Still I fought with my last dose of strength until I had no choice but to let go.

"My Starlight."

My eyes fluttered open and though I still floated underwater the image of him was so clear beside me.

"They made you. But they cannot break you."

His mouth didn't move with the words as he cupped my cheek and brought his head to mine. Our lips met, and I was content to stay here, but we only got a second before we were ripped apart.

I gasped and water didn't flood my lungs.

It took a moment to feel the ground under my hands where I knelt.

"Please stop," I begged. She was trying to mess with my head. Get me to see Nyte as the enemy and show me there was another path for my heart.

My head angled back and I knelt under the harsh judgment of the still figure. My heart became cold. All my short life I'd yearned to discover if I had parents. But it seemed all gods were merciless and cruel, and I was merely their failed creation.

I only had one purpose; to right the world. They would never forgive me if I didn't let Nyte go.

It was another god who spoke next—the deep tone of the God of Dusk, and I cast my eyes over his dominating sculpture.

"You have flesh and you bleed. You have feelings and a heart that beats. We created you in the image of mankind and you are capable of their flaws. We brought six guardians together to raise you and teach you the ways of the species. Yet still you abandoned all you were destined for. Your heart calls to darkness, and you cannot give yourself to it again."

"The dark isn't frightening. It can love too."

"There will come a time when your heart is tested, and you must not choose to sacrifice yourself for it."

"I don't know if I have the strength to let him go," I confessed quietly.

"Look not for strength, but righteousness."

"I need my memories, please."

"They cannot be given back, my child, as you bargained them to us and it is absolute. But the mind is a powerful tool. All is never lost."

The glow of the key discarded beside me returned and loneliness swept in; no energy pulsed through the space except what was bound to me.

I didn't want to cry but tears fell before I could force them back. There was part of me that passed the years believing I didn't need to know who my parents were, that I didn't need their love. Now having the answer and knowing I would never gain such affection, I mourned for the lost child in me.

But there was a single flare of hope that my search wasn't over. The confirmation that I had been a child in the past, and I had been raised by six guardians, as the God had said. So I straightened, breathing a long inhale to compose myself.

When I turned, I saw the light leading out of the temple, as if the doors closing had only been an illusion. Who waited beyond them pulled me with more eagerness to be outside than in.

I breathed in the cool air and found Nyte sitting on the steps with his back to me, leaning his forearms on his thighs. He didn't speak, or even look at me, but I joined him.

"I would go inside and ask for their blessing, but they might just find a way to cast me to hell sooner rather than later."

"Probably," I said. "And that job is mine."

His mouth twitched, but something was preventing the break of a smile.

I said, "The gods weren't any help; I might be just as damned as you are to them. But I want to visit the Guardians . . . to know if they think any differently or could help."

He only responded with a nod. His thoughts seemed elsewhere.

Nyte's tone turned so haunted. "When you died, I called to the gods. Any gods that would listen, and I was answered by Dusk and Dawn. They said they would take you back. I can't face going inside that temple, and I almost fell to my knees watching you disappear into it just now because it's where I had to bring your body. Walking out of there all those centuries ago . . . watching those doors close with you inside . . ."

Nyte didn't finish, but the slam of his grief and sorrow was enough to prick my eyes. I reached out a hand, and his unclasped to entwine with mine as I shuffled closer.

"I'm sorry," I said, not knowing what else could soothe the sharp pain slicing both of us.

Nyte sighed before his forehead fell to mine; his other hand cupped my cheek.

"Even if you hate me. Fight me. In the company of your rage, your defiance, your heated passion. It is my peace, because you're alive to throw it all at me. And only when I'm around it do *I* feel alive."

I didn't know what to say. There were no promises I could give when our paths rocked so uncertainly. He wasn't looking for a response when his lips pressed to my forehead and he stood, seeming to bury any insecurity with it.

"I didn't think they would help, but it was worth a try," Nyte said.

I followed him down the steps.

"What do you know of the prophesy . . . When falls night?"

"That it's a fickle and convoluted thing. I've never been a fan of riddles, and one tied to fate serves no purpose other than to bring out madness in men."

His hand slipped around my waist without warning and I held his arm as the familiar pull through starry shadow took us away.

"So what do we do now?" I asked, hoping he had something else.

He took us to the castle rooftops again and my stomach flipped as I eyed him suspiciously like he could push me off in an attempt to train my flying this time. The bastard gave a wicked side smile reading my apprehension, but it was a strange relief to see after the kernel of vulnerability he let show at the temple.

"When you came back, I was surprised it was in Alisus at first. Until I remembered that's where one of the Guardian Temples is—there's many of them throughout Solanis. Perhaps your parents knew Vesitire wasn't safe and the king would find you there if you wandered without memories."

"Considerate of them," I grumbled sarcastically.

Nyte reached through the void to retrieve his stunning black sword again. My shoulders slumped as he looked to the key I held expectantly.

My key became a blade and Nyte's eyes twinkled in satisfaction.

"Don't slip off the edge," he taunted. "I might not be fast enough to catch you this time."

My eyes narrowed to a glare. "I'd catch myself."

"We'll see."

I moved first, using steps Rose had taught me before. Nyte sidestepped my vertical strike, but I spun to clash blades, giving off a beautiful flare from the key against his obsidian. Pushing off it, I reeled into a focus that came to me by instinct. Nyte began to push back, dancing with me.

We pushed and pulled through the bitter air for some time. I became lost to it, *enjoying* the feeling of release through the movements that answered his like it was a rhythm we'd found before. Our blades cut a symphony through the silence, and each time our eyes met with the passion of battle a pulse of energy expanded in my chest, racing through my blood.

When our blades locked again, Nyte spun his arm, nearly disarming me, but instead of claiming victory, he claimed me. His arm wrapped my waist, drawing me flush to him as a surprised gasp left my lips.

"No matter what the gods have to say, you are incredible, and powerful, and they won't admit it but they fear you," he said huskily, before bringing his mouth to mine.

"They're only disappointed I didn't turn out to be their perfect maiden despite their efforts."

"Disappointment only comes from their own egos. Gods are very proud and very selfish. They fear you because you do not fear yourself and therefore they do not control you. It is the greatest power you'll ever hold."

PART
THREE

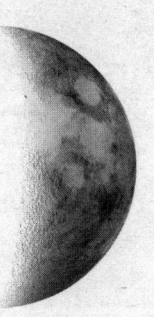

20

Nyte–Past

When three weeks passed since he had last seen Astraea, Nyte broke his own damn defiant stance to seek her out in Vesitire. She had become a plague in his thoughts. Devouring all of them to remain the sole focus more times that he cared to admit. Every time he paced a room, broke something, flew high, tried to do *anything* to eradicate her presence in his mind, the suppression only made it worse.

So he'd spent the last hour high on dark, simmering rage, thinking that maybe if she didn't exist for him to find, he could forget her.

Until he laid eyes upon her as he spied, crouched and blended fully into the darkness, atop a tall building.

Just like that, his mind calmed. When seconds ago he had wondered if he would snap to end her once and for all when he found her.

The peace only lasted for a few seconds before he watched a man—a celestial—approach her on the street below. Nyte quickly assessed his towering wings and the dominant way he carried himself. Then what sealed his assumption was the glint of the moonlight against a circlet that peaked downward at the center of his forehead.

A High Celestial. One of four.

He would have to get closer to distinguish the sigil on his jacket. Nyte's ability would work to slip into his mind, but unlike anyone else, this celestial was sure to feel it if he tried.

The man reached for Astraea, and Nyte didn't realize his fingers around the chimney had tightened until he clenched only stone debris in his hand. The hold he pulled her into was near intimate. Nyte should have looked away, but he couldn't. What overcame him he had no right to feel, nor did he want it.

He couldn't help tracking her every response though he was on the verge of doing something reckless. Thinking she would lean into him, Nyte braced to leave before he snapped. Yet Astraea laid a hand on the High Celestial's chest, a signal for space, which he didn't grant right away. His palm went to her face now, and Nyte *broke*.

Slipping into her mind, he said, *"Over a hundred years, I've never been able to find you. So I have to think this exposure is a calling."*

Astraea reacted to his voice, too abrupt that it made her companion survey the street as well as if she picked up on an impending threat. His brown hair half tied back in a knot, leaving a few strands around sharp features and a shadow lined jaw.

"Took you long enough," she sent back, but gave her attention back to her company.

"Come to me," Nyte said, then took off.

He landed high on a mountain and slipped into the snow-covered woodland. Then he waited. Nyte could tell a lot about a person by how they navigated the dark. Would Astraea hesitate with fear? Shy away with uncertainty?

A candle flickered inside him before he saw her. Astraea's footing was gentle, careful but bold. He sought her through the shadows while he watched from behind a thick tree. Her hair was a beacon against her surroundings and stark clothing, but her magick awakened faintly to glow the markings of her skin. Astraea glided through the woods like a fallen star, utterly exquisite. Confident in her light and unafraid of the dark, perhaps even curious.

Through the shadow that climbed her body, he felt her like a ghost's touch. Her breath drew shallow, stopping her walk. The beat in her chest amplified as she observed the moving darkness, lifting a hand as if to greet it.

"I found you," she said through her thoughts.

"I see now what has been occupying your time," Nyte said, stepping out from his cover.

Astraea watched him now, and the darkness drifted away from her.

"Auster? He's not a new distraction," she answered.

Nyte's jaw locked, and to distract himself from something ugly stirring within, he turned to continue his walk.

He knew the name.

"The High Celestial of the House of Nova," Nyte drawled. "You're involved with him?"

"You could say that," she said, but it was a low murmur that took his interest.

"He seemed . . . affectionate."

"He's my Bonded."

That slammed his steps to a halt. He didn't realize how close she'd come until she knocked into his side with the abruptness of his stopping.

How could that be possible? Nyte had been sure the she was his last time he saw her, but now he was doubting again.

"Are you—?"

"No," she cut him off. "We haven't completed *that*."

The topic made her uncomfortable, and Nyte wondered why.

"You're a powerful match."

"Yes, so everyone likes to remind me."

"So what's stopping you?"

"Are you always so direct about people's personal lives?"

No. In fact, he'd never cared to inquire about anyone before.

Nyte shrugged, continuing his walk. "I'm curious how it works. A match of power, is it not? Why wouldn't you want to strengthen yourselves."

"Are you really clueless? Vampires and fae have a Bonded too—" she paused to contemplate. "Which are you exactly?"

"I'm intrigued as to what your fables say about me. No scepter, but there might be some truths."

She huffed a laugh. "No beard either."

"I've never been fond of them."

"They say you're death, actually. None of our species."

"It's not far from the truth."

"I think it is."

They broke out of the trees, coming to a wide open glade covered in snow. At the farthest edge, Nyte headed toward the small cabin.

The door was pitiful and wouldn't keep out any chill. Nyte had to duck through the threshold.

"What is this place?" Astraea inquired, scoping around.

"A cabin."

"I can see that."

He didn't want to expand; he'd only come for one thing and then they would leave.

Astraea reached for something on the crooked mantle and Nyte reacted before he could stop himself. He caught her wrist.

"Do you always touch what isn't yours?" he said irritably.

She eyed him carefully. "It's just a wooden figurine."

Nyte didn't look at the bird carving. He stepped forward, forcing her back with the hold he still had on her until her back met the wall. He tuned into her heart, picking up speed and skipping beats like a song off tune.

He let Nightsdeath linger at the surface, and watched as she glanced at his ears, then his neck, until finally his eyes, and through this lens she became so dangerously bright.

"Do you know why people truly fear the dark?" He canted his head, hooking a strand of her shining hair. "Because it requires trust." The cabin flooded with the shadows Nyte drew in from every tree, rock, and creature. Cloaking them in pitch darkness but unable to smother the light that glowed between them from the whimsical markings over her skin.

"You can't scare me," she said, but the breathlessness gave her away.

Nyte leaned in close until his breath fanned her neck. It was a compulsion; he he was repelled by how insufferably bright she was yet wanted to claim her so no other could.

She was his war.

His to end.

His to break.

His to protect.

"Then let go of the light," he said in a low, taunting tone.

Astraea did. The glow of her shallowed until they stood in his peaceful embrace. Where everything began and everything ended.

The dark wasn't just trusting.

It was tempting.

A keeper of sin and lies.

It was dangerous.

Yet she stood here with him. A willing little lamb in his trap.

"You've proved your point," she said.

"I don't think I have."

Nyte's hand wrapped her throat, but in the same breath, she flared to life. The key glowed and wind blasted through the cabin as she slammed it to the ground. For the first time in his life *he* was caught off guard by how quick and dazzling she could become, and the force of his magic strained against hers.

They stared off in a battle of wills. Night against starlight. He tried to hold onto the darkness he'd pulled together as her light pushed it out. Maybe he could overpower her, but this place would become dust, perhaps the forest around them too, if one of them didn't yield.

So he let the shadows return.

Both of them straightened when the magick around them cut out. They collected their breath after the exertion. In full battle . . . they could be catastrophic.

"Don't provoke me again," she warned.

A sinister thrill rattled in him with that.

"Don't entice me," he said.

"I could turn this place to ash in a blink."

"Is that what your light does? Burn?"

"Like your darkness, it does many things. I just happen to be in the mood for fire."

"How so?"

"What?"

Astraea's heartbeat was so fast he became entranced by it.

"What is it about fire that excites you?"

"Perhaps I just want you to know what hell will feel like before I send you there."

The curl of his mouth wasn't foreign when he made men tremble at the cruelty of his smile. But what awakened in his veins at what she evoked was so new it became an addiction.

"You are a volatile, stunning thing," he mused.

Nyte backed away, turning to pace to the far end of the cabin while Nightsdeath slumbered again inside him.

"How do you do that?" she asked, closer than he expected her to come after he'd invaded her space. "Turn all dark and frightening, I mean."

"You said I couldn't scare you."

"No, but you terrify others."

Nyte kneeled by a small chest, opening it to rummage inside.

"I don't do much to invoke that," he answered. "Fear is choice. What is it that makes something frightening?"

"Unpredictability."

"So you're not affected by me because you know all I'm capable of?"

"No . . ."

Nyte paused, flicking a look up, but she seemed just as puzzled as he. Astraea should be afraid of him. Yet he believed her when she said she wasn't. Her brazenness around him wasn't just arrogance. She was smart enough to know fear wasn't a weakness. It was necessary.

He found what he was looking for and straightened again.

"We came here for a compass?" she observed flatly.

Nyte dusted it off. "You should learn to think beyond the ordinary means of an object."

"It's magickal?"

"It can be."

"Do you always dance around straight answers?"

He flashed her a devious side look, then tossed the compass to her.

"Magick deals in bargains," he said. "I didn't think I would have to explain that to you."

Astraea examined the intricate gold casing.

"So what does it require?"

"I'm not sure, actually. My brother and I won it in a game of cards years ago. He said it was an item of the Wanderers Trove. It's supposed to lead you wherever you ask—any place rumored to be hidden or lost, you'd find the way with that. We never really got the chance to take it anywhere and discover how to activate it. Besides, it's not like there's anywhere we could have gone."

Nyte knew there was much of the land to be explored, but their leash to their father was short. He planned to snap them both free of it someday. He had the patience to get it right.

"I can take it to Auster—"

"No."

Her blue eyes flicked up at his abruptness.

"It's a very high value item. I'm not risking you cutting me out of this alliance if you find what you need with your *Bonded*." He took a pause with the taste of ash in that word. "You came to me for help, and I think it's about time we made it official."

"What are you saying?" Astraea already knew, so he left his silence as confirmation, which dropped her arms and turned her face defiant. "I'm not bargaining with you."

"Then give it back."

Nyte stepped toward her with a hand out, but she jerked back, pulling the compass to her chest. His eyes twinkled in amusement at her stubborn frown.

"The Cratonis Bargain then," she said begrudgingly. "It prevents either of us from betraying the other until we find the source of the quakes."

Nyte lifted a brow. "Are bargains part of your training, maiden?"

Astraea folded her arms, leaning against the precarious wooden table. Nyte blocked out the memories of him and Drystan around it from a long time ago. This cabin held much of their childhood with Drystan's mother. Before they grew older, and she shed all warmth for Nyte when she discovered the monster he would become. It was then that their fantasy shattered. Nyte was not her true son, and he was shunned by the only nurturer he'd known when he was young. Drystan always defended him, and Nyte harbored a guilty conscience that she all but abandoned her own son too, eventually.

"Like you said, magick deals in bargains. I'd be a fool to not read up on them," Astraea said, pulling him back to their present from the past he'd tunneled to.

Nyte took a long breath to drown the threatening flashbacks.

"It requires giving what we most desire from the other that cannot be claimed back," he said.

Astraea straightened, and if he wasn't beginning to read her easily he might have dismissed the thought that she appeared nervous.

"What is that for you?" she asked, giving him her back.

His tongue traced across the two teeth that had sharpened at the mere thought.

"Your blood, of course."

Her shoulders locked at that, but she'd known it was coming. More dominant than his raging craving right now was his curiosity about what her desire from him would be. He could slip into her mind to find out, but watching her squirm to spill it herself was far more exciting.

"For this to work you need to be honest," he said with a hint of amusement.

When she turned to him, the color on her pale cheeks and the way she couldn't seem to hold his eye made him *very* curious.

"Don't get inflated with arrogance about it," she snapped. Nyte could hardly suppress his smile.

"It can't be that bad."

"I only want to know . . . *shit*."

Under all the titles, esteem, and power, Astraea was just a person. One who now covered her eyes in embarrassment and paced the floor with tangled thoughts. It was humbling to see, distracting for a moment.

"I promise not to tease you about it," he said.

She still cast him a scowl.

"I want you to kiss me," she blurted.

Of all the things he'd imagined, this hadn't even made the list.

"I'd have thought your desire would involve something sharp lodging in my chest."

"It does," she grumbled, hating herself for what she wanted. "But I know that'll achieve nothing and this . . . it's a mere curiosity to know if I'm completely broken."

"You're not broken to crave lust, and your choice in suitor is faultless," he added with a wicked gleam.

"It's not that . . . it's that I wonder if I *don't*." The rose coloring her cheeks spread. She added in a grumble, "And you wouldn't be my first choice; you just happen to be a convenient one."

"There can't be a lack of prospects who would gladly go to their knees for such a request from you." Though he had an urge to hunt down any she allowed to touch her.

"There's none Auster wouldn't hear about."

By the gods, he despised that name the more he heard it.

It was another unexpected confession. Nyte laid down his weapons before his enemy for this moment of vulnerability he never could have anticipated walking into.

"Have you never . . . ?"

"I have . . . but I just have never felt *good* about it. Sleeping with Auster."

Astraea looked at him, and her face washed with horror like she was only just realizing who she was divulging this too.

"We should just choose a different bargain. The Fecarrah Bargain would make sure I couldn't draw blood from you, at least. Or—"

"Astraea," he halted her scramble for a way out. "You don't have to be ashamed with me. There's nothing wrong with not wanting to be intimate with your Bonded. I've seen it before."

That lit a light in her eyes and Nyte didn't expect it to warm in his chest.

He couldn't deny there was still a note of resistance in him. He was being too soft on his enemy, but for this plan to unfold in the long run, this temporary trust was necessary.

"You have?"

Nyte nodded, coming a little closer.

"A few times, in fact. Some tie the Mating Bond for power and live as friends. Others have parted ways without ever completing the Bond."

Astraea mulled over his words, and he watched her in fascination. Nyte had never met someone he didn't *want* to breach the mind of because the puzzle was far more enticing to put together slowly, delicately. The star-maiden was a picture worth painting with precision to capture the finest details.

"So, are we doing this?" he asked carefully.

Nyte could be patient. He was damn good at it.

"Who goes first?" She still couldn't meet his gaze and something about that frustrated him.

"Are you sure you want to do this?"

Finally, her eyes flicked up, and he was lost in the spark of challenge in them that instant.

"Yes."

"Good."

He moved before she could rattle with another twinge of uncertainty.

The moment his hand grabbed her jaw and his lips met hers . . .

Nyte was overcome with a rage of want—no, nothing so easily sated or forgotten; Astraea became a *need*. As essential as the blood that coursed faster through his veins and as necessary as the air they could hardly draw around the kiss that turned to a near feral demand he wasn't prepared for. When she gave a breathy moan his arm circled her waist, lifting her onto the table, and their bodies pressed together.

She was made for him. It was undeniable.

But their perfect existence was crafted for destruction, not bliss.

Right now, he didn't care if they cleaved the world in half with the passion that ignited between enemies.

The ground trembled, turning violent.

Astraea leaned back, planting a hand behind herself, but they didn't stop with the dangerous quake that rattled through the cabin, tumbling things from the mantel.

He couldn't break away from the heat of her despite the very land that quaked around them like a warning from the gods against it.

"Nyte," she breathed his name and his cock ached at the sound of it.

He kissed along her jaw, down her neck. "My turn," he said, voice husky with pure wild lust the like of which he'd never felt before.

Astraea's hand tightened to a fist in his hair in anticipation. Nyte couldn't hold back anymore.

The moment he tasted her blood he knew he'd fucked up.

It was his greatest desire and he'd never been tested to the very limits of his control when blood turned him feral. He'd indulged in human blood before and it was a sweet craving, but this . . . *her* . . . she was euphoric. Her blood was transcendent, and he didn't know if he could stop.

Astraea's moans only encouraged him. Her thighs pulled him closer and clamped tighter. The wreckage continued to mount around them with the quake that lasted longer than ever before. He didn't care if the stars were collapsing too. All he knew was her.

The way her hips ground against his hard cock made him thrust against her too as he kept an arm around her to press them impossibly tighter when it never seemed close enough.

"I think I'm going to . . ." she lost her words but he knew what they were.

He could only groan through his mouth still wrapped around her throat with his teeth deep in her flesh. Nyte was losing his damned mind to thoughts of his cock being buried inside her too.

Astraea's blood wasn't just like any other celestial's.

It wasn't even just because she was the star-maiden.

She was *his*. In every way. Forged in his bones and written in his soul. It was dangerous to think of Auster right now when his murderous thoughts turned despicably villainous to keep the High Celestial from taking her. In this moment he would wreck the realm and kill anyone who stood in his way.

Nyte pulled out of her flesh with a pained groan. Against her neck he said in a low, husky murmur, "Come for me, Starlight. Show me how bright you shine for your enemy." Then his tongue lapped over the small puncture wounds he'd made.

His name cried from her mouth with a release that shook her body and he almost exploded in his damn pants too. Nyte held her tightly as she rode the waves of her climax. He didn't want the moment to be so fleeting and clung to every exhilarating fucking second of her wrapped tightly around him. They stayed catching their breath as the world around them settled too.

The last trembles of the land were a reminder of what they'd done. He had to remember it was not for pleasure—only a duty. An alliance.

He felt the bargain like a new tether within him. They were protected against one betraying the other until they found what they needed to stop the quakes.

Nyte deemed her steady enough to keep herself propped up as he stepped away. Astraea wouldn't look at him immediately hopping off the table. The sight of his bite mark on her collar surged a primal need in him all over again. She fixed the neckline of her jacket to conceal it, which ground his teeth. He wanted her to wear it openly so every creature would see Nyte's claim on her.

"I didn't mean to . . . I mean I didn't expect . . ." Astraea was embarrassed, and that disturbed him.

"It means nothing," he assured. "Nothing but confirming you do have needs and lust is simply natural."

She chuckled with resentment that turned dark in him.

"Then I'm fucked up and twisted to have it surface with my enemy and not my Bonded."

He wanted to rip that term apart unless it was said in regard to him. Nyte hadn't even met Auster and he wanted to kill him. With Astraea's blood coursing through him he trembled with volatile rage replaying his proximity to her. The obvious affection he had for her.

"I was just an experiment," he said, matching the acidity in her tone. He had to remember that being her enemy trumped any alignment of power. "I'm confident you can find it with another. But to further ease your mind, a bite from a fae or vampire is supposed to evoke pleasure when it's done willingly. It is why many humans seek out the blood vampires."

Even as he said it, the darkest, most selfish and insidious part of him wanted to kill whoever she chose to finally bed before they could even get that far. Perhaps it would be his new favorite way to torment her when this was over. He could follow her, let her fulfill her desires mindlessly with men who could never give her enough, not everything she would crave, then see how many bodies he could leave in her wake before she discovered it was him.

"We don't ever speak of it again," she said firmly.

Nyte's teeth clenched. "It's already forgotten."

"Then I'll find you again soon so we can track down a mage for that damned compass."

Astraea's boots crunched over shattered ornaments on her way out. He watched her back right until she left through the Starlight Void, engulfed by beautiful darkness.

Nyte stayed a moment longer to untangle his thoughts.

Being wrapped with Astraea in the heat of her pleasure was something his mind was going to loop in torment for a while.

He pinched the bridge of his nose with a groan, pacing to the mantle. When his sight fell down, he sank to his knees to pick up the small bird carving.

It was the only thing he had of his mother's. He'd been clutching it as a babe when his father stole him away in the night, supposedly saving him, before crossing worlds to escape one so powerful.

That's all he knew. Perhaps all he would ever know.

21

Astraea

Every time I gained a vision of the past I battled two minds in one body. My fingers brushed my lips as I stared in the mirror, skin prickling with the remnants of Nyte and me discovering our passion as enemies. It was as damning to the world as it was igniting to our souls.

Thinking of what I'd said about Auster as that spirited, curious version of me . . . it made sense to my feelings now. Maybe I even found it a relief to know I had been reserved about my attraction to him in the past too. He was no doubt beautiful and Auster radiated power and protection. It was me who was completely and utterly broken not to want him the way he wanted me. That filled me with guilt and despair. Wondering if I simply wasn't trying hard enough, wasn't letting myself see him as anything more.

"You didn't tell me about the bond you suspected," I said with Nyte lingering behind me. I reached for the dress ribbons I'd abandoned.

"You despised me as it was. There was no reason to tell you when I didn't think anything would ever come of it."

"When did it change?"

He approached as a looming shadow in the mirror's reflection. His fingers caught the laces of my dress and he took over.

"There are a few more things you should see before we skip there."

I was growing impatient. Needing the whole story not just chapters, desperate to turn the next page while Nyte held the book.

"Did you wear such darkness just for me?"

I traced my fingers over the black lace bodice.

"It was my preferred color before it was yours."

"It's color*less*, love. And it's my favorite on you *because* it is yours."

I tacked back to the memory. "You agreed to help me, but you still wanted to kill me at the end of it."

When he finished with the tie, his hands slipped to my waist.

"I'm sure you had your own plans on how to betray me too once we achieved the goal of our alliance."

"You never found out?"

"No."

There was only so much Nyte could give me. His own version and plan of events. For now, I was so eager for the next page of his story that I wanted to abandon today. This reckless plan.

"I need more," I said.

"You're exhausted today. It's going to take time. I'm willing to give you all I can but not at the cost of your health. We'll take it slowly while you adjust to each memory, and hopefully you'll find your own somewhere in between."

My impatience irked me, but I understood. I thought I'd done a good job at hiding how tired I was today, thinking it was just a bad day because of my blood deficiency.

It slipped my sight to the bottle of silver tonic Agetha had given me in Althenia. I should take it; there was no reason for anyone there to harm me.

I swiped it from the table, hesitating to catch Nyte's curious eye.

"Can you tell me if this is safe to take?" I asked him.

He approached, taking the small bottle from me. "Where did you get it?"

"A healer," I said, hoping he didn't query deeper than that.

"You don't trust them?"

"I do, I just . . . never mind." I reached for the tonic but Nyte pulled his arm back.

I watched him pop the cork off and sniff, then take a sip. His expression soured and I bit my lip from amusement at the reaction.

"Safe, yes. The taste, however . . ." Nyte cringed handing it back to me.

I relaxed within. It was a potion from Althenia and Nyte didn't know that to be a reason I shouldn't take it. That was confirmation enough that neither could be manipulating me through it. Staring at the swirling silver liquid, anger simmered in me. I despised how Goldfell had made this so difficult and that I questioned the help.

Drinking the tonic, the taste was bitter but I could hardly register it considering my resentment.

Nyte's fingers grazed my chin, tearing my glare up from the empty bottle as I thought of Goldfell. Of how he would place his pill of control on my tongue and I'd been his willing victim.

"Are you all right?" Nyte asked tenderly.

"I will be." That was a promise to myself.

I would be no one's pawn again and it was time to make those who thought to try see there was steel behind the guise of a delicate maiden. Starting today.

"Can we get this over with?" I asked quietly.

His mouth leaned to my ear. "I don't want it to be this way," he said, his breath like sand scattered across my neck, which inclined a fraction.

"I'll be bleeding in a hall of vampires particularly attracted to it."

"I'm rather looking forward to the test of their restraint," he said nonchalantly. "I would enjoy getting to make an example out of one. There won't come a second chance, not even a hesitation, for any advance made against you."

"That's a little harsh," I said.

His head tilted a fraction. "Don't tell me you've grown merciful for those seeking to overthrow you."

"I don't need you to fight all my battles."

Without warning, his mouth came down on mine with a firmness I yielded to instantly. I had to bite back my embarrassing whimper of a protest when he pulled away too soon.

"I will always fight them *with* you, not for you."

Held by the sun burning in his irises, I wanted to believe the promise of the world in them. Wanted to give in to everything he might offer. But I couldn't escape the nagging thread that it came at a cost. Maybe one day it wouldn't feel so cowardly to accept what our alliance could mean, but right now, how could I ever feel equal when I hadn't the chance to discover who I was myself.

"They're waiting," I said.

With that acknowledgment my stomach tightened the knot that had formed since waking this morning.

Nyte scanned every inch of me. As though he was savoring it for the last time. "You are absolutely magnificent," he said. "And brave, and resilient. I may be the villain to all those we face today, but I will never be yours. Even if you choose to see me that way."

I didn't know what to say to that, so I was glad when he saved me from needing to by stepping away, extending an arm to the door.

"Time to tempt the damned and the deprived."

If it wasn't for Nyte walking by my side rather than awaiting me down the aisle, the setting of the throne room would have spiked my nerves high enough to sway my vision with the thought of a darkly twisted wedding. Though I suppose binding my life to the devil I walked side by side with was far more permanent.

Nyte's hand grazed my lower back; it was his gentle influence on my emotions within that soothed the sharpness of my panic I appreciated more. Soul and blood vampires gathered down each side of the hall. Perhaps some of them were fae but I couldn't distinguish without checking for both a shadow and a reflection. It was the furthest concern right now.

Only when we met at the dais did I glance sideward to find Zath, Rose, and Davina.

"No one will get a step toward you before their knees break on the ground," Nyte said to my mind.

"That's not my concern," I thought back.

"Stage fright?"

"Something like that."

When we stopped walking, I faced him. *"Only you and I exist in this room,"* he said. *"To me, only you and I exist in this world. It's been an empty three hundred years I don't plan to repeat."*

I gave a barely there nod. My throat was too tight for words, and my mind was racing to think of anything but what we were about to do.

"This union between our notorious Nightsdeath and the esteemed star-maiden will be most legendary." Tarran's voice crawled across my nape as we past him.

To my surprise, he kept near the back, leaning casually against a pillar like he awaited a grand show.

Nyte's hand gave mine a gentle squeeze, and though he kept his expression neutral for the crowd, there was no mistaking the hatred he bore for Tarran. Whatever their history, it went beyond me.

He gave me his attention as if the room of spectators didn't matter to him. I wished I could feel the same, but I was hyperaware of every set of eyes.

Nyte unfastened his sleeve, beginning to roll back the material to expose his forearm. His eyes didn't leave mine as he brought it to the sharp teeth he'd exposed to cut himself. My hand lashed out before he could, heart leaping up my throat with what was about to happen.

"Can I?" I asked, painfully choked out of nerves.

My hand reached into a pool of glittering black, retracting with my storm-stone dagger from the void. The material of it I now knew was fatal to vampires if aimed at the heart.

I held Nyte's forearm in my hand, angling the sharp tip of the waved blade over his skin even though it twisted my stomach to harm him.

"You had no trouble plunging it through my chest," Nyte mused.

I flicked up a scowl which quirked the corner of his mouth.

My blade cut deep enough to bead crimson along the purple steel. It was like my senses became acute to him, and while I might have otherwise been horrified at the notion of drinking blood, his filled my nostrils with a sweet copper tang my mouth parted to.

"How fast will you heal?" I asked to distract myself a few seconds longer when I'd finished scoring his flesh.

"A couple of days. Stormstone is a particularly irritating material to be cut or stabbed with, even for me."

Nyte's hand cupped my nape as his arm raised to me. My pulse drummed hard in my ears, my breath became labored. This was insane, and I was fully convinced I was out of my damned mind to go through with this.

Just before my lips could meet his open skin, my sight flicked to Rose. Her expression, trying not to twist with disgust over what she was witnessing, pinned me firm, and I coiled inside. Zath appeared pained by her side, like he wished this circumstance was different but there was nothing he could do.

Tasting Nyte's blood again was as powerful as I'd expected. This time and the last my existence felt broken into finite threads that searched for something equal and promising to bind together with. Every fiber of my being was searching for *him* and I became addicted, feverishly addicted to the essence of Nyte, believing I would never find completeness unless he found me back.

I might have moaned with the pleasure rocking through me, completely unaware now of where I was, who was watching. I didn't care. My back pressed to something so warm and safe.

"If you don't stop I'm seconds from bending you over that damned throne," Nyte strained in my mind.

I registered his arm around my waist while I had the other clutched in my grasp, drinking from him. He held me against him while I drifted on a cloud of euphoria.

My eyes snapped open to that awareness and I let him go. I stared at the impression of my teeth on his skin while I scrambled to piece together where I was. *Who* I fucking was. My heart raced to a dizzying speed. I hadn't anticipated how much his blood would affect me, and I still had a task to do.

I wiped the blood at the corners of my mouth and stared at the crimson on my thumb. Nyte swept my hair out of the way to expose my neck. His lips pressed softly but I was numb to it.

He turned me in his hold as I finished whispering words I hoped I recalled right.

"Are you ready?" he asked, inching sharp teeth and hungry eyes toward the veins throbbing against my flesh.

"Yes," I choked out.

Nyte didn't hesitate. My brow pinched tightly and my eyes fluttered the moment he sank his teeth into me. The heat from before gathered quicker between my legs and I was shamelessly teetering on the edge of a blissful finish from the rush of lust infusing my adrenaline. I had to keep chanting to myself to stay present.

He seemed to lose himself too, groaning quietly against my skin and, *stars,* I wished we were alone. That this was different circumstances. That we were different people.

When he pulled out my flesh his breath shuddered out of him. I reached fingers to the wound, swiping my own blood onto my fingers.

Then I touched the thing I held and finished my final verse.

Nyte locked still against me.

"What is that?" he asked, but he already knew. He could feel what I'd done before he had a chance to tie the mating bond.

His head only pulled back enough to rest against my forehead. He stared down at my hands.

At the feather—his midnight feather—I held.

"The Primeera bargain," I said through my tight throat. "Complete command of another. Far stronger than your basic blood bargain to have will over me. Our blood combined on an item belonging to you."

"Oh, Starlight, what have you done?"

He let me go, stepping back and those golden irises became unreadable to me.

"Kneel," I said.

Nyte's eyes flexed, fighting it for as long as he could.

Then, when he lowered with clear resistance to my command, murmurs broke out among the crowd.

"What is happening?" a soul vampire demanded.

He only got a few steps before I said to Nyte, "Stop him."

Nyte didn't even have to look away from the intense stare we'd locked on each other. The low growl of outrage from the vampire told me Nyte had seized his mind against movement.

I dared a look over, and my sight snagged on one vampire I didn't expect to be leaning against a pillar near the back, watching with amusement on his face. I'd thought Tarran would be the most outraged, at the front to bear witness to all of this, and it was almost a disappointment to see him *smiling*.

"Now make them all kneel."

"Are you sure you know what you're doing?" Nyte taunted to my mind.

I didn't. This plan I'd conjured only knew the present with no steps paved ahead. Only defiance and determination that I wouldn't be another pet. Never again would I allow my choice to be made for me.

"I'm going to walk out of here, and you're going to make sure no vampire can come after me. Then I forbid *you* from coming after me, Nyte. Until I break this bond, you will not follow me."

"How could you allow this to happen!" another vampire barked.

"She's the star-maiden," Nyte said calmly. "We shouldn't have underestimated what that meant."

I couldn't decide if I was glad about his cool demeanor. That he didn't pin me with loathing and betrayal, or maybe that would have been easier to bear. It could have prevented the swell in my chest that wouldn't let me do this without *regret*.

I was the star-maiden, and it was time for me to stop underestimating that too.

When I turned to the onlookers of furious vampires on their knees before me, I delighted in the power I had over them. With Nyte at my command, they would be helpless to stop me. My hand reached into the void again, and the power that hummed through me with the weapon in my grasp quelled my anxiety.

The key came to life as its true staff form, the faint purple glow winking out when the stars did.

"Rose and Zath are coming with me," I said, glancing Rose's way, and only then did the two of them snap out of the stun that blanked their expression. Rose nodded once, the fierceness in her returning.

My head dropped to Nyte again, and so much conflict waged inside me to see him on one knee in submission to the betrayal I'd inflicted on him.

"Order them to free Calix," I said coldly.

Nyte's jaw locked in defiance. "No."

"Order. It."

The bond within us strained hard with the demand. Hurting him but not me. I was prepared to keep amplifying it if he kept denying it.

With fury lined reluctance, he asked a nearby couple of guards to release Calix. My insides calmed when he did. Despite everything, I took no joy in hurting Nyte.

"If you're going to shine, may as well blind them with it," he said to my mind.

My shoulders squared, turning from him to face the crowd. Vampire rage choked me when I looked at over them, but I didn't let it show.

"My name is Astraea," I said, letting the power of the key soothe my senses like we were one. "I am the daughter of Dusk and Dawn. The star-maiden. And I'm back. There was once a time this land knew peace and I plan to bring it back. You'll either become a part of the new Golden Age, or you'll become dust, forgotten in the old."

I didn't get two steps off the dais before Nyte's low voice, shadow-touched and daring, echoed through my mind and caressed my spine.

"Run, Starlight. Run far and fast. But when I catch you . . . you'd best be ready for it."

22

Nyte

Astraea was the most exquisite thing to have ever lived. I was soaring with her blood in my system, which was the only thing keeping me from wrecking everything in my path because she was currently venturing away from me.

I couldn't deny that what she had done was utterly brilliant. A fantastic announcement to the world that she was back.

"How could you not have seen that coming?" Tarran drawled at my back.

I stopped with my hand on the door to my father's old study.

"Amazing, wasn't she?"

Heading inside, I had to make tremendous effort not to do something deadly and impulsive to the soul vampire that followed me in.

As an elder vampire, one of the oldest alive, he had a reputation and influence I had to navigate carefully. When I was free and known across the land by my notorious name, Tarran wasn't a force I considered a threat. I knew of him, but he was quiet back then. It seemed that in my absence he had found an opportunity to gain power, and from my findings, he had a lot of it in follower numbers where the vampires were considered.

I gravitated toward the window as if her distance from me was straining a tether. My mouth curved when I saw her, chest clenching with such pride I wanted the pain to linger. I savored the last flickers of her silver hair before she disappeared out of sight over the curve of the frosty courtyard with Rose, Zath, and to my absolute displeasure, Calix.

Tarran said, "It was quite a spectacle indeed. Though I'm surprised you allowed it."

"She's the star-maiden. We never should have doubted that, even if she's still finding herself from before."

What he couldn't know was that I'd been hoping for her to escape. Waiting for it. Though I never predicted the bargain she would trick me into. I adored that about her—the unpredictability of what Astraea could be planning.

"What is your plan now that we've lost our greatest ally?"

This was my part to play. Assuring Tarran I still had things under control no matter what Astraea did.

"I haven't left Astraea since the early days after she came back; I'm not going to start now."

He knew what I meant. "You'll continue to follow her?"

"She didn't say anything about infiltrating her mind," I mused, fixing my stare out the window and replaying the breathtaking sight of her. "I'll know all of her movements and plans. We'll have her soon enough."

"When she feels you there, she might block you."

"Don't underestimate me, Tarran. And it's in your best interest to tame the restless vampires away from this. Astraea is smart enough to have pulled off this bargain; she'll know she hasn't gained an escape from me, only a head start."

I'd lost her once. This world would end before I lost her again.

"My lord, you might want to—" Elliot halted in the door he'd entered without so much as a knock.

Usually I wouldn't mind, but locking eyes with Tarran made him regretful of that. It was no secret the vampires hated the turned—seeing them as an abomination of their species and I guess that's why I could sympathize with the Golden Guard.

"What is it?" I asked sharply.

"Drystan is here," he replied, but my spine straightened at his tone. Elliot added, "Nadia is trying to kill him."

When I found my brother and the rogue, I was quite irritable Elliot had made it seem more urgent than the childish display I stood witness to.

They *were* fighting. Perhaps it seemed vicious enough to the others who stood with me, but I found it mildly entertaining.

She chased him while he darted around the drawing room. They'd wrecked the map and crushed the figurines I was quite fond of on the table. There were claw marks on the wood too, and at least three chairs were in splinters.

Nadia picked up another, throwing it, and Drystan was too cornered to avoid the impact of that one. It slammed him to the wall and broke into pieces.

"Stop this," I warned. My command trembled through the room and she wisely stopped herself before taking another step.

"You're quite strong," Drystan groaned, rolling back his shoulders.

"What do you think you're doing?" I asked, targeting Nadia.

She straightened, gathering her breath not from exertion but anger. Nadia had so much of it bottled inside her I could practically feel it emanating from her. It made me curious, because I didn't think Drystan was entirely the cause, merely one volatile trigger that unleashed some of it.

"Welcoming our guest," she said, keeping her heated stare on my brother like she anticipated another round.

"Next time, allow me," I warned. Then I said to the others, "Leave us."

Elliot read my silent command, edging tentatively toward Nadia like she was an explosive that would detonate on him too any minute. She tore her glare from Drystan and I felt a stroke of heat from it falling on me for a second before she marched from the room.

"I don't know what I did to piss her off so much," Drystan said when we were alone.

He straightened his jacket and ran a hand through his hair, staring after the ghost of her like she lingered on his thoughts.

"She doesn't like the power you have over her."

"I have never used it."

"But you could."

His hazel eyes slipped to me then, and my chest felt the mutual understanding. Drystan knew the centuries I'd lived through as the monster lingering in people's nightmares without ever needing to terrorize them.

"So the attack doesn't matter, only that you hold the weapon," he said.

I didn't wish this life on Drystan, but he'd brought this upon himself.

"Your mistake was ever picking it up in the first place," I answered, pacing around the table and stepping over the pieces of Nadia's rage.

"She's not going to stop wanting you dead," I said. "Unless you know of another way to break the blood bond."

"There is no other way."

I quite liked Nadia's spirit. Admittedly, I wanted to figure her out just like I did each of the Golden Guard after their game. What made them compete in their selected trials to be in the Libertatem. Who they'd lost or hoped to return to. But with her passionate drive to end Drystan, I might have to put her down instead.

"Why did you come?" I asked.

"Have you shown her the day in the library yet?" he asked.

My brow curved curiously. "Why are you eager for her to have that memory?"

"She should know."

"I thought you didn't have concern for her anymore—so what is your gain?"

Drystan shrugged. Then circled back to my question.

"I came to tell you, rumor is father has been bragging about a way to kill you—and he plans to use Astraea to do it."

Heat torched through me so fast I risked causing far more destruction to this room than Nadia.

"You know where he is?" I snarled.

"I said I heard *rumors*."

"Where?"

"Here and there."

I was so fucking far away from being able to tolerate a verbal dance with him.

"He has no army. No power."

"He has an answer to a once impossible feat."

My true death. I didn't know what it would take, but the fact that Astraea was mentioned made me want to hunt him down like a savage beast if that's what it took to find him and rip the black heart from his chest.

"You have no leads on where he's hiding?" I asked.

"I've had some of the transitioned on the lookout as spies. It's curious how untraceable he's become."

"Magick?"

"I had that thought, yes."

He could be cloaked, stealing the identity of someone else through one of many means of magick.

"You never did find the final item of the Wanderers Trove, did you?" Drystan asked.

"No."

There was a monocular out there that could unveil anything hidden by magick, but we'd never been able to find it.

"A shame," he said.

"So you came here to warn me?"

"You said we were working together on finding father? I'm waiting for you to start pulling your weight."

I'd been too distracted with Astraea. I still was. She was the only thing I wanted to care or think about but that was a luxury I couldn't afford right now. While she was gaining her freedom and challenging herself, this could be the distraction I needed to use my sharp edges in her absence.

"I still have the compass," I confessed.

"You said you broke it in your foolish rage," Drystan grumbled.

It had been the first thing to make Astraea and me realize our doomed fate. The thing we'd thought was broken and useless had been warning us the whole time and I *had* thrown it against a stone wall and watched it shatter. Then witnessed the mockery when it laughed at me as the pieces vibrated against the ground and reformed back into the enchanted item.

"It might take us to him if we can find the right mage to enchant it," I said.

"You could have told me this before. I would have been on it while you've been gallivanting with the maiden."

"She's been learning her powers."

"Too fucking slowly," Drystan snapped.

"Watch yourself."

"You've been too precious with her when you know she's not so easily breakable. The more you treat her like glass the longer she'll believe she is."

"Not anymore," I assured him.

I'd pushed her in the woods and feared I'd gone too far. But she was magnificent. Watching her defiance and power unleashed filled me with awe to see again after so long.

"Just meet me tomorrow with the damned compass."

23

Astraea

We traveled for two days without much conversation. At least, Rose, Zath, and Calix might have exchanged words but I was too lost with thoughts storming my mind to contribute.

I didn't know how many hours had passed since we set off today after a short camp in a freezing, damp cave. Twigs snapped under my boots and I stumbled occasionally over rocks but my tunneling focus barely registered any of it. My pace had been a punishing walk since then, driven by terror that the hall of vampires I'd mocked would be chasing. Or worse, that Nyte had humored me, watching in sadistic entertainment as I thought I'd bested him when really the blood bond hadn't worked. The thought of *him* chasing us exhausted me with spikes of fear and excitement.

"I've left you to march in your silence long enough. Please tell me we have a purposeful direction." Rose's tone was careful, and I wondered what I'd said since leaving or what my expression displayed that had brought on the unusually tentative approach from her.

"We're heading toward Alisus," Zath informed her.

From the chime following us, I spared a look back to Calix who trailed behind, eyes fixed on the ground with his wrists still bound in front. I didn't want to feel the sympathy worming its way through my resentment toward him, but there it was. I tore my sight from him and tried to forget his presence for now.

"Astraea." The firmness of my name accompanied by the shake of my shoulders snapped me back to the woodland surrounding us.

I met Rose's concerned hazel eyes.

"Sorry," I breathed, scrambling to pull myself together. "Nyte couldn't be known to let me go willingly or the vampires wouldn't trust him anymore."

"You didn't tell him of your plan?" Zath asked.

"No. I had to do this for me."

"It was amazing what you did. I'll admit I had my doubts for a while, but damn did you shock us all. Brilliant, really," Rose said.

A nervous laugh escaped me. I couldn't believe I'd done it and glee burst over me. Starting to come around to myself, I reached down to the sodden hem of my gown. I tore the material right up to my corset bust, creating a second tear up the other side before the front part came away completely. It exposed my leather pants, and I slipped my stormstone dagger into the sheath at my thigh.

Rose was already more dressed for the travel than I. She glanced over at me with approval.

"If we're not opposed to a little theft, I'm certain I can get you better wears," she said.

I shrugged. "I'm fine. I knew I would have the few weeks' travel back to Alisus."

My boots kept my feet warm from the snow and my cloak was thick enough, at least. Rose nodded, then we carried on our trek.

"We need to get out of the woods before nightfall," Zath said.

By the time the sun vanished and the stars awoke, we'd found a quiet inn, making sure there was no sign of vampires before paying for lodgings. Rose watched me rummaging in my pockets.

To her concern, I said, "Of all the things Nyte would want revenge for, I doubt it will be a few stolen trinkets."

I handed over a sparkling red necklace and the innkeeper beamed though I couldn't be sure of its worth.

"Hell no," Zath said, snatching back the necklace.

The innkeeper yelped, reaching after it.

I frowned at Zath, puzzled.

Rose gawked at his hand as she explained, "That is made with rubies which could buy a place twice the size of this establishment." Then she began sifting through the other items I'd brought.

"How do you know that?" I asked; my cheeks warmed by how little *I* knew.

Rose flashed a wary look to Zath that I found odd. "It's not that uncommon to know the value of certain well-known jewels."

She fished out a small bracelet with white and purple crystals. Rose handed it over and I smothered my protest. I liked that one.

The innkeeper scowled at the exchange but was only met with Rose's sharp stare.

They slapped two keys to the table and grumbled, "Only two rooms. One with two beds; one with a double."

We exchanged looks to decide who would be sharing. My sight lingered on

Calix and I thought about how leaving him with either of them would only beat him down more. Both of them hated him for what he'd done.

"I should share with Calix," I said, hoping Rose and Zath wouldn't mind sharing.

They passed a look, but it was quick and if I didn't know any better I would have questioned their unease.

"We should eat," Rose said, breaking the tension.

My stomach gave audible agreement as we headed into the main room.

"Can I, uh, have these off?" Calix asked; lifting his arms and slipping his sleeves past his shackles. I winced at the red abrasions.

"Shit," Zath muttered. "Did anyone get the key?"

I blanched at the oversight. Calix's eyes closed for a long second of hopeless irritation.

"Tough luck," Zath said, clapping a hand to Calix's shoulder with a smug smile. Calix met the amusement on Zath's face with daggers.

"Allow me," a new voice crept up, one I found naggingly familiar before we all turned.

Nadia's flaming red hair was a surprise to see. Then my pulse skipped a beat thinking my bargain hadn't worked when I'd ordered Nyte not to let any of his vampires follow me.

"How did you follow us?" I asked with trepidation. There couldn't be another reason for her being here other than by Nyte's order. She had become part of his . . . truthfully, I didn't know what Nyte regarded his close circle as when he would reject the term *friend*.

Nadia shrugged. "It was easy; you're not the most skilled at covering your tracks."

She approached Calix, and he retreated an inch as she reached for his hands, snapping the chain between the manacles easily. We watched in surprise as she broke the lock on one wrist, then the other, the metal clanging to the wooden floor.

Calix rubbed his wrists gingerly. "Thanks," he muttered.

"Did Nyte send you?" I asked.

"He won't even notice I'm gone. Or he'll be glad I am."

"Why were you with him at all?" Rose asked.

"I'm starved, aren't you? What were you saying about food?" She shimmied past us and into the main room.

The rest of us traded uncertain looks, not sure what to do about the transitioned vampire that had followed us.

"We can't trust her," Zath said. Rose agreed with him.

"We don't know what she wants yet," I said. "Let's just eat."

We sat at a wooden bench soaked with ale and wine. My nose crinkled at the sour scent of alcohol and bodies that warmed the air. I was eager to retire for the night.

Our stew arrived and we ate. Rose, Zath, and Calix must have been thinking the same as me as we apprehensively watched Nadia eating just like us, lost in her bread and stew.

"I thought you drink blood?" Zath was the one to voice what all of us were wondering.

"I do," Nadia said with a frown. "Are you offering dessert?"

Zath stiffened against a shudder to that.

"But you can survive on human food still?" Rose inquired.

"It's like a bland meal now, I guess," she said, chewing on a bite of bread. "It fills a hole, but I couldn't survive without blood."

"Human blood," Zath said.

"Actually, the transitioned can survive on any blood."

"Even another vampire?" he asked.

Nadia nodded. "Except another transitioned. Their blood is just foul."

"How long has it been since you . . ." Calix trailed off, shifting nervously in his seat.

Nadia propped her chin in clasped hands, giving him a sweet smile.

"Drank?" she supplied. "I would never pass up an offering. You might enjoy it, you know? It can be pleasurable. Though I will admit there's something sweetly addictive about fear."

Now it was my turn to shudder. Nadia was a dangerous creature when she had an effortless beauty and allurement to her.

"You want to kill Drystan," I said. Her attention drew to me. "What does following me have to do with that goal?"

"I might have chosen the wrong alliance at first. I thought being one of them, telling them what I know, would get the golden guard to help me convince Nightsdeath to put down his brother. But they are foolishly loyal to him, and the notorious villain of the land is nothing but a weak and selfish coward."

That flared a defense in me, tightening my grip around my spoon. Nadia seemed to notice my reaction with bored disappointment.

"I really hope you have a mind of your own to see what needs to be done," she said.

"And what's that?" Rose asked.

"We can't allow Drystan to have an entire vampire army at his disposal," she snapped. "You have no idea what we're capable of."

Nadia stood, grabbing the next man in her path. She pushed him down onto the bench and straddled his lap. We all tensed at the sudden boldness as she grabbed his face. He was young and handsome, staring at her with stunned adoration as she smiled.

I grew uncomfortable witnessing the affection around our meal as she leaned in close to whisper in his ear. Then before I could take another blink, her sharp fangs sank into his neck.

"What the fuck are you doing?" Zath hissed, pushing up from across the table.

I was shocked still, not knowing if I should stop her. Would she kill him?

The man tensed at the first sting of her bite and my neck tingled, my body flushed, recalling how it felt to be drank from. By Nyte, it was sinfully pleasurable.

He relaxed and I imagined the pleasure taking over. He gripped her hips, needy for her.

It only lasted a minute before Nadia released his neck and her tongue lapped over the wound. She kept his face in her hands as she spoke.

"You don't remember that bite," she said seductively.

"I don't remember," he repeated, completely under her spell, and I blanched witnessing the compulsion.

The flush of his neck faded quickly along with the two neat puncture wounds. The speed of healing for a human was impossible.

"You kissed a pretty girl, and that's all."

"Yes," he said cupping her cheek. He'd become enamored with her in minutes.

"Good boy," she purred, slipping off his lap. Nadia picked up a knife from the table, pressing it into his palm. "Now go stab this through the hand of the man with the white scarf over there."

"Stop," I said as her victim stood without a second thought.

She didn't listen and we watched in horror as he walked over to the person she'd indicated, knife clutched tightly with purpose.

"You've proved your point," Zath hissed.

"I don't think I have," Nadia sang.

I couldn't watch this; pushing up from the bench, I wouldn't make it in time to stop him, but Zath could. He lunged, grabbing the young man who struggled against him and commotion ensued.

"He won't give up until he achieves the task," Nadia said, reaching for her wine.

I knocked it from her hand in a flash of anger. "Then fix it."

She met my defiance, and I thought for a second she would fight me. But she huffed in irritation before swaggering over to the fight that had erupted with Zath pinning the young man down and the near victim shouting curses of accusation.

Nadia crouched, gripping the young man's jaw. Once she attracted his stare she spoke. He stopped fighting.

My next breath released all the tension in me. Witnessing the power of compulsion Nadia had was chilling.

"Now can you imagine the power he holds?" Nadia said as she returned, her tone switching so dark and cold I shivered at the whiplash. "If Drystan were here, he could command me to do whatever he wanted and I have the ability to compel the mind of anyone to keep them silent."

"There has to be another way to break the bond to him," I said. My mind was reeling. We couldn't kill Drystan; I needed him on our side and hadn't given up hope of that. "Has he forced you against your will before?"

"No," she said, folding back into the bench as if nothing happened. "But I can't live with that possibility. I won't be anyone's puppet after I had my whole life ripped away from me."

I sympathized with her on that, sitting back down with her as Zath returned, disgruntled and pinning Nadia with a hateful stare.

"How do you know it is his blood that has been used for the transitions?" I asked.

"Because I saw it."

"Did he harm you?"

"No, he was actually . . . kind. Not in the sense that he checked in all the time and made sure we were comfortable, but he made sure our treatment wasn't as cruel as we expected, given the way we were torn from our homes by soulless."

"Do you have family?" Rose asked.

"Not anymore."

None of us pressed her to expand upon that somber statement.

"He doesn't deserve to die for being the blood that changed you when it could have been someone far worse," I said.

"If you won't help me then I'll tell more transitioned vampires. Someone will get the job done."

"Then why haven't you?" Rose challenged.

"Like I said, he wasn't as cruel as he could have been and I didn't want him to die by some rogue. I came to Nyte thinking he was planning for it anyway, but he's lying to himself."

"So you're not completely twisted and heartless," Zath grumbled.

"Not completely," she repeated with a deceptive smile.

I was rattled by the lingering ultimatum that if Nyte didn't kill his brother, she would. "Don't do anything yet. Just let me figure something out," I said.

Stars, if she killed Drystan . . . Nyte might try to guard himself against exposing how he still cared for his brother, but I could see that he did. I didn't want to imagine what it would do to him if Drystan was killed.

After dinner, we headed up to our rooms but Nadia said she would find elsewhere to rest.

Down the narrow halls of the inn, I was taken aback by my surroundings. Tight brown walls, the clamor of the night downstairs, and the lingering scent of alcohol. I didn't realize my vision had turned blurry boring into the sad chipped wall until Rose called my name.

"What's wrong?" Zath asked.

Seeing my expression, both of them scanned me head to toe as if I could have sustained an injury in the few seconds they'd glanced away from me.

"The last time I was—" my throat tightened. "We were with Cassia when she died. The place was similar."

Would all such well worn and bustling establishments slam me with the flashback of that night, or was it possible some were different in their atmosphere?

"Shit. Sorry, if you'd told me the value you were carrying we could have chosen somewhere better," Rose said.

Calix gave a hollow laugh. "She would have hated that."

My chest constricted. He was right. Cassia didn't like fancy things and places. Not when she spent her days suffocated by them, as she'd told me many times. I smiled at the memory; this is exactly the place she would have chosen for a night of cheap alcohol and common people games. It was just the type of run-down establishment we would so often sneak into back in Alisus town.

I shook my head. "This is perfect."

We said goodnight to Zath and Rose before parting to find our room.

Twin beds were made with a few feet of space between them. The roof slanted and as the midnight sky grew darker, the snowfall came heavier against the single window that could be seen from the bed. A desk occupied one side of the room next to a small dresser.

Calix started a fire while I took off my boots and cloak, laying them in front of it to dry off. Then I sat by the flames, finding peace watching the tango of flame. He joined me, but neither of us spoke for a peaceful while, lost in our own thoughts.

Mine drifted to Nyte—wondering what he would be doing and if he was angry with me. Then my mind sped with what to do about Drystan and the target he had on him from the rogue vampire. The whole army he'd created that could want him dead too if they knew the power he held over them.

"We're going back to the keep, aren't we?" Calix asked distantly.

"I should see Reihan, pay my respects," I said. The mood between us was suffused with sorrow and heartache.

We'd been here before. After the influence of wrath left me in the maze and we'd stood staring at each other with so much pain we didn't know how to release or comfort each other.

"He wanted me to come after you too," Calix admitted quietly. "When I returned with Cassia, we kept it quiet when it was already announced she'd made it to the central. I knew it was you, and I couldn't believe you'd gone there in her place. At first I resented you for impersonating her, but then I realized . . . you had to be one of the bravest people I knew to even try it. When you weren't trained for it, you stepped in to give our kingdom a fighting chance and I understood. I felt the pride I knew Cassia would have."

My lip quivered but I swallowed my grief.

Calix said, "Reihan was distraught. I'd never seen him like that before. But he told me we had to get you back; he was still very passionate that you had to succeed and return to him."

The ache behind my ribs grew and my breaths were shallow with the pain. I couldn't fathom a father's loss of a child. Nor Calix's of his love. I'd lost my best friend, and ever since my world still often felt empty.

As I leaned my chin on my knees tucked tight to my chest, I began reflecting on a past that felt like a lifetime ago. Who I was before I entered that game was a woman I mourned for now, someone I didn't ever want to be again but who I was grateful to, thankful for her resilience in enduring what she did for me and finding the strength I have now.

"Goldfell said he had a standing agreement with Reihan, do you remember?" I asked. I didn't know why my mind found that piece of information among the chaos of that day.

Calix's brow pulled together as he tried to recall.

"He was a high member of society and very rich. Probably did some kind of trading with the reigning lord," Calix concluded.

It seemed very plausible, only I was curious to know what it was Goldfell could have supplied to Reihan.

"You don't have to come," I offered. "You wanted to start a new life in another kingdom. I can ask Nyte to get you through the borders elsewhere."

"I want to come," he said. "One last time."

I didn't respond. Fatigue started to weigh on me and I slipped into bed, watching the snow gather on the slanted window.

Calix sat on the edge of his bed with his back to me.

"How can you be sure . . ." he paused as though warring with asking me. "How true was it that Cassia loved me? How can you be sure that it wasn't just an infatuation? Being the only man close to her, with her believing she didn't have long left, I could have just been the only option."

All this time Calix had been harboring the insecurity that Cassia's love wasn't as true as his and it took me by surprise how much that disturbed me. I rolled onto my side to watch his slouched back as I thought.

"You weren't her only option. She was the reigning lord's daughter with no shortage of attention. She was beautiful and charismatic and her company was infectious. She could have chosen anyone in this kingdom, slept with as many as she wanted since she knew her days were numbered, but she waited for you."

I watched the words hit him hard. The small comfort that he wasn't alone in his devotion wasn't the balm he hoped it would be; it was another wound. Something I couldn't heal and didn't think anything ever could.

I laid back again to watch the snow and my thoughts drifted to Nyte. After all I'd done, with the lingering prospect of Auster even though he didn't know of our meets, it struck me all at once to imagine his turmoil. His uncertainly about my feelings. Yet at the same time, I couldn't find the words to describe what I felt for him anyway.

I counted snowflakes like they measured something greater. I wasn't conflicted in my feelings, only terrified about how to guard them and keep them locked tightly away. Against Auster's warning, I had to go to the Guardian's Temple. I had to know if they could help when they could be far closer to parents than the gods. They were people who walked this land too, and had raised me like I was merely a child of the world like all others. My heart yearned for someone to talk to that wasn't part of my battle here—the war in my heart or around me.

24

Nyte

I'd given her enough time without me.

Seventy-one hours was even too many.

I sat, tipping my head back, and while I could reach her at any moment, slipping my eyes closed and giving over to the task completely would make it all the more tangible and I was *starved* for her touch.

It didn't take long to find the brightest star. Before she discovered me there, I scanned her surroundings to know where she was. They were heading for Alisus. Smart girl.

Finding Calix trailing them particularly stirred my loathing. As far as I was concerned his days were still numbered, stretched longer only on Astraea's mercy, and I fucking loved her heart. Even when it defied me it was a beam of light against my darkness.

The flash of red hair I saw was unexpected and filled me with dread and anger, however. What was Nadia doing with her? And how had Elliot and the others let her elude them?

They stopped by a stream, and I took that moment to watch Astraea bend beautifully, cupping hands in the water and bringing it to her lips.

"Come home, Starlight." How present I could become for both of us depended on her mind being open to me. For now, she didn't want to see me, but there was a part of her that at least wanted to hear me, to my great pleasure.

"I'm going home," she answered.

She didn't truly believe that. Alisus was all she knew, but it was not her home.

I pushed her barriers a little harder and she yielded enough to feel my touch along her collar, shivering to it.

"I miss you," I murmured.

"It's only been three days."

That was far too many with the years I'd been without, but I didn't expose myself as a pining fool completely.

"You were absolutely radiant declaring yourself," I said, making it a believable whisper across her ear.

Astraea's body was singing even to the phantom presence of me, and it took every bit of my willpower not to damn everything and follow her already. I would behave. Give her this venture to find herself before I helped. We would always be stronger together, she would see that soon.

Her head turned, and just like that she gave me what I wanted, the clear opening to her mind that was as close to kneeling right there by the water with her as I would come. It was only then that I started to feel her surroundings through her mind. The bitter air nipping her cheeks, how her hands were cold from the water, much colder than the rest of her. The rush of the stream and the song of faraway birds. Her companions were chatting or minding their own business while it seemed they'd stopped for a short rest. It gave us this moment alone with them entirely unsuspecting of my intrusion.

"Seeing you kneel for me was very satisfying," she said aloud, but quietly now that she could see me.

I couldn't fight the curve of my mouth. "Which time?"

Her pink lips parted. Both of us felt the rush of desire to remember her spread out for me on that dining table. She was a temptation just by breathing.

"You're insufferable," she grumbled.

My fingers grazed her chin. "Come back to me. I'll kneel for you any time you ask."

I knew she wouldn't come back. Not yet. I asked only to feel the yearning pull inside her. It soothed a wicked beast that paced within me, tormenting me with the knowledge that she truly wanted me gone. That she could leave me. But her expression couldn't lie to me no matter how hard she tried to resist the twitch of her brow, the flicker of her eyes, and most preciously, the gentle uptick in her heartbeat.

"I need your help," she said, reluctantly, but it was music to my ears.

Those four words, I decided, were close to my favorite in the fucking world from her.

But while I was close to falling at her damned feet, having Astraea bend for me was thrilling.

"What are you willing to owe me for it?"

"More bargains?"

"Always."

"What do you want?"

The sadistic side of me was rejoicing in the game.

"I thought we'd talked about this," I said, leaning in closer until our mouths were just shy of meeting. "Monsters can want frightening things and gain them in pretty ways. You wouldn't know what you'd sold until it was in my hands."

Her breathing came delightfully shorter.

"Like my soul?"

"Already mine."

I kissed her, only for a second before she added resistance to my reach that numbed her surroundings to me again. I clung on enough to meet her adorable scowl with a wicked smirk.

"What do you need?" I asked.

"Past the borders of Alisus."

"Done. Anything else?"

"What happened to wanting something in return?"

"You've already opened your willingness for it to be anything. I won't forget to collect." Her lips parted again to voice a protest. It silenced with the brush of my thumb along her lower lip.

"What does the rogue want?"

"Nadia? Same thing she tried to gain from you."

"She really is hell-bent on ending Drystan."

"It seems so. What do we do about her?"

"I'm trying to seek out my father with Drystan now. Then I'll deal with her. Unless she's a threat or an annoyance to you, I'll send Elliot and the others to dispose of her."

"She doesn't deserve to die."

"I don't think she'll let go of her vendetta and it's a risk I won't take. I should have ended her the moment I learned of it."

"But you didn't because you know why she feels so strongly about it. As do I."

I kissed her head. Her soul was so precious it hurt.

"If she harms any of you—besides Calix—I won't have the patience of mercy before I come for her." Before she could protest I claimed her parted mouth. "Be safe, Starlight. You know how to call for me."

As soon as I slipped away from her and opened my eyes to the dull brown office my mood became sour.

I couldn't stay idle for one fucking moment without her near or I was sure to be villainous for no reason in these vampire infested halls. That wouldn't be ideal. I didn't mind the reputation I'd gained; it was the truth even if their terrors about me were often amplified by the unknown. The unpredictability of what I could do when few would care to know the motive behind heinous actions. There was always a purpose.

So Drystan would be my distraction.

25

Astraea

I never thought I would see the gates of Alisus Keep again. My feet planted, unable to go any farther with my heart speeding so fast I thought it might collapse me. A warm hand slid into mine, giving a squeeze. Zath's gentle smile was a calming sight, while Rose on his other side was taking in every aspect of the Keep.

"It's a lot . . . *brighter* compared to Pyxtia Keep," she assessed to herself.

"Not as vibrant as Fesaris Keep," Nadia said, observing with folded arms. "So many plants and flowers in Fesaris the colors were sickly, I'm kind of glad to be away."

I'd never been and knew little of what could make each kingdom look and feel different. It was fascinating to hear about.

When we got to the gates, the guards chatted to Calix while my heart thundered. Reihan emerged from the keep and my knees weakened. He headed for us immediately and the guards let us pass.

"Astraea." The heartbreak in Reihan's voice cracked when it had always sounded so mighty. Unshakable. Death broke even the strongest wills.

What pulled us into an embrace was not the warmth of a reunion, but the chill of grief. I hadn't appreciated how much she looked like him until now. His eyes were a lighter shade of blue but the shape of them was Cassia's. Then he broke a smile and it slammed in my chest to remind me of Cassia too.

He wore a top hat on his jet-black hair; I'd never seen him wear such a thing but perhaps it was for the cold or a token of his mourning.

"I'm so sorry." The words barely came out of me. Choked and muffled against his chest.

"Oh, child," he said, resting a large hand on the back of my head.

I melted at the fatherly comfort of him, blessed in such a dire moment that I was so glad I'd braved to come when there were fleeting moments that tried to tell me I wasn't welcome here anymore without Cassia.

"Come, let's get you out of the cold."

Inside the Keep, the familiar walls were both a burden and a gift. I tried pushing away the sorrow to find happiness, hearing Cassia's scolding in my mind that would tell me to stop wasting my energy on things that could not be changed.

"This is Rosalind," I said when I knew the halls were clear. "And Zathrian."

Reihan didn't seem that surprised. He didn't stop walking nor did he give her a glance. "My congratulations on your win," he said.

"Cassia was a good friend of mine. I'm so sorry for your loss," Rose said.

His posture remained stiff as he walked, hands clasped, and I let Rose walk with him to exchange condolences and tell him of their correspondence all these years.

"You should have let him kill me," Calix said, barely a whisper.

He stopped walking with me and I searched his eyes, becoming colder than the winter wind breezing through the archway hall the longer I couldn't find anything in the brown depths that countered his words. Not a single flicker that was glad to be here.

"Cassia knew her life was ending; she never would have wanted yours to as well."

"I thought I could handle being back here but I don't think I can."

"I held her soul," I admitted. "The whole time I was in the central, until the very end, she helped guide me through and I never realized. Now she's joined the stars. She's seeing the world like she always wanted and she sees *you*, Calix."

"Then she'd be telling you to kill me too."

Something in me snapped. Before I could process the heat of my actions the vibrations of slamming Calix to the wall shot up my arm and my magick awakened.

It reached into him from my connection to his chest, finding something warm and bright and dragging it out. Calix gasped then stunned still. We both did, as a flare of white and gray light hovered in the space between his chest and my palm.

"A few more inches and you'd be dead," I warned. "Say right now that's what you want and I'll send your soul to join her. But let me tell you it won't be as poetic as it sounds. The stars are dying, and you might be one of those unfortunate souls that never gets to find life again. Cassia would have given anything for the many years you still have in this damned realm to make a difference. You let her down by regarding your life without care."

We stared off for a few moments. He said nothing, but he was thinking deeply.

"That's a fascinating and frightening trick," Nadia said in awe, bringing her head much closer to examine the glow of Calix's soul. "What happens if I touch it?"

My hand thrust against Calix's chest before she could be brazen enough to find out. I wasn't sure if it could harm him.

I pushed off him, winking out the brightness of his soul outside his body, and found Reihan studying me apprehensively. I'd come here expecting to explain what I was to him, though I supposed the demonstration would make that a little easier now.

I brushed myself off as the tingling sensation of the magick within me subsided fully.

"I'm quite hungry," I said, heading toward them. "And we can't stay long."

Reihan nodded but his mind was still on the spectacle he'd witnessed, quiet and trying to process as he led the way to the dining hall.

"When I heard the star-maiden was real . . . and that she had returned—" Reihan stared off, seeming to continue his conclusions in his head.

"I didn't know who I was," I admitted with shame crawling my spine.

It began to retract when Reihan's furrowed brow smoothed out and he cast me a warm smile. His hand guided the small of my back and the tension within me broke its stiff walls, feeling that touch as his acceptance. It was a liberation I didn't realize I'd been on edge for.

In the banquet hall, I sat next to Reihan on his left, and when my eyes cast opposite for a second I met deep blue irises. Cassia was laughing about something her father teased her about, the sound of it like her ghost skipping through the room. The vision of her broke when the chair groaned across the stone.

"I can't sit there," Rose protested to the servant who'd offered it.

"Please," Reihan offered kindly but the curve of his mouth was forced and broken.

Rose wanted to object again but caved to the weight of his expectant stare. Then she met my eyes, and I wished I could do something for the sorrow that was tangling around us all.

The food became a distraction, especially since my stomach had been hollow for hours, and I piled helpings of chicken and vegetables onto my plate.

"Does the . . . uh, soul stealing thing starve you or something?" Calix asked gingerly, eyeing my stacked plate from beside me.

My eyebrow hooked at him. "Soul stealing?"

"Well what would you call it?"

I hadn't given it much thought. That my ability could have a name.

My mouth quirked in amusement. "We haven't eaten in hours, but I think using magick could be having an added effect, at least while I'm gaining it back."

"All this time," Reihan muttered.

I cast a sheepish look. "I wouldn't have kept the secret had I known."

Reihan dropped his eyes from me and my gut sank with them.

"Don't apologize," he said, but something changed in him. "How long will you stay? I'll have guest rooms set up for you."

"A few days, if that would be okay?" I said.

I'd only come to visit the Guardian Temple—the place I'd fallen to—but I wanted a little more time before I said goodbye to Alisus again.

"Of course. Then where do you travel?"

I hadn't told any of them where I planned to go next. If I didn't get any answers from the guardians, I thought I would go back to Althenia for a while this time.

"To Althenia. I think the celestials will come out of hiding soon."

"How soon?"

I didn't expect his tone, like he feared it. The celestials would be their salvation yet his response indicated the opposite.

"They're ready if war breaks."

"They could come for you."

I stopped eating, trying to figure out the source of the urgency in his prompts.

"You don't have to be afraid of them," I said.

Reihan nodded, but the disturbance didn't leave the creases of his aging, tanned skin. I couldn't blame him for being uneasy. The humans had never seen the celestials since they locked themselves away behind the veil centuries ago to save their species and regain their strength.

Knowing I was the cause of their suffering and would be again the more I came into my magick . . . it was another matter of urgency that drove my need for answers against my clashing existence with Nyte.

I finished my food, weighing in my mind where I wanted to go after and wondering if I had the strength. But my chest warmed three times like it did when Cassia guidied me through the Libertatem, and I took that as a sign of her spirit still with me in some way.

So I asked, "May I visit Cassia's room?"

26

Astraea

Everything was exactly like I remembered. Grief crashed into me but I kept walking through Cassia's room despite the rising storm. The color blue, which she favored, was littered throughout and it was like she watched me through every note of it. I don't know what I'd expected, but it felt right to be here.

I laid on her bed and mapped her starry ceiling, pretending she was lying right beside me as we'd done so many times.

"I don't know what I'm doing," I confessed as though she could hear me in those painted stars.

The silence was cold and heavy. I rolled over, hugging myself against the lonely chill. Until my chest warmed again like a pulse of three beats and I felt I must have been conjuring it from memory and desperation.

This time it made me remember . . . Cassia kept a diary.

I'd seen her writing in it in my company; she was never shy to tell me how she loved to write her thoughts and plans, finding it gave her wonder-filled mind reprieve and sealed her promises to herself in ink.

I looked in drawers and around the room, growing heavier at the thought I wouldn't find it. Perhaps she'd taken it with her to central and it was lost in the belongings I'd never recover. Until my eyes were drawn to the edge of her bed, and I knew . . .

As I lifted the mattress, my eyes lit up at the familiar deep blue dyed leather journal. The stamp on the front was a constellation I traced the points of.

For a while I merely sat on her bed, hugging the journal to my chest and trying not to cry. I wondered if she would protest against me reading her thoughts, but my chest kept warming and maybe that was her permission.

I just needed to hear her, even in silent words.

Just before I could flip open the pages, Cassia's door creaked open tentatively.

Rose entered as gentle and lost as a ghost. I didn't disturb her. Letting her wander around, observing and reflecting on our friend in her own ways.

"Seems fitting," Rose said, quiet to the peace of the room like we were careful tourists in the remains of our dear friend's life in our physical world.

"Everything in here speaks to her personality," I said with a glance at the roof. Rose followed and smiled.

"You had more in common with her."

I shook my head. "There are many commonalities that can connect a person. She might have loved the stars like me, but she was a warrior like you."

Rose regarded me then; her brown eyes became thoughtful and this gentleness was rare from her.

"You're a warrior too, Astraea. You just haven't had the chance to prove it yet. Even to yourself."

I gave her a smile of gratitude. I was trying to see that in myself.

"I think I'm going to stay in here tonight," I said.

"Can I stay with you?"

"I'd like that."

Rose lit the fire and we sat on Cassia's bed. Neither of us were tired yet.

"Are you not worried Calix will try to turn Reihan against you?" Rose asked.

"I don't think so . . . He loves Cassia still, and I have to believe his amity with me is true to her memory."

"What are *you* going to do about him?"

For the first time, I felt real authority. Calix's fate was in my hands right now and I had a choice to make.

"I'm not sure yet," I admitted. "I spared his life for Cassia. She truly loved him and despite the very bad choices he made . . . it was all to try to save her. How can I fault him for that?"

"Nightsdeath said it was his fault Cassia died."

"His name is Nyte," I cut in. "Nightsdeath is just a dark part of him."

"He is all darkness."

"Maybe. But he's a person."

Rose might never understand why I defended Nyte, but at least it seemed like she was starting to accept it.

"What's that?" Rose asked, breaking me from my thoughts.

Her attention bore down on the diary I clutched.

"Cassia's thoughts and dreams. I don't know if it's wrong to open it."

Rose didn't immediately say it was, and I slipped her a look, finding her pinning the book with a frown of contemplation.

"No one else knows about it?"

"I don't think her father or sisters would have left it there if they'd found it."

"What if it could tell us something she never got the chance to?"

My heart skipped. I had thought of that. Cassia had shown me pages within it before. She'd expressed to me what she was writing sometimes, but still I wondered if some things were private and this would be an invasion.

"You said Reihan is like a father to you too . . ." Rose trailed off.

"He is."

"He seems . . . afraid of you."

That sank in my gut. "A lot has changed about me. I guess I'm not the person he used to know and he had the right to be wary."

"I guess," Rose said, in a way that didn't seem convinced by that reasoning.

I pushed the diary across the bed. "You read it."

For a time unmeasured I sat dangling my legs off Cassia's bed, enjoying the gentle strokes of the fire, and listening to Rose's voice take on a soothing tone as she recited some things from Cassia's diary. Though my heart was melancholic as I glanced at the familiar things around me without their owner, the tales of her weaved through the room. I found myself giggling at things I already knew. My eyes would tear up with more touching things to come from her pages. For a while it was like she was right here with us.

"She really loved Calix," Rose said quietly.

"Yeah," I whispered, watching the tango of fire. "Which is why I have to let him go. He was going to try to start a new life but seeing him here . . . I don't think he'll ever let *her* go."

We shared a pained look of agreement. Even though Rose didn't care about Calix, for our friend, we couldn't disregard him completely.

"She thought you were special," Rose went on.

My brow pinched at that. "She had the biggest heart."

"It's more than that. Listen—" Rose shifted behind me and I cast a look back over my shoulder. Rose recited Cassia's words, *"There's something about Astraea that is magickal. I can feel it. And when I look at her, she's so ethereal I wonder how she can't see it. Sometimes I imagine her as an angel. One with beautiful silver wings like the ones in father's office."*

My pinched brow of sorrow smoothed out with those final words.

"Wings?" I repeated like it could be wrong.

"It's what she wrote," Rose said with a shrug.

She showed me the diary and I was taken by the sketch next to that page. My fingers brushed over the charcoal lines of the feathers.

Were there celestial wings in Reihan's office now?

Adrenaline sent my heart thumping hard and I stood from the bed.

"It's the middle of the night," Rose argued, anticipating my intentions.

"I just want to see."

"You should ask him tomorrow."

I shook my head. "Cassia would always say it was the one room out of bounds to her. She would talk about the celestials with such fascination like she *knew* they were real even when no one had seen them in generations. This must be where she got that belief from."

"I'm coming with you," Rose said, slipping into her boots.

I didn't protest as I headed for the door.

We avoided the guards that were sparse at this hour. I knew where the office was since I'd passed by with Cassia many times.

Down the next deserted hallway leading straight toward the office, a body jumped out of nowhere into our path. The key was in my hand in a heart-beat and my next breath choked in my throat, but my attack tensed my body against unleashing when the violet glow revealed a familiar face.

"I love a secret mission!" Nadia gushed in a whisper.

"Shit, why did you do that?" Rose grumbled, letting go of the hilt of the dagger on her thigh.

"If you'd thought to invite me, I wouldn't have had to."

"It wasn't exactly a planned venture."

Nadia assessed us head to toe. "What is the venture?"

"Just be quiet and don't touch anything when we get inside," I said, passing her on my way down the hall.

I listened first, straining my hearing against the wood.

"There's no one inside," Nadia confirmed.

"Can you hear better . . . as a vampire?" Rose asked warily.

"Hear, see, smell, taste; honestly aside from the whole bloodlust annoyance, it has a lot of perks."

She said it with a nonchalant attitude, but I had a feeling it still wouldn't have been a choice she'd have made.

"I'm stronger too—want me to break in?"

"No," I said quickly. She could be quite impulsive. "He can't know we were here."

"Ughh," Nadia groaned, reaching into her high ponytail. "The *human* way it is, then."

We watched her use two hairpins in the lock with fascination.

"I could have done that too," Rose commented.

I slipped a curious look but she only shrugged at it. There was a lot of Rose I still had to figure out.

Nadia cast a victorious, feline smile at the unmistakable click of the door unlocking.

Inside was dark, ominously so. The only light to flood in right in front of us on through a long window made the prominent desk and tall back seat appear as daunting figures of judgment even though they were vacant.

"You should have brought a torch," Nadia said, already across the room. I figured her vampire sight was a little more advanced than ours.

To my command, the key flared to life in its staff form and I smiled proudly. "I did."

"What is that thing?" Nadia asked curiously.

I didn't know how to explain what the key was. It could do many things—*an extension of my magick,* as Nyte had called it.

"Astraea," Rose said my name with a note of dread that slithered down my spine before I turned around.

My heart stopped.

I didn't feel my movements but as I got closer to the wall Rose stared up at the light from the key revealed unmistakable finer detail with every step.

We stared at celestial wings.

Huge, breathtaking wings.

They had to be a life-size replica. They couldn't be real.

I didn't bask in their beauty; I had to know for certain.

My hand was compelled to reach for them, to touch those shimming silver feathers . . .

I gasped sharply when my mind flooded with images the moment I did.

A grim, horrifying reel played for me, showing that I was no longer in that office.

I was somewhere so terribly cold. In a small square cage high off the ground. There was no color, hardly any light. And worst of all, it spanned years of lonely isolation.

"Astraea!" Rose snapped my name and I plummeted back into myself with a harsh shake of my shoulders.

"They're real," I breathed.

Oh stars . . .

"And I think . . ." I shook my head, dizzy with the confusion and pain of what it meant. "I think they're still alive. The celestial they belong to."

I thought I might be sick. Sinking to my knees I tried to scramble for any reason for why Reihan would have someone's wings. Perhaps he'd won them, or bought them from some sick poacher. The explanation for why he owned them could be a mere innocent though ignorant admiration of the celestials. Right now, it's all I could believe because the alternative I couldn't fathom.

Reihan was like a father to me. Always so kind and warm, even though I knew there was a side to him that had to be firm and sometimes harsh in order to rule the people of Alisus.

"Someone's coming," Nadia hissed at the door. "They're far away enough that we can get down that hall before being seen but we have to go *now.*"

I wasn't ready to leave. What else could I find in this room? I could discover where he'd bought them and begin to trace the poacher. What if they were still at large, capturing innocent celestials that ventured out of their safety behind their veil?

Rose pulled my arm to get me to leave but one last lingering look at his office chilled me with a sense of foreboding. This enlightenment to what cruelty lurked in the world showed that Nyte had been right about what he'd told me on the rooftops in the city during the Libertatem; battles came around and ended, but war was ever-present.

PART
FOUR

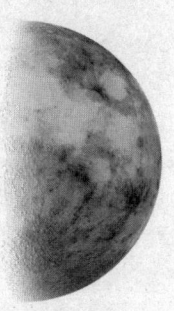

27

Nyte–Past

The summers were becoming shorter each year, and this winter was beginning to feel endless.

Nyte stifled a shiver from the cold whistling through the cracks of the long neglected library they'd ventured to in a corner of Arania. He plucked a book from the old shelf, squinting with little interest at the small script. Astraea's light laughter drew his eyes to her as she sat unbothered by the dust of the old seating she reclined on next to Drystan, their noses stuck in books likely far afield from what they'd come to this hopeless abandoned library for.

Over their time spent trying to scour the land for any knowledge and following any leads to seers, mages, and tricksters . . . he'd watched the pair become concerningly close. Only for the mischief that was tangible between them. If his father knew they'd been meeting with the star-maiden for so long, Nyte didn't think his rage would spare their lives for this.

Nyte kept to himself as much as he could, but as the months turned to years and the years passed suddenly too fast, he found the days, or weeks, she wasn't around became hollow. Astraea also kept their meets secret, and both their travels were passed off as a truth wrapped in a lie: that they were hunting each other.

"I don't know what you could find about the realm's history that could be humorous," Nyte muttered.

When Astraea flashed those silver-blue eyes at him, twinkling with mischief, her attention on him fluttered in his chest.

It did so often and he tried to ignore it, but the small truth that he allowed his dark mind to hold was that he enjoyed it.

"You know, I've often wondered if you're capable of a smile," she replied.

Drystan didn't look up from his book as he said, "So have I."

Astraea was leaning into him, turning the pages of the book in his palms when he didn't do it fast enough and giggling over whatever they were looking at. Nyte couldn't understand his feelings at the sight. He'd never had such light occupy his mind without the itch to expel it.

The star-maiden was unbiased to what Drystan was—a blood vampire. She was raised to be neutral about all species even though both the soulless and shadowless had begun siding with his father to overthrow her in masses growing larger each day.

"This is the last library we know of," Nyte said, approaching them.

Astraea's face fell with this news. She knew already that they were running out of options to discover the origin of the quakes and how to stop them.

"There's one temple left," he hedged.

They'd been to all of them. Yet he wondered why Astraea had often diverted from the one he thought they should have tried, or at least she could have, a long time ago.

Her feet swept off the table she'd perched them on, and she ran a hand down her face. Nyte stilled with the urge to do something for the distress rising in her. He could feel them, the shifts in her that had grown stronger in their time spent together.

He was becoming so acutely in tune with her it was frightening. He'd never feared anything in his life.

Nyte asked carefully, "Why won't you reach out to your parents?"

Astraea huffed a laugh. A mocking sound.

"They've never been *parents*. They are gods, nothing more."

He'd never expected to find himself on common ground with his enemy.

"You are the Daughter of Dusk and Dawn. They might help."

"I am a duty, not a daughter. Created, not born. Raised by six guardians, not parents."

"Nyte is created too," Drystan said casually with half attention as he kept flipping through his book. "Technically."

Nyte's jaw locked, wishing he wasn't here right now.

"Hardly the same," he grumbled.

"What do you mean?" Astraea asked. The interest she harbored wasn't simply for knowledge about him . . . but rather it was like she exposed a side of herself that was longing to find a relation to something. When those who surrounded her in Vesitire and Althenia could never understand what she was.

"Nightsdeath," Drystan answered her.

"Maybe you should take a walk, little brother," Nyte said tightly.

Drystan looked about to protest, until he looked up and saw it was an instruction, not a request. He groaned under his breath, thumping his book shut and kicking his feet off the table.

"If something terrible is lurking in dark corners to devour me—"

"I'll make sure you're commemorated bravely."

Drystan sauntered off with a huff. The silence between Nyte and Astraea grew uncomfortable.

"He shouldn't have said anything," Nyte said, wanting to strangle his brother.

Astraea was still their enemy, and he wasn't foolish enough to think she wouldn't turn on them as easily as Nyte could her. Once they found the answer they were looking for, he was prepared for the battle to rise between them.

"You don't have to tell me," she said, dropping her sight to brush over pages aimlessly.

Her disappointment tugged a thread within him, clamping his fists by his sides. Would it matter if she knew things about him? When it came time, he supposed it wouldn't. It would be his power against hers and knowing the origins of him couldn't grant her an upper hand.

Nyte sighed, gravitating toward the old leather seat. He sat beside her, sinking down and not anticipating the small size that had them nearly touching. He'd thought being near her would keep the tension locked in his body. But instead, he eased.

"My full name is Rainyte," he began, picking a book from the stack for a distraction. "But it didn't feel right to keep when it belonged to a child named by his mother he was torn away from. But nothing is chance, and that child was bestowed a gift that would become a curse. *Made* into what would become the realm's nightmare by the name of Nightsdeath."

He stole a glance, finding her delicate face thoughtful.

"So you see, we're not so different after all," he said quietly. "Only you are made of light, and me of dark."

"Some might call that balance. That you were created for something good after all."

"Or destruction. Created to bring nothing but terror."

"Not everyone is afraid of the dark."

Nyte mapped every inch of her face, resisting the urge to reach for a strand of glittering silver hair that hung loose from her braids.

"No one fears the dark. They fear what can lurk within it."

"Hey, look what I found!" Drystan's voice echoed from down a bookcase.

He came into view waving a parchment.

Nyte hooked an unimpressed brow. "A map?"

Drystan smiled, mischievous. He set it down, saying, "Kateran Keep."

They watched the paper, and to his surprise, the ink started shifting. When it finished, the full keep came into clarity. He'd never seen such an enchanted item before.

Nyte swiped it up faster than his brother's protest could stop him.

"Vesitire," he said to it.

Nothing moved.

When Drystan huffed a laugh in satisfaction, Nyte almost tore the damn parchment.

"It doesn't like you, give it here," Drystan said.

Astraea plucked it from his fingers first. "Vesitire," she repeated for him.

It didn't answer her either.

Drystan's grin was insufferable.

Astraea said, "It must only answer to one person at once. Perhaps it would switch if Drystan gave up ownership as it seems to have attached itself to him."

"This place is centuries abandoned," Drystan thought out loud. "It's past owner could be dead, and it was just waiting for the next."

"It's an item of the Wanderers Trove," Nyte realized.

"Like the compass that doesn't work? Is there anything else?" Astraea asked.

Nyte drew a long breath, leaning back to try to recall the story he'd learned from an old man in a tavern once. He'd thought it was just a drunken tale for entertainment that engrossed the room at the time.

"I think there's a monocular telescope. They say it can reveal lost islands or doors or items. It uncloaks anything hidden by magick. These three trove items make someone a master traveler and treasurer."

"We need to find that," Drystan said with a giddy edge.

"Not what we need right now," Nyte said.

Drystan rolled his eyes as he folded and pocketed the map. "You're not very fun."

Nyte ignored him, halfway to lifting a book from the table when a loud sound, like a roar mixed with a wail, shot him and Astraea to their feet in alarm.

"What the hell was that?" Drystan said.

"What else did you touch?" Nyte demanded.

"Nothing!"

It sounded again and Astraea's key glowed to life in the appearance of her legendary staff.

"We should get out of here," Nyte said.

Contrary to his warning, Astraea headed through the bookcases.

Toward the creature's sound.

She was impossible. Yet Nyte followed after her. Perhaps some action would help to ease his boredom that had been growing over the last few months of travel and no findings. Nothing at all except suffering close company far too often with Astraea and Drystan, who'd bloomed something of a near intolerable friendship.

"This is not a good idea," he warned, but he knew there was no dissuading her.

The bookcases in front of them exploded and Nyte's power struck out on instinct. Waves of his darkness surged toward the threat but it was repelled by a huge white feathered wing. Nyte wasn't thinking when his arm hooked around Astraea, pulling her to him to avoid the counterattack from the beast that came with just as much force.

Pressed to the nearest bookcase, he watched the power blast by, trying to decipher what it was when it looked like what he could conjure—smoky darkness littered with stars.

"It's a celestial dragon," Astraea said with wonder, barely audible over the commotion.

The creature wailed again.

"Run!" he barked at Drystan.

His younger brother took off but Astraea pushed off him to face the creature.

"Are you planning to talk to it?" Nyte said sarcastically, charging his dark energy.

"It's wounded," Astraea said, so entranced by the giant threatening creature Nyte was ready to kill.

He examined the huge beast that had wrecked dozens of bookcases around it. Its mighty wings hung lazily. Someone, or likely it would have taken several people, had sawn away at its shoulders and they were shorn of many feathers. Some were bare like long fish bones. Nyte pitied the mighty creature that had been overpowered by mere mortals, who took away its ability to fly.

"Someone clipped them?" Nyte concluded.

"It's barbaric," Astraea seethed.

The dragon cried out again and they winced at the sound.

"We're either getting the fuck out of here or I'm killing it," Nyte warned.

"Don't you dare." Astraea pinned him with a lethal look of warning.

Nyte internally groaned. Of course this wasn't going to be an easy out.

"A dare is a musical challenge to me, Starlight."

Astraea appeared ready to fight *him,* but the dragon's chest expanded and its neck straightened, ready to blast another round of what he assumed to be some kind of shadowfire at them.

This time, Nyte circled Astraea's waist and traveled through the void to evade the attack. They stood behind the dragon as it finished breathing fire. It must have felt them as it immediately swung around and they had no choice but to dive out of the way as its lame wing came close to projecting them across the room. More bookcases were torn through, but before Nyte could cast out his power to avoid the rain of sharp wood stakes and books, a gale of light encompassed them as a shield from Astraea.

"Thanks," he said through a breath.

"Don't mention it." They fumbled up to stand over the wreckage around them. "I mean it, don't."

With the next roar, he wondered if it was his own adrenaline that thought the beast was getting more pissed off. Nyte didn't think when he took Astraea's hand and they raced through the library.

"Over here!"

Nyte swore at the sound of Drystan's voice echoing from somewhere lower and distant. He hoped his brother was safely outside but a part of him knew he wouldn't be that fucking compliant.

They winced at the loud tumbling of stone as the dragon tore through walls to follow hot on their trail. Nyte's intuition of the darkness felt the prickling of its approach across his nape just in time to duck into the next alcove and pull Astraea into him. He held her tightly to his front and they panted hard to catch their breath.

"Remind me why we're not just killing it?" Nyte snapped.

"Celestial dragons have been believed extinct; we can't just kill it!" she hissed back. "It's only attacking because it thinks we're a threat. You can't really blame it for the treatment it's endured by mortal hands."

"Right, and you want to become smoke and ash for what?"

She pushed off him, and Nyte cursed all the hells as she ran and he after her.

"Just let me handle this. Don't get in my way."

He had a lot to say about that, but he kept it to himself. It wasn't that he thought her incapable; what he despised was the acknowledgment that *he* was incapable of leaving her in danger.

They skidded into a smaller hall that had been torn down. In the center was a giant nest like the dragon had made themselves a home here. Nyte could kill his brother right now, standing in the middle of the dragon's den, a dead end with no door on the other side. But what he stared down at . . .

"Stars above," Astraea breathed in awe.

It was a celestial dragon egg. A stunning stark black with silver etchings.

"You decided to come to the one place that'll piss it off more for our trespassing?" Nyte snarled.

The crashing amplified and if they didn't get the hell out of here now they were going to—

Nyte's magick expelled from him out of instinct. Darkness struck the creature behind them and its roar turned to a cry of pain.

"Stop!" Astraea said, advancing forward, and Nyte jerked, almost following her.

He studied her and the beast with a laser focus, ready to disregard her request to strike it again if it so much as showed a flicker of attack. Right now it huddled into itself and the viciousness it found them with fell, revealing a frightened, beaten animal.

Nyte watched Astraea raise a hand and when the beast snarled Nyte's shadows swirled his fingers.

She wasn't afraid. Astraea's metallic tattoos glowed brighter the closer she got, like her magick was recognizing the dragon as kin. Then she spoke. Words not of our language or any he'd heard before. The soothing speech was as delicate as it was fierce. Like an enchanting song that, even though it was for the dragon, Nyte felt hypnotized by, resisting the urge to kneel to her. It calmed the beast, who laid down its head as if it *bowed* to her.

"She's in pain," Astraea whispered, her voice choked with emotion, and Nyte turned stiff.

He was in pain. With the star-maiden's distress and he didn't know how to be rid of it. This ache inside him *for* her.

"We have to leave it," Nyte said, approaching her and the tired dragon.

"We can't." When she turned her head to him and her silver eyes glistened with tears, he was slammed with the pressure to stop them from falling.

Nyte was utterly compelled by her, reaching without conscious effort to touch her wet cheeks. He didn't know what this was, only that he couldn't stand this sight and needed to eradicate anything that could invoke this sadness in her.

"What do you need me to do?" he asked, and it was like he gave her all the power over him with that token.

Astraea's sight weighed to the ground with sorrow before casting back to the dragon. She reached out a hand and Nyte's whole body tensed when she made contact with the beast. It gave a huff like a dozen horses at once, then a soft whine. Such a contrast to what had chased them moments before.

It was then that he understood the creature. When agony turned peaceful things sharp. It broke out claws and teeth and all it took was one vicious reaction from the pain to be condemned to that reputation.

"We can't leave her here like this." Astraea sniffed, wiping her tears on her sleeve, and looked to where Drystan still stood by the egg. "She's only held on this long to guard it."

Nyte understood what she was asking. What needed to be done, but Astraea didn't have it in her to kill the beast even to end its suffering.

"Take it. I'll meet you outside," Nyte said.

Astraea's eyes held him with gratitude he didn't deserve. He was only doing what he was known for, after all. Death.

"Can you make it painless?"

He gave her a nod, and it was in that moment he realized the trust she gave him was genuine and without doubt. As he watched her say her silent farewell, calming the beast more so that it settled down like it understood it was all over, Nyte didn't expect the feelings that lingered when she left with Drystan carrying the egg.

She trusted him.

Why did that feel more terrifying to him than the thought of her as the enemy?

He didn't know when it had happened, but that term—*enemy*—seemed fitting only in politics and duty now. For somewhere along their quest, he'd been silently, unwittingly, ensnared by the beautiful poison of her that tasted precious and valuable but it turned a steel guard to fragile glass.

He cared for her.

No—that felt too little for what he was willing to become for her. When he knew he'd be a shield if danger was near. Or a sword if a threat advanced. *Shit,* he would even take her in his arms if it would stop those tears from falling.

He'd felt the racing in his chest before. It was like the adrenaline of war and that's what she'd become. His war. Something he had to fight against because it was not their destiny to be anything else on mortal opposite sides of everything.

Dark and light.

Vampires and celestials.

Him and her . . . it was a twisted, dark mockery that taunted the bond between two who could never be.

Nyte grew bitterly resentful and turned his focus to the dragon. He had to admit, a part of him despaired at the end of such a magnificent creature's life, and more so because it had spent its last centuries in lonely misery. Nyte came to the sinking thoughts he could relate to in its torment.

Approaching, the beast tracked him with large purple eyes with slit pupils. He reached out a hand and was hit with so much pain and suffering his teeth clenched tightly. While he distracted the creature's mind, his shadow magick crept around the dragon. While it could cause immeasurable agony and terrifying hallucinations, his darkness could also be peaceful and gentle. The beast's eyes grew tired and shut. Its loud heartbeat slowed.

Just before the silence of death fell, Nyte's mind was battered with impossible images.

He saw Astraea, but she appeared different somehow. So lost and fragile.

Then he looked up at a tall barrier of rippling starlight that felt like his magick but he didn't know what it was dividing.

He was shown Drystan, but his brother's usually bright hazel eyes were so disturbingly cold and loathing.

Then he heard the roar of a different dragon, seeing one with membranous wings and red tipped talons and horns.

Finally, Nyte saw himself . . . kneeling in a small crater around deserted ash-clogged land, but it was his cry, a sound of the most absolute agony, he didn't know could tear him apart for what—*who*—he cradled . . .

Nyte ripped his hand back, but it was too late to demand what it all meant.

The echoing terror of that final vision drummed hard in his chest.

Nyte didn't know what to think. How to feel. He wandered out of that library feeling vacant until the freezing air hit his face. Glancing up, Astraea and Drystan huddled close on the snow covered steps. She held the dragon egg, examining it as his brother was studying a book, and they chatted quietly.

"It's done," he said, words that were almost lost in the whistling wind, but Astraea heard him.

She stood, hugging the egg to her body, and Nyte didn't care about anything anymore. Not the dragons, nor the quest to find the quakes.

He couldn't explain why he never wanted to let Astraea out of his sight again and resisted a strong pull of gravity to her right now.

"We found something else," Drystan said, coming up beside Astraea.

Nyte barely registered his brother. He couldn't take his eyes off the star-maiden.

"Are you okay?" Astraea asked carefully. Her face pinched in concern, as if it was killing the dragon that disturbed him.

Astraea unexpectedly stepped toward him, and his whole body turned taut at the arm she circled around him, only one while she still cradled the egg but her warmth seeped into him. He didn't know what to do.

"You're a terrible hugger," she mumbled.

"Tell me about it," Drystan said.

Nyte glanced down to see her small smile to that, and he relaxed, thinking of nothing but right now.

She was safe.

Right here.

She wasn't going anywhere.

Nyte held her. Slipping an arm around her shoulders and his other hand cupped her head on his chest. He'd never felt this before. Every muscle in his body eased and he didn't want to let go. He wanted to draw her tighter when it suddenly didn't feel like enough.

He wanted her alone—like that time in the cabin she'd been wrapped around him. Nyte didn't know what love was, but he thought, just for a few vulnerable seconds, that he could come to find the answer in her.

An answer he couldn't want.

"Thank you," she whispered.

"What else did you find?" Nyte asked. His throat tight.

Astraea took that as her sign to let him go, and the coldness of her absence was like a lash of punishment for craving her warmth when it could drift away at any moment.

"A diary, I think, but the text is in a language neither of us have seen before. It's *old*," Drystan said, squinting at the pages. "This was also inside."

He held up a transparent piece of paper the likes of which Nyte had never seen before. It had an intricate drawing of a dragon on it but Nyte thought there was a constellation through it.

"What does it do?" Nyte asked.

Drystan shrugged. "We've been puzzling over it."

It seemed the least of their concerns right now. "What do we do with *that?*" Nyte pointed to the black and silver egg.

Astraea held it protectively, marveling over the silver swirls that reminded him of her metallic tattoos.

"I think it could be alive," she said. "I just don't know what it takes to hatch it. No one knows a lot about the dragons, even the celestials. It's been over a thousand years. For now, I'm going to place it with a guardian I know will keep it safe."

Her brow crumpled and Nyte knew she was reflecting on how long the beast inside had been suffering. Even he felt sorrow, but it was sleeping peacefully now.

Astraea slipped her sight to him, and her small smiles felt so precious all of a sudden—like he had to capture each one and store it away for safekeeping because they could be numbered. This world wouldn't survive if that was true.

It had been Nyte's primary order to eliminate the star-maiden. Now he feared she might be the only thing that could save the world . . .

From *him*.

28

Astraea

Drystan knew how to hatch the egg. It was the only conclusion I had and what Nyte had shown me of the past was what his brother was waiting for me to see.

I figured he'd found out from the diary, somehow translated it. So much was unveiled to me in that one memory that my mind was spinning faster than it ever had.

The map—it all made sense now. I dipped into my pocket for the enchanted item I kept close. It was invaluable and yet Drystan had given ownership of it to me.

I couldn't figure out his motive yet but suddenly I was cursing myself for coming to Alisus. As much as I wanted—needed—to see the guardians, my heart was urging me toward this new path. I felt so close to discovering more about the celestial dragons and that became an exhilarating rush.

I walked the halls of the keep like the fresh air would help me sort through my tangling emotions.

The temple.

The dragon egg.

Both had to wait for one other thing I needed to confront while I was in the keep. Though as I headed to find Reihan, I wasn't entirely sure how to approach the subject of the celestial wings in his office without exposing our infiltration that would break his trust.

"Sleep well?"

Those two words stroked like a lick of smoke at the tip of my spine. Nyte's illusion was *very* convincing, strolling by my side with his hands casually in his pockets.

"I hid the egg in the maze," I said, still in disbelief.

"You did."

"The map . . . we were there when Drystan found it."

I kept replaying the memory that held so many clues to the present. It hurt to see how close I'd been with Drystan, even feeling it through Nyte's obser-vation of us, yet the younger brother I knew in this life often regarded me like I was nothing at all to him anymore.

"Yes."

"I need to meet with him again."

"Is that a good idea after the last time?"

I winced recalling the outburst that had come over me. Though it had felt damned good to unleash at the time and I couldn't promise it wouldn't happen again.

"I'm sure you'd enjoy the reaction it could pull out of me."

"Absolutely. I'm restless to taste your rage and feel your power again."

"Are you not angry with me?"

"What for?"

"The humiliation in front of everyone—the bargain I placed on you."

Nyte merely shrugged. "Trust I feel not an ounce of embarrassment at what you did. I'm still glowing with the pride of it and it was genius to my advantage that the vampires think you escaped and I had no choice. But you and I both know it's only a matter of time before I come for you."

I shivered at that.

"The bond I made could kill you if you do."

Nyte reached for my hand and I let him pull me into the shadows. It was too convincing; he was too damn tempting. I was taken back to all the times he'd come to me like this, unable to truly reach me.

"I've told you before, I'm well acquainted with death. To reach you, it's the last thing that would stop me."

My hands met his chest when his circled my waist. *He's not real.* It was all I could chant to myself to pretend this didn't count as anything.

"How do I know you're showing me the truth?" I whispered.

Auster and Rosalind's doubt had nagged at me several times.

"Come back to me; we can bind a truth bargain."

Nyte chuckled at my groan.

"I've had enough of bargains for a lifetime," I said.

"For two lifetimes."

"None in the third, then."

"Deal," Nyte said low, before tipping my chin up to him and leaning his mouth to mine.

I was lost to him that second. Shamelessly, my hands curled into his jacket, pressing into him tighter, and before I knew it I was *frustrated* with him for not being real.

I broke away with that unwanted disappointment. I'd made the spectacle to show the vampires I wasn't weak, and I'd left Nyte's side to prove it to myself.

"You don't look too well," he observed, scanning my face like it would reveal deeper details about my troubles.

I cupped my forehead. "I'm fine, just a little tired."

"You need to eat and rest. I'll come for you now just to make sure you do."

I tried to pull on a mask of absolute health with a charming smile. He knew what I was doing, but he said nothing, perhaps anticipating I'd bite back at the coddling.

"Do I get a tour?" Nyte asked, tipping my silver hair over my shoulder.

"You've never been here before?"

"I've never had reason to. Alisus has actually had the least vampire problems."

I thought to ask Nyte about what had been disturbing my mind since last night.

"Have you ever known of celestials having their wings . . . taken?" My stomach rolled at the mere thought. Picturing Nyte's stunning midnight wings on that wall ached in my chest.

"Yes. It was punishable by death to be caught selling or even in possession of celestial wings. Some poached them just for triumph and decoration. Like all crimes and evil, the law doesn't stop it from happening. Sometimes it even tempts the hunger of the wicked more."

"Does it kill the celestial?"

"Not usually. But it's an unimaginable pain to have them sawn or torn off, and they don't often recover mentally from the ordeal." My horror filled gaze met his. Even Nyte displayed his abhorrence for it. "Why do you ask?"

I paused to contemplate what he might do or say if I told him what I'd found.

"If there was a pair of wings and I touched them . . . would I know if the person was still alive?"

Nyte's arm pulled me against him again. His eyes searched mine, filling with concern.

I was distracted for a moment by the real force of his touch. Then by the fact that my hair stayed over my shoulder when I thought the illusion that he'd touched it would be broken. Those were the tells I'd learned when I reflected on his illusion appearances.

"You can manipulate things from afar now?" I concluded.

Nyte's hard frown of interrogation smoothed for a second of twinkling satisfaction.

"I was wondering when you'd notice," he said with a low gravel to his tone. Nyte's hand headed lower, toward the cut of my skirt. Heat gathered inappropriately between my legs. "I'd still much rather be with you in person, but I could demonstrate how real of an impression I can make now."

"How?" I said, letting him continue his sinful roaming when it dulled my headache for a moment.

"I drank your blood, you drank mine. It's a far stronger connection for me. Magick is . . . pliable."

Nyte twisted with me, pushing me against the wall in a small alcove with a low growl, and my face pinched when he hooked under my knee to press himself into me tighter.

"I think I've stayed away long enough," he purred.

"I could still banish you with a thought."

"Do it. I dare you."

I was on the verge of it when these dares and silent battles awoke a dormant language between us. But I wasn't going to entertain him so easily.

"Have you seen Drystan again?"

"I don't want to hear his name, or anyone's, when I have my cock pressed against you."

"Technically, you don't."

I whimpered at the firm drag of him against my core.

"Stop," I rasped, becoming hyperaware of how this would look if anyone wandered down here.

Nyte smiled wickedly. He kissed the edge of my jaw.

"Is that really what you want?"

No. I wanted him to finish what he'd started when the temptation of him was right here.

"Please," I whispered. I had pitiful resistance.

His hand reached between us, slipping under my skirt, and his other hand clamped over my mouth anticipating the moan I couldn't bite back when he circled between my legs.

"You are so wet," he growled. "While I'm bending your mind to come for me on my hand here, I have my fist around my cock, imagining it inside you instead of my fingers."

I choked on a sharp inhale when he curved two fingers inside me, stretching me full. My hips rocked against his hand, chasing the pleasure faster with the rush of adrenaline that came with knowing anyone could come by.

"Best be quick, love. How scandalous you would look here."

His thumb pressed against my sensitive bud as he fucked me harder, faster with the curve of his fingers. What was driving my lust wild was the thought of him touching himself to the same rhythm—thinking of me and how I felt wrapped around his fingers.

"Are you hard for me?" I whispered. Nyte planted his other hand by my head as I pulled his head down and he watched his hand working under my skirt. "Wishing your cock was fucking me instead."

"Yes," he rasped, like he was as close to a release as I was.

I tightened around his fingers, teetering right on the edge. This was so different and daring but it felt so good and real I didn't care.

"Fuck."

"Come for me, Nyte," I said across his ear.

Reaching my hand down I dragged the heel of my palm down his hard cock and that pushed him over first. He tensed against me, and picturing him sitting in his room or office, hand pumping his cock and releasing to every thought of me, sent my orgasm crashing over me in waves.

My head tipped back against the stone wall with a silent cry and I shuddered violently. Nyte kept fucking me as if he was spending himself inside me.

We both came down in a panting mess, his his forehead buried in my neck.

"That was unexpected," he said, breathless. "But absolutely thrilling."

I shivered with his fingers pulling out of me. Pressing my palms against the wall, I tried to scramble the pieces of me back together as my leg unhooked from around Nyte.

"Miss, are you all right?"

My pulse leaped up my throat—literally. I coughed and swallowed to force it back down to be able to respond to the guard who had come out of nowhere. Nyte chuckled darkly, not even moving for the company that stood right in front of me because only I could see the scandal of Nyte pressed against me, mouth hovering at my ear.

"Better respond," he taunted, kissing my neck.

That bastard.

"Just fine, thank you," I barely squeaked the words, needing him to leave when I couldn't move.

"Should I get someone for you?" The guard asked in concern for the flustered mess of me.

"No, I'm just taking a moment."

Leave me the fuck alone.

Nyte wouldn't stop trailing his lips along my collar. I could banish him, and there was something twistedly wrong with me that I didn't.

"If you're sure, ma'am."

I nodded, a little too eagerly, but with a wary look over, he continued on his way.

My hands flattened on Nyte's chest and pushed the moment he was gone and I scowled deeply to his smirk of amusement. It didn't put much distance between us.

He tucked a strand of hair behind my ear. "I miss you."

"Then you need more things to occupy yourself."

"Trust I could be in the midst of a war outnumbered five to one and still be missing you. Do you forget the centuries I've waited?"

He knew how to make me forget everything that should be driving us apart.

Nyte backtracked our conversation. "Why did you ask about the wings?"

"Reihan has a pair of silver wings in his office," I said, scanning the hall.

"But before you jump to any conclusions I'm going to find out why. I don't believe he knows of such laws when two human lifespans generations have passed since people saw celestials wander freely. They've been thought extinct or even an old fable."

Nyte's silence was frightening. His jaw worked like he was trying to hold back his impulse to disregard all I tried to defend. He might be their greatest enemy, but Nyte was disturbed by the idea of the celestials being poached for their wings.

"If there's even one hint he knows more than he lets on, trust your instinct. It's never led you astray, but sometimes your good heart tries to ignore it because of something you don't want to believe."

I nodded. Then, with a drop of disappointment, I said, "I need to go."

"I'll always answer your thoughts if you call. But if you long for me—"

"You'll become an irritating, tangible force."

His smile lifted my spirit. "Always," he said. Then kissed me firmly.

Nyte was gone when I opened my eyes and became lonely in his absence.

29

Astraea

I spent the next hour looking for Rose and Zath but found no sight of them, nor did my inquiries to passing guards produce answers. Beginning to grow anxious, I turned the next corner and found Calix heading toward me.

My relief at finding a friendly face turned to tension when I looked over his uniform.

"You're staying?" I asked.

"I had a change of heart," he said, but it was distant. Emotionless. "The reigning lord sent me for you."

"You said you wouldn't be able to live in this place with the constant reminder of her," I accused him.

Something didn't feel right.

"This is her home. It's the best place to keep her memory alive."

I couldn't figure out what might have changed his mind so suddenly. When we'd arrived he looked ready to leave. He could hardly stand to look around the keep.

"What happened?" I asked.

"Nothing. Let's go."

"Why would Reihan send you for me?"

"He's requested you join him for dinner."

That should be harmless enough. I would be able to ask him what he knew about the celestials and it might lead to an explanation about the wings in his office. Yet as I walked with Calix, I couldn't banish the unsettling feeling in my gut.

"Have you seen Rose or Zath?" I asked him.

"No."

I slipped a look up to him at that short answer. He wouldn't look at me and my walk slowed a little.

Your intuition has never led you astray.

"I'm not actually hungry," I said. "Can you tell him I retired for the night?"

Calix hooked my elbow when I tried to turn back. My pulse slammed.

I ripped my arm free as I spun to him, hovering my hand over the key at my hip as I took backward paces.

"What's going on?" I asked.

As I stepped under the open archways, the snow fell around me in the small open courtyard. Memories of Cassia's last training session flooded me from this space.

Calix didn't answer, merely waited with a steely expression before glancing around me. I chilled at the sight of the guards surrounding the archways.

"Astraea—" Calix said my name like a hint of a plea but he was interrupted by a voice I wished wasn't responsible for whatever the fuck was happening.

"You have no idea how long you spent here as a blood supply," Reihan said as he crept out from a shadow cover.

I didn't recognize him. The demeanor. The cruel smile foreign to his kind face.

"Why are you doing this?"

I didn't know what his intentions were, but from the armed guards blocking every escape around me, I knew he meant to capture me, at least.

"You'll find out soon enough, maiden. Now, do you want to come easily or is this going to be difficult?"

My answer pulsed warmly in my hand when the key expanded to a glowing staff and I firmed my stance.

"You don't want to do this," I warned him. Even though betrayal was stabbing in my back, I didn't want to hurt him. "He'll come for me. And he is not merciful."

I shuddered to think what Nyte would do.

More than just killing Calix and Reihan—what if he destroyed the entire keep in his wrath?

Noises of a struggle rattled my composure. I knew before I saw them that my odds had been damned.

Rose and Zath were dragged out and pushed to their knees. Not Nadia. Though I wasn't surprised, as she was gifted at appearing and disappearing.

"You're not going to let that happen," Reihan said. "Or I start cutting them into pieces."

"Why are you doing this?" I said, my voice reduced to a heartbroken, pathetic whimper.

This wasn't the man I knew. Cassia's father was warm and safe and welcomed me just like any of his daughters.

"You're going to help me end Nyte once and for all."

I blinked at that. It didn't make any sense—why would Reihan want Nyte dead so badly as to risk all of this? It wouldn't stop the vampires or save his land.

My heartbreak sharpened to anger that aimed my daggers of hatred toward Calix.

"How could you?" I seethed.

When Calix said nothing, gave no reaction, I broke.

The key pulsed a flare of light that shot at him. It slammed his chest and maybe I was a weak coward for not adding enough force to it to kill him.

The other guards drew their blades and I didn't know if I could take them all but I felt myself beginning to reel into a focus that would damn well try.

"Fly, Astraea!" Rose shouted.

Reihan's hand connected with her cheek and she cried out from the brutal force. I'd never seen Zath so angry, and he lunged, almost reaching the lord before he had to turn his focus on the three guards who were attacking him.

I couldn't leave them here.

Through my magick I felt the ice of the ground. My hand moved—a vertical swipe then my palm upturned—with magick that awakened in me; the snow formed into dozens of ice shards floating the perimeter. I might have admired the spectacle of it were I not trembling with the effort it took to hold it.

But dark thoughts started to trickle into my mind with the display of power I wielded.

I could kill them all.

Send every spear of ice shooting around the square at once. I wondered if I should be horrified by my contemplation—that the only thing that spared the blood of these soldiers on my hands was the fact that I wasn't confident enough yet in my precision to spare my friends in the attack.

My heartbeats of deliberation became my downfall.

Fire exploded in my shoulder from the piercing of an arrow. My knees crashed to the ground and my consciousness started slipping rapidly.

I'd experienced an arrow shot before but this type of seizing pain was something far more incapacitating. It set my blood boiling beneath my skin but my agony was silent to the world. I couldn't open my mouth to release the screams tearing me apart inside.

"The arrow is laced with Nebulora. It's a poison to your kind," Reihan said. He crouched by me and I could do nothing but kneel in my broken misery. "Rainyte won't be able to feel you for a while."

How did he know his full name? I tried to shake my head but it was as heavy as stone. So I gave up, unable to tell him that that was what I was afraid of. That Nyte didn't need to know exactly what was wrong. It was only a matter of days that he would be content not to hear from me before, perhaps thinking I was blocking him on purpose, he defied my bond to come for me.

Reihan took me in his arms and I couldn't fight it. I was losing my senses one by one. Unable to hear like I was drowning. Not feeling anything except the spreading pain through me. I could only see the blurry white sky until I was carried under the archways.

"Oh maiden, how elusive and smart you are. I severely underestimated you and never thought our paths would cross like this."

"I don't . . . I don't understand."

"Shhh," he said gently. "You will. Sleep for now."

30

Astraea

Every time I woke it was a punishment. I didn't know how many days had passed. My mind was foggy, my throat was dry, and I couldn't peel myself from the hard ground I lay against. I had a cushion under my head and a blanket, but I was freezing.

Today was a little better. I came around enough to know my shoulder was bandaged but it ached so much with every movement that I often wanted to fall back asleep to escape the pain. My skin was slicked with fever. Maybe it was infected, or maybe I was still suffering the remnants of the poison Reihan had called *Nebulora*.

My eyes opened and I could finally get them to focus but I wished to be oblivious instead when the sight of the iron poles crushed my spirit. A tear slipped out the corner of my eye as I lay staring at them, wondering if I would ever be free of cages, or if I would always be this little bird easily captured in the palms of others.

I pushed myself up, gritting my teeth with the screaming pain of my dormant muscles. Panic rattled me when the ground beneath me *moved* and I gasped, thinking my disorientation was swaying my balance. Until my sight slipped out past the bars and horror doused me, seeing the true ground was far below. The cage I was in was suspended high in some kind of underground prison hall. Cells lined high up the walls too but they were vacant.

"Astraea."

The whisper of my name was timid but it shocked me like a siren. I winced with a sob at the sharp stabbing in my neck, whipping around toward the direction it came from.

I wasn't alone.

It was both a relief and absolutely horrifying to discover that inside another suspended cage a short distance from mine was a woman. She was beautiful with blonde hair and green eyes but the hollowness of her face along with the worn scraps of clothing she wore made it clear that she had been here for some time.

"How do you know my name?" I asked. My throat was hoarse and my voice barely came out in a croak.

The woman frowned, then her expression saddened, and I didn't know why I felt like I had disappointed her. She inched closer to the bars facing me.

"It's me, Katerina. I—we were friends."

That fact slammed into me, and my hand braced to catch me from the wave of dizziness.

"You don't remember," Katerina concluded, and the small glimmer of hope on her face wiped away completely.

I was overcome with guilt. "I'm sorry."

She smiled sadly, sitting back against her cage with her blanket. "Don't be. I was part of one of the first groups that left Althenia to look for you five years ago."

"Look for me?"

She nodded. "Auster and the other High Celestials decided to send groups of us to search for you when we all felt the quake of your return to land five years ago. Did they find you?"

"Yes," I whispered vacantly.

All this time . . .

My people had been looking for me when I'd been cluelessly locked away in Goldfell Manor. Celestials were risking their lives in search of someone who was of no help or use to them.

I thought about Auster now with more guilt that I hadn't made efforts to see him again in weeks. He'd risked so much for me.

"Why did he capture you?" I asked. This couldn't be about me. I had to figure out what Reihan had been doing.

"For my blood," she said. "I believe he trades it to vampires to keep them away."

Stars above.

It was so cruel and heinous I struggled to believe the man I knew was capable of it. Reihan was like a father to me, so loving and kind and . . . did he know about me before?

My eyes stung and my heart might have been bleeding for how deeply I was wounded inside.

Goldfell was taking my blood, and it was more valuable than ordinary celestial blood.

Things I didn't want to believe started to come together so clearly that denial wasn't an option anymore. My head rested against the cold, sharp metal.

Five years ago, Cassia got confirmation from a healer.

Something Rose had told me during the Libertatem. A truth.

Only with their infused remedies was she given more time than everyone thought.

A partial lie. Cassia's years weren't extended by any magick from human mages.

You'll find I have a rather upstanding agreement with the reigning lord.

I blinked hard with the final recollection of Goldfell's words and the conclusion dawned on me.

He was trading my blood to Cassia's father. It's what kept her alive.

I couldn't find it in me to be resentful or angry. All I felt was overwhelming sadness and betrayal. Because I would have agreed . . . if Reihan had told me, asked me, I would have given Cassia my blood for the rest of our lives if that could have kept her with me.

My tears fell but I couldn't make a sound.

"We'll get you out of here," Katerina said fiercely. I had to admire her spirit, more resilient than mine right now despite her years of captivity.

I had to be strong for her. For my people, who had been strong for me.

"I'm getting *you* out of here," I said, staring at the grim dark walls and beginning to calculate a way out. Whatever it took.

"Does someone know where you are?"

My first thought was that it was only a matter of time before Nyte found me somehow, but then I remembered Rose and Zath and my head straightened.

What had Reihan done with them? Now my anger was creeping over every desolate feeling. If he'd harmed them . . . I hoped my dangerous, vengeful thoughts wouldn't need to be translated to action. That he'd merely locked them up too so they didn't try to help me or warn Nyte.

"My friends are here with me," I said.

I had to push out of the drug. Getting to my knees, I tried to take in everything I could about where we were. It was a simple underground room with no windows. There were more cells around the perimeter of the ground floor, and I had to wonder if they had put us up here as some sick twisted joke.

"Do you know if we're still in the keep?" I asked.

"I think so," she said. "I've heard the guards talking about it."

I needed my key. Just enough strength to reach into the Starlight Void and retrieve it.

So I folded my legs, cupped my hands, and sat straight, slipping my eyes closed. I had to focus. My mind was hazy like I couldn't see through the fog. My headache worsened and I could barely hold this upright position. I kept trying.

The harsh grinding of metal against stone snapped my eyes open. Across from me on the balcony perimeter stood Calix, and rage flushed through my body when I met his eyes.

"You spineless, deceitful bastard," I spat.

His firm expression didn't flinch.

"Your blood kept her alive," he said.

So Calix too had only just found out what extended Cassia's years. I didn't answer him. Calix could burn in hell for all I cared now. I should have left him to Nyte.

"Where's Rose and Zath?" I demanded.

"I don't know."

My teeth ground. "Fuck you, Calix."

"Astraea—"

He stopped speaking when Reihan entered behind him. Like a good obedient dog, Calix dipped his head before stepping aside.

I wanted to keep my anger hot and coursing, but seeing him conflicted me with so much pain because I still wanted to deny he'd wronged me and my people so despicably.

"I didn't want to do this," Reihan said, and there might have been a time my soft heart would have fallen for those words too easily.

"It's never about want," I said. "You know what you're doing is barbaric."

"There is a cause to all things no matter how extreme the method."

"Cassia would be disgusted with you. All of this. She never would have *wanted* it."

He didn't respond. It was like he'd come to examine his pet in a cage—to know if I was still too feral to touch.

"How many have you killed?" I asked with deceiving calm.

"It changes nothing to know that."

No. But now I knew he wasn't just a deplorable man, he was a murderer of innocents.

"It's not Nyte you need to fear," I said. "It's me. When you came for *my* people."

"Aren't we all your people . . . maiden?"

My eyes narrowed on him. "I don't condone evil. In my time, people like you would have had their souls wiped from existence by the soulless in treaty with the celestials for *peace*."

"Your time is over."

I smiled, but there was nothing friendly in it.

"My time is just returning."

What I'd hoped would gain a wary reaction from him only seemed to invoke a thrill. I couldn't decide if he was just taking sick enjoyment in my fight, or if he was waiting for it to return so he could break my spirit.

"I'll be seeing you without bars soon. You might come to find our goals align more than you think."

Reihan left and there were few times I'd felt such a bottle of rage inside me that I couldn't unleash.

I didn't expect the bigger twist of betrayal to be from Calix. I should have known he was capable of this. He'd been willing to sacrifice me before and I guess when the opportunity came to win back favor with his lord he did it again.

"I should have let Nyte kill you," I said to him.

He didn't even flinch, like he had no emotions at all left to feel anything.

He said, "Rest, Astraea. You need to build your strength."

31

Astraea

They took me out of the cage but I could only glare at Calix across the dining table.

"You need to eat. For the blood you're losing," he sighed, like I was a defiant child. I was close to picking up the plate of delicious food and throwing it at him.

They'd taken at least two cups full from me and I fought the dizziness as I relied on the tall back of the chair to keep me upright. Then they bandaged my wrists and brought me here to eat helpings of red meat to *recover*.

"Burn in hell, Calix. I look forward to sending you there."

He barely reacted, only dropped his eyes like he could hardly stand to look at me.

Calix surveyed the small room. We weren't alone. Two guards stood by the door and I didn't doubt more were outside. They were afraid of me, and though I felt weak and helpless physically, part of me retained a sense of power and satisfaction that they remained wary of me.

"Can you please eat?" He tried again.

I was planning to, if only to get some strength back. My slowness wasn't resistance, I was merely simmering in my hatred toward him and too tired to move.

He groaned, pushing up from the table and coming around to my side. I hoped he would turn to ash with the stare I kept on him. I was restrained in shackles that had created thick red abrasions. More Nebulora, I assumed. If he got close enough I might just muster the will to attempt to strangle him with the chain between my wrists.

Calix started cutting up the meat as if that's what was stopping me.

"You try to feed me and I'll bite your damn fingers off," I warned.

"Trust me, I don't want to."

He speared a piece, and gave me a cautious look over before setting the fork back down on my plate. When he moved away again, I reluctantly lifted my hands that felt like heavy stones, taking the fork and bringing the meat to my mouth. It was as delicious as it looked and my head tipped back to savor it as I chewed.

Reaching for another mouthful, it was pitiful how much effort it took me to simply eat. I might have been embarrassed, but that was drowned under everything I was calculating to try to get out of this. I wasn't weak, not really. This was all cheap and dirty tactics to put me at their mercy.

"What does he want from me?" I tried. "A few cups of blood to sell isn't going to last long."

Calix sat back down opposite me, once again looking to the two guards like they would object to anything he said.

"Is it true that you and Nyte . . . you're the reason the land shakes every now and then?"

Sorrow clenched in me with the reminder. "Yes."

"And Nyte. He . . . he can't be killed?"

"Why do you care?"

"If there's a way, you have to take it."

Pinning him with a glare, I wanted to hurt him. Badly.

"Is that what he's tried to tell you?"

"When falls Night, the world will drown in Starlight—Cassia would recite that riddle. I know he's made you care for him, but he's going to kill you again if you don't find a way to kill him first."

"You don't know anything," I hissed.

"Astraea." He said my name in a jarring soft plea. "You spared me in Cassia's name. This is me trying to return the favor. Whether he wields a weapon or not, Nyte is *killing* you. Every day he's too fucking selfish to admit there is *no* you with him."

"You think we don't know what is happening because of us?" I snapped.

"Then you have to hear what Reihan has to say. At least learn how to do it and then decide if you have the strength to stop history from repeating. If you don't end him . . . someone will end you, if not Nyte himself. Just like before."

I would not break. I would not cry.

Every time I was reminded my soul couldn't have what it yearned for I came closer to wanting to burn everything to the ground because it wasn't. Fucking. Fair.

"Screw you, Calix. You'll never atone for all you've done and I hope you never get to see Cassia again in the stars. I'll make sure of it."

That made its mark. For the first time Calix showed fear. There were no threats nor words that could strike him as hard as the promise that he'd never reunite with Cassia. He knew her as well as I did, how much she believed our souls watched over those still living at the end. Perhaps he believed it now—it was all he had left. The belief that when his time was over here, he would be with her again.

"I'm only trying to help you," he said quietly, but he blanched, seeming to realize what I was capable of taking away from him.

"Sure doesn't fucking feel like it," I grumbled.

My wrists were becoming itchy beyond belief and I still shivered though my skin was slick with sweat.

I finished eating, sad when I chewed on the last piece. I reached for the cup of water and Calix stood. I watched him carefully as he came around. He lifted my cup before I could, and placed his own in my hand.

It was so quick I paused to process the maneuver. Calix wandered around the back of my seat, taking a sip out of my cup before seeming to aimlessly wander again.

I glanced inside the cup he'd given me with suspicion. It looked like water, but he could have put any poison in it, knowing I was desperately parched. When I didn't taste anything that would trigger alarm, I couldn't help myself greedily gulping it down.

"Let's go," he said, hooking my elbow and pulling me up.

The cage they suspended me in could be craned in to the balcony, and the sight of the open door waiting to capture me again filled me with despair. Calix leaned in to remove my shackles. As much as I despised the closeness and teetered on the dangerously unhinged idea of screwing the consequences and trying an attack, I had to be smart and he could incapacitate me easily like this.

"Rose and Zath are detained in another cell block, where I think he's keeping other celestials," Calix murmured, so quietly I almost missed it under the loud chafing of metal as two humans reeled in my enclosure.

My eyes dared to snap to him as he unlocked my second binding. He didn't look back, but my heart sped with the information and I had to tempt him to give another piece.

"Nadia?" I asked.

"He hasn't found her. She seemed to escape somehow."

Would she have gone to Nyte to tell him?

I had no choice but to walk into the wobbling cage, taking cautious steps to adjust my balance.

"Is this really necessary? The height?" I groused.

I'd never been at sea, but this was how I imagined shallow waves might feel. So I decided I was no longer enthusiastic to try a voyage one day.

"I think it's in case you reached your . . . wings," Calix said, eyes trailing over my shoulders like the idea was daunting to him.

"How considerate of your lord to give me flight practice."

It wouldn't have made a difference. Suspending the cages like this was only a mockery. To display his prized trophies like perfect trapped birds.

"Hang in there," Calix said, once again almost inaudible as my cage started to reel away from him on the edge of the balcony.

I couldn't figure him out. He'd been so hot and cold that I didn't know what of him was true anymore. He was only trying to clean a fraction of his conscience for Cassia.

"Did you know . . ." I tried to tell myself I didn't care. What did it matter? "What Reihan was doing with the celestials? Or that he was using my blood?"

"No," he said quietly. I wanted to believe him, but I didn't know if it made any difference to the sting of betrayal even from someone I knew hated me. "Like you said, Cassia never would have allowed this to go on."

I turned away from him with the grief that weighed me down to my cushion. Then it was just me and Katerina again as I shivered and folded my blanket up to my shoulders.

"You don't look so well," she said, sitting like me against the bars.

I was feeling better after the meal, but still so tired.

"I don't have a lot of blood as it is," I said with heavy eyes that contemplated sleep.

"What do you mean?"

"That it's not the first time I've been used like this," I whispered. Then it hit me all at once. How I was right back to where I started.

"Oh Astraea, I'm so sorry for all you've been through."

"Me too. For you. And everyone else who tried to come for me."

Guilt would never be enough for all that was growing in me because of the stranger's sacrifices.

"Zephyr wouldn't stop until we found you."

My eyes slipped back open then.

"Zephyr? Not Auster?"

She smiled but it held something like uncertainty. "Him too, of course, but Zephyr insisted on leading many of the searches himself. He cares for you a lot."

That knowledge was unexpected. Zephyr had been easy company, though I hadn't had as much time as I would have liked to have had with him when Auster kept me close in his own province of Althenia so far.

"You and I . . . were we close?"

I realized I couldn't fully trust anything she might say. I had no memories and that made me frighteningly vulnerable.

"Yes."

There was something hesitating, held back, in that single word. She didn't add anything else. Anything people told me about my past life could be riddled with lies or only half truths.

"Did Auster find out about me and Nyte?"

"Eventually, yes."

I had a feeling it wasn't by my confession nor Nyte's.

I closed my eyes and thought of neither.

"We're going to get out of these damned cages," I said, with my determination growing and my rage simmering.

I was fucking tired of being trapped in iron. So I focused on stilling my mind, feeling and bonding with my magick to learn to reach it past the numbness and pain of the Nebulora. In the calm of my thoughts, Nyte's words trickled back as I thought of the cage around me.

If you ever find yourself in one again you're going to have the means to break it.

The fire burning inside me from the poison hissed, rebelling to my will to pass through and claim back the magick it guarded.

My name is Astraea. I am the daughter of Dusk and Dawn.

I had to retreat from my battle to reach my magick when my skin slicked hot and I trembled, panting with the exertion, but I was so far from giving up.

I am the star-maiden, and my light is eternal.

32

Nyte

My younger brother was already grating on my nerves with the way he walked, one hand in his pocket while the other tossed and caught the compass absentmindedly over and over.

"Can you stop that?" I hissed.

"Still as easily irritated as ever," he grumbled, pocketing the compass. "When you showed father the other one . . . from your realm, what did he say?"

My mind conjured the image of the item with a twisting in my gut.

"He didn't have a lot of time to react under the circumstances." I didn't know what kind of ground we walked on with this temporary common goal, but I supposed if it was glass doomed to shatter at the end, there was never a better time to ask questions that had taunted me for years.

"Why did you bring it to me?" I asked. "Why did you keep visiting me under the library all that time?"

I didn't expect the answers to come easy. Drystan's jaw shifted in the glance I stole as we walked through the quiet streets of a town near the edge of Vesitire.

"I realized that one of you had to be triumphant, and I guess you were the slightly lesser evil."

"Then why did you act on his order to seek out Astraea when she fell?"

"I was going to kill her."

My steps slammed to a halt. Drystan stopped a few paces ahead, dragging his bored sight to me.

He said, "Well I didn't, did I?"

"To get back at me?"

"To stop a cycle that will never end," he snapped. "You will always choose her."

I couldn't deny that, nor could I get him to understand, because my feelings for Astraea could not be placed in mere mortal words. No language could move another person to fathom even a fraction of all I carried for her.

"She was your friend; she trusted you even in this life."

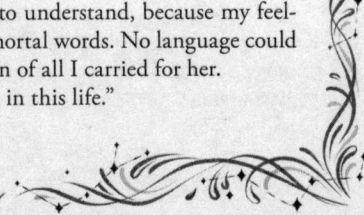

"And whoever is truly after her in this one didn't kill that arrogant son of a bitch in the Libertatem."

"Draven?"

Drystan's jaw worked and he avoided my eye like he hated to expose himself.

He'd killed that player.

"Why?"

"Because he would have killed her at the end to take her key, and I didn't think she could contend with him then."

"You gave her your map."

"That was obvious."

"Then why pretend you don't care for her?"

"Because I fucking don't," he said coldly.

Yet his heart was betraying his mind.

"She has something I need, that's all."

I was beginning to itch with a promising wrath as I heard about more and more people who wanted to *use* my Starlight.

"What is that?" I asked through gritted teeth.

Drystan held me with dead eyes for a second before he turned away and continued his walk down the snowy street of a town just outside the central. He declined to answer my question.

"The person who killed her handmaiden, however . . . they had to have been after her," Drystan reflected.

"You couldn't find a trace?"

"I did. You're not going to like what the identifier was though."

"There's nothing about it I could like."

"There was a silver feather."

"A celestial? That had to have been from one of them just watching her."

"Didn't you say her own people had attacked her in the past?"

"Until she was adamant she was mistaken about that first assumption."

Drystan cast me a look over his shoulder that said I was being complacent.

"They have no reason to harm her."

"Don't they? What if others found out about the two of you in the past and condemned their maiden?"

"They've been hiding for centuries waiting for her return. Auster would have caught wind of any upset or movement against her."

As far as we knew, only my father and Auster had found out about us. The High Celestial wouldn't have wanted that abhorrent scandal to get out—worse than their maiden sleeping with the enemy, the fact that she'd rejected Auster as her bonded for it was a secret I had no doubt he protected vehemently from getting out.

Drystan merely shrugged. "That's what I found. If it was vampires, I don't know what they sought to gain from trying to kill her either."

I had to calm myself right now. It was taking everything in me not to defy her bond right now and go to her with the thought of that threat still lingering. Every moment she was out of my sight was haunting.

We came to an establishment like Goldfell Manor. A place where the higher members of society came to gamble, drink, and fuck.

Apparently Drystan knew a mage inside. I listened in on his conversation with one of the ladies who leaned into him with eager flirtations that he indulged.

"They'll be a moment," he informed me, returning with two glasses of wine.

Impatient ire pricked my skin but there was nothing I could do but take up a table with Drystan.

"Not in the mood for a game?" Drystan said, indicating the card tables with his chin.

"No."

"Sour as ever."

"If you knew where Astraea was all that time—did you know of the abuse?"

Not knowing might be safer for both of us, but I was trying to figure him out since everything I'd thought was being contradicted when it came to how he felt about Astraea now.

"I knew that Goldfell was selling her blood to keep the vampires away from his establishment, yes. I didn't know his hand could be cruel too. He doted on her any time I saw her."

My hand tightened around my cup.

"I didn't expect the alliance he'd make. He was smarter than I thought," he continued.

"What alliance?"

Drystan cast me a look over the rim of his cup, like he didn't believe I wouldn't know.

"Shit. I thought you just hadn't told her to spare her heart."

"What fucking alliance?" I snapped.

"You should really be nice to people when you want something."

The only type of kindness pressing on my mind right now was imagining my hands around his throat.

"Nice trick in erasing his name, by the way. I wonder where you got that idea," he said sarcastically.

Now I was really itching to strangle him.

"Drystan, my love, you've neglected me for years and I don't anticipate this to be a social call given your company."

The interruption came from a tall person with dark skin and gold eyeliner complimenting yellow catlike eyes that had to be an enhancement of magick. Their black shirt was open to expose a toned chest and they held a glass of wine as they approached, seemingly having been interrupted from some private affair they didn't mind provoking anyone's speculation about.

"Nadir, this is my brother," Drystan introduced, sitting back and allowing them to trail an admirable hand along his chin.

My brother had no preference for gender in people when it came to his sexual relations, and there was no denying that these two had been involved before.

Nadir's lips parted and they gave me a second intrigued assessment.

"The notorious Nightsdeath." They drawled that name with a deep air of wonder but still a trickle of fear. Then their attention fixed back on Drystan with a soft look of adoration. "To what do I owe the pleasure of your esteemed company, Your Highness?"

"We need you to enchant an item for us."

Drystan held up the compass and Nadir took it, setting down their cup on our table. They flipped it over.

"The Wanderers Compass?"

Drystan nodded. "Can it find a person?"

"Of course. The Wanderers Trove makes sure nothing that is lost is forever and nothing that is hiding can stay so."

Nadir took a long drag of a pipe offered to them by a woman in a feathered nightgown. So maybe it was quite like Goldfell Manor, but this place was far more eccentric and bold in its affairs.

"Who shall I spell it to obey?"

"Me," Drystan and I said simultaneously.

He cut me with a look. "We wouldn't be here without me."

"I would have found another mage," I countered.

That earned a disgruntled huff from Nadir. "Good luck finding another that will touch that thing. One wrong move and it can curse the mage responsible for tinkering with it," they said.

"Wrong move?" I inquired. I didn't think there could be any repercussions from using the item.

"Items like those of the Trove are never meant to fall into nefarious hands. It can sense ill intent."

"Such as?" Drystan prompted, also curious.

"The compass never used to need a mage to activate its power. Until the previous owner began using it to find people to kill them. Always a specific type. The compass would point them to any child-free, blond, and unmarried person as their prime victim. They say he raped and killed eight before the compass stopped working and never helped again."

Drystan and I exchanged a look.

He said, "We are hoping to track down our father and kill him."

Nadir took a long inhale, then another drag of the pipe, as if to collect a plea for the ask.

"A very risky request given the intent. What shall you give me in return?"

"What do you want?" I asked.

"A vial of the star-maiden's blood."

"No."

"Deal."

My sight blazed at Drystan's agreement.

"It's not ours to give. Her blood runs in me right now, you can have mine."

Nadir contemplated my offer with a tip of their chin.

"Are you Bonded?"

"No."

"Then it's hardly as powerful to me. Only the Bond truly makes you one source. Your blood, your soul. It's as powerful as it is vulnerable to the likes of you. A god, are you not? The one who cannot be killed."

It was like they mocked me with that last sentence, knowing something I didn't and that itched my skin toward violence, which I did a commendable job of suppressing. I didn't know what they were trying to provoke out of me, but I didn't appreciate the probe into my Bond with Astraea. Forged or not.

"The offer is my blood or nothing," I said firmly.

Nadir challenged me with those yellow eyes primed with amusement. I thought about testing their mind, but decided it was best not to risk getting what we came here for unless they kept resisting.

"Very well."

Nadir took the compass and claimed they needed peace to work the spell. I undid the button of my sleeve, rolling it up as a woman came around to my side with a small knife to collect my blood.

"Did you ever try using the compass to find her killer?" Drystan asked curiously.

"Yes. It didn't work. For a while I thought it might mean they were dead, and I can't decide if that would be worse when I've been counting on revenge for centuries."

"How did it not work?"

I shrugged. "The mage spelled it, and it never moved."

"Then they could be dead."

"It should have at least taken me to the remains."

"Unless they're dust or shadow."

That was a fair point to make. I'd erased all physical trace of many bodies in my wake. The thought that I could have unintentionally already killed them ground on dark nerves.

"Who did Goldfell sell her blood to?" I asked again.

Drystan sat back, contemplating whether to be kind and tell me or test the limits of my patience.

"I thought it was rather obvious, given that you knew about the reigning lord's daughter."

That's all it took for the weight of what he implied to slam into me.

"Reihan Vernhalla?"

Drystan's look of disappointment over the fact that I didn't figure it out sooner was all the confirmation I needed. In truth, I was loathing myself right now for not thinking of it sooner.

"Goldfell heard about his daughter's condition, and he knew from the vampires that Astraea's blood was no ordinary celestial's. I don't think it would have kept Cassia alive forever without some greater consequence for attempting to evade her fate, but it extended the human's years, at least, and she was Astraea's friend. I figured if she'd had the choice, she would have given her blood anyway."

"The point is she had no choice," I growled. Thoughts of her being controlled and taken unawares boiled in me. She was magnificent and powerful and her first years back had made a mockery of the goddess she was.

She's alive, and she's with me now. It was taking everything in me not to slip through the void to her this second.

"She's heading there right now," I said, so low and dark while my vengeance was stirring. "I'm going to fucking kill him."

"Can you really blame him for wanting to save his daughter?"

"Yes. When it required taking something against Astraea's will and pretending he *cared* for her."

"I think he did, truly. Goldfell was a powerful man and Astraea's blood kept his daughter alive for a while longer. What would telling her have done other than upending her world and what she knew, and Astraea would have had no one to help her then. Time and order; you of all people know destiny works in often cruel ways."

The woman finished taking my blood. More than I thought was a vial but I didn't fucking care right now.

"You should have told me that sooner," I growled. "Astraea is with the lord right now and I'm not leaving her there a day longer."

33

Astraea

I tried to meditate, but it seemed I needed a lot of teaching to even come close to mastering silence of the mind. Even though my thoughts were foggy right now, they wouldn't stop battering my head.

Groaning, I gave up, massaging my temples.

"You can do this," Katerina encouraged.

I was enlightened by her to the fact that my past self had conquered the effects of Nebulora and had been able to find my magick through it. With my hopeless attempts that weren't so much as slightly warming my skin with magick, I was beginning to lose trust in that fact more than anything Katerina had told me so far.

"I haven't even felt my full power yet in full health, never mind pushing through this. Everything is heavy and cloudy."

"Now is the time. Find it for you and for all of us, dammit."

My head turned to her, stunned and mildly irritated by her tone.

Katerina giggled. "Sorry, it was worth a try. You preferred to give and take tough love a lot as your old self."

I huffed a laugh with her. "I don't know what I prefer now."

It was a lie, I thought, as I remembered how responsive I became to Nyte when he was harsh in the woods, attacking without holding back.

The scraping of metal and stone would never fail to make me wince, but my heart skipped a beat when it came from below this time.

Two humans dragged someone in and my cage wobbled as I stepped closer to the edge. My world silenced at the blood that trailed them—at the gruesome sight of the man's torn back. Two sharp, bleeding lines. My hand covered my mouth and the other gripped the bar with the wave of dizziness and sickness that overcame me.

I couldn't believe what I was seeing. That all the times I'd stood above in this keep my people were being barbarically stripped of their wings and held captive for their blood below.

My eyes filled with tears of grief and agony at first. But they quickly turned hot. My pulse spiked. I watched them drag the man who couldn't walk through the door at the opposite end and I snapped with rage.

"He's not getting away with this," I snarled.

I took deep inhales as I sat back down, crossed my legs, and straightened my spine. I dove deep within myself to find what I needed to break free of this damn poison. Meeting the raging fire around my magick with more willpower than ever, I gritted my teeth painfully and reached through it.

My name is Astraea.

I pushed with everything I had through the haze of my mind. My pulse raced dangerously. It was like passing a hand through scorching fire, which took me to the very edge of my resistance. Every time I'd come this close I'd had to retreat when it threatened to devour me completely. It could kill me . . . or free me.

I am the daughter of Dusk and Dawn.

A whimper escaped my lips but I let the inferno take me within and gripped the magick behind it with everything I was.

I am the star-maiden.

That light magick . . . I became it.

My eyes snapped open and my world was touched in starlight. Shimmering and beautiful, but dangerously lethal. My skin warmed to banish all chill and I found my silver markings glowing. My hand lifted and the Starlight Void opened for me, as natural as breathing. I reached inside, gripped my key, and stood as it came to life in my hand, flaring a stunning purple and touching in my chest like an embracing alliance.

"You did it," Katerina said with an air of wonder.

"We're getting our people the hell out of here."

The key answered me, and with a cry I swiped horizontally and expelled a sheet of light magick that cut through the bars. The floor fell away but instinct awakened in me, like I was unlocking skills I'd known before, and exhilaration pumped through my blood.

I jumped before I could fall the long way down. The key disappeared into the void and my hands wrapped around the top bars. Half of the cage clamored so loudly against the stone that it wavered my focus in a wince and pierced my ears.

Now, we were on a countdown before guards flooded in from the commotion.

It was only now that I came to the terrifying conclusion that while I might know how to do this, I hadn't accounted for my current lack of physical strength in my brazenness. My arms tore in pain from the lack of muscle but I couldn't fall; I didn't think I would survive it.

"Where's your wings?" Katerina asked with a note of panic from seeing my struggle now.

"I can't—," I wheezed.

I tried to focus and find them but right now my panic and the remnants of the Nebulora made it impossible.

I sobbed from the pain as I swung my legs, enough to gain a push, let go, and barely manage to grip the next bar. Three more to go. Then the biggest challenge would be whether I could pull myself up to the top of the cage.

By the time urgent voices sounded, about to burst in, I cried out at the last hurdle to pull myself up. It took every ounce of physical strength that I had to pause for breath that was hard to draw with my midriff being crushed by a thick pole I was bent over. When the blackness at the edge of my vision passed, I seized all my determination to swing my leg around until I got in the position to balance myself on top of the cage just as the door below slammed open.

I retrieved the key, not sure if it would work, and I aimed it and called my magick through it. The bridge of light it produced could plummet me down if it was as hollow as it looked, but I was out of time for caution.

I jumped.

Landing on the strip of light I released a delirious noise of relief and shot across. The voices were commanding each other on the ground, and it was only a matter of time before they burst through the balcony I landed on too. But I made it across, and then it was only my adrenaline pushing through every tired muscle and sharp breath cutting my throat.

I reeled in Katerina's cage despite the pain lancing through me with every heavy pull. I couldn't manage the whole way as my arms gave out and I heaved a dry sob.

"Can you jump from there?" I asked through wheezing gasps.

"Yes."

Using magick was a temporary reprieve even though it drained strength from me after. In the moment it coursed through my body, I felt dangerously invincible. It could destroy me if I didn't remember my limits.

"Ready?"

She nodded.

I cut through Katerina's cage the same way as before and she almost didn't make the leap across. Both of us shot arms out for each other and by some miracle from the gods she tumbled my way instead of the opposite. We crashed to the balcony ground in a tangle of limbs and agony.

Then the door tore open.

I angled my arms and pushed myself up as they wobbled. Flicking my sight up, I saw four men file in, braced with swords.

"I don't want to hurt you," I panted, managing to clutch the key staff and use it as an aid to rise.

The closest man gave a chuckle, but it wasn't fully arrogant as he eyed the key carefully. As if it was the only threat but the person who wielded it was nothing more than a cockroach to crush.

"You're the one who's going to get hurt, girl."

"Stop," I warned.

He didn't listen.

I had no choice.

All it took was lifting the key and slamming it to the ground to split through the slab between us. The other three shouted and managed to usher themselves back before the stone balcony crumbled. The one who'd advanced was swallowed in the crumbing debris that fell with him.

"We have to go," Katerina said, pulling my arm, but I couldn't help the seconds of regret that tainted me when I saw he wouldn't survive that fall.

Then I squared my shoulders, knowing this was the world I lived in, and that it was at war for peace.

We jogged across the balcony until we found stairs and ran down them. When more men tried to intercept us I used magick to get them out our way until they started retreating.

Then we emerged into a new large space like the one we'd been held in but horror slowed my jog until I stood in the center, turning to see every cage on the ground level, then the second level, then the third.

They were all. Full.

Dozens of captive celestials edged timidly out of shadow, peeking through their cages at our abrupt intrusion.

"It's the star-maiden!" someone called out.

It snapped me back from my reeling shock. Voices broke out, most of them muttering the same thing with a growing buzz of *hope*. Hope that they were getting to go home.

"Astraea!"

I gasped, spinning toward the direction of my name, and my eyes filled with overwhelming relief at the head of pink hair I saw. Zath was with Rose, to my immense relief.

Rushing over to them, I examined Rose head to toe. Aside from tousled hair and a few scratches, likely from her resistance, she appeared unharmed.

My eyes dropped to in concern to where Zath was clutching his abdomen but he waved me off before I could say anything.

"Just a nasty beating, I'll be okay," he said.

Even Rose looked at him with worry.

"I have to get you out," I said, mulling over *how*.

My hand lifted to the lock, and threads of magick pulled out of me to break it.

I was learning it was so many things. Like clay to a sculptor and paint to an artist—it could do many things and was my craft to learn.

When my magick retracted back into me, however, I didn't know how much longer I could go on in my current state and I glanced helplessly around all the cages.

Rose's hands were on me the moment she was free, as if knowing my stability was about to fail.

"We have to get you out of here. We can come back with more forces for them," Rose said quietly.

I shook my head, watching Katerina at one of the cages and the bright hope of the tattered older woman within one . . . I couldn't leave them another moment in here.

"You can't fight anymore," Zath said softly in a plea. I'd never seen him so concerned for me.

"I have to."

Taking a long breath that felt like fire expanding in my chest, I used the help of my key to walk, trying to gauge how I was going to do this. One cage at a time? That would take too long, guards would flood the room soon.

Then I realized . . .

"Where's all the guards?" I asked.

Surely Reihan would have guessed this was where I would go. We should have been swarmed by forces by now.

Someone approached, a single set of feet running toward us, and I spun to them.

Calix slowed his pace, holding up his hands, but he didn't keep his eyes on me; they scanned around and above and if I didn't know any better I would have believed the ghostly expression that was disturbed by this sinister place.

"I'm going to kill him," I seethed.

"Wait—" my step was halted by Rose and my incredulous look sliced her instead. "I hate to say this, but we might not be alive if it wasn't for him."

"What are you talking about?" I snapped.

Calix was a traitor and a liar.

"Reihan ordered us killed. Calix took us before they could but we couldn't leave you. So he brought us here since they wouldn't come looking, and kept us in the know about you until we could figure out a plan. But you seemed to have done that all on your own, as impulsive as this is. I kind of like your style."

I tried to smile at the small attempt to ease the racing adrenaline in us from realizing that this was far from over. We had to get everyone out of here alive.

"There's an attack outside the keep," Calix informed.

My brow pulled together, then relaxed with a wash of cold dread as I asked, "Nyte?"

Calix quickly shook his head, approaching tentatively as if I still might turn on him. In truth, I hadn't fully let him off the hook yet.

"I think they're fae."

My eyes widened and hope bloomed in my chest. Had the resistance come to aid?

It bought us time to get everyone out of here.

"Do you have keys?" I asked Calix.

His face fell apologetic and I could have groaned to see the shake of his head.

"Magick it is," I said through a labored breath.

"You hardly seem capable to tackle them all. We can wait for help," Zath protested.

"We don't know how many fae there are. This could be our only chance with the distraction they're making for us."

I practically hobbled to the center of the room. *I would rest once everyone was out.* And could only hope what it took wasn't my life.

So many eyes watched me. Hollow, tired faces that for some reason looked at me with the kind of hope they'd thought was lost.

Focusing on my breathing, I reached for the power of the key, unable to muster enough magick without it right now. Power crawled over my skin like thin prickling water. It hummed in my veins like new life, and I was just the vessel. Then it spilled from me in threads that searched for the cage locks. Starlight swirled around the room and though it was beautiful I was trembling to hold it, direct it. Those threads wound their way around every cell like I held them all in the palm of my hand and all it would take is one . . .

Pull.

They all broke at once but I wasn't prepared and had not trained myself to reel the magick back into myself safely. It pummeled into me like a rebounding attack.

Rose caught me before I could fall.

"You did it," she said, a certain wonder in her tone.

I could hardly stay awake, but I had to see. The voices grew louder yet they were all muffled. I was close to passing out. But I watched in wonder as some still had their wings—stunning, large silver wings. They helped each other from the higher cages and my chest beat with so much pride and joy.

"They're going to be okay; now we need to start getting everyone out," Rose assured me.

I nodded. The key staff slipped from my grasp, but my hand raised in time and the Starlight Void opened to keep it safe. I let Zath hook my waist and help me walk.

In the familiar halls of the keep above, my heart ached at the memories I had here that now felt tainted. I could distantly hear the clamor of steel and shouts of battle and my fear awakened my adrenaline to push through some of the fog threatening my consciousness.

We made it to the grand entrance before we stopped.

"Oh Astraea," Davina sighed, rushing to me.

I could have broken in the embrace she pulled me into.

Over her shoulder, I trembled at the sight of the vicious fighting.

"We have to stop this," I breathed.

"We're handling it," Davina said. "We need to get you out of here."

"Not yet." Reihan's voice chilled down my spine and I turned.

My body was weak but I straightened. No matter what, I would protect my friends.

"It's over, Reihan," I said.

"We didn't even get the chance to talk, maiden," he said. So calm and unbothered by the fighting that was happening.

I didn't know who I was staring at. Something had been wrong since the moment he captured me and I couldn't untangle what it was.

Reaching for my key, I thought that if I kept the magick flowing through me I would be able to fight him. Whatever punishment I had to face when I let the power fade would be worth it to save my friends. My people.

Bodies crept out from behind the reigning lord but they weren't guards. Not uniformed, and when I tracked the ground . . . I discovered them to be shadowless. Then I looked in the glass to confirm some were soulless by their missing reflections but what I found instead . . .

My heart stopped. Then sped. It felt like the ground crumbled from under me slowly and I couldn't move.

"Vampires," Zath muttered.

It all made sense now. World-shattering sense.

There was no time to deliberate my horror when the vampires attacked.

Rose and Zath fought with steel they had to have picked up from fallen guards. Davina shapeshifted into a large black panther to tear through bodies with her powerful claws and jaw.

None of them came for me, because I was pinned by the hungry stare of the villain in front of me.

"What do you want?" I asked. My throat was bone dry. "My blood?"

"I have enough of that for now."

My grip tightened on the key as he took a predatory step to me.

He said, "I want an alliance, Astraea. I have the answer to the dire problem of the world. The one you couldn't find all that time ago—a way to kill Nyte before he kills you."

My head shook vacantly.

Reihan took one more step and I braced to shift the key—

He cried out and my sight snapped down in utter shock to the blade protruding from his abdomen. It retracted but I barely caught a glimpse of Calix who locked eyes on me with blank terror.

With goodbye.

With a plea.

My mouth opened but I didn't get to release my scream. Reihan moved impossibly fast, hand lashing around Calix's throat.

"No—!" I was too late to save him.

I didn't hear the snap of his neck, but watching death glass over those familiar brown eyes and his whole body go limp in Reihan's hold . . . I fell to my knees as his body was let go so carelessly to crumple to the ground.

My vision came and went but I couldn't think of anything but that final request in Calix's eyes that now stared hauntingly at me. I only had seconds to react, crawling to him and placing a hand over his hollow chest.

The last warmth of him engulfed my palm before shooting up my arm and settling in my chest.

"I'll make sure you see her again," I whispered to his soul.

I didn't cry, but his death crushed another piece of me inside. We might have had our differences, but in the end our love for Cassia kept us bonded. I mourned for him.

I barely looked up in time to see Reihan slipping away down a hall, blood dripping from his wound.

Loathing torched my blood. Rage and vengeance and pure fucking spite.

I went after him against all alarms to let him go this time. To come back when I had full strength. But my anger knew no limits.

Down the hall I braced against the stone wall a few times to catch my breath. I reached deeper and deeper for more magick even though I knew the danger.

He was right. Here.

I had the chance to end him.

In the room I cornered him in, his guise was revealed in the mirror reflections along each wall. This was where Cassia would have lessons in ballroom dancing and a few times I'd had the joy of participating.

Reihan stood with his back to me in every perfect detail.

But it was the fallen king, Nyte's father, who stared at me with a wickedly amused smile through every reflection.

With a cry the key became a bow and I aimed a light arrow in seconds. It pierced the top hat he wore, spearing it into the mirror that cracked, now adding a sinister tone to his image.

"What did you do to him?" I yelled in anguish.

When the king turned he wore his own flesh now, and my heart withered with what I was about to learn.

"The reigning lord is dead. But you should be thanking me after his exploitation of you. That was truth I uncovered for you."

I blinked, then shook my head. He was trying to warp my mind.

"What do you have to gain in killing him . . . in being here?"

Shock smothered my fear of him. I couldn't believe it. He'd played the part so well when we'd arrived, but the cruelty this past week had never really been Reihan.

"I knew you would come here eventually."

"Why kill the reigning lord for it?"

"I enjoyed taking his place for a while. Having some semblance of what I once had before you destroyed it, and perhaps I came to enjoy it more. Here, the lord had true power and respect. It made me realize once and for all that what I had was always because of my son and without him most would not have feared me. But that will change. I no longer need him."

"He's your *son*." It came out in a pained breath of incredulity after hearing him lack any care or ounce of love for his own child.

"He's a failed experiment. Though I will admit he served his purpose well for a while. Before you got in the way."

That brought my resentment back in a surge of heat.

"He's every triumph you'll never achieve. Every power you'll never feel. You've always needed him, but he has never needed you."

"Your affection for him is admirable despite the people he's slaughtered. Your people."

"By your order."

"My order is a word, his actions are the crime."

"Your word is a poisonous manipulation. And I won't let you hurt him anymore."

Forming another light arrow I lifted my aim, but the king's words halted my release.

"Bond with Rainyte."

It was such a jarring statement I frowned, puzzling over the motive.

"You know of a way to kill Nyte," I said, becoming slowly doused in dread. "Does that have something to do with it?"

The king boldly took a step toward the arrow pointed at him.

"We don't have to be enemies. There is a way for us all to get what we desire. I would vow to reign as an equal to you and the High Celestials. No more war, no more conquest, no more failing magick. All you would have to do is give him up. He will always be destruction to your order."

My heart cleaved in two for Nyte. To have a father so hell-bent on ending him now that he no longer served as a ruthless soldier to his gain.

"You're absolutely despicable," I said through gritted teeth. "You are the plague to my *order,* not him."

The king moved and I reacted too. I realized all his words had been a distraction from the dagger he unsheathed and threw. It scored across my arm, knocking my arrow out of his path. From the lance of searing fire I knew it was laced with Nebulora.

A new voice intruded and if I hadn't caught his reflection behind me, I would have thought it a trick.

"Harm her again, and I'll kill you where you stand."

Auster stepped in front of me, standing off against the king, and I couldn't believe he was here. How had he known I was here and in trouble?

"Heroic of you to come for your maiden, Auster Nova," the king said with a hint of amusement, like he'd anticipated it.

"Leave," Auster ordered.

The king met my eyes with a gleam in his. He stepped forward, the only exit was behind me.

I intercepted him.

I was so fucking angry that I couldn't contain it anymore.

"You don't get to walk out of here," I said.

Then I struck, hand cast out and with the added power of the key, the king flew back, slamming into the wall of mirror that rained down in a lethal waterfall.

"Astraea, you're going to hurt yourself," Auster reprimanded me, but right now he was only in my way and I couldn't fathom why he would try to stop me with our enemy right in front of us.

The king groaned pushing himself up. I expected him to be more incapacitated by the blast. Then the mockery of laughter tightened in my bones.

"The gods granted me one more thing when I got inside that temple. It seems your creators are reevaluating who they entrust the world to," the king said.

"What are you talking about?" I hissed.

"The key doesn't affect me as much, because they granted me the will to use it without harm."

Dusk and Dawn were really growing my vendetta against them. My grip around the key tightened like he could snatch it from me right now. Why would the gods who are supposed to be on our side grant such a catastrophic power to him?

They created me. This key that made me both astronomically more powerful yet also completely vulnerable. Now they'd granted it to the hand of my ultimate enemy.

In case I didn't choose right. Because *their* ultimate enemy was Nyte.

My Nyte.

I despised those gods and didn't care if it damned me to declare it.

My anger had been simmering but it skipped straight past boiling and I *erupted.*

A scream tore from me. Magick expelled from me.

The mirrors shattered and the walls exploded with the velocity of the power that blasted from me and from the key flaring brightly.

I am not a maiden just to serve.

I am not a weapon just to gain.

I didn't stop until I fell to my knees, panting and slick with sweat when my energy dwindled to embers.

Every breath was like ash and flame. Every focus of my eyes from the destruction around me pounded my head sickeningly. I didn't know what I'd done to the king or Auster but I couldn't see either of them.

I'm dying.

There's too much light.

I was so engulfed by it that I felt wholly set on fire.

I yearned for the darkness and it came for me.

It spilled over my splayed fingers cutting into shards of glass on the ground. I couldn't lift my head for the boulder it felt like but within my blurry focus I saw him, wondering if I was mistaken about the dark angel that approached through the reflections of the shattered mirror pieces.

Until Nyte crouched before me, taking my face in his hands.

"There you are," he said, so softly but it was the type of calm that hid panic. "You saved them all. I came thinking I'd be turning this place to rubble to get you out, but you did so by yourself."

I managed to look up then.

"Nyte," I said through breaths that felt numbered and if they were . . . I wanted to give them all to him anyway.

"I'm here. I've got you."

"Is everyone . . . safe?"

"Thanks to you, they will be."

My head was pounding, my muscles were on fire, and the air was too thick to breathe. I tried to blink and find focus and though it was all dust and rubble, no one else was with us when I thought to warn Nyte about his father . . . Auster . . .

My head slumped with the effort to look for them. "I can't hold on."

Nyte took me into his arms and stood.

"I'm right here. You're going to be fine," he promised.

My heart cried when that's all I wanted and also everything I was afraid of. That he would always come, and I could never stay away.

34

Astraea

I took a long deep inhale, glad it didn't burn or pulse in my head like I anticipated. I stared at a slanted wooden ceiling that had a single window. It was dark out, and the stars were blurry from the pounding rain against the glass, but the sound was peaceful. I almost wanted to go back to sleep.

Until I remembered what I'd faced before getting here.

Who had brought me here . . .

Nyte's presence wrapped me in his embrace and my head fell sideways. He was so beautiful laying there on his back with his head facing me. I reached for the lock of dark hair that had tipped over his eyes in his sleep but then my body tensed.

Something wasn't right.

His chest . . . it didn't rise.

Nyte wasn't breathing.

"Nyte." I barely choked out his name as I shot up. Gripping his shoulders, I shook him. "Nyte!"

Still no response and my pulse ran frantic while my body seized in panic. I straddled him, blinking fast against the pooling in my eyes because Nyte wasn't moving.

He couldn't be dead.

He told me he couldn't die.

Oh gods, had his father come when I lost consciousness?

No—we weren't Bonded and I was sure that was somehow needed for his plan to kill Nyte.

"Nyte, please," I croaked. "Wake up—"

I gasped at the same time he did.

Nyte drew a long, sudden breath and his eyes snapped open. His heartbeat thumped under my hand now and mine was knocked around off beat because . . . *what the fuck?*

"Astraea," he breathed, disorientated, like my name was an anchor.

He held my hip and I leaned down, unable to hold back the need to press my lips to his.

"Why did you do that?" I cried angrily now from the worst fright of my existence. "What happened?"

"Your . . . your bargain is pretty damn powerful."

I pulled back, scanning over his face and realization washed me with such guilt. Then more outrage because he could have *left* me had the magick been strong enough to take him for good.

"You shouldn't have come for me. I was making it out—"

Sweat slicked his brow and his teeth gritted together as he pushed himself up. His breaths were labored but he cupped my neck and held me with fierce eyes.

"I once held you in my arms as you fucking *died,* Astraea. As you left and took my heart with you and the only kernel of good ever to reside in my soul. I can't do it again—I *won't* do it again. So no, a blood bargain won't keep me from coming for you. There is nothing I wouldn't destroy in my path to you when you are in danger. I was too late once; I won't be again."

All my anger dispersed at once, opening a hollow void that filled with his pain instead.

Nyte's energy was drained completely, his eyes could hardly stay open. I held the back of his neck now to help him lie back down and his skin was dangerously hot. Panic surged in me with the beat that began to slow under my palm.

"I release you from that command," I rushed out. "I want you to come for me. Always."

"Thank fuck," he rasped.

"How many times did you . . . die?"

"Doesn't matter," he said, running a soothing caress over my thighs straddling him. "How are you feeling?"

"Better than you."

He smiled, and my chest fluttered. I didn't want to miss him, but I realized now, having him right here not as an illusion, that was a denial I was tired of fighting.

"I had to give you my blood again," he admitted. "I almost thought I might have had to—" Nyte stopped himself.

"What?"

He shook his head, but it was slow and tired like he could hardly find the strength.

"That's part of our story. You'll see."

I lay down with him, tucked into his side.

"You need to drink from me."

Nyte's next attempt to shake his head was weaker than the last.

"Please, you'll recover faster."

"I'll be fine in a few days. Dying is just . . . more taxing when it's multiple times in succession."

"I'm sorry," I whispered. "I didn't want to hurt you, I just wanted—"

"To best me. And you did. I'm proud of you for it."

His weakness was tearing me apart. He might be known as the realm's nightmare but for some reason I feared for it without him.

"It wasn't Reihan," I whispered. "At the keep—it was the king."

Nyte's eyes slipped open and his brow furrowed.

"Are you sure?"

I could only nod. My throat seized tightly as I recalled what he'd said. How was I to tell him what I suspected his father could do? Turn our Bonding from something that should be promising into a nefarious scheme.

"He can use the key without harm. He gained that at the temple in Vesitire."

Nyte pinched the bridge of his nose. "If I could kill gods, I would risk damnation worse than hell for my soul to do it."

"Reihan's dead," I said quietly, as I was only just now getting the chance to really settle that fact. "So is Calix."

My heart shattered. Calix had tried to save me. My hand raised to my chest harboring a final vow to him I had to see through.

Nyte's fingers ran up my spine in comfort.

"I'm sorry. They meant a lot to you."

"I know you couldn't forgive him for what he'd done, but Calix saved me in there in more ways than one."

"Then for that, I hope he gets to join your friend."

Cassia. I would make sure they got to shine together.

I angled my mouth to meet his jaw, planting soft kisses that tensed the muscles in his neck. "I want you to drink from me. I can't bear this."

"Are you seducing me into it?"

"If I have to."

My leg hooked over his middle and his hand traced up from my calf and over my knee. His eyes fell closed again. I continued the path of my lips against his soft, tanned skin. Nyte pulled me over him but not with the demand he usually would. He was so weak, worse than when he was struck by lightning.

When I got to the hollow spot of his collar I opened my mouth and bit down. It drew a pleasurable pained sound from his throat and I smiled, kissing there afterward.

"You've been through a lot and need your strength," he protested.

"You have the restraint to only take what you need; I'll be okay."

"I'm about to lose all restraint with you if you keep doing that."

"Doing what?" I said coyly, and dragged my teeth further up his neck.

His hand gave a frail squeeze of warning but I didn't listen. He needed this and I wanted to give it to him.

I sat up, untucking my shirt from my pants. When I folded out of it, Nyte's eyes fluttered open to the sight of me bare-chested above him.

"Now I know I must be alive," he murmured. "Hell would not be this kind to me."

His hands traveled up my sides and one cupped my breast. I sighed with the pleasure, tipping my head back. I shuffled down a few fractions until I felt his hard cock beneath me and my hips moved against him.

"Fuck," Nyte said, the snap of his restraint.

Despite his fatigue, he pushed himself up. His arm circled my waist and I squealed as he flipped me onto my back. I didn't get to draw a breath before he kissed me hard, pouring everything he had into showing me how much he wanted me regardless of his need to rest. His thigh hooked under my knee, spreading my legs farther apart to fit himself in perfectly. His cock pressed into the heat of my core with shallow thrusts that rubbed the stitches of my pants torturously through my slickness.

Nyte slowed our kiss not out of want, but exhaustion. His forehead leaned to mine as he caught his breath.

His fingers reached up, tracing along my collar, and the phantom eruption of pain from the arrow laced in Nebulora tingled my skin. My sight angled down to see the scar before his lips replaced his fingers.

"He's going to feel what he did to you a hundred times over," he muttered. I shivered at that the dark promise.

"I don't expect you to give me your blood," he said.

"I want to." I was close to *begging* for it. As I remembered how he'd taken from me in the bath, my hips couldn't help lifting for more relief against him.

"You are incredible," he growled, pressing his lips over the faint scar where he'd last bitten.

My hands tightened in his hair when his mouth closed over my neck and his teeth sank into my flesh. I drew a sharp inhale with a silent cry. The pain quickly numbed and pleasure overtook me. It was a blissful, near delirious high that entwined threads of me with him each time.

Nyte's body pressed me to the bed harder and my hands trailed down his back, adding pressure where his wings would be. That caused him to groan around my throat as the hand not cupping my nape curved over my ass, grinding his hardness against me, and I whimpered because it wasn't enough.

His fingers worked on the ties and buttons of my pants and he peeled the material from my legs. Then he teased my core and I cried out while my body arched into him. Needing him closer. My nails clawed into his back when he circled my apex.

I lost all care for decency then, lifting my hips and working against the movement of his hand. With the pleasure roaring through me from the bite, I raced toward a climax so fast it overcame me out of nowhere.

"Nyte," his name pulled from me in a pained cry as sparks quaked through my body.

His teeth pulling out of me caused my whole body to give a violent shiver. Nyte gathered his breath before his tongue lapped over the wound and I tensed with the sensitive burst of pleasure.

"Such a good girl," he rasped against my throat. "Thank you."

"Did the blood help?"

"Very much so, but it will take a few hours to fully bring me back."

Nyte's hand slipped out of my pants, and I watched, entranced as he brought his fingers to his mouth.

"Gods, I missed you," he said in a gravelly murmur, then leaned down to kiss me hard. "And what a pity it is I can't yet show you just how much."

I shivered with thoughts of what he would have unleashed upon me if he had full strength and control right now, but I was blissfully content with this.

"I missed you too," I confessed.

Nyte's look of surprise, then a flicker of relief, ached in me. I decided then I couldn't keep these feelings from him. Not when it was like he never expected his to be reciprocated as strongly. I'd tried to keep reserved in my feelings for him only in my fear for the challenges that seemed destined to keep us apart. Now I was beginning to realize it didn't matter how many fractures may split my heart, it belonged to him anyway.

"What's wrong?" he asked gently.

"Nothing," I said. Then changed the topic away from my sinking gut. "What happened at the keep after you arrived? Where's Rose and Zath?"

"Safe. I think I might have actually seen them embrace when the fighting was over."

"Are you sure she was well?"

"Could have been the result of a hit to the head making her delusional about who she was seeing, I suppose."

I huffed a laugh, but I was glad Rose might be starting to take off her armor with Zathrian. They were both important people to me.

"Can I use the same the excuse?" I mused, tipping my chin to peer up at him.

Nyte barely shook his head, and I thought he was only hanging on to his consciousness for my sake as he lay back down beside me. He needed rest.

"No more pretend, remember?"

I smiled, content, but I wanted to wash after the captivity.

"Is there a washroom here?" I asked.

"Don't leave," he said.

That answered my question and I shuffled to the edge of the bed before he could reach for me.

"I'll bring something to cool your fever. You're going to sleep."

"You're being too good to me. Maybe I should be concerned."

"Don't remind me. I'll come back with hot towels instead to counter the kindness."

He almost broke a smile.

"There's a bathing room down the hall. We're in a pleasure house, you should know. Please don't be enticed into someone's room. My jealously can be as dangerous as my wrath."

"You *were* lacking—"

I squealed as he lashed out for my waist but he was slow enough that I managed to jump off the bed in time.

I flirted with my eyes as I fitted into a robe.

"Trust I am well and truly satisfied. Should that change, I'll come straight back."

"You know how to call for me."

I nodded, and his tired eyes concerned me. Under all the notorious names and villainous traits, he was just . . . *Nyte*. A person who had limits. And though his care was selective, he protected those he gave it to with everything he had.

"Astraea," he called as I reached the door. "Did you get to the temple yet?"

"No."

"Tomorrow, then. We'll go together."

Nyte looked so peaceful and glorious lying there with the cover over only his lower half. The contours of him were mesmerizing against the moonlight with a small flicker of flame from the brightness of his irises.

"You can call for me too, you know," I said, leaning my head on the open door.

"I'm always calling for you, Starlight."

35

Astraea

I left Nyte to rest, heading down the hall toward the small women's bathing room of this establishment.

Before I reached it I was surprised to find Drystan leaning against the wall.

"Did you keep my brother in his cycle of torture for a while, at least?"

I scowled at him. "He's fine now."

Drystan's eyes dipped to my neck with that, and my skin heated with his knowing look.

"Pity."

"What are you doing here?"

"I guess he didn't fit in a moment to tell you of our time together. You're welcome, by the way. If I hadn't mentioned Reihan's deal with Goldfell for your blood he wouldn't have come so quick."

"You knew all this time?" I accused.

"I did. It seemed harmless enough at the time. Your blood kept vampire activity against the humans down immensely, and your friend alive. I figured the day you came to know about it, you would have a right to feel betrayed but you would understand why the reigning lord did it."

My heart ached. "I don't know what I might have done."

If I'd had the chance to face him for it.

Drystan said, "Nyte showed you the day we found the dragon, didn't he?"

My pulse skipped recalling that memory. It was tragic to stand in front of Drystan having seen how close we once where. Now, he could hardly stand my company but he needed something.

Then I realized . . .

"You know how to hatch the egg." His unwavering expression was confirmation enough. "It was in the diary and you managed to translate it over the years, didn't you? Is that why you wanted me to see it?"

"Smart girl. I don't know if the egg is alive to hatch but yes, I know how to do it."

"Tell me."

My palms clammed with exhilaration at the prospect, but Drystan's hooked brow told me he wasn't going to give up that information without a gain.

"Meet with me tonight?" he asked.

My chest pounded with the decision. Would Drystan lure me out to hurt me?

"Where?"

"You'll see. Bring the little rogue, and don't tell any of the others. I'll know if you do."

"Nadia?" Last I gathered she was very keen to hold the ticket for Drystan's murder.

"You want to mend anything of the past, I'm giving you this one chance of trust," he said flatly.

He pushed off the wall, passing me, and I twisted after him.

"I'll be waiting on the rooftop at midnight," he said before disappearing around a bend.

Shit. I didn't want to fail him when it could be a chance at getting him to trust me. Yet it could be a trap for something nefarious and it was a secret I had to keep from Nyte.

There were voices inside the bathing chamber, familiar, and when I entered relief relaxed my tense shoulders when I saw the pink hair of Rose first, then Nadia's flaming red tresses, Davina's long, crowning dark braid, then one other . . .

They all turned around one by one, submerged in the large round tub big enough for at least ten people.

"Lilith?" I beamed at the extra unexpected head of stunning green hair and small curving horns.

I couldn't believe the beautiful, kind fae, who helped me at the manor Nyte had taken me to after I fell in the lake long ago, was really here. I didn't know how or why, but she was a flutter of tangible joy. Lilith beamed brightly seeing me, her smile stretching her freckled complexion.

"You're all here," I said, wondering if I'd fallen asleep in Nyte's arms and this was a wonderful dream.

"Oh Astraea, I'm so glad to see you well!" Davina gushed, floating over to the side of the tub nearest to me. "None of us could sleep worrying about you after the sight of you at the keep. Rosalind was just about to hatch a plan to barge into your room and steal you."

Stripping off my robe, I climbed into the bath from the steps. I sighed blissfully at the steaming milky water lapping my skin. Recalling how sore I'd been trying to escape that cage, I guessed Nyte's blood had nursed me back to full health.

"I'm okay now," I assured. "Thanks to him."

"He has a good heart," Lilith said. "Even if it's hidden in darkness."

That caught my intrigue.

"You know him too?"

Was there anyone not in league with Nyte?

Lilith gave a sheepish smile. "My father is the leader of the fae resistance in Alisus. He would have been killed or under the king's order long before he even claimed the crown if it wasn't for Nyte saving him and others. My father also sent him to meet Lucinda, my human mother."

"I didn't know." I thought over that for a moment, but it only caused more confusion to surface. "Why are you here?"

"I'm part of the resistance," Lilith said. It was like she'd grown into a whole new confident person since I'd last seen her. "Or at least, I want to be. My father has been trying to keep me out of it but then I heard a commotion. I met Davina and she said the star-maiden was in trouble and I . . . I didn't know who you were for certain when you came to my manor months ago, but I had a strong suspicion. So I knew I had to come find out if you'd made it through the Libertatem after all since Pyxtia was announced the winner." Her tanned skin crumpled at her brow. "Oh Astraea, I'm so glad to see you."

I didn't know what to say. There was so much to get straight in my mind I didn't know where to begin.

"I didn't know I was the star-maiden when I was with you," I admitted quietly.

"I know," she said. "I'm sorry you don't have your memories."

I smiled with sad gratitude.

"That was an unexpected turn of events at the keep," Nadia said, unbothered.

"How did you get away before they could capture you too?" I asked.

"I'm particularly good at evasion and escape. Davina was already heading here and our paths intersected."

My look slipped to the fae; Davina gave a sheepish smile. "You told Nyte not to let any *vampire* follow you."

I couldn't be mad. In fact, I was so damned relieved she was here.

Recalling the absolute chaos of events that had unfolded at the keep, my thoughts snagged on the end right before Nyte found me.

Auster had been there. It seemed even more incredible now that I had a calmer mind. Where was he now?

"Have any of you seen Auster?" I blurted.

"Who?" Lilith asked.

"The High Celestial?" Nadia answered with an edge of bitterness.

"No, we haven't," Rose answered.

"Should we?" Davina curved a brow.

Though I was so happy in all of their company, the many directions of voices made my head spin.

"He was there just before I . . . wrecked the place, I guess. Then Nyte came," I explained.

"Probably ran off then," Davina said, a little smug. "He's always been afraid of Nyte."

"Can you really blame him?" Rose grumbled.

Davina didn't respond but her mouth stayed with a small curl.

I had to tell Nyte about my meetings with Auster. Despite Auster's warnings, I didn't believe he'd start a war over me simply because I was going there to learn. He was far more understanding than the world wanted to believe he was.

"Cassia's father . . ." Rose trailed.

My grief pummeled me like a fist in my stomach.

"He's dead," I whispered. "It was never him. It was the king this whole time using some enchantment in a stupid hat, which I should have detected sooner."

"Shit," Rose muttered. She rubbed her forehead. "Zath and I should have seen it."

"What do you mean?"

"We'd visited a hat shop during the Libertatem—we didn't know it was enchanted—and I was tricked into giving a lock of my hair. They attached it to the hat with magick and when they put it on . . . they stole my whole appearance. Only with brown hair."

"I wondered about your natural hair color," Davina said.

"The pink suits you," Lilith admired, twirling a lock of her own unique green tresses.

Rose was growing comfortable with the new female companionship, and I was so touched to see them all together. The only one who felt out of place was Nadia. Not because of what she was, but even more so than Rose when I'd first met her, Nadia kept her guard high and buried any troubles under a constant drive. But sometimes when I looked at her . . . I thought she harbored the most lonely soul I'd ever seen.

"My blood," I said. "It had been keeping Cassia alive for longer than she should have had."

"The reigning lord used you?" Rose said in shock.

"I never knew. I wish I had, because I would have given it willingly. But I guess he had an agreement with my . . ."

"Abuser," Rose inserted.

I winced, dropping my eyes.

"Yeah. And telling me about my blood would have exposed what I was and that would have diminished his control over me. Perhaps given me a drive to leave him."

A hand took mine under the water and I locked eyes with Lilith's gentle hazel gaze.

"You're the most resilient person I know."

That meant more to me than I could form the words for.

"Yeah, yeah, the star-maiden, our savior and protector. Goddess of Justice and peace," Nadia drawled sarcastically.

I might have been stung by the comment once, but glancing her way, I didn't take it personally.

Rose furrowed an angry brow, however. "What is your problem?"

"I don't have a problem," she said icily. "It seems like no one here has a fuck-ing problem."

She floated to the steps and climbed out, fitting a towel around herself. I thought about Drystan lingering in the halls as she stormed out, but I figured he had the sense to stay far out of her path.

"She's . . . spirited," Lilith said carefully.

"People lash out when they feel alone and scared," I said.

"Well it's not like she's making a team effort," Davina muttered.

Lilith looked at her with a soft smile. Davina quickly averted her eyes, turning shy. I'd seen her this way before, but I didn't want to make any as-sumptions about her possible attraction to Lilith.

Rose tracked back to the revelations of Cassia's father. "I have no doubt she would have been outraged by what her father had done even in her best interests. But she was very depressed about her shortened life. You saved her body by providing the blood she consumed, which neither of you knew about, but more importantly, and this is why she loved you, you saved her spirit right until the very end."

My lip wobbled with that and Davina floated over to me. Her head rested on my shoulder in comfort. "Now we're going to do the same for you, Astraea. As the Maiden Tribe."

"The Maidenettes," Lilith chimed in with a giggle.

"Team Maiden," Davina countered.

My brow crumpled with overwhelming joy while they went back and forth with more names and laughed about them all. It felt ridiculous, but at the same time, it felt like I finally had a place in the world.

"Mind if I join you?" a timid voice said from across the bath house.

My eyes lit up. It was Katerina.

"Of course," I said.

She smiled, coming around to the tub, but hesitated with shyness about removing her robe. All of us read it, averting our gazes to allow her to undress, and the waters were milky enough to hide our bodies underneath.

"This is . . ." she said through a breath of pleasure when she was submerged to her shoulders. "Is it strange to say I think I could orgasm from this?"

The tension eased as we all broke into laughter.

"I thought the same," Davina answered with a grin.

"I never thought I'd feel a hot bath again," Katerina admitted.

My expression fell in sorrow, but I smiled. "How is everyone?"

"Healing. It will take time. They'll be heading to Althenia tomorrow, but a lot will have to travel by land without their wings."

I'd never thought to ask her before, but now I wondered . . .

"Why were you in that cage next to me—in a separate room from everyone else?"

Katerina distracted herself with the water. "Because I'm the Bonded of Zephyr, the High Celestial of the House of Luna."

I was gawking at her now. She was practically celestial royalty.

"Why didn't you tell me?"

She couldn't lift her eyes, like she kept them down in shame while her brown irises glittered with tears.

"Because it doesn't matter anymore," she whispered.

"Of course it does," Davina said gently.

Katerina only shook her head.

"He won't want me once he sees," she said. Then she sniffed hard before turning around.

My hand covered my mouth with a cold wave of sickening shock. They'd taken her wings. The magnificent silver pair in Reihan's office flashed to mind and I was overcome with nausea. They were hers. I could feel it now like connecting an old intuition.

All this time Reihan had been kidnapping my people and keeping them captive for their wings and blood. I couldn't decide if I was relieved or *angry* he wasn't around for me to confront. I don't know what I would have done or how I wouldn't have survived facing the heartbreak.

"It won't matter," I said, reeling back from my initial horror. "He doesn't get to take a single thing more from you. No matter what, you're a celestial just as much as the rest of them."

Two long, thick lines tore like jagged lightning on either side of her spine. The skin wasn't like a fading scar, it was a deep purple and I didn't think that would ever change.

"You don't understand the harsh ways of their ruling. I won't be worthy of him anymore."

"You're worthy of far more than that. If he doesn't accept what has happened to you against your will and help you heal, then he never deserved you at all."

Katerina nodded, but she wasn't fully convinced and I understood the doubt. But I was committed to her. To all of them. Right here and now I couldn't explain the tether I felt winding around each of them. We needed each other, and I would protect them with everything I had.

36

Astraea

I shivered waiting upon the rooftop of the establishment, flexing my gloved fingers to work up my courage before Drystan arrived at midnight. I had one task to do before then.

Nyte had shown me how to do it before, and sorrow weighed on me to be here again when it felt too soon for another goodbye to someone who'd had far fewer years than they were owed.

I steadied my breaths and remembered what it had felt like to pull Cassia's soul from its safekeeping inside me. It was like drawing a final warm breath that wasn't mine. This particular ability was an honor and as I dragged forth the sphere of light from my chest I marveled at it.

"Hi, Calix," I whispered to it. "You might have been a stubborn, prickly bastard at times . . . but thank you for loving her. You didn't deserve to die the way you did but I hope you find your solace in the stars now."

It didn't emit any emotion or reaction back, but I felt the familiarity in it. Whatever souls were made of, I believed Cassia's and Calix's belonged to each other. My cupped palms raised, letting the glowing light fly, and I cherished this moment, watching them reunite in the sky.

When he reached far beyond where I could touch them again, his soul flared where it belonged. It was like they joined to make one constellation.

"Of course," I whispered to myself. "Cassiopeia."

The name of their constellation.

"Your magick seems to be coming back strong," Auster said, jolting me from my silent moment with my lost friends.

My sight fell back down to find him. "Where did you go? After the Keep?"

"I figured you didn't want Nyte knowing I was there."

I pursed my lips. Actually, I thought it might have made things easier for Nyte to have seen him there—to know Auster had come in aid of me—and then I could have begun to explain how I'd been going to Althenia.

"What happened to the king?"

"He is a king no longer."

"I don't actually know his name."

"No one does. They say Nyte's mother erased it in their realm, which carried into this one. He doesn't even remember it himself."

I was stunned by that revelation. Then I thought back to how Nyte had erased Goldfell's name. I could hardly remember what he looked like anymore either.

"Honestly I don't know where he went. After your attack, he disappeared."

I would be foolish to think I'd harmed him enough in my rage.

"Did I hurt you?" I asked with a wince.

Auster chuckled softly, coming closer. "No. I'm used to your magick enough to know how to defend myself. I was glad to see it."

"I'm sorry I haven't come back to Althenia. I have some things I need to do here first."

"I understand. I'll always be waiting."

I appreciated his patience.

"But Astraea, I can't wait forever."

My stomach tightened with the alternate meaning now. The bond between us. I couldn't have them both and I'd selfishly hoped I wouldn't have to choose so soon. I knew with certainty how I felt for Nyte, but I hadn't enough time to know what I could have had with Auster and whether I was throwing away something that would be better for me. Even for Nyte. As painful as it would be to admit.

"I know," I whispered.

My body tensed as Auster closed the distance but I didn't let it show. He was trying; I owed him that back at least. His fingers brushed my skin and my lips parted at the feel of it. I couldn't place it, but my pulse sped and my mind throbbed faintly as though it was trying to push through a memory and maybe it was me who didn't want to see it. Whatever flash of the past could unveil.

"So this is what you get up to when my brother is occupied or incapacitated."

I drew away from Auster like we'd been caught naked together. To Drystan, it might have looked like we were tempted.

"It's not what it looks like," I said, turning to find Drystan leaning against the chimney of the roof.

"What does it look like?" he taunted.

"I was just seeing she was safe," Auster interjected.

From his stiff tone, I could tell he wasn't remotely fond of Drystan and from the prince's darkening gaze, it was more than mutual.

"You wouldn't know how to keep a thing safe if it wasn't for your precious veil."

"You've let them call you *prince* all this time but you're nothing more than a powerless, blood-sucking bastard child."

Drystan didn't react, but I did. My head whipped around at the hateful comment.

"I think you should leave," I said.

Auster's eyes flexed around the edges with that. I knew what he must have been thinking, that I was defending the enemy. But I'd come to realize neither of them were my enemy. I was the only neutral territory, albeit because of my lack of memory, but I wasn't entirely clueless.

"I'm not leaving you with him," Auster protested.

Drystan said, bored, "You already have. If I wished to do her harm I would have done so when she was running around like perfect prey in the Libertatem and where were *you*, Auster?"

The High Celestial's jaw worked and for a second I thought I caught a spark of light at his fingertips. I hadn't seen his magick yet . . .

"Come back to Althenia with me?" Auster asked, soft to me but restrained hinted at ire from our present company.

"I can't right now. I have to go to the Guardian Temple tomorrow," I said.

Auster's brow furrowed. "You shouldn't."

My face matched his. "It's where I fell to. It's my best place for answers and they raised me."

"Not very well."

I was taken aback by his sharp tone but Auster recovered, sighing and wearing me down with concerned eyes.

"There are many who believe it's because of them you didn't receive the guidance you needed."

"They were *chosen* to guide me. By the gods *you* worship so dearly."

"Even gods make mistakes."

Drystan drawled, "What he means is they let you be your own damn person rather than the poised and pure maiden in white the celestials expected you to be."

"You know nothing of our customs," Auster snapped.

"I know they're archaic with an air of superiority that's long overdue to be broken."

"For your kind to savage the land? Shadowless and soulless creatures."

"Don't forget the nightcrawlers," Drystan said. "Don't forget the ages of control you kept over the realm with thanks to your wicked *creatures.*"

I caught intrigue in that last part, wondering what it meant. The celestials used the vampires?

"Ohh, a snack," Nadia's voice sang from behind Auster.

Her green eyes peered up as she circled around him, amusement cornering her mouth at Auster's dark reception.

"Trust me, it wouldn't be worth the indulgence," Drystan murmured.

"Because you'd be dead before you even got close," Auster said.

Nadia boldly reached up to touch his wing, seemingly innocent and curious. Auster shifted to face her, hand not reaching for his sword, just hovering, ready to use whatever power lingered under his skin.

Admittedly, I was hoping she kept provoking him so I could see it for the first time.

Drystan had inched closer with the rising tension too, eyes tracking Auster like he would lunge between them if he tried to attack Nadia.

"I'll ask you again, Astraea. Please come back with me now," Auster said, not taking his sights off Nadia who smiled deceivingly sweetly, hands clasped behind her back.

"I will. Soon," I promised. "I just can't tonight."

His disappointment shifted to me for a beat. Then he backed away from the vampire.

Auster didn't speak, only gave a nod, and I hated that it seemed I was always letting someone down. Torn apart by two sides, and I was losing hope each day that I could ever please them both.

When he left and the last wrap of air from his beating wings breezed around me, I sighed deeply.

"Don't let him cause you guilt," Drystan said. "He wants you. He always has. He doesn't always have your best interests in mind."

I wanted to trust Drystan, but I didn't know if *he* had my best intentions in mind anymore either.

"What did you want to meet me to discuss that I had to keep from everyone?" I asked.

"First it requires the egg."

I eyed Nadia questioningly and she started to look as wary as I was.

"Why am I here?" she asked.

"You'll get your purpose, little rogue."

"You didn't have to invite me here and make it easy to kill you. Takes the fun out of it."

It was like Drystan enjoyed her hunger for his life. There was a spark in his eyes that spoke something to her without words.

While they were distracted with each other, I reached into the void for the dragon egg. It would never fail to evoke awe in me and awaken a humming vibration of my magick every time I held it.

"It's alive," I said, hushed as though it were a sleeping child in my arms because it felt so precious. "It has to be. I can feel it."

"We're going to find out. Tonight," Drystan said.

"And if it is?"

"You can tell them how you did it and even that I told you, but nothing else. Before we leave you'll both swear a truth bargain to me."

"Like hell I'll bind myself to you another way," Nadia snarled.

"You're going to get what you want. But first, you'll need to yield this dose of trust. A foreign concept to you, I know. Get over it."

Her lips firmed, arms crossing to match Drystan in an intense stare off.

"What does it require?" she asked.

"You offering me your blood through a cut you make yourself. As much as biting into your pretty neck is highly tempting."

I shivered at his tone that hinted with seduction toward Nadia. She gave no external reaction to it but that only seemed to entice him more. It made me curious about vampires feeding on each other. Did they find it pleasurable in certain circumstances? Nadia was once human; did that make her blood more desirable than a born vampire's?

"At least you have the sense to call me pretty," Nadia said sweetly.

Drystan pinned her with a look and produced a small dagger. She held his stare and unsheathed her own at her thigh.

"This had better be worth it," she muttered.

"Or what?" he challenged.

"I can get *very* creative with my murder methods."

I was still reeling from my uncertainty while I hugged the egg tightly as Nadia cut her wrist. Drystan's eyes darkened as he stalked to her.

Distracting myself by tracing over the contours of the shell, I skipped over my options before I would offer my blood too. Would Nyte see this as a betrayal? I didn't know how long or how severe this lie would have to be, but I had to hatch this egg. If there was a chance the dragon was alive within . . . it could change the tide of the war.

So when Drystan came to me next, I held out my hand, and hoped my trust given now wouldn't become a regret learned later.

37

Nyte

The breath I drew when I woke speared in my chest with panic. It started ever since I'd been free from my underground prison. Sometimes I was pulled from the depths of hellish nightmares, other times the sleep had been restful, but the moment I woke was when a flicker of terror seized me. All because of her.

I pushed up from my stomach-down position with a tightness growing behind my ribs. A confusing torment that I was still there in the cave behind the veil, and Astraea was still gone. It left me unable to breathe.

With the cold, empty wrap of the room, my teeth clenched with the sharp pain attacking my head as I got out of bed. I'd fallen asleep. I hadn't meant to despite Astraea's scolding.

Astraea.

She wasn't back, and somehow I knew it had been far too long and she should be here with me.

I'd fallen asleep.

I tried to pull myself together, getting changed numbly. Sweat trickled down my skin. It wasn't from the exertion of dying; I was in perfect health. No—my dizzy sweeps came from a disease of the mind that had crawled its way into parts of me that became overwhelmed with fear. Riddled by treacherous anxiety.

I can't lose her again.

Bracing a hand on the table, I scrunched my eyes shut, beginning to tremble with anger at myself when I was only delaying myself from her longer in this pitiful state.

I'd breathe right again as soon as I saw her. Right in front of me. Safe and unharmed.

Thinking of her I reached for the thread of her that was bound to my soul. The only bright piece of treasure in such a dark and twisted place.

I wrapped my whole being around it as I pushed through the void to find her. To my relief, I felt nothing bad in the essence of her that lived eternally in me.

When the world stopped moving and my feet felt ground, I didn't know where I was.

I didn't care.

The head of stunning glittering silver hair that faced away from me weakened my knees with the weight of relief.

"Astraea." Her name barely escaped me in a breath with my throat still so tight. My pounding heart started to calm as she turned.

I took a long, contented inhale when her icy blue eyes met mine. On the exhale I began to take in more of where I'd found her.

We were on the rooftop of the establishment we took lodgings in. I would have been confused yet when I looked at what Astraea was cradling . . . I was slammed by shock.

She'd done it. Astraea had hatched the celestial dragon egg.

"His name is Eltanin," she said preciously, like she was holding a sleeping child.

The small beast was breathtaking. A dragon with feathered black wings and feathers that ran over the crown of its head right down to its very long tapering tail that wrapped around her wrist. It had flickers of violet on the leathery skin of its legs and chest.

"How did you do it?" I approached carefully, in awe of the creature but more so of her.

"It needed moonlight; then I had to *hear* its name if it was willing."

"Is that where you've been all night?"

She nodded.

I needed to touch her, slipping a hand over her waist. It was an invasive habit I hoped she would never grow repelled by. I couldn't help it, when it was the only thing to truly settle the beast of fearfulness that was always clawing in my chest, my mind, my soul, when she wasn't within reach.

Her existence felt too fragile. I'd lost it once before in the blink of an eye.

"Drystan told you," I assumed. That's why he wanted me to show her that memory. "What did he want to gain from it?"

Astraea dropped her eyes to the sleeping dragon, patting a careful hand over its head.

"He wanted to see if he could bond with a dragon," she said quietly, with a hint of fear, and I pulled her close.

"He won't get to take him from you," I assured.

Even if he wanted to, if the infant dragon had chosen Astraea, I thought it would be pointless to try to take him from her.

Astraea didn't respond, seeming to lose herself in thought looking over

Eltanin with a pinched brow. Something else weighed heavy on her mind that she didn't speak.

"They don't age like most creatures," she said. "He won't be so little for long. Every full moon they age. It takes four to six for them to stop growing."

The dragon gave a yawn, emitting a sound something between a caw and a rattle. One eye slipped open as if checking whether it was worth waking fully yet and I was taken by the starry purple of it, split by vertical pupil.

"He's beautiful," Astraea murmured.

The dragon was, but I couldn't stop watching her. How dearly she admired this creature in her arms. I leaned in to kiss her temple.

"It's freezing out here. Are you sure he's not got the power to cause juvenile destruction if we take him inside?"

"I'm not sure, actually," she said.

As we moved, Eltanin seemed to object, climbing with sharp claws on his four feet up her chest, over her shoulder, before burrowing in her hood, his tail circling her neck now.

I smiled as she giggled, cringing with the feathers tickling her skin. Every time I saw Astraea it was a gift, but right now, I was utterly enamored.

It was hard to imagine the small, adorable creature that could fit in her hood now would grow to a huge, terrifying beast in four to six short months. I thought about the one we'd faced in the library so long ago—even in its agony it was terrifying. Astraea had no idea of the weapon she had allied with tonight. Even if it never attacked, for her to be the only dragon and rider in existence was going to shake the continent.

"Do you think it breathes fire that burns?" she asked in wonder as we headed inside.

"The one in the library we found—its breath was like shadowfire. It can burn in a sense but not like amber flame. It would drain the life from anything that it touched. Rot it, essentially."

"It looked like your magick," she said. "The dragon's breath in your memory. You could feel it."

"Yes. It was peculiar."

"Then perhaps it should be bonded to you instead."

"We don't know if it has the same magick."

"I think he will," she said, and it was like a new spirit had lifted her this night.

In the main room of the pleasure house, I wanted to suggest we just retire for the night.

People sought more distance than necessary as we passed. I was used to the dejecting nature of my presence and didn't pay it any attention. Their separation from us made it easier to find Astraea's companions.

"I think they're scared of Eltanin," Astraea said, leaning into me.

"I don't think they've noticed the beastie in your hood."

He blended in like fur in her dark cloak.

"There's our little Stray," Zath called over. He was drunk.

Zath's personality became far bigger with alcohol. Rosalind wouldn't look at me, but I thought the edge was taken off her usual thick distaste around me. She even smiled to Astraea.

"Oh my stars!" Davina gushed, hands covering her mouth as she bounded over.

"Is that real?" Lilith shot up from the bench too, eyes locked over Astraea's shoulder.

"His name is Eltanin."

"Eli!" Zathrian announced the new nickname. He jostled Rosalind into his side. "We're godparents."

Rose didn't seem enthused by the way he wrapped an arm around her shoulders and imposed the declaration on her.

"*We* aren't anything," she said flatly.

Zath waved her off. "You'll come around. Let me see our godson!"

"How the hell did you get a baby dragon?" Rose asked, but she was curious enough too.

I let Astraea lose herself with her friends and their admiration of the dragon. It would be interesting to watch it grow and I imagined how mighty they would look ruling side by side.

She was magnificent.

I leaned sideways against a wooden pillar mostly cloaked in shadow—an attempt to make my presence as small as possible.

Drystan wasn't here upon my quick survey. I expected to find him flirting with some man or woman.

"Not one for social scenes either?" The rogue's voice trickled from the other side of the post I leaned against.

"I'm enjoying myself just fine," I said.

"You look like you're contemplating turning this place to ash," Nadia countered.

A table of three men kept sparing wary looks in our direction. I'd have admitted their attention was starting to grate on my nerves, until they stood and shuffled out.

"See? You'll quieten this place down in no time. Keep doing that."

"Doing what?"

"Standing there."

"How do you know it was me? You're not exactly the most approachable either."

"They're human men and I'm a beautiful woman."

"That could kill them in the blink of an eye."

I watched a slow smile of satisfaction curl her face as she leaned like my mirror reflection, watching the crowd.

"Vampirism has its perks."

I dreaded to ask, "Have you seen my brother?"

"He's been good at avoiding me; I have to give him credit."

"If he hadn't changed you, someone worse could have," I said. "We might have our differences and a lot has changed in him. But if he wanted to use the power he had over you, he would have by now."

"Doesn't mean he won't. Perhaps he's biding his time. You've led many armies and fought in many wars. Your strategies are legendary yet you're blinded by the fact he's your blood. He has an army ready to command, and you'd be a fool not to consider he'd turn on you with the might of it and he's just waiting for his chance."

"Perhaps. But if that time came I would kill him myself."

Nadia slipped me a look. She didn't believe I would. I didn't like to dwell on *what ifs*. To calm my rising irritation, I found Astraea.

The little dragon had awoken, prancing around the wooden table while they marveled over the creature. A nearby table evacuated in their cowardice regarding the unknown.

I could relate to it—a pitiful realization.

It coughed a small cloud of black smoke, and I was curious about it. Wanting to feel it even if satisfying that curiosity got me hurt.

"Seems pointless," Nadia commented, watching the group with me. "For a celestial to have a dragon for a pet when they both have wings."

It was a peculiar thing. The celestials were like kin to the dragons from what I knew, but the dragons would often bond to the fae—it acted like a treaty of nature.

Astraea met my eye with a grin from watching Eltanin knock over cups and snap with juvenile innocence at people's fingers.

"I think he's hungry," I said to her mind.

Her face fell as she looked at the dragon with new consideration.

"What does he eat?"

"My brother coaxed you into dragon motherhood without adequate instruction?"

She cast me a flat look; I couldn't suppress my hint of a smile too.

I said to Nadia, "You might be the best candidate to take the creature hunting."

"I'm not risking suffering the consequences of whatever untrained power could unleash from that thing."

"I think it could hardly char bread."

"Yeah? Well, you take it."

I shrugged. "Suit yourself."

The ground rumbled and I straightened. The quake shook through the establishment as a dormant warning that awoke to rattle through my bones. It turned time to stardust slipping through my fingers as I gravitated toward Astraea in the commotion.

She met my look with concern; our thoughts aligned but I didn't care. Not about the many ways this world would try to tear us apart. As long as she still called for me, I would always come.

If the sun never rose again, I would come for her in total darkness.

If magick died out for good, I would run, or walk, or crawl.

If a void split and tore us apart, I would step through worlds to reach her.

I took her face in my hands with the ground raging its warning, and I sealed those promises with my lips on hers.

PART
FIVE

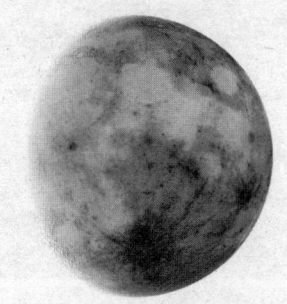

38

Nyte–Past

Every year the nights stole more hours than the days. The winters stretched to freeze longer than the summers warmed. The quakes became more frequent—from once every quarter year to nearly every month.

Astraea was in tune with the stars, Nyte was too but she didn't know that. Both of them could see the gaps between them were growing.

The stars were dying.

"I don't know what else we can try," Astraea said with exasperation, throwing herself down on the bed of the bell tower.

They met here frequently. To plan, or at least that was the expectation. Over time, they often forgot why they started meeting in the first place. They'd end up spending the days playing chess, or cards, or riddles as a particular favorite of hers.

Those pastimes were avoidance from the fact they were failing in their task. If they didn't allow themselves those moments, they might have driven each other or themselves insane long ago.

"A game of checkers?" Nyte asked.

She tried to suppress her half smile under the glower of her eyes. Nyte knew she was tempted to say yes, but they'd been avoiding setting their minds back on a new strategy for too long.

Nyte reached for the compass on the dresser.

"Can't believe we got hustled by those men for this," he grumbled to himself.

It reminded him he had hunting to do for the scam. That could take his mind off the hopeless task for a while.

"I can," Astraea countered.

Nyte opened the protective case of the compass. It was still, but occasionally it would flicker. They'd tried to pin it on a map and followed several directions toward temples, libraries, and other places they thought could hold the answer it was supposed to lead them toward.

They'd wondered if it was something that moved. Perhaps a creature in their realm that was never supposed to be.

Nyte tossed the compass to her and she caught it with a gasp that escaped from her unawares.

"Drystan hasn't been able to stop thinking about dragons," Nyte said.

It had been years since they'd discovered the egg and put the beaten down beast to a peaceful rest. His younger brother was less insistent to accompany him to meet with Astraea when he'd become engrossed in translating the ancient language and learning what he could about the dragons. It all seemed pointless to Nyte—the dragons were all gone now.

"Has he discovered how to hatch an egg?" Astraea inquired.

"Not that he's told me. I think he'd have come to you to go get it back if he had."

She placed it somewhere neither of them knew of for the utmost safekeeping, she'd said.

Astraea stood, examining the compass as she paced around the room.

"It's like it's mocking us." She scowled at it. Nyte could hear the faint flicker of the needle hand. "Perhaps we should try one more mage."

"We've tried three who all say it should be working."

She rubbed her temple as she kept walking back and forth as if it would untangle the threads of her brilliant mind and reveal an answer.

He'd learned so much about the star-maiden it was unsettling. Not as many things about her personal life, which they both kept closely guarded even after all this time. Their enemy wall was only down for this impossible task.

But he'd discovered so many more insignificant things that held more value to him. How she would pace endlessly in thought and it was like he could see the cogs of her mind turning. How she always wore her stormstone dagger on her right thigh and it was a subconscious habit to trace the black-winged cross guard like she did right now. How she could look up from staring at the floor for so long and pass a whole internal conversation over her expression as she came close to figuring something out.

Astraea stopped walking. It was the sign she'd found an answer, even if pending confirmation. Yet Nyte didn't receive the usual spark in his chest he usually did when she met his eyes ready to spill her theories, because from her wary expression, her thoughts weren't positive.

Wordlessly, Astraea threw the compass back to him.

He caught it effortlessly, looking just in time to see the needle spin again.

Confused, he looked up in question but Astraea fixed her sight on the compass, her lips now parted and eyes slightly wider.

"What's wrong?" he asked, stiffening with trepidation.

"Throw it back to me," she said distantly.

He did.

Astraea swore.

Now he was concerned.

"No—that doesn't make any sense. What the fuck does it mean?" she ranted, pacing again.

Nyte couldn't stand it; appearing in her path, he took hold of her shoulders. His skin crawled at her ghostly look.

"What is it?" he demanded.

"*Look,* Nyte," she snapped, taking his hand and slapping the compass back in his upturned palm.

He was about to snap back at the prickly violence but he watched the needle move.

Pointing to Astraea now.

"What are you trying to say?" he asked, but dread was beginning to coil in him to prepare for denial.

Astraea held out her hand, taking the compass more gently. In her palm, the needle spun to him.

Nyte frowned. "So are you the problem or am I?"

She clenched her fist around the brass and went back to pacing. He was becoming so dizzy with her antics that he sat in one of the low open arches for air.

"*We* are. But how?" she whispered, calculating. Then she stopped abruptly, turning accusatory. "What are you?"

"This again?"

"You've never truly answered."

She looked at him now like she didn't know who he was at all anymore. That disturbed him.

"I did. You just never took me seriously. I was born fae, but I was made vampire and the wings are just an added gift." He said the last word with bitter sarcasm.

"Made," she repeated. Recalling that he'd told her that. "How?"

What he hadn't told her before . . . was that he wasn't from this realm. Her realm. He didn't need her to think of him as more of an invasive pest on her land than she already did.

"Tell me," she pressed, softer now, like she sensed his guard rising.

He'd never cared about what people thought of him before. His methods, his motives, his existence. Yet right now he stared in the face of vulnerability with her, and he wasn't used to this feeling.

Nyte stood, turning to brace a hand on the stone and look out over the capital city.

"I wasn't born here," he said.

"In Vesitire?"

"In this world, Starlight."

He needed her reaction, but his body tensed to brace for it as he turned around. She studied him, waiting for the lie.

"What are you talking about?"

"My father brought me here when I could barely walk. Through some kind of portal like a mirror."

Astraea was slammed in shock, eyes darting around as she tried to fathom how it was possible.

"So you're the reason things are falling apart here?" she said, rising with rage and accusation, and he could feel her energy growing dangerously. "All this time you knew, and you said *nothing?*"

"How was I to know that could be the cause?"

"Because you've never *belonged* here. It's so fucking obvious."

He didn't expect that comment to strike him. Words never did. Yet somehow she'd gained the ability to turn hers to knives that bled him.

Nyte knew he didn't belong. Maybe for some reason . . . he still had a kernel of hope that was a wicked lie of his mind and he could still find somewhere he belonged someday. Through travels with Drystan, perhaps. If they ever got to escape their father's shackles.

"When did you first notice the quakes?" she demanded.

"I've never known a time without them."

"Shit."

The air charged and he could hardly stand her distress.

"Why does it point to me when you hold it?" she asked, mostly to herself, reeling with troubles.

Nyte focused his mind on her conclusions too. He watched her. Every movement of her leg exposed her thigh from the high cut of her gown. She liked light wears and putting her beautiful silver marked skin on display . . .

"Fuck," he muttered. He didn't know if it meant anything, but he had to show her.

"What?" she said, spinning to him.

She'd never seen his skin. Not enough to see the resemblance of his gold markings to hers.

Nyte reached for the fastenings of his jacket, and Astraea's body turned rigid as he began to undress; debating if she should turn around or flee. When he peeled out of that, he spared only a glance, delighting in the warmth spreading over her cheeks, but the curious thing didn't look away. He reached for the hem of his shirt and pulled it off.

Her uncertainty washed away under a wave of shock that parted her lips.

"Your tattoos . . ." she trailed off in a breath.

Nyte couldn't stop assessing her every flicker of emotion under the scrutiny that prickled over his skin. Static grew between them as she came closer carefully, never taking her eyes off his arms, chest, and shoulders like she was studying in a map.

His teeth clenched tightly when she was close enough to touch. He wanted to touch *her*. So fucking badly it disgusted him. He shouldn't—couldn't—want that from his enemy.

Astraea's hand lifted, and the moment she brushed his bare skin his magick awakened to her. His soul stirred with her near and it wound him in torture and bliss.

She traced along his bicep, circling around him. Over his shoulder blades. Nyte's eyes closed for a second to enjoy the slow trail of her fingers he didn't want to crave.

"They kind of look like mine," she said quietly.

Her anger was gone, stolen by wonder, and the space between them somehow became delicate.

When she faced him again, her light blue irises flicked up to him.

"What are you, Rainyte?" she asked, not expecting an answer.

I'm yours, he wanted to say. Two words that were as dangerous as a declaration of war, but they were true, even if he didn't want them to be.

"My mother was a goddess," he admitted. "Of stars."

Astraea backed away a single step with her shallow gasp.

"Like me?"

"Perhaps. I don't think there was a maiden in that realm. Not like here. There are different laws of magick, different gods and spirits and monsters in many places."

"Do you think that's why solar magick is failing? Because you are a son of a star goddess and I a daughter?"

"You're the Daughter of Dusk and Dawn, technically," he said. "But perhaps. Or maybe the *gift* I received of Nightsdeath has something to do with it."

Astraea was burdened by something else then. Sorrow.

"So we're back to the start, then," she said. "For one of us has to kill the other."

That couldn't be the only way. Nyte was hit hard by a refusal to believe it. There was a time he'd wanted her dead. For all intents and purposes, he still should. Even if it was still a goal of hers he'd let go of the fight for it to be his.

There was only one problem . . .

"I can't be killed," he told her softly.

Her brow pulled together. "All beings can be killed by something."

"A mortal god, like you or I, can only be killed by something we're made of."

His eyes dipped to her hip where the key was a short baton strapped there. Astraea angled her body like he might lunge for the only weapon that could kill *her*.

On the contrary. He looked at the key now with the most terror to ever rise in his chest.

"We can't tell anyone about this," he said, showing his fear made her relax, trusting he wasn't about to turn on her.

"Agreed. Until we figure out how the hell to fix it."

That helped him breathe a little easier. There had to be another way to solve their clashing existence.

"You should, um, get dressed," she said, swiping up his shirt and holding it out to him.

Nyte wanted to trace the pink coloring her cheeks. The compulsion caused him to grip her wrist instead of taking the shirt and her lips parted with the fright. His chest was pounding in a rhythm it never had before.

Reckless, taunting thoughts circled his mind. When it came to killing or crime, or apparently being in close proximity to the star-maiden, he had fucking poor resistance.

"We've damned the world anyway," he said, pulling her to him and claiming her mouth.

Astraea was stiff against him and he was bracing for her to pull away and likely slap him. Or take her dagger to his chest.

She didn't. Her body softened to him like clay piece by piece. She molded around him and they fit together too perfectly. She kissed him back and that was a mistake for her because now he couldn't stop.

An addiction took over him in an instant. Absolutely feral because she kissed back this time from nothing but desire for *him*. Not to prove something to herself and bind a bargain.

Her hands slipped over his side, around his back. He didn't know this kind of igniting of skin against skin existed and *fuck,* the thought of both of them stripped and bare to bask in the full heat of it was a glorious temptation. Nyte swept his tongue over her lips and when she opened for him to deepen the kiss he groaned as her nails dragged over his skin.

This was what madness felt like. A slow obsession that had always been climbing and all it took was this final push.

The taste of her exploded in him. Right now, his whole existence before the day he met her became questionable. His purpose, his gravity, it all became forces revolving around *her.*

"Nyte." She sighed his name, and his cock twitched to it.

With his strong arm hooking around her waist, Astraea lifted herself into his arms so gently it was undeniable their magnetism worked for each other. His tongue traced over the vein in her neck that pulsed for him to claim but he wouldn't. Not yet.

He risked losing his restraint; pressing her against the wall next to the archway he kissed her deeply again. Greedy for so much more of her.

"We can't," she rasped with a hand on his chest.

It took everything in him to stop, leaning his forehead to hers and gathering measures of sanity back in every breath.

"Why?" His voice was thick with lust and her legs tightened around him.

Nyte groaned, squeezing her thigh and pressing himself to her core to make her feel what she was doing to him by denying them both.

"Because if you take me in that bed . . . it'll start something that can't end well for either of us."

"And if I drop you and take you hands braced to the wall right here?"

"Nyte," she breathed his name and it was only another strain on his faltering control.

"I want to do the worst things to you. Things you never could have thought of but would crawl back to me for again."

"I'd never crawl for you."

Nyte moved to add friction between them, dragging his aching cock over her core, but it was as tormenting for him as it was for her.

"We'll see, Maiden," he said, then he couldn't stop the impulse to open his mouth on her neck, dragging his sharp teeth just shy of piercing her soft flesh.

Astraea gasped, her magick hummed to life, and his body tensed to the current she shocked through him like lightning. His hold slackened and her feet met the ground. Astraea pushed against his chest and slipped away from the cage of his body against the wall.

Her cool eyes met his with a warning, but Nyte couldn't suppress the small smile that found great delight in her resistance. Until he remembered she would be heading back to her *other* Bonded. What if she decided to forge it with him and he would be helpless to stop it?

"Do you love him?" The question slipped out of him.

She knew who he meant of course. Nyte's fist clenched in anticipation of hearing something he wouldn't like.

"In some ways, yes."

"What ways?"

He was desperate to know even though it might be crossing a line.

"He's my bonded. I grew up with him and he's been a loyal and dear friend most of my life. I'll always love him."

"Does he think you're more?"

"No. But he hasn't given up hope we could be."

If Auster was right in front of him, Nyte couldn't be sure he wouldn't break to kill him without logical thought. It would incite a war but he didn't care.

She was worth waging war for whether here or between the stars.

Astraea threw all logic and consequence from his mind.

"Our quest isn't finished," he said.

"No," she whispered. "I think it just got a lot more complicated."

39

Astraea

Eltanin had made something of a home tucked in my hood. We were both craving the extra warmth against the bitter winter air as he was surprisingly very warm.

"Best hope he doesn't get the impression he can keep using you when he gets bigger next month," Nyte mused.

"He'll be able to keep himself warmer then. More feathers." At least I hoped he would.

The temple we stood outside of was more like a small castle. I couldn't stop staring at the magnificent structure that was so tall I had to crane my neck back to see even though we stood at the opposite end of the massive circular courtyard before the entrance.

Nyte kept close to me, but we hadn't spoken of the memory he'd given me last night. I spent the morning reflecting, tracing his gold markings and feeling myself being pulled impossibly closer with each new glimpse of the past, made even more precious in his own thoughts and feelings. That night we'd learned of our clashing existence that should have sunk me in despair, given me enough reason to push Nyte to arm's length with all that was repeating in the present. Yet all I felt was defiance to change our fate.

"Do people use it?" Zathrian asked from behind me.

I wondered if their distance was because Rose held a stare like knives on Nyte which kept Zath and me on edge with what she might do or provoke out of him. Nyte didn't help when it was often like his receptive stares back were goading her.

It was Rose who answered. "It's said to be haunted by spirits and curses anyone who tries to enter with ill intent. But people still worship around it for the Winter Solstice."

I twisted around to her in surprise. "How do you know this?"

"There's one in Pyxtia too. People make paper dragon figures and burn them in bonfires for Winter Solstice as they believe the age of the dragon will come back with her—you," Rose corrected, shifting on her feet like acknowledging the legends she grew up with were about *me* made her nervous to remember. "I guess they were right."

"I love Star-Maiden Day!" Davina said excitedly.

"Me too," Lilith gushed. "The fae cast coins into wells like wishing upon stars. Then of course we get drunk and dance the night away outdoors."

The concept seemed wonderful, but I was cringing inside because of the name. "My birthday," I said.

Nyte's hand hovered on the small of my back. "Yes. This side of the veil it's known as the Winter Solstice. I imagine the celestials still celebrate it as Star-Maiden Day."

I remembered Auster's disappointment when he learned Nyte hadn't told me about it already. I didn't understand why when Nyte spoke of it now with ease.

"Hardly something for anyone else to celebrate," I muttered.

"I worship it every day, but once a year, the world recognizes your brilliance too," Nyte said, low and personal away from the others nearby. "Many have never forgotten, and never given up hope you'd return."

I was building up the courage to tell Nyte about Auster. This time when I went back to Althenia I didn't want it to be behind his back. After this visit to the guardians, I decided I would tell him.

My eyes trailed back to the building, then they fell down, and I was awash with dread, blinking at the golden circle I stood within.

"Strange," Rose muttered, examining the ground with me. "Pyxtia's temple has the same woven circle outside, but ours has a magnificent painting of a white dragon within it."

This one had nothing.

"Uhh, should we be concerned about them?" We all turned to Zath's carful alert.

Long past the gold-painted circle, guarding the entrance now, stood three cloaked figures with pointed hoods.

"They're keepers of the temple," Davina said. "They should be harmless unless you try to bypass them to get inside."

"I need inside," I said.

"They have to find you worthy," Davina said.

Should be easy enough as the star-maiden, I thought.

"Let's get this over with," I muttered under my breath. A crawling unease was beginning to prick my skin.

Even as we got closer to the keepers, I still couldn't see any flicker of skin from their tilted-down hoods. I walked ahead with Nyte, and stopped when they finally looked up.

They weren't creatures of flesh, only bone. Ice crept through my blood at the depthless skull eyes that seemed to lure me in.

"Why have you come, maiden?" A low, echoing vibration sounded those words and silenced the wind around us.

"I need to know why I fell here," I said.

"You have abandoned your duty since."

"I hardly had a choice."

Nyte's hand slipped into mine, and with the touch my rising temper cooled within. I thought the faceless keeper before me might have shifted his head a fraction as if observing our hands.

"Even now, you are not ready to dedicate yourself to being what the world needs."

"I wouldn't be here if I wasn't."

"They mean because of me," Nyte said calmly.

"This doesn't have anything to do with you."

His hard eyes turned soft on me. "You know it does."

We didn't have time to navigate more obstacles. I was running out of patience.

I slipped the key free; flipping it, I caught it in its full staff form it had transformed to.

"You either let me pass, or I do so by force. But what I won't do is turn away from answers I need for my *duty*."

A tendril of pride fluttered in my chest like a gentle passing of Nyte's emotions within me.

"Very well, maiden. But you must go alone."

Nyte pulled me to him, cupping my cheek.

"You know I'll be waiting right here for you," he said quietly, trying for privacy.

"I know."

Then he added to my mind, *"You always know how to call for me. And you know there's nothing that can stand in my way to you the moment you do."*

Nyte let me go and I rallied the courage to go ahead without him in my next breath.

The keepers parted and I ascended the long temple steps as the doors groaned inward by some invisible force.

Inside, I'd never felt so small and intimidated by a single space before. There was nothing ordinary about the colossal columns that circled the perimeter toward a lower center hexagonal platform. I came to one of five descending staircases.

My chest tightened with anticipation as I tried to gauge all I could but there was so much to take in. Light flooded the space from a domed roof and greenery climbed the aged cream walls and pillars. Down on the platform there were six statues. I kept my senses on high alert and the key warmed my palm as I headed down. It was so eerily quiet with only intermittent sounds of water dripping somewhere and the faint scuff of my boots.

I reached the platform and surveyed the statues. They stood in three pairs. The second thing I noticed was that each pairing had a different animal painted in front of them. A serpent, a panther, and a raven. The third thing I noticed was the diversity around me. A male nightcrawler from his taloned bat-like wings next to a human woman I deduced from her rounded ears. A celestial male from his feathered wings next to a vampire female, but I couldn't tell if she was a soulless or shadowless. Then finally a fae male with dark, curled horns next to another vampire female.

Nerves bubbled inside me, but they were overpowered by something tighter in my chest. Excitement. The kind that sped my pulse with eagerness, but it was wrapped in threads of sadness and uncertainty.

These were my guardians. The people who raised me in this world. I blinked away the prickling in my eyes, hoping my memory of them would come back.

I hadn't had two parents. I'd had six. And I couldn't remember all they'd done for me.

My sight weighed to the ground in sorrow. At the center point of the gray cracked stone, there was a six-point star in the middle. I gravitated to it, puzzling like it was a riddle before me. The hole wasn't a perfect shape, near circular but more like a rock had plummeted down to create the crevice.

It only took trailing my eyes to the stone at the top of the key staff in finding two puzzle pieces that would fit together.

Hope bloomed in my chest.

"Here goes nothing," I said to myself.

Flipping the staff, I gripped it tight, my adrenaline threatening my composure as I considered what I could unlock by doing this. I *had* to try.

Holding my breath, I lifted with both my hands until the rock slammed into the slot. A perfect fit that erupted the world around me in a flare of light my eyes winced shut at. Energy slammed into me, then left me feeling weightless.

When I dared to open my eyes, I gasped.

I was still in the temple, but it was like the walls and roof had dissipated away and became an open ground of endless sky and mountains and *life*. So much life radiated here, but not like in my world. This place had a peaceful but almost sad aura.

"Astraea," a soft feminine voice said behind me.

I whirled around in fright, and my heart slammed against my chest finding the six figures, the statues given flesh, before me. At least in appearance when they could be spirits with hollow forms.

"Where am I?" I asked.

"The land of guardians. Where those of us who have fulfilled our sacred duty get to pass in peace," the woman said.

She was the human, I assumed. Her hair was long and raven black and she had dark eyes to match. Beside her stood a male, with dark brown short hair and bright hazel irises, who wore an equally warm but saddened expression as he held eyes on me. I couldn't reciprocate when the towering, leathery wings behind him made me balk.

"She should know this," another feminine voice said bitterly.

The red-haired beauty stood cross-armed, pinning me with a frown of disappointment but I didn't think it was aimed toward me. Somehow, I knew to look down to discover her missing shadow. A blood vampire. The male at her side wore a similar steely intimidation in his green eyes and had silvery hair like mine. I was awestruck to discover his celestial feathered wings were black when I'd only seen those on Nyte before.

The two pairings were so unfathomable in the world I knew with all species at war.

"You're my . . . guardians?" I asked the red-haired shadowless. Her lips firmed like the question angered her.

"They make us spend nearly a century raising her only to take that all away?" A new voice snapped, talking to the others about me as if I couldn't hear. He was the tallest and I found him so beautiful with dark reddish disheveled hair, curving horns, and green eyes. Though my speculation about him being fae from the statue above was wrong. *He* was the other vampire. Soulless. From his missing reflection in the lake surrounding the hexagonal platform.

A female with short black hair with silver tresses framing her face curled an arm around his bicep. She had both a shadow and a reflection. Fae.

One from each species stood before me—I had been raised by them all to be fair and unbiased.

"It's not her fault," the soulless female said.

"I'm trying to find my memories," I whispered. That snapped all their eyes to me.

I hadn't known what the concept of my *guardians* would mean when I confronted it. If they would be just as parentally unattached as the gods who created me. Only seeing me as a duty. Yet as I looked over them all I couldn't explain the waves of emotion at being in their presence that were overcoming me. I didn't have the pictures . . . but I missed them. I mourned for them.

"Oh, our little star," the human said, stepping away from the others to approach me.

The nightcrawler followed and she stopped in front of me, hesitating to raise her hands. She touched me carefully like she didn't know if a touch could be physical here.

It was, and the moment she held me I couldn't help but break a sob, pulled into the arms of someone who felt trusting and warm, like a mother I never had.

"I don't know how to remember," I cried.

"Shhh," she soothed, smoothing a hand down my hair. "We're here now."

"Can you help me get my memories back?"

"I don't know. But I do think there is something you could find here."

She held my arms to pull me back and gave me a saddened smile.

"I'm so lost," I confessed. I'd been trying to be brave and strong and convince those around me I could be what they wanted but those walls came tumbling down here. "I don't know if I can be what they need."

"You are everything they need," the red-haired shadowless said, approaching too. "We didn't raise you to be anything less."

Her reception wasn't as warm as the human's; her affection was a little sharper, but I appreciated the balance.

"It has to start with believing in yourself," said the celestial male.

"I'm trying," I said.

I was relaxed in their company; unexplainably I knew I could be my most vulnerable here and it would be safe and secret with them.

"You're holding onto your past. Both in this life and the one before," the nightcrawler said. "It's always been your greatest flaw—you've always been the hardest on yourself and your capabilities."

The guardians weren't old in appearance—immortality had preserved their youth—but I felt like a child among them. Their child. It was unconventional, but I understood now this was what I was missing most in my short life since returning. To know if I'd had parental love and I never could have imagined it was in the form of not blood but guardianship. It was whole and promising all the same.

"None of you had children of your own?" I asked, keen to know more of the history of the guardians before I came along. How they met their partners, and why they'd been chosen to raise me by the Gods of Dusk and Dawn.

"A story for another time," the woman said with a smile. "Unless you remember first. But this is about you right now. You're as much of a daughter to all of us as any of blood could be."

"Can you come back with me?" I said, a child's plea, but I yearned for them to come back and guide me again.

My glance over their dropping expressions sank that small dose of hope.

"Our time has passed in your world now," the soulless male said.

"It doesn't feel like mine," I admitted quietly.

The woman cupped my face, planting a kiss on my forehead, and I bit my lip to keep it from wobbling when it felt like goodbye.

"It will," she assured me.

"What about Nyte? Is there really no other way than for him to leave?"

Her expression saddened. "All of us have faced improbable odds. At our time it was like your world now—our species didn't get along. We fell in love, then were guided by your creators to the temple in Vesitire where we were granted the sacred duty of raising you when you would arrive to bring a Golden Age to help us all see peace. You did well, Astraea. You ushered in that time and led triumphantly. It is Rainyte who stepped into a world that was not his and along with a meddling god's gift it made him too powerful of a contender for your magic and the age of peace began to collapse. His father rose a vampire rebellion and your clashing existence shook the balance of magick—the celestials wouldn't have stood a chance."

"Why are we all dancing around telling her the truth?" the shadowless female snapped.

Her companions shot her warning looks but they didn't discourage her. When she looked at me, I braced for the impact impending in her green eyes.

"You have to kill him, Astraea. Before, by his hand or not, he kills you."

I shook my head. "There has to be another way."

"Astraea," the fae female said. "You have to kill *Nightsdeath*."

"I can't," I shouted. The world we stood in trembled at my cry of defiance. My eyes prickled and I swallowed down the marble in my throat. "The world might have crafted us as weapons against each other. But we refuse to be used as such."

Why bond two people destined to create such catastrophe together? There had to be a *reason* our souls called to each other. A reason that while a bond could be denied our hearts claimed each other first.

The human cupped my cheek. Her expression warred with what she wanted to say, pinched like she shouldn't speak.

But she did.

"There is a prophesy that speaks of a Godkiller—"

The ground quaked, so suddenly and violently that we clutched each other tightly.

"Stop, you'll condemn yourself," the nightcrawler male said, slipping a hand around her, and the concern he bore down on her rattled me.

"What do you mean?" I asked.

"Death shouldn't always be feared. No one is born evil because of their shadow, or reflection, or wings. And no one is wholly righteous because of their blood either," she continued. "Trust yourself, always. Don't fear the darkest path for it will always lead to the brightest light."

The warning rattled harder under our feet.

"You said each of you defied great odds to be together," I backtracked, but it was a fragile grasp of desperation when my heart was shattering where I stood.

"We weren't facing catastrophic imbalance," the shadowless female countered. "Merely enemy outrage."

"Merely," the celestial male repeated with a playful huff. Meeting the snap of her scowling stare at him with twinkling adoration as his hand slipped absentmindedly around her.

I wanted to know their stories. Each of them. When their love for each other was so absolute it pulled at a yearning in my chest . . .

For Nyte.

"The hardest battles make the strongest soldiers, and if conquered together, it creates something transcendent and immortal," the human said.

"Our time is up," the fae female informed me.

"I still have so many questions," I rushed out, panicked.

"I know you do," the human said, embracing me again.

The nightcrawler laid a hand on my shoulder. "I have every belief in you. That stubborn, defiant, and kind mind of yours can't lock those memories away forever. When you come back here, you'll remember us."

I clenched my teeth tightly to keep the tears from surfacing to waver my vision. I looked over them all again, filling with more motivation to get back my past to know all they'd done for me.

The celestial male took the hand of the shadowless female and turned to walk away.

The soulless male curved an arm around the fae female, exchanging a loving smile before they followed.

Then the nightcrawler male interlocked fingers with the woman.

"Cassia was right," the woman said somberly. "If there's one thing you're not allowed to give up on, it's love. After all you face, it's the peace you deserve when not everyone can brave the dark to find it."

My brow pinched with that and I was slammed with relief I didn't know I needed.

"What about the world?" I asked desperately at their fading forms.

"You'll find a way; you always do," the nightcrawler said. The final echo before they were gone.

A single, silent tear slipped down my cheek when I stood alone.

I almost fell to my knees for a moment to gather my thoughts, but the ground trembled beneath me, and I shifted my stance to brace.

It only got worse, but there was nowhere I could run to. Water surrounded me and it was only then I realized that while the guardians had walked over it I wasn't confident I could do the same.

The platform began to crumble and I gripped the key, yanking it out of the ground with a cry. It sucked me back into the mundane and comparatively cold surroundings of the temple in my world. The guardian sculptures didn't move, but the ground beneath my feet still trembled.

Before I could take one step to race up the stairs, I was falling.

The ground gave way beneath me and darkness swallowed me whole. No stones touched me. It was like I was falling through oblivion. A space of lost time and endless wonder.

Down and down.

All I could do was close my eyes and embrace the confidence I'd gained in coming here. The defiance to follow *my* path of destiny, not one the world was trying to pave and condemn me to that separated me from everything my soul cried for.

My name is Astraea Lightborne.

I embraced the fall, curving my body in a dive and locking my shoulders that broke with tingles over my skin.

I am the star-maiden. The Daughter of Dusk and Dawn.

I breathed clearly, giving myself over to the flare of magick that wanted to expel. I fell like a shooting star. But this time, I would rise.

I am not weak. I am not alone. I am not afraid of myself.

Wings expanded from my back.

Then a voice broke through my tunneling focus. My name—but it was the shallow, fearful plea of it that snapped my eyes open and tightened an urge in my chest.

Nyte called for *me.*

Then his pain . . . it lanced through me, and my body twisted, stopping my endless fall with powerful pulses that strained my shoulders. I cried out with the effort, but I needed to get out of here.

If there was one thing I would *not* give up on . . . it was him.

40

Nyte

I went over the probability of me being able to kill three keepers to follow after Astraea. The repercussions wouldn't matter; I could handle further damnation to reach her. What stopped me was that I didn't think they were creatures that *could* be killed, and I knew Astraea would be rather furious with me if I put her friends in danger as a result.

So I stood there for a while longer after she disappeared through the entrance and made sure these things knew I contemplated their death, at least.

"She'll be okay," Davina chirped next to me. Her contrasting cheerfulness grated against my sharp ire.

"Maybe you should try your way in," I said to her, low enough the keepers shouldn't be able to hear. Perhaps in a small rodent form, Davina could scuttle past their feet.

"She needs to do this on her own," Lilith replied from my other side. "She's stronger than you think."

"I know," I said. None of her friends knew her better than I did. Astraea was brilliant and cunning and truly I had no doubt in her.

Getting out of the keep, and saving all the celestials there, was breathtaking proof I was right to have every confidence in her to handle herself if ever a real threat emerged. If I didn't, I never would have let her leave my side.

It wasn't her capabilities that I considered just now. I just didn't want her to feel alone. Never again. Especially now when I couldn't be sure what she might learn from the guardians she always regarded fondly in the past. Not like the gods.

"Maybe I could get in," Zath said. I had to admit I was glad not to be the only one who just wanted her to have company.

"We're all right here if she needs us," Rosalind said flatly, the one out of all of them who retained a steel exterior over her emotions.

I knew I was the reason why. Sometimes it was fun provoking her when all it took was a look. Though I was also aware it couldn't continue. It meant something to Astraea that Rose and I get along and I was willing to try if she would stop spearing me with ice from those hazel eyes. I admired her resilience. Maybe one day we'd get along well enough for me to admit it to her.

"Besides, she's probably safer in there than out here with you," she said, casting me a look as she turned away from the temple.

Just like that, the hope of finding amity between us seemed unlikely again. In a breath, I intercepted her path.

Zath shifted as if he would leap between the small space left between us.

"You can say or do whatever you goddamn like. But *never* question her safety with me."

"I'm not questioning anything. It's fact, isn't it? Something has been keeping her upset despite her obvious care for you. What are you doing to her?"

"If we're airing out other people's business how about we face the fact of the murder you committed to be in the Libertatem."

I'd kept quiet when it wasn't my secret to tell, but she'd danced with my darkest past and I was going to dance with hers.

"What is he talking about?" Zath said, distracted from his defensive stance against me.

"You know nothing," she seethed up at me.

"You didn't win your trials so you swapped the information that was to go to the central, but someone found out before it left, didn't they? Who was Eryn to you, Rosalind?"

"Stop."

"The keep messenger boy, but you had a relationship with him, didn't you? He found out what you did and feared what would happen to him for delivering the wrong papers. You got into an altercation—"

"I didn't mean to," she said, barely a whisper.

Her heartbeat was picking up and I didn't know why I eased off before the memory I'd dragged out and crafted into a blade could truly hurt her.

I was growing too soft. How irritating.

Instead, I calmed the anger she'd provoked out of me when I saw the horrified look over what she'd done in her eyes.

"You did what you had to; it doesn't make you a monster," I said. "But don't ever throw things you don't know about us at me again."

Her sight dropped and I stepped away, letting her explain the rest to Zath who looked her over with new eyes of concern and disturbance.

I understood—death and murder littered their world every day and they slept peacefully. Yet finding out they'd shaken bloodied hands became a haunting burden.

"I pushed him . . ." Rose admitted. "Harder than I meant to when he was fighting me in the woodland. Then he tripped and fell, hitting his head on a sharp rock. He didn't get back up."

I walked aimlessly around the huge gold-painted circle on the ground, listening in to their conversations out of curiosity though I already knew the full story from Rosalind's mind. I knew how much the event had scarred her.

"I don't remember how I got there but I delivered the note myself. Then, when the selected profiles came through, I left as soon as the borders opened before they would have hunted me down," she finished explaining.

"Now you can't go back," I said.

"No. I think the reigning lord would call for my death."

"Probably."

"Your concern is endearing."

I fought a smile. "I taste the hate you harbor for me. Am I supposed to care for you?"

"I don't hate you."

I slipped a suspicious gaze at her.

"I want to kill you."

"Careful, Rosalind. Those are sweet words to me. They're often the last I hear before I hold the person's heart in my palm."

"You're a twisted bastard."

"Is this a battle you want to keep expending yourself on? You'll exhaust yourself before I ever give one fuck about your humorous attempts on my life, let alone your perceptions that mean nothing to me."

Zath talked to her privately and something he said caused her to concede this time. I could admit I appreciated her strong will. It had clearly served her well. I didn't know if she would ever warm to me and I didn't crave it. Astraea did, and it was only for her that I did anything.

"Nyte," Lilith warned, eyes cast behind me. I picked up on the sounds of an impending intrusion as the two fae did.

I used the void to get closer to Lilith and Davina. The approach came through the forest—distant breaking of branches and scuffling rocks. Then the air whooshed with too many gushes of wind to be anything natural.

"Celestials," I said.

"Do you think he's finally come for her?" Davina whispered to me.

My jaw locked with the assumption I hoped was fucking false. Dealing with the High Celestials coming to claim their maiden was a power struggle I wasn't in the mood to face right now.

"It could just be the last of the captives from the keep," Lilith offered, but we all knew they would have no reason to pass this way.

"It's not," I said, slipping a hand into my pocket like it would keep a grip on the monster within me that was already priming.

There was no mistaking the distinct energy of celestial royalty that dropped from the skies.

Zephyr Luna, Aquilo Sera, Notus Aura, then . . .

"It's been too long, Auster," I greeted with a venomous edge, but I smiled. "I haven't seen you since the war three hundred years ago."

"Not long enough, if you ask me," he said.

"I'm afraid you wasted a trip; as you can see, Astraea is not here. You should have sent a messenger ahead."

"We know she's here. You can spare the act."

"I don't have an act; would you like one?"

Darkness tipped my fingers and I examined them. I just had to buy time. Stall them until Astraea came out because I would be damned if they had some plan to steal her away before she could choose if she wanted to go.

"You're not getting to poison her mind a moment longer," Auster snarled.

He hadn't changed. The silver circlet peaked on his forehead, the shoulder-length wavy brown hair half tied back, and worst of all, the hideous glare I felt was crafted to distort his expression this way just for me. One thing was different . . .

"Nice hand," I commented.

His right fingers flexed but the left never would again having been replaced by solid silver. He'd had both in flesh last time I'd seen him, days before Astraea's death. I knew from battle it had been his dominant side for wielding a weapon and he must have taken some time to retrain with his right hand instead.

Auster took a few steps across the courtyard toward me and I was glad he did. For now I knew it wasn't just his hand he'd lost, as that left arm didn't move with his walk like the right did.

"Everyone lost something back then, and everything is on your conscience, *Nightsdeath*. Especially Astraea's fall, and you're not getting to harm her again."

It was my turn to erase some distance between us but I had to be careful. The air was charging with a dangerous challenge of dominance and I couldn't kill him; it would erupt a war far more savage than our history holds.

"Astraea is a person with a choice—I'm not holding her, but until she says she wants to leave, she's not going anywhere with you."

"She already has."

At first I thought he had to be taunting me. My flare of denial started to fade with Auster's irritatingly smug look.

For some reason I knew I would find the confirmation with a glance to Rose, and the guilty shift of her eyes to avoid mine, then the way she lingered a familiar gaze on the younger celestial close to Auster . . .

Oh, Starlight, what have you been up to?

"Doesn't mean she will now," I said coolly.

My lack of reaction served to provoke him more.

I couldn't decide how I felt about the revelation Astraea had been keeping that secret from me. Could I blame her? No. It only hurt that I'd somehow failed to acquire her complete trust in me but I didn't yet know what Auster could have told her.

"Step aside, Rainyte. You might not be allowed to enter the temple but I am. I'm not waiting for you to whisper more poison thoughts into her mind and manipulate her."

The allegation that I would ever manipulate Astraea in such a way drove Nightsdeath to the surface. The darkness despised the celestial's brightness, but I held the reins against the impulse to eradicate it.

"If you want to get to her, you'll have to pass me."

"Do you think we've been idle all these centuries? You've been our greatest focus, with no effort spared to figure out every weakness you harbor."

My head canted in amusement. "I'm flattered. I haven't given you a second thought since the war and could still put you down a hundred times over."

An arrow fired, but I'd anticipated it from the faintest signal Auster gave with his head. It didn't aim for me, but I'd blinked through the void to catch its path before it struck Davina and that pissed me off even more.

I snapped the stick in a flash of rage but I became distracted for a split second at the ominous dark pull whispering from the arrowhead. It was a dark iridescent stone. Not obsidian.

"Your origin is fae, is it not?" Auster said, taunting me with the knowledge. "I bet you're susceptible to materials that harm them like obsidian does to celestials, and stormstone does to vampires."

"What is it?" I asked Davina, who fixed wide eyes on the arrow head.

"Iron can weaken us but that feels stronger," she said in fear.

"It took a long time to find anything from your origins, but I'll admit it turned up some fascinating things. I don't know what they call it, but we discovered it was a mineral found in the coldest of places and with our combined magick we've been able to recreate the properties. We've tested it on the fae, a few who had betrayed us to join the king's army, and since I'm merciful, I'll warn you it is highly effective in incapacitating the fae."

"Attack me all you want," I said, beginning to tremble with murderous restraint. "Attacking any of those behind me will be your last fucking mistake."

Auster's chuckle dragged like knives in me. "Don't tell me three hundred years has grown a heart in you."

"Tread carefully, Auster. It's not my heart that makes me dangerous; it's the one I protect."

"You've never protected her," he said coldly.

"I have nothing to prove to you, so why don't you retreat until Astraea is finished inside. Then we can talk."

"I don't trust you for a second. You've been hiding her from us all this time since she came back and gods know what lies you've spun in your favor with her memories gone."

"Your efforts to find her five years ago were weak. Even my brother found her before any of your kind did."

He looked like he wanted to counter that statement. He was restrained only by a a flash of bitter resentment that might have spilled something he didn't want me to know. That took my curiosity.

I couldn't infiltrate their thoughts as easily as I could anyone else's, as their minds were protected by what I assumed to be from Starlight Matter. Too much could drive them insane, so if I had the will and reason, I thought I could likely shatter through the measure.

"Step aside, Rainyte. This doesn't have to be a fight."

Our time was up, and I only hoped my Starlight would come out very soon.

"That's not going to happen, so do what you have to."

I wasn't particularly in the mood for a fight, but I supposed Auster had riled enough energy in me for it. I saw it more as a game—protect the fragile things behind me and collect the lives of those who tried to harm them.

Auster might have anticipated that, as he drew his bow and arrow and aimed it for me just as he gave the signal for a dozen of his warriors to advance. The four High Celestials stayed firm, braced against me.

"You really need to fight me four to one?" I asked, distracting them as I listened to the clang of steel from Rose, Zath, Davina, and Lilith. They were great fighters in their own right.

"We don't have to fight you at all," said Zephyr, the only one who didn't pin me with the same loathing as the others.

I knew him vaguely. He had been close friends with Astraea and she spoke of him fondly.

"If a single one of your people draws blood from them, they die," I warned.

I wasn't one for senseless killing, but I had little mercy. I thought my proposal to be fair.

"Then surrender," Auster said.

"You speak like a child; that hasn't changed."

Lilith was the first to get hurt with a slash to her arm from the celestial she fought and my rage darkened my vision in the flash it took to cross the space and snap his neck. While I was here, I disarmed another, swiftly lodging a dagger in his shoulder, which crashed him to his knees with a cry.

Davina was mesmerizing with the way she moved like wind, throwing the daggers from the unique weapon she'd designed herself. Rose and Zath fought back to back but the odds of four celestials against two humans were hardly fair. I should even the scale.

The celestials hadn't drawn blood yet from the humans, but I was beyond mercy now. I wrapped shadows around the neck of one and my own hand of flesh around the other. Both of them choked, clawing for air until they drew their last breath and I tossed their bodies aside.

"All this time and you couldn't train better soldiers?" I taunted over to Auster. His people began to hesitate and retreat.

The High Celestial pinned me with such hatred I could almost feel the tangible heat of it. The feeling was mutual, but I wouldn't expend such physical energy toward it.

More celestials emerged from the woods. Far too many for me to defeat alone when I had Davina, Lilith, Zath, and Rose to protect.

"It's over, Rainyte," Auster said. He always used my full name ever since he learned of it. As if he knew there had to be a reason I despised for why I didn't use it myself. Even now, I never gave him a reaction but I itched for his throat each time.

"Astraea still breathes, and I still stand. It's never over."

"Both can't be true in our world for it to return to the peace it was. This time, the abomination you are will be the thing that falls."

My chest drummed with the all-consuming adrenaline right before the break of a battle. It could be over fast. I could kill every celestial here before they could even reach Astraea's friends. But these were her people, and I had to keep an oath not to kill them all when she might condemn me beyond her redemption. Astraea held the reins to my ever slipping humanity.

So I let them attack. They wouldn't kill Astraea's friends; all I had to do was fight long enough for Astraea to come out. I wouldn't let Auster get to her alone when he could take her away beyond the veil in a blink through the void.

"Did you not learn from the last time you challenged me and lost?"

"You'd taken my Bonded right against her will."

"No Bond is a *right*. It was your ego that couldn't accept she'd chosen me."

"You forced it upon her!"

The sky broke with a boom of thunder. Auster had the power of storms. He'd attacked me that night Astraea found her wings and I didn't tell her though now I wished I had. For I didn't know they'd been meeting in secret, and though he didn't deserve it, it was for her sake I didn't want to taint her impression of him with that knowledge.

Did she not know about his direct magick of lightning?

His brothers had other strong abilities. They might rely on cosmic energy to wield it, but their gifts were of nature. The celestials were blessed from multiple deities to keep peace.

"You're only angry like a child because your attempt to turn her against me didn't work back then," I said.

Tearing at old wounds made it feel like no time had passed at all.

"That was only a result of the Bond you'd shackled her into."

"She still had full will to want to stay away from me. She could have taken your offer to try find a way to break it."

I taunted him. Buying time. *Come on, starlight.*

As soon as she came back they would stop attacking.

In my distraction an arrow whizzed past me. It struck Davina through the abdomen and she screamed with the pain. Lilith rushed to her with a horror-stricken expression, catching her as they fell to their knees.

Fury boiled in me.

I was about to channel to them when fire, the likes of which I'd never felt before, erupted in my shoulder. So much that it stole my vision, my orientation.

I underestimated what they were willing to do. Clenching my teeth, I broke the stick of the arrow in me with the head still embedded. The material seized me still like poison flooding my veins.

Another archer aimed for Davina again and all I could do was make it in time to take that hit too. This time the explosion in my chest felled me to one knee. *What the fuck is this?*

"She'll never forgive you for this," I rasped, gripping the arrow stick and managing to pull this one out fully. The iridescent stone glistened with my blood.

"She has before," Auster said.

Another arrow struck my chest. Then another. And another.

I coughed, splitting blood over the stone on my hands and knees.

"I don't mean hurting me," I said through short gasps. I was faltering. "You shouldn't have harmed her friends to distract me."

I had to hold on, but my heart was slowing. Dying felt like slow laps of sleep; inviting to numb the pain. I fought it with everything I was, but there came a point when the pull under was inevitable.

If something happened, I didn't want her to believe I'd abandoned her. That I'd let them take her. So I called her name in my mind. Over and over even though it only seemed to rebound.

"Astraea."

Darkness.

Agony.

Silence.

Then . . .

My brightest star.

I felt her. A prideful burst of energy expanded in my chest and brought my consciousness back enough to pull my head up. Auster looked down on me with satisfaction but I didn't care. He wasn't important.

Despite the three arrows in my chest, I found the will to turn around.

All was still, so tensely still.

Until up from the temple shot the most magnificent flare of light. Everyone had to shield their eyes against it. What came gliding down after was pure triumphant energy.

The star-maiden.

With her breathtaking silver and violet wings and if I wasn't already on my knees I would have fallen to them like everyone else did now.

Astraea's eyes glowed, her expression was ethereal, and she was dressed in gold and white and purple. Her feet gently touched the ground and her wings tucked in like a goddess descended from the heavens. The energy of her magick was breathtaking but it subdued as the brightness of her eyes and the glow of her key faded out.

I was so tired, losing the fight against the stone torching my blood and slicing my skin; my head bowed. Pride kept me awake; her presence kept me alive.

"Astraea," Auster said from beside me.

"What happened?" she asked softly to me.

She'd disregarded him to kneel in front of me, lifting my head. I couldn't believe the sight of the stunning angel.

"We have company," I said, barely able to get words out, and I cursed my helplessness.

"I can see that. What did you do to piss them off?"

"I think I do that to him just by existing."

Her smile was pained until she examined the arrows in my chest.

"Astraea," I groaned.

"Yes?"

"These arrows really fucking hurt and I could use your help."

"What are you willing to owe me in return?" she taunted playfully, but reached for one arrow stick.

I gave a breathy chuckle. "Absolutely everything."

"I would have thought it would take more to incapacitate you," she said with an edge of worry.

"They're not just ordinary arrows."

"This is going to be painful."

I nodded, gritting my teeth with the pain that scattered blackness across my vision when she ripped the first free. A firm hand was planted on my shoulder to keep me from falling forward. It was Zathrian.

"Don't die here," she whispered to me, reaching for the next.

"I'm trying," I said.

For her, I could defy the pull of death as long as possible.

"You need to drink—"

"No." I halted her, but groaned to the next searing pain of the second arrow being pulled out. One left. I spoke the rest to her mind. *"Don't offer me your blood here. Your people will disgrace you for it."*

"You need it," she argued vehemently.

"This time, yes I might agree. Just not here."

"You won't make it elsewhere."

"Astraea, you must come with us. We've come to take you home," Auster said, authoritative but wary of her.

"You have to be mad to think I'd see this and go with you," she snapped.

If I wasn't so debilitated right now, I would have shown surprise at her sharpness, her confidence, addressing him like that.

"We mean no harm to you or your friends. After what happened at the keep, you would be safer with us while the fallen king still seeks vengeance," Auster said.

"Last one," Zath muttered apologetically, taking over while Astraea held my head and was distracted by the High Celestial.

I did groan to the final explosion of pain that almost pulled me under completely.

Astraea's hand slipped around my face, her thumb brushed my lips, and I didn't know when she'd cut herself but the moment her blood was on my tongue it took every fucking ounce of willpower not to break in my state—to let the instinct take over that would have made me sink my teeth into the mesmerizing vein of her wrist without a thought of permission. My hand lashed out to her thigh, squeezing in warning, and I heard the shifting behind me. They wouldn't be able to see that she was giving me her blood but I imagine Auster anticipated I would grab Astraea to use as a hostage right now.

"That was a very dangerous thing to do," I said to her mind.

Her thumb slipped out of my mouth and the trickle of her blood I got was enough to give me some strength to grapple for consciousness a little longer, but I was teetering on starvation for her now that I had to focus on control.

"You can't die here. I need you."

My existence wove around those three little words. *I need you.*

"We've expended many resources for you. Come, Maiden," Aquilo said.

He was a bastard. Astraea favored him least, from what she had told me in our past. I could feel the echoes of her anger and fear but I was still helpless to promise I could get us out of here if she asked me to.

"She's not going anywhere with you," I said, standing even though it felt like lifting rocks on my shoulders.

I would fight until I couldn't anymore. Bleed until there was nothing left.

Hearing the next arrow fired at me, I managed to catch it, but not the second nor the third that came in succession.

"Stop!" Astraea yelled; her staff slammed to the ground and whether she meant to or not it scattered a vibration of warning energy under everyone's feet.

The arrows dragged me back to my knees but Zathrian caught me before they slammed me to the stone.

"You can't take much more of this," he grumbled.

I kept track of Astraea and the High Celestials. She cast her sight sideways, finding Lilith using some kind of her magick that glowed a faint green around her arrow wound. A change shifted in Astraea, it was familiar but had been dormant until now. She'd always been protective and head strong, and seeing her friend harmed too brought her palpable outrage to the surface. She targeted that gaze on Auster, but he barely flinched.

"Why?" Astraea asked. There was no kindness in her voice.

"They fought us," Notus replied, always the calm and indifferent bastard.

"You attacked first," Rose countered.

"These are my friends," Astraea interjected. "An attack on them is one on me."

"They side with our enemy," Aquilo seethed.

"Then I am your enemy."

The air became thick and ice cold. Looking at Astraea now, it was hard to remember she only had five years of new existence, when it was like she'd never left at all with the authority and challenge she embodied. I was so fucking proud.

"You know nothing, Maiden," Aquilo said. I wanted to rip his throat out so badly my fingers flexed against the stone.

Auster said, "We won't take this to heart given your . . . circumstances. It's our mistake in harming your friends, which we hope you can forgive."

I decided I wanted to feed Aquilo's throat to him. They mocked her with those words, belittled her confidence.

"You should leave," Astraea said.

"You'd turn away aid from your people for him?" Notus said bitterly.

"We are not needed here, brothers," Zephyr said as the voice of reason. "We came to see she is safe after the attack at the keep and to bring our people home. It's clear they need us more right now and Astraea can take care of herself."

He was the only High Celestial I might have had a shred of respect for. Astraea spoke of him more fondly than Notus or Aquilo and I trusted her judgment.

My vision blurred when Zathrian tore out one of the arrows but I thought their forces began to turn away.

Astraea could have left, but she's right here.

"Oh Nyte," Astraea said, sinking down in front of me again. "You really have a penchant for torture in provoking them."

It was mildly embarrassing how many shots they managed to fire through me, but I blamed the new material they'd crafted that was a fucking hinderance, being able to incapacitate me faster and more effectively than anything else.

"They could have struck me with a dozen more and it wouldn't have stopped me if they'd tried to take you."

I would have let Nightsdeath take over and shown them the true villain I could become with the right motivation to get her back.

"Can you travel through the void?" Astraea asked.

My vision came and went; I didn't have long before I would pass out.

"I don't think so," I said. The last words I could utter, and they felt like lead on my tongue.

I feared falling unconscious only in case Auster could be waiting for the moment I was to storm back and take Astraea from me. I tried to speak, but I knew it was too late. Astraea took one of my hands, a soothing reminder of what was waiting, as Death gripped the other, and welcomed me home.

41

Nyte

I t wasn't often I woke to such peace and I knew from that feeling alone that Astraea was near. Very near. I breathed her scent in a long inhale, registering the soft feel of her under my head, and a warmth hotter than flesh at the side of my face.

Her fingers combed through my hair and I stifled a groan, deciding this awakening right here was the best in my entire existence. My eyes slipped open for the final piece of this dream, and the angel staring down at me really did make me question if I was even alive.

"You've been out for a long time," she said quietly, brushing a lock of hair from my head, which she held in her lap.

I spared a glance around but only took in gray jagged stone around us, illuminated by a small fire. Then I remembered the events that had unfolded after the temple.

"Zath helped to get you here. I really need to learn how to travel with someone through the void. I could feel it but . . . you said traveling through it was risky even at the best of times."

"Thank you," I said, it was barely a breath in my weakened state, but I was coming around. I took her hand over my chest, and it was all the strength I needed.

"Do you think they hate me now?" The sound of defeat in her small voice had me pushing up, propping on one hand.

I tipped her chin up, unable to bear the weight on her that bowed it as if she'd done something wrong.

"You were absolutely incredible. If they have any ill feelings toward you standing up for your friends then they're a problem," I said. "One word and I'd end them all. Or at least make them remember it's *you* they bow to, and that you will never bow to them."

Astraea yielded a small smile that relaxed the tension in me, ready to charge at her every whim.

"Always finding answers in violence," she mused.

"I find my answers in you. What I do is entirely dependent on your wishes."

Astraea leaned in to kiss me, and *fuck,* I loved it when she did that.

"I'm going to go to Althenia once you're well," she said gently, like it might detonate a fuse in me.

I wouldn't deny the idea sparked something volatile, but I knew this time had to come. I had to let her go.

"Auster said you'd been meeting with him," I told her. Part of me hoped he'd been lying to provoke me, but the other part knew it was the truth.

"I'm sorry. It's not that I didn't trust you, but he said . . ."

"You don't have to explain it to me. How did you feel with Auster?"

Her brow furrowed, seeming to try to answer that to herself first.

"Sad, like I broke something I don't know can be fixed. Also . . . wary."

"That's not giving me assurance to let you go with him."

"Let me?" she challenged. I loved the fiery flicker against the ice of her irises when she adopted this playfulness.

"I could tie you up."

"Is that a fantasy of yours?"

"It would be a fantasy if I'd never done so before."

Her lips parted, searching my eyes for the lie.

"That's not fair," she pouted. "Taunting me with lost memories."

"Would you want me to—?" I leaned into her, forcing her to lie down slowly. My hands gazed along her side but shadows crept along her stomach, lassoing around her wrists. She tried to wriggle from my touch but gasped when the shadow bonds locked her hands above her head. "Restrain you?"

The answer was in the desire fluttering her eyes.

"Yes."

I leaned down, kissing her lips softly, then her neck. "Good."

Letting the shadows ease from her wrists, Astraea's hands slipped down my abdomen, dipping under the hem of my untucked shirt. Her fingers against my skin were fucking bliss.

"You can't come with me to Althenia, can you?" she asked, wandering her touch absentmindedly.

My fucking heart skipped at her want for me.

"I'm not welcome there. I'll only reflect badly on you for bringing me there."

"That's not fair." She frowned.

"We also don't know if you can open a pass in the veil for me."

Astraea began tracing my chest and I was in an utter state of rapture that the thought of hiding in this cave with her for days was the most appealing thing in the world.

"I think I could," she said thoughtfully.

"Your confidence is stunning."

She smiled to herself this time but it quickly fell. "What if I don't belong there for all I'm choosing against them?"

That meant me. I wanted her to say it—*I choose you.* There's nothing I wouldn't give for those words. But more than that I wanted her happiness, and this wasn't it.

"What do you want to do?"

Astraea slipped her hand around my back while her knees tightened around my hips, drawing me down closer.

"You're everything I shouldn't want," she whispered.

"Yes."

"So why do I want you so badly?"

"Even the most pure and precious things can be lured by darkness."

"I don't think it's just your darkness. I think it's your heart."

"Because it's yours," I said.

Astraea kissed me, firm and unexpected. Every time she moved for me first, I turned into a pining proud fool for her.

"Before you settle on your choice, you should give Auster more of a chance. To be sure."

"You don't want that," she accused, maybe even taking offense.

I gave a resentful laugh. "I would rather the world burned to ash, but that would be entirely villainous of me. I'm trying not to corrupt the world's hero into condemning it for me."

"You think too highly of yourself."

"You begged me not to leave."

"I didn't *beg.*"

"It's one of my favorite things from you, so I think I'd remember."

Her lips parted with an adorable scowl and I smiled in amusement. Before she could say something snarky I claimed her mouth and then we were lost. Or found. We were stars colliding and night defying.

I hadn't been able to give her everything when we'd woken after the ordeal at the keep. I died seven times before Astraea came around. It was a record I hoped never to beat or even come close to again.

Now, everything came pouring out of me and I hoped she had the same blazing desire to receive it. Her back curved, pressing us tighter. Those fucking hands of heaven locked in my hair to pull me closer and I was driven so wild with everything I wanted to do to her that I didn't know where to start worshipping this goddess wrapped around me.

The ground trembled beneath us and I wouldn't be surprised if it was a direct warning from the gods.

It only surged me with defiance and a dominant need to show them she was *mine.*

Slipping my arms around her back, she lifted so effortlessly to me, straddling my knees. I stood with her, pushing her to the wall, and she moaned, opening that pretty mouth for me to devour her deeply.

Astraea's hands moved to glide over my ribs before clawing at my back. Such a needy girl. I broke our kiss abruptly and was burned by the passion in her icy eyes.

"I need you to undress for me before I make ribbons out of the only clothes you have until we reach a town."

She shivered against me and I reluctantly let her go, bracing a hand on the wall instead to watch. Everything around us still shook and Astraea observed the falling debris as she undid the fastens of her leathers.

"Do the quakes always last this long?" she asked with a hint of fear.

"No. The longer they are, the more they're affecting the magick."

"Maybe we should stop—"

I reached for the button of her pants, then pulled the ties.

"We could," I murmured, kissing her jaw, her neck. Drinking in every sweet taste of her flesh. "But we've tempted fate this far, why stop now?"

Astraea peeled out of her leather jacket, then I helped fold her out of her shirt just as the quake stopped rumbling.

I groaned at the perfect sight of her bare chest that would never fail to turn me into a crazed male for her. I sucked one of her nipples and she pushed her chest into me. Such a good fucking girl. I gave the other the same attention and her arousal filled my senses. I breathed the drug of her deeply, becoming more and more unhinged to be buried inside her with each breath. Hooking my fingers in her waistband, I kneeled, freeing her stunning legs from the leather as I did.

"How much do you want this?"

I was priming to unleash on her. Everything I never got the chance to do the other night.

"More than anything," she said through a delightful short breath.

I lifted under her knee to hook it over my shoulder, then I bit into her thigh, piercing the flesh. Astraea gasped from the surprise, hand flying into my hair and grabbing a tight fistful. I only took a mouthful of her exquisite blood before I licked over the puncture wound. My eyes flicked up, finding her lust-clouded sight on me.

"Did that make you needy for me?" I asked, kissing along her thigh. I loved the way her hand tightened and her brow twitched in anticipation the closer I got to her center.

"Shit, yes," she mewled.

I groaned, savoring that sweet begging I would never tire of hearing.

Then I couldn't hold back any longer.

Astraea's cry echoed through the small cave and I gave no mercy. Needing her to scream louder as a declaration to the world that she was mine. That only I could make her feel this good.

My tongue passed through her hot core and the taste of her exploded in me. Sucking on the sensitive bud gained the most reaction. Astraea ground her hips into my face like she couldn't get enough. I let her use me as she needed, cupping under her ass for encouragement, and she didn't hold back. Her arousal coated my mouth and chin as she chased her pleasure, and my cock was fucking aching to be touched.

I slipped a finger into her tight heat and swore at the slickness pooling out of her. Enough that I added a second easily.

"Oh, just like that, please." I turned nearly feral with that. Her wish was my fucking command. She was close to the precipice and I needed it like a starved man.

I sucked harder, driving my fingers into her faster with a slight curve with the right pressure to make her body sing until she began to tense for the orgasm and her channel sucked my fingers deeper.

Astraea climaxing was a blessing from the heavens no creature from hell deserved. She cried beautifully, and I held her tightly pressed to the wall as my assault strung out every euphoric tremor of her release.

I slowed as she came down from her high. Every gentle flick of my tongue caused her body to spasm from the sensitivity, and I delighted in the wicked torture. Astraea moaned with my fingers slipping out of her and I sucked every last taste of her from them.

Her eyes were wild on me, looking down with her chest rising and falling and she wasn't finished. Good. I wasn't even close to being done with her.

"On your knees and take out my cock," I ordered.

Astraea didn't miss a beat, sinking down with me and working her nimble fingers on my buttons and ties. The relief when she freed my cock was a burst of pleasure itself, but she wasted no time in gripping my base in her pale hand, tightening as she pumped in slow, tormenting strokes. I wanted her mouth wrapped around it, and if I didn't ask I knew she would in a moment. More so, I wanted to be deep inside her so desperately it was a carnal need.

Perhaps it was the lingering, resentful thoughts of Auster. He was good for her, safe. I was nightmares and devastation but she couldn't deny which kept her feeling the most alive.

"Turn around and put your hands on the wall."

She did as I ordered, giving me her perfect ass, and I coaxed her hips back while nudging her knees farther apart. Astraea shuddered with a pained moan as I passed my fingers through her soaking heat, using her release to cover my shaft. I shifted up on my knees, kissing between her shoulders and wrapping a hand around her throat. My cock lined up with her entrance. Astraea pushed her hips back, taking the tip of me into her body, and I groaned against her skin.

"Impatient," I growled. Then plunged all the way to hear her sing for me and it was mind blowing. I had to take a second fully seated in her, clutching her body bent perfectly in my hold.

"Don't hold back this time," she rasped.

"You think I've been holding out on you?"

Pulling out to the tip, I began fucking her in slow, savoring strokes. I wanted her to feel how perfectly every piece of me fit with her. Then again. And again. Slow punishing plunges she cried out at, beginning to anticipate it to meet me stroke for stroke.

"Do I feel good inside you?" I whispered across her ear.

"It feels . . . *oh gods—*"

My next deep thrust altered her words.

"We've talked about this," I said, a low graveling warning before I plunged in again and stayed seated in her. "The only gods around here are you and I."

"I want you . . . to fuck me as Nightsdeath."

I stilled with a dark, pleasurable shudder at hearing that. It was unexpected, but the darkness inside me rattled to be desired.

"Are you sure it won't frighten you?" I taunted, trailing the vibrations of my words down the column of her neck that inclined for me. Begging for my teeth. My mark.

"I can handle you."

She was the only creature in the world who could.

Nightsdeath crept to the surface, but I kept control. It was urges and dark promises that impressed on my consciousness. Nightsdeath was like choosing what emotions to turn off and which to amplify. If I had no control, I had no humanity.

It was most dangerous around Astraea, who was so beautifully bright that she repelled the want for goodness. But the defiance to crave it could also translate to the most euphoric bliss in the throes of passion.

Astraea gasped like she felt the change in me, the embrace of a monster. Shadows replaced my hold around her neck so my black-tipped fingers could hold her hips in place.

"How hard can you take it?" I asked, trembling with the restraint required not to give in to abandon.

"Just fuck me."

The beast in me purred at that and my cock glided in and out of her, and I marveled at the sight of where we joined.

"I want to mark you," I growled, pressing my lips to her shoulder before my teeth scraped there.

"Please."

"So willing for me."

With my next deep plunge into her my teeth sank into her skin with the ease of an apple. Then I was lost in her. High on the taste and scent of her, my hips slammed into her hard and fast and she clawed at the wall with her cries of pleasure. I licked her wound when my mouth pulled away and my abdomen tensed with an impending release.

"Come on my cock," I ordered, fucking her like no sane person. She made me crazed, entangled in madness. I didn't think any amount of her would ever be enough and that made my chase with her an eternal flame.

Her channel gripped me like a vise and I was so fucking close. Another snake of shadow wrapped her middle before the tip reached her apex, rubbing her sensitive bud with every powerful thrust that had us both slick with sweat and ready to collapse.

Astraea's noises were heavenly. The call of my name shattering through her release was a god's blessing bestowed on me. With my next slam into her I came too, seeing stars and darkness and her, her, *her*.

"Fuck," I rasped, struggling to collect myself back from an orgasm that continued to rip through me as I braced one hand next to hers on the wall and the other around her body as the shadows dispersed and Nightsdeath was put back to rest.

"That was . . ." Astraea didn't finish her words. She didn't need to.

I kissed along the column of her neck in the comedown of our shared euphoria.

"You are utterly exquisite."

I slipped out of her, and we gathered our breath.

"There's a lake just through the trees," Astraea said, turning around.

I took her hands as I stood, and from her blood and the adrenaline we created, I felt brand fucking new. As I hooked under her thighs, Astraea's smile bloomed, lifting into my arms, legs circling my waist.

As I carried her out, the night was bitterly cold but bearable with the heat of our worked bodies right now.

"Your light is warm; if you can find out how to channel it right, you could save us a freezing bath in a minute."

I was too enraptured with her body around mine to feel the woodland beneath my bare feet. When we got to the lake, Astraea clamped around me tighter as I walked into it.

Shit, it was fucking freezing. I almost retreated, but thought that this could be a good training exercise for her magick.

"This could wait until morning!" Astraea gasped, trying to let me go when the water lapped past her ass.

"It won't be much warmer then, anyway," I said.

Her teeth started chattering, her body shaking but locked around me. I stopped in the pool where I could still stand but sank down to submerge to our shoulders.

"You could heat around us," I said through short breath. The water was like small knives to our skin.

"I—I don't know h-how," she chittered.

"Focus, love."

Brushing hair from her face, I warmed her ear, her neck, with my breath. Anywhere I could. I tried reaching her with my magick to give it a gentle awakening. When her silver markings started to glow, she was the most breathtaking sight in the dark.

"Good girl," I whispered. "You're not just a vessel to power, you *are* the magick you harbor. Trust yourself with it, and command what you want."

Shimmering light spilled around us like she bathed us both in starlight. Fucking exquisite. Astraea glowed like a goddess, her tattoos, the glittering strands of her hair; she was in every way a pure fallen star.

"My fallen star," I said to her, kissing the constellation on her chest.

We both shuddered at the warmth that weaved through the cold. Our bodies relaxed against each other and I groaned with the pleasure, no longer wanting to make this swim quick but wanting to stay here for hours. To take her again and again in these waters imbued with her magick.

After a moment of peaceful silence and soft touches, Astraea broke it.

"How did the celestials manage to overpower you at the temple?"

My anger simmered at the recollection.

"They've been busy these past few centuries. It seems they've created a material that incapacitates the fae like stormstone does to vampires, and obsidian the celestials."

"Why would they want such a thing against the fae? They are their allies."

"I don't think any two groups can wholly be considered allies anymore. They know I was born fae and they were right to assume whatever this new material is that it would incapacitate me more than stormstone or obsidian. It's also safe to assume they know many fae joined my father's army over the years, so I guess they wanted to be fully prepared."

"Most of them were forced against their will," she argued.

"Yes. But war doesn't spare the innocent. It views everything that's multicolored through a black-and-white lens. It is not fair nor merciful. It hears no reason."

"We have to make them. Be the voice of reason if we must."

I adored her fierce will. Astraea was in every way a fit leader, then and now, she just wasn't always what they wanted her to be and that made me love her even more.

"I'll be right by your side. I'll do whatever you ask of me."

"Whatever I ask?" she repeated coyly.

My cock jerked from that tone alone.

"Unless you order me away."

"What happened to giving Auster a chance?"

"I already changed my mind."

"Jealousy suits you."

"This isn't jealousy because you're undeniably mine. I mentioned Auster so you can finally accept that with a clear conscience. I'm very patient and you are very worth the wait."

I kissed her throat, refraining from scattering bite marks across her body.

"You held back again in the cave," she accused breathily.

Our stares tangled in desire and thrill.

"I didn't fuck you hard enough?"

"You haven't shown me everything you can do."

"I would never give everything at once. We have eternity, and I have infinite ways to pleasure you. Next time, I want you to feel my magick inside you."

I kissed her hard and she curved into me. My cock prodded at her core from our position.

"There's something I've been wanting to ask you," she said before we could lose ourselves again. The serious edge made me give her my full attention for it.

"You can ask me anything."

"Did you really kill Drystan's mother?"

Guilt locked my body as I sighed. "Yes. It was an accident long ago, shortly after you died."

Every time she learned something heinous about me I always counted my breaths for her reaction, believing it would be the next sinister truth that would make her see the monster I am and leave me.

"How?"

"I'm not proud of who I was back then. Vicious nightmares need peaceful dreams . . . and you were gone."

Her delicate brow pulled together and her fingers threaded through the back of my hair.

"I'm here now."

I sighed, running a hand up her spine in complete gratitude for that fact.

"His mother tried to kill me first, knowing I would be sent for her when she planned to leave my father and abandon Drystan. Nightsdeath didn't give a second chance to her attempt at ending my life, futile as it was. I didn't realize what I'd done until I was kneeling by her body and her lover's coated in their blood. Nightsdeath has no brother. No one to consider."

"You've been Nightsdeath around me."

"That part of me is both repelled by and addicted to you, I can't explain it. You make me volatile but in a way that either drives a need to kill you or a desire to claim you."

Astraea pressed herself to me with a playful smile. "The feeling is mutual."

42

Astraea

I passed through the celestial veil alone. Well, as I'm sure Eltanin in my hood didn't classify as what the celestials would consider to be company. I traveled on foot this time as I couldn't help my desire to explore the feeling it gave me for a while longer. Surrounded by a storm of darkness and shimmering starlight, I couldn't place why it was so welcoming, familiar. It awakened my magick and embraced the call. The key staff in my hand glowed with my silver tattoos and I felt so light and *powerful*. Even Eltanin purred like this force soothed him.

Emerging on the other side, I was immediately met with the sight of the four High Celestials, flanked by a number of guards that seemed excessive.

Did they not trust me not to bring Nyte here?

It had been two days since the temple. I hadn't told Auster I was coming, and the fact they were waiting for me regardless crawled my skin. Had they sent spies to watch me?

"We weren't sure when you would come back," Auster said, breaking the tense silence we stood off in.

"Seems like you did," I countered.

"I can feel when you're near."

I recoiled internally at that, often forgetting that even though our Bond wasn't claimed, it was a lingering connection between us. That enlightenment pressed on a sore spot for both of us.

Admittedly I came here built up on annoyance and anger for the attack on Nyte and my friends, but now, faced with the sadness Auster tried to hide under a steel mask, my guilt was breaking down that wall.

"I'm not your enemy, but I'm not his either," I said.

"I know."

Notus and Aquilo could hardly hide their distaste toward me but I didn't care for their approval anyway. I'd learned that the High Celestial with long red hair, a few strands loose from a half tie highlighting green eyes, was Notus.

Aquilo had cropped black hair with dark eyes nearly as depthless. Whatever their reasons for disliking me in the past, it didn't seem like they were likely to set aside their indifference. Zephyr was the only one to offer kind eyes and a partial smile.

"What is that?" Notus demanded.

He must have caught a glimpse of Eltanin, who tickled my neck to crawl onto my shoulder with the new commotion.

"His name is Eltanin. He's a celestial dragon." Dipping into my pocket, I lifted a piece of dried rabbit to him.

He was surprisingly gentle at taking food now and I wondered if it was because of the training of Nadia, who I'd seen with him often. Despite her initial refusal, and though she still denied it, she had quickly become engrossed with him.

"Impossible," Aquilo accused.

"Do your eyes deceive you?" I said flatly.

I decided I liked him least of all. He presented himself as so bitter and challenging and I was going to give it right back if he kept testing me.

"It's remarkable," Zephyr said, taking a step forward.

"Where did you find such a creature? No one has seen them in over a thousand years," Auster said.

"It's a long story," I said. Literally, it was. I'd held him in his egg for the first time centuries ago and it was bittersweet to think we'd waited for each other all this time. That right now was when we were truly supposed to meet.

"If you'd stay a while, we'd love to hear," Auster said, the first time his tone started to warm to me.

I smiled with a nod. I didn't want there to be a rift between us. Despite my heart being Nyte's, I still cared for Auster and wanted to help him find the happiness he deserved too.

The guard retreated and I wished his brothers would too but they trailed a few paces behind us as we headed toward the bridge that would take us onto the Nova province. My sight cast past it, however.

"Can we visit the Luna province?" I asked.

Zephyr's brow lifted in surprise; he looked to Auster for an answer, which I didn't like.

"If you wish," Auster agreed, but I got the impression he would rather I decided to go back to his land.

I didn't know what it was about the snowcapped mountains of Zephyr's lands that felt compelling.

Taking Auster's hand, we stepped through the void to get there fastest. Luckily I was already dressed for the colder temperature with winter thick on the other side of the veil.

The castle here was high between mountains, made of beige stone but glittering spectacularly with the ice and snow. A wide waterfall fell from the height with a river running through the fortification. It almost looked like an island floated in the sky.

"Can we go there?" I asked Zephyr.

"Of course." He seemed receptive to my eagerness, but still wary of Auster who kept close to my side.

"Did I come here often . . . before?" I asked.

"Yes. Whenever you came back to Althenia you would spend time here and of course on the Nova province."

It wasn't surprising I clearly didn't favor Notus or Aquilo's lands, or I wasn't welcome there. I was curious in this life, however, and made a note to visit even if just to piss them off because they had to host me.

"Actually there's a place you might find more intriguing than another boring castle," Zephyr said with a knowing smile.

It turned me giddy and I followed without regarding Auster. The streets here were so tranquil and beautifully snow-covered. A carriage pulled up, silver and pulled by two magnificent white horses. Except . . .

"They have wings," I marveled. I had never believed such a creature existed.

"Pegasus," Zephyr told me, coming around to stroke the mane of one. "They're very rare in our age. Sacred to our people."

I thought back to the time I'd gotten to ride a regular horse on my way to the Libertatem. I might not have mustered the courage were it not for Nyte. Even though he'd only been in my mind, the memory was as real to me as if he'd physically been there, pressed tightly behind me and helping to guide the beast.

I wondered if riding the Pegasus would be more like dragonback, something I was excited to experience when Eltanin was big enough.

"Want to ride?" Zephyr asked, tipping his chin to the carriage.

Beaming, I all but skipped up to it, taking Auster's hand for help. My gut tightened in anticipation and Eltanin gave a small caw, burrowing in my hood deeper. He could fly alongside, and I should be encouraging it; he was becoming quite the lazy dragon.

I clutched the side of the open double facing carriage as the Pegasus walked. Their wings expanded as they picked up speed, then my stomach tumbled to the leap they took into the air. They were so smooth in their flight that it was like we were gliding. Eagerly I peered over to drink in the snowy province below us that expanded with so many homes, forests with hidden communities, and mountains.

"How is your own flying coming along?" Auster asked.

His eyes had tuned soft on me and I sank back into my seat.

"Good, actually. Once I felt what it was like to fly I think it came back to me quite easily."

"I am glad," he said with a smile.

"And your powers?" Zephyr asked.

My fingers flexed subconsciously at that; the key was now a small baton strapped at my hip.

"I'm getting better at reaching that too."

"Is he treating you well?" Auster asked with a stiff edge.

"Yes. He's careful with me." That wasn't a lie despite the time I'd provoked him into a battle after seeing Drystan. Though I kind of wanted to unleash like that with him and our powers again.

We landed high and I hopped out the carriage on my own, eager to trace my hand down the beautiful wings of the Pegasus I might not see again for a while.

"This way," Zephyr said, already strides ahead.

I bustled after him heading toward a small woodland around the bend of tall rocks. My breath was stolen when I saw it wasn't ordinary. The ethereal glow of the nature here gave off an enchanted energy. A quiet pocket of magick.

So much glowed in the brightest neon colors, which I'd only seen by Starlight Matter enhancements. Lights flew around—insects—which immediately caught the interest of Eli, who jumped suddenly from his cozy nest around my neck. I grinned watching him chasing after the small life around here.

"What is this place?" I asked, wandering into the greenery that was untouched by the snow.

"There are a couple of spots like it around Althenia; no one really knows why they bloomed, though some speculate they're places where the spiritual veil is thinnest. I believe you liked to come here because you're the star-maiden."

"We call them Light Nests," Auster added. "Many come to them to heal and find spiritual guidance."

That took my interest as I trod carefully. When I touched the soft bark of a tree, small waves of energy lapped over my skin, the silver lines and swirls on me came to life, adding another glow to the ethereal space.

"Do you think it's possible to reach guidance from a spiritual realm such as . . . the realm of the guardians?"

Auster looked me over curiously. Then he frowned at the grass he walked over, which was brighter than any I'd seen before. I followed, touching and weaving through the trees between us.

"Your guardians did well in raising you to be an unbiased and fair ruler, but I think even your parents thought their own hearts meddled too often."

I didn't expect Auster not to be fond of them.

"What do you mean?"

"The guardians let your rebellions thrive when they were supposed to teach you discipline."

I turned tense at the way he spoke of me like a child out of line. The guardians had been kind and genuine—I'd never felt the kind of safe attachment like I had when I'd been around them. As if no matter what I confessed, they'd help me find a way.

"My *parents* seem to have given up on me anyway," I muttered resentfully.

"They only want what is best for you."

"They wanted a perfect creation. A person they could control the world with. They should have given up their supreme forms to be here themselves."

"Don't reject those who made you and want to better the world, Astraea. Not for him."

It always came back to Nyte. It always would.

"You have to accept he's part of me."

"Then *Bond* with him!" Auster's outburst shocked me.

Zephyr shifted awkwardly before turning, following Eltanin's antics to appear uninterested.

"Now you're encouraging me to bond with him?" I said bitterly.

"I can't bear it, Astraea. Being around you with that chance, even if just a thread, that you could still choose to bond with me instead. So do it; let us both heal from the fact that it would never have been me. It's the only way I'll believe there's no hope for us."

That confession tore through me.

"I'm sorry," I whispered.

Auster shook his head. "Don't be. Just get it over with."

His words stung. "Nyte showed me a memory—"

"Please don't speak his name," he snapped.

I winced. "He showed me something I'd told him once. That I loved you and always would. We were friends. I didn't want to lose that then and I don't now."

"I am trying. Which is why you have to do this for me to move on."

How could I tell him that I couldn't bond with Nyte? Not yet. His father was at large with a way to kill Nyte now if we forged that bond and became part of each other.

"I will."

"Now."

His persistence made me uneasy but my guilt about hurting him made me understand why he wanted it over with. I hoped he was right, and that once Nyte and I were bonded, we could heal from it as friends even if he would never warm to Nyte.

"Such a thing shouldn't be rushed into," Zephyr said carefully.

It was the first time I'd seen Auster direct a hostile stare at one of his brothers. "This has nothing to do with you."

"We're all here to counsel her. Let us get past Star-Maiden Day, at least."

"It doesn't need to wait. She's made her choice," Auster argued.

I interjected, "And that means I choose when it happens. I'm sorry this hurts you, but it shouldn't take this for you to accept that our bond is gone."

"It's not though," he said, in a low tone that had me balking along with his step toward me. "So long I can still feel you, the essence of you that reaches for me, it's fucking torture. I want it gone and the only way that happens is if you bond him."

"Or you both declare your rejection," Zephyr countered.

I stiffened at the dark look that flexed around Auster's eyes from that. "This is none of your fucking business."

"We can reject it?" I asked.

"I won't," Auster said firmly.

"Why not?"

"Because the only way I'm letting you go is if it's impossible to bond you, or you're dead."

Auster began to leave after hanging those haunting words in the air. My throat tightened at them and my vision swayed. I didn't know why they impacted me this way. It felt like panic, fear.

I spun to go after him but Zephyr caught my arm.

"Let him be for a while."

It was a relief to hear that when I didn't want to face him after that but I wondered if I was being selfish, hurting him more than he deserved and this lashing out was justified.

"It would have been so much easier if I could have fallen for him, instead," I whispered. It ached my soul to acknowledge that, but it was the truth.

"Easier to everyone but you."

"Is that not what being a leader is? The star-maiden?" I pulled my arm free, pacing in a restless growing resentment. "No wonder your brothers see me as nothing more than a stubborn, rebellious child back then and now."

When Zephyr didn't respond I stopped walking to scowl up at him. I didn't expect him to be standing there watching me with an amused smile.

"This isn't funny!"

"I didn't say it was," he said through a chuckle. "Stars, I've missed you, Astraea. You haven't changed; you've just been hiding."

I blinked at that. "We were good friends, weren't we?"

"You could say that," he said somberly now.

I ran a hand down my face. "Everything would be so much easier if I just remembered."

Zephyr's mouth firmed with that. "I have to believe everything has an order and that you will, when the time is right."

"I don't think time is ever right. It can't be stopped, or reversed, or pushed faster. Time gets the blame for things we do or that happen in a way that is unfavorable to our current circumstances. Or how we feel better about the things we let get away when they were desirable."

"Or how we push through the hardships believing time has a plan—something better waiting in its passage. You're right. Sometimes I think time is used as a means of hope, and that there's a reason for why we don't achieve what we want in the present, or have lost what's in the past. Have faith, Astraea. It might be the last light you have to make it through the dark."

My shoulders slumped. Peering up at Zephyr, I felt both yearning and unsure about what I wanted right now.

"Can I—?"

Zephyr already crossed the few steps, pulling me to him in an embrace. I sighed with the wrap of comfort, deciding to trust that our past friendship was true.

"How is Katerina?" I asked, flooding with concern that I hadn't inquired sooner. "And all the others that were saved?"

Zephyr tensed before he broke our hug. "Everyone is healing. Glad to be home and alive, at least."

I got the sense he wasn't telling me everything. "Can I see her?"

"Probably not best right now."

"You're her bonded . . . she was worried about what you would think about her lost wings."

I backed a step, suddenly awash with a cold chill. Had she been right in her fear that he would reject her?

"I want to see her," I demanded.

"You can't."

"I'm going to the castle by invitation or not."

"She's not there."

Now I was retreating, regretting that embrace and how easily I felt myself trusting that he was an ally. Not like Notus or Aquilo.

"Astraea, there are things you don't yet understand or remember about our ways here. This is what I meant by having faith. Being patient."

"This seems pretty damn clear," I said. My fingers brushed the key at my hip. "What did you do to her?"

His jaw worked. He knew the truth wasn't what I wanted to hear.

"She's exiled from all four provinces."

My mouth fell open. "How could you?"

"She is safe—"

"How would you even *know?*"

Oh gods . . . I should have believed her fear, helped her, offered to let her stay with me and Rose and the others.

"Because I wouldn't exile her to an unknown fate," he hissed.

He had a fucking nerve to be angry.

"Wings don't change anything about a person."

"It makes a celestial powerless. Impure. At least that is what our laws have dictated for millennia. There was a time black wings were more common because it was a *curse*. There's a reason Nyte is so villainized because of them. A celestial's wings turning black was a mark of their sin that they'd slain another celestial, or had their shadow stolen—been cursed essentially. Though since that's not happened in over a century some believe that was a myth. Either way, the High Celestials in past decreed black wings would be torn out and those celestials exiled. Over time if someone had them poached, people often believed it was because they were black and they'd had them ripped out themselves to hide their sin. So it became part of our laws to exile them all."

My mind spun with all that information on top of my outrage over Katerina's exile.

Zephyr's eyes turned pleading. "Celestials are prideful and arrogant— we've always been known as the species chosen by the gods, that were depicted as their perfect mortal image. It's always been the role of the High Celestials, four individuals, to keep our species thriving and pure."

I shook my head. "None of this makes me see what you did as *right*. What does that make me? I am the star-maiden, a direct daughter of gods. What if I say no to this?"

To my surprise, Zephyr relaxed, almost smiled. A stark contrast to my building fury.

"Like you never left," he said to himself. Zephyr took a long breath, closing in a step toward me. "Please don't do anything reckless. There's more you're yet to see and understand. If you take this to Auster it will disrupt a lot you don't want to shake right now. Can you trust me?"

"I barely know you."

"That's not true and you know it."

I let him take my arms. Shit, I wanted to believe how I felt was real and that I could trust it—trust him.

"I love her with all I am, Astraea. She's half of me. Nothing could change that even if she's not with me now."

Time. Order. And faith. It's all I had. All I could hope was that I wasn't being led astray by my own intuition to be patient with Zephyr like he'd asked, and that I'd have the strength to challenge all the High Celestials on this cruel, unjust law when the time was fucking *right*.

43

Astraea

I f I opened my eyes, all I would see was darkness.

An irritating kind caused by the strip of black fabric Nyte tied around my head. He'd truly lost his mind with the training measure.

"The idea is to hone your senses more acutely. Reach a deeper connection to your magick."

"I've been reaching it just fine," I grumbled.

"You've been excelling impressively, but you're capable of more."

That was somewhat frightening. Nyte spoke of the well inside me like it was catastrophic, but even I had limits.

I clutched the key as a blade, readying for combat on a high mountain fringe at the edge of Alisus. We were heading back to Vesitire on foot with Zathrian, Rose, Davina, Lilith, and Nadia.

"On your mark," he called to me.

Pinning the direction of his voice, I took a long breath and braced my stance. My magick awakened and I listened to it, seeking out his energy through it like threads of power that touched him.

Then I attacked.

My first few attempts sliced nothing but air. The cuts of my light magick whistled through the wind. Then when my key finally chimed off his obsidian blade, I dove deeper into a well of concentration to keep track of him. Without my sight to lock his golden eyes for target, I became magnetized to his gravity.

Where he moved, I followed. Our dance became a breathtaking push and pull that stunned me with exhilaration every time our weapons sang together.

Lost in only him, I neglected to account for my surroundings. My heels slipped off the high ledge and I gasped. Nyte caught me from the fall with an arm around my waist.

Instead of pulling me away from the edge he leaned in until his warm breath tricked across my cold face.

"Fly, Starlight."

He barely grazed my lips with those words before he let me go.

I pushed the key into the void and extended my arms, enjoying the free fall in complete darkness and the prickling sensation of my wings slowly weighing on my shoulders.

Somehow I could sense the ground was near and I twisted, reaching my hand down to feel the snow before I shot high again.

When I felt the mist of breaking through the clouds, I removed my blindfold, and was swept away by the most breathtaking sight.

The sun was setting at this hour.

It was a picture of tranquilly and new beginnings with the glow of the sun spilling over the clouds, which gave an illusion of an endless expanse of tree canopies ablaze.

"Beautiful, isn't it?" Nyte said, hovering close.

I thought that word wasn't enough for the painting of a burning sky above us in streaks of amber.

Nyte flew in front and pulled me close. He kissed me and I soared. Then he let me go and I fell.

We raced gravity heading down. Wings splayed, my gentle landing made me beam in exhilaration. I didn't voice my arrogance, but I considered flying a conquered skill.

Except when I straightened and found Elliot, Zeik, Kerrah, Sorleen, and Nadia, I turned stiff. Nyte landed behind me.

"I thought we'd play a game to put your skills to the test," he said, his tone haunting and daring.

From the way they stood in a half circle, waiting with predatory amusement, I had a bad feeling about what this *game* of his would entail.

Nyte's hand snaked around my waist; his breath caressed my ear. "We're going to play Catch the Maiden."

I swallowed hard. "It's dark now."

We were in the Undying Forest North, a place that was known to be lurking with nightcrawlers.

"Exactly."

Nyte held the key out in front of me.

"We have bets to catch you and I'm planning on it being me. Strike them in any way and they'll stop chasing. Strike us all and you win."

My chest began to pound hard and fast, priming for this deadly race.

He was wicked in his methods. Completely mad. Yet I was growing hot with an adrenaline that was exciting.

"I don't want to hurt any of you," I said.

Zeik said playfully, "We don't want to hurt *you*."

"Speak for yourself," Nadia said with a gleam in her eye.

I shivered.

"We won't go easy on you," Kerrah added. "So don't hold back on us."

My wariness dissipated and I smiled, thrilled for the challenge.

Nyte's voice vibrated darkly below my ear. "Run, Starlight."

I took off in a sprint past the Guard in that second. Feeling for my magick, my skin came alive with it for the moment any of them found me. Or a night-crawler attacked me.

That added real danger that kept me sharper than if it'd only been a sport. I honed my senses, reaching further with my magick to detect energies around me.

The first to try me was Kerrah.

She raced beside me thinking I didn't know she was about to lunge. They said they wouldn't go easy, but this felt like it.

Deciding on arrows for this one, the key shifted to a bow. Crafting a light arrow, I stopped abruptly right before she could pounce. I knelt on one knee to angle my aim, tracking her high jump, and let my arrow soar.

It hit her leg, passing right through as the magick faded.

"Shit. Nyte downplayed how far you've come in combat so he could win. Bastard."

"Sorry." I winced at the bleeding hole in her leg, but she would heal quickly.

I took off running again, darting through the trees and jumping over the obstacles of loose branches and forest debris.

My blood roared and I was so alive and free. I don't know what it said about me to be enjoying this type of thrill. I didn't really care.

Zeik was next. He didn't hide, appearing in my path directly. Did he think he could grab me? Incapacitate me with the impact of slamming into him? That might work; he was built like stone.

Time for a new a test of my magick.

Pushing the key through the void, I cast my hands out flat in front with a movement that conjured a step made of light. Zeik blinked at it but I made another as I stepped on that one, then another, and another. Until I leaped off the top one, spinning in the air. As I landed behind him in a crouch, my palm cast out again with a flare of magick just as he turned around.

Zeik's cry was loud as he plummeted to his knees.

"It was barely a warm touch," I said to his overreaction.

"It nearly burned through my leathers," he complained, examining his chest.

"But it didn't. You're welcome."

I grinned at his grumbles then left him.

This was the most fun I'd had in a long time.

Sorleen was the most nimble. Quiet. I didn't feel her approach before she leaped out of her tree cover. She almost landed on me but I pivoted in time, unsheathing my stormstone blade to pin her to a tree with the point of it at her throat.

To my surprise, she smiled cruelly. Triumphantly.

I realized why too late.

Nadia closed in at my back and if I turned to face her I would be vulnerable to Sorleen. They'd made a tag team. *Shit.*

I only had a few seconds to react, and this was a test of my magick, after all. I had to create an impairment.

With a deep breath I dropped my blade to conjure a sphere of light instead, back to the basics Nyte had made me do over and over. It did become as easy as breathing, and as that orb grew and disturbed the air to a swirling gale in a heartbeat. This trick became a force that made me realize . . . *I am power.*

Sorleen shielded her eyes and Nadia was lost in the hurricane of forest debris. I hoped this wouldn't harm them too badly but the blast would be unpredictable. My legs braced, shifting to let go, then the light erupted in a shockwave that slammed into Sorleen and Nadia.

Panting, I swiped my dagger, sparing only a moment to find Nadia and Sorleen peeling themselves up with pained groans.

"Sorry!" I called as I ran away.

There weren't limits to attack, were there?

I was enjoying the quick test of my mind and magick. How they came together in the face of obstacles to calculate the most effective way out. This game was like a riddle of survival and my soul was rejoicing.

Elliot was still left. Then it would be just me and Nyte. My skin pricked in delight at that thought. Him chasing me. Getting to face off with our magick against each other again. The feel of his darkness against my light was incomprehensible. Dangerous yet absolutely euphoric.

The next obstacle was neither of them.

I skidded to a halt in a small clearing at the sight of three sets of taloned wings easing out from behind trees.

"Well what do we have here?" one sang.

"A delectable snack," another said, a woman this time.

"Oh I think she's far more than a snack. Can't you scent it?" the third said.

"A celestial." Fuck, a forth came out of the shadows.

Okay, four untrained, but likely savage in attack, vampires. One star-maiden. *I am power.*

My stormstone blade is what they feared as it could incapacitate them quickest, and kill them swiftest. But they hadn't seen my light.

The late arrival was the first to lunge with a snarl like his restraint had snapped. I ducked under his arm, twisted around his body, and my dagger scored across his wing. His wail pierced my ears, distracting me for a cursed heartbeat that was enough for another nightcrawler to attack.

The woman pummeled into me, straddling me, and all I could do was brace myself against her shoulders as her teeth snapped at me. The nightcrawlers could appear civil and in control, but it was like the moment their bloodlust took over they became nothing more than creatures driven mad by it.

I had to let her go, and her teeth came shy of piercing my neck until my palm thrust to her chest and a flare of light scorched right through her heart. She died instantly, but I realized my error when she fell as dead weight over me and I was trapped.

Pushing her off took everything I had but I was soon dragged by one of the others by my collar. I tried to scramble for my magick but too much was happening at once. He hauled me up to my feet from behind and I reached through the void for the key.

Feeling it was a breath of relief. My hand gripped the hilt of the sword I'd made of it and I spun with a cry, surging a force of light through the blade that cast out in a beautiful but lethal expanding circle.

I thought I'd only cut through the body of the one that held me, but as I twisted to face the impending attack of the last two nightcrawlers, I met their wide eyes before their bodies fell. Cut in half.

I'd done that before, I remembered from the last nightcrawler attack at the fae resistance camp meeting.

"Impressive." That single word licked up my spine. It wasn't spoken by just Nyte; I recognized the deep, sinister echo of Nightsdeath.

I thought I'd have Elliot to face before him, but he was alone, stalking toward me like a predator from the other side of the clearing.

"Did you just stand by and watch me?"

His small smile only curved one side of his mouth.

"It was entertaining."

"Glad you enjoyed the show." I was still gathering my breath. Debating if I should run.

"I'm going to enjoy this one a whole lot more."

"No using the void," I warned.

"Fine."

That single word struck in me like a declaration. I got one glimpse of Nyte leaning to break into a run before I twisted, my sole digging into the wet grass and nearly slipping.

I ran faster than I thought I ever had before. I could stop and attack, but I was twisted to find pleasure with him chasing me. I focused on nothing but the obstacles of the forest to get away.

"You can't outrun me," he taunted in my mind.

"I can try."

"You want me to catch you. I can taste it."

I couldn't even deny that.

A wall of dark smoke rolled in from both sides in front of me. I gasped, conjuring a gale of light just in time to break through it.

Movement caught in the side of my vision. Shadow wolves. They raced alongside me, crafted of Nyte's magick.

They were fascinating but I couldn't let them distract me. I tried to mimic his trick, breathing steadily without faltering my pace and crafting stags made of light that chased the wolves. When they caught them, Nyte's magick that animated the shadows hissed under the trampling hooves of light.

Nyte's darkly amused chuckle vibrated through my mind and body.

"You are cunning. And absolutely bewitching."

I broke through the tree line into another clearing, intending to race right across, but I gasped, slowing only enough for it not to be painful, when I collided with the angel of death that dropped down in my path.

"You didn't say no wings," he said huskily, then his lips slammed to mine.

I was already so breathless and high on adrenaline that I became dizzy with the way he claimed me. Harsh and ravenous. His hand grabbed a fistful of my hair, angling my head back more to kiss me deeper. He devoured me. Stealing every breath from me and yet I couldn't stop even if he claimed my last. When he broke away abruptly, my knees weakened and I was delighted prey in his hold.

"You have no idea how fucking magnificent you are. It's my purpose to show you. I have to make you feel even a fraction what I do when I look at you. This deep, unending obsession."

My skin tightened with desire for him, wild and feral right now.

"So the student becomes the master?" I said playfully.

Nyte's smile caused a flutter of pride in me. "Almost."

"I had fun. And I think that was a breakthrough to realizing what I can be capable of when I have no time to think or doubt. Thank you."

"I am irretrievably yours. That means pushing you to be the best you can be. Don't thank me for serving that."

His grip on my hair loosened. Nightsdeath retreated in him to bring back the tan complexion of his ears and neck. Returning his golden tattoos and dulling the amber flare of his irises. He kissed me softer this time with the arm circling my waist pressing us tighter.

"Nyte," Elliot's voice broke us apart. "You'll want to see this."

Nyte's brow furrowed but he nodded, taking my hand. Whatever Elliot had come across must be why he wasn't party to chasing me down.

After following Elliot for a few minutes Nyte seemed to detect something that I couldn't at this distance. He slowed our pace.

I found out what it was a few cautious strides later. Nyte pulled me carefully behind a tree far before the large clearing where a group gathered.

Not fae. Even though I could barely make out anyone else, I couldn't mistake the red hair and swagger of Tarran.

This was a meeting of vampires. Dread rolled in my stomach over what they could be plotting for their war.

I used my thoughts to speak to Nyte.

"You didn't know of this?"

"No."

His reply was short as he seemed to be trying to figure out what they could be scheming behind his back. They were talking but we were too far away for me to hear. Not too far for Nyte, but his expression gave little away.

I didn't need conversation when the next person to join them made me step back. My foot snapped a branch and every nerve in me stunned still as Nyte's hand pressed me tightly to him with the error.

A few heads turned, then some of the group started heading our way and Nyte swore under his breath.

"Get out of here," he hissed to Elliot, who nodded, taking off as starry shadow swept around Nyte and me and pulled us through the void.

My heart slammed when we stilled and I spun to Nyte back on the mountain fringe.

"Drystan has been meeting with Tarran?" I cried.

I knew he'd been involved with him before from seeing them together after the Libertatem, but for some reason I had naively thought his alliance had dropped Drystan now that Nyte was back.

"And a few more of the Elder Vampires."

"What does that even mean?"

"I'm not sure yet. I recognized a few, some of the oldest soulless, shadowless, and nightcrawlers. I believe they each have a leader like Tarran is for the soul vampires."

"Is this bad?"

"Depends on what they're up to. We might have had more time to catch a lead if you hadn't called them over."

I glowered at him. Then ran a hand down my face.

"How could we have missed this?" I said, mostly to myself. How could *I* have missed what Drystan had been up to? He was far more cunning than I'd given him credit for.

I paced. Back and forth. Back and forth.

There were so many sides that I didn't even know where *we* stood.

The vampires wanted power.

The fae wanted retribution.

The celestials wanted peace.

Or did they?

All this time they had been living in perfect peace beyond the veil. Why would they want to come out at all?

"You're going to wear steps down the mountain if you keep it up," Nyte remarked.

I found him leaning against a large rock, arms folded, watching me.

"Why are you not more concerned?"

"Not all of us show it by mapping our tangled thoughts on the ground."

I rubbed my temples instead. Continuing my train of thoughts on the war to figure out what the hell we were supposed to be doing other than waiting for someone to start the battle.

"Why haven't the vampires attacked yet?" I wondered out loud.

"The celestials are still in hiding."

"There's an empty throne right now and the Elders haven't moved in to claim it."

"They know it's not empty, it's yours."

That might have been true in theory, but right now I was barely an obstacle in their path to take it.

"Why did the vampires rise up against the celestials?"

"There had been unrest among them before my father started gathering an army of them. He saw a potential alliance with those who had a particular grudge against the celestials, and in turn many also resented the fae since they were close and respected by the celestials."

My mind started to lay out a history puzzle that felt important. I had to know the very roots of the war.

"The Elders could have recruited their own and started an army."

"My father was very . . . *hungry* to overthrow you and the celestials. He had me. He told them how we walked through worlds. He used me to demonstrate power. I can kill a room of men in a blink. I can force them to bow. Warp their minds to submit. For a while a lot of those who resisted his cause were brought to me and I bent their will and perspectives. There's a reason I am the villain of this realm as he wouldn't have grown his alliance with them without me. I did villainous things, Astraea. That will always be in my capabilities."

He gave me a hard stare like I would condemn him here. No matter what he told me, I still couldn't see what he wanted me to do. I saw a child that had his own will stripped away under the iron fist of a cruel parent. I saw a fae with nowhere else to go, who then gained a brother to protect. I saw someone who did what he thought he had to for survival.

"You aren't your past," I said.

"We are all ever changing products of our history."

I wondered what that made me when my history was hidden in my mind.

I asked, "What about Tarran and the others back then?"

"I never saw them."

"You don't find that odd? That they wouldn't make themselves known, ally with your father, to take power or even kill him to use you themselves?"

Nyte's expression turned thoughtful, staring at nothing in particular.

"I've never really thought about it. My father's army was growing rapidly. Word spread about what he wanted to achieve and with my help, it wasn't long before he was a known force to reckon with. They thought of him like a god since he'd traveled through realms."

It wasn't making full sense to me either. Nyte's father gathered an army of vampires but the Elders didn't participate . . . like they were merely observing, waiting for something.

I knew Tarran wouldn't trust me. I couldn't approach him and merely ask what he was planning.

"We should try asking Drystan," I said.

"He'd know we were here. If they're up to something, it gives away our advantage of surprise."

"We have no advantage if we don't have the first clue to what we're up to."

I gave an exasperated sigh. Nyte appeared in front of me, pulling me into his arms, and it diffused a lot of my anxiety.

"Don't worry too much. It's nothing we can figure out right now. You have Star-Maiden Day to prepare for."

"It seems ludicrous to be celebrating such a thing with the threat of war at their doorsteps."

"Let people have their moment of joy, love. It may be all they get to make it through the long year ahead."

"What will you be doing?" I asked quietly.

"Missing you, of course." He smiled at my sad frown. "Don't worry about me. Elliot and the others will drag me out to get recklessly drunk."

At least he wouldn't be alone. The thought of them enjoying the holiday together warmed me in my chest. Part of me was even envious of their humble plans compared to the extravagance of a ball that was rattling me with nerves.

Nyte pulled back, lifting something in his hand to me. My mood sulked at the black strip of fabric.

"You cut our session short with your uncoordinated footing," he said, suppressing his amusement.

"It's dark now anyway."

"Not dark enough."

44

Astraea

"Y ou bring trees indoors?"

I stared up at the giant pine tree in the temple Auster brought me to. It looked . . . sad. Taken from its home of soil to be caged by stone. It was odd to feel a connection with an inanimate thing of nature.

"It's a tradition of the festive season running up to Star-Maiden Day. It's still to be decorated."

"Decorated?"

"It's fun. You used to love this time of year."

I'd never seen Auster so relaxed and almost *giddy*. It was a relief that our tensions from our last encounter hadn't lingered, but I was also kept on edge since it could return any moment.

Celestials entered through the side arches with their arms full of gold and silver sparkly items. Everything was laid out around the base of the tree taken from its natural place outside and potted. I'd seen nature indoors before but it had been much smaller plants and flowers.

The celestials bowed to us when they stood in a line. I hoped the tautness that locked my body to the formalities here would ease over time. I'd once again been requested to wear an elaborate white and silver gown that made me stand out anywhere I tried to go.

A few shrieked when Eltanin spooked them, racing out from under one of the benches at the sight of the glittering ornaments and ropes of shimmering material.

I covered my mouth from my laughter as he dove into the assortment, finding entertainment in them like toys. His juvenile antics wouldn't last long at all. Soon he wouldn't even be able to fit through the door.

"He'll make a great helper," Auster mused.

He guided me toward the tree with a hand on my back as the other celestials started plucking ornaments and hanging them on branches.

"What is this for?" I asked, picking one out of Eltanin's mouth. I copied the others, looping it over the branch.

"It's supposed to be a blessing to welcome spring when winter passes and the decoration is just for joy and wishes."

"Wishes?"

His brown eyes sparkled. "You'll see later."

I didn't know how much time had passed as I lost myself in the activity. It had been a while since I'd become so eagerly engrossed in a task that was so carefree and *fun*. It reminded me of how I could never put down a puzzle or riddle until I'd finished it. I laughed at Eltanin flying higher than I could reach and trying to copy what I was doing. He was getting too smart too fast, and my pride swelled watching his progress.

"Can he speak to you?" Auster wondered.

He dangled a gold star close to my silver bauble.

"Not yet," I said, watching him fly with a rope of what I now knew to be called tinsel. Another celestial flew up to help him wrap it around the wide expanse of the tree.

"You think he will?"

"I don't know, actually. Apparently in the past I knew how to speak to them but perhaps I can't anymore. Or perhaps he's too young or some never speak."

Something I'd said caused Auster's silence, drawing my attention to him.

"How do you know you could speak to dragons?"

My pulse skipped. Had I not told him of it in the past? Of course . . . he never knew of my secret meetings with Nyte and I internally cursed, scrambling for a diversion.

"It was in a book—I assumed you knew," I lied quickly, bending down for a gold ornament shaped like a box with a bow. An imitation of a present, I thought. Convincing enough that I shook it to listen for a tiny gift inside. I pouted that it was hollow.

"I did not," he answered distantly, like he now thought back on the past version of me.

I grew with unease that he could do that. I didn't know why it made me far more anxious to wonder what memories Auster had of me—of us—more than I was worried about what Nyte could recall.

"Probably won't matter," I said, brushing it off.

Auster and I reached for the same stray silver bauble. Our fingers brushed and I retreated to let him have it. He picked it up, passing it to me with a genuine smile that fluttered in my chest.

Nyte wanted me to be sure. To give any feeling that might surface for Auster a chance. So I didn't shrink away from our proximity. We stood together, and I followed his sight up.

"There's a spot near the top," he said.

I rolled my shoulders subconsciously, then my wings unglamoured to reach the perfect place with the tree now full and beautiful. Eltanin gave an adorable noise flying over to me as I hooked the final ornament. I didn't go back down, instead I flew back to take in the whole sight of the tree that now looked so strange but breathtaking. Though something felt missing.

"There will be a lighting ceremony later," Auster said, like he could read my thoughts.

That sparked my intrigue, and the image of the tree glowing with lights flooded my mind. My lips parted; it felt like the first time a memory had come to me so easily. Just that single picture.

My feet met the ground and Auster walked down the aisle toward me. He looked upon me like *I* was the magnificent tree.

"Will you dine with me beforehand?" he asked.

I smiled with a nod, actually looking forward to his company over food and then the ceremony later; I didn't fully know what it entailed, but I was excited to find out.

It was the first time I'd come here and forgotten the passing hours. The burden of war and vampires didn't touch here and though it was peace; I would always harbor a note of guilt that this was like pretend to me. I had friends on the other side of the veil that kept everyone here safe and there was a world of suffering beyond. That's where I belonged more.

Zadkiel waited by the main doors with a warm smile that I returned.

"Will your friend Rosalind be coming back with you sometime?" he asked as we headed back to the Nova fortitude.

"I asked her today, but she claimed to want to train with my friend, Zathrian."

Some enthusiasm fell from his face. I added, "I'll tell her you asked for her."

"No need," he said. "She just seemed to find herself at home here, that's all."

I agreed. This place had that effect on people.

"This other friend of yours is welcome here with you, of course," Auster said.

"He—uh . . ." I didn't want Auster to dislike Zath before they'd even met. I'd asked him if he wanted to come but he was very hesitant. "I think he's respecting his loyalty to Nyte."

I hated that there was this divide, but I understood. I could only hope time might make it smaller. *Have faith that time has a plan.* I was trying, at least. Zath hadn't admitted that was his reason, and Nyte would tell him to come if he wanted to, but Zath was fiercely loyal and though Nyte might not see it, he made an impression on more people than he realized.

"I see," Auster said tightly.

Shit, I shouldn't have said anything.

"I hope we get the chance to meet on the other side of the veil sometime, then," he continued, after a pause.

I smiled, though it felt like tension had grown. I had a feeling it would be like this for a long while with Auster every time we met—hot and cold, learning who we are now versus who he remembers.

We headed straight for supper and Zadkiel left us again though I wished he'd joined us.

Auster sat at the head and I was on his right. The placement didn't sit right with me. Perhaps it was because I was beginning to see more and more of what made him royalty here. A king without that title. What did that make me on these lands?

Traditionally my place was lower than his, but I tried to convince myself there was nothing in the table placement.

Nyte made me feel like the world was mine. He never let me forget I was the star-maiden and should own that. On this side of the veil it was harder to believe with the High Celestials displaying their leadership as if I wasn't needed and was merely a *symbol* for the people.

As we ate, he told me more about the festivities around this time of year. People loved to have bonfires and sing and drink. It was such a season of joy that I was swept away in his stories and the way he told them for a while.

Auster loved his people. He spoke of the celestials so highly. Of his advisers and how the provinces were run. I found it fascinating if daunting, but I would have time to see it all for myself and learn the order here.

I laughed with him and indulged on celestial wine that tasted so sweet it was addicting. It numbed all my nerves and after we'd finished eating I wasn't in any hurry to be anywhere else.

Leaning back in my seat, I was entertained with Auster throwing scraps of meat for Eltanin to catch. The juvenile dragon was so content and at ease here.

"Will you stay the night?" Auster asked gently, like he already anticipated I wouldn't.

"I should get back—we're trying to figure out what the vampires are planning."

The mention of the vampires distracted him from the usual disappointment he showed when I would decline to stay.

"Have you discovered anything of importance?"

"Nothing yet. There's a fae army I don't think the vampires are aware of. They're ready to fight with us."

Auster mulled over that information with a hand under his chin, elbow propped on the arm of his chair.

I'd given him that information as a ploy to learn things from him too. "The material you used to harm them—what is it?"

"We're not sure of the name, only that we were told by a seer where to find a shard of the rock that was deadly to the fae. Then we learned how to recreate the effects. All we've had is time to build our efforts to take back the entire continent. The vampires and their allied fae won't stand a chance."

He was so confident that it should have stoked me with relief and even pride, yet my chest constricted with foreboding. I was overcome with a strong need to prevent it ever being necessary they should have to use their newfound weapon against the fae.

"A lot of the fae are not in the opposing army by choice," I said.

"Many are. There are always bound to be innocent casualties in war."

"What if there are vampires who are as opposed to this war as we are?"

"Astraea." He said my name in a way that pricked my irritation like a scolding. "We were once like gods to the people in Solanis. The celestials were respected; we kept full order for the fae, humans, and vampires to survive. We gave the blood- and soul-thirsty creatures purpose and they became too greedy. They will always be unpredictable."

So are all people, I wanted to counter. Something in the way Auster spoke told me he would hear it, but not regard my defenses. The vampires were wholly condemned to him.

"What will you do with them when the war is won?" I dreaded to ask.

"There will be none left to even worry about again."

My world stopped spinning for a second. It was unfathomable . . . he couldn't seriously be considering the annihilation of an entire species? That was not justice but a massacre, simply for the way they were born.

"That can't be the only solution," I protested.

"Let us worry about that."

"I will not," I said, more firmly as I stood. "Everyone wants to call me the star-maiden, the savior. Then that's what I am. I speak for and consider all life."

"You haven't been here," he said harshly, as he too stood up.

"I might not have all my memories but I'm not naive. Evil isn't born, it's made. Just because someone wronged you doesn't make everyone your enemy."

"Someone?" he seethed. I hadn't seen Auster this angry before, but I'd triggered it in him now. We both backed away from the table and he stalked to me. "We've been hiding for three hundred years to gain back the magick *you* weakened to the point the vampires would have annihilated *us* if you didn't die and the veil was created."

The daggers of blame speared me one by one until my back met the wall.

He searched my eyes with that blazing anger, recalling all that time ago. Until he sighed, and it all diffused out of him when he came back to the present.

"I'm sorry," he said, cupping my cheek. His thumb stroked my skin. "I don't blame you. I just want you to understand this is what we've been waiting for. Your return to our side to help us stop this once and for all. War isn't easy, it should never be. It takes a lot of sacrifices and those of us who lead need to be willing to make the hard choices."

All I could do was nod. There would be no reasoning with him right now. I hated to submit. Hated *myself.* I wanted to argue—to make him see I would not be a bystander to this war. I didn't want to hear it spoken of like something I didn't need to understand, only accept.

I wanted to fucking *remember.* Maybe then I would know what Nyte saw, why he believed in me so passionately. Was it pitiful that in moments that shook my confidence all I wanted was him? Just a single look at Nyte was often enough to set the dying wick of my candle ablaze.

"Let's not let this ruin our day," Auster sighed. "Come, you'll enjoy the lighting ceremony."

I didn't know what to expect, but standing by the tree in front of a crowd that made the giant hall feel too small now, I couldn't place my feelings.

Auster made a speech and people listened to him with adoration in their eyes. His brothers were here from their own provinces, but they would have their own version of this happening throughout the week too.

Zephyr hovered close to me while Auster was still speaking.

"How are you finding all of this?" Zephyr asked under his breath.

I spared him a glance. He was as formally dressed as me and the High Celestials. Always in white with their province color. I noticed the seal on his coat this time—each celestial had a different constellation and I made a note in my mind to research them. I had the constellation tattooed in silver on my chest carved into brass and pinned at my shoulder too. It's what decorated the banners in the street for this time of year.

"It's . . . a lot," I admitted. I'd never been such a spectacle for so many eyes.

As well as my elaborate white gown, they'd convinced me to wear a halo crown that was stunning, it just felt too much. They added glitter to my face and silver liner over my eyelids that made my irises brighter.

"You're doing great," he said, looking out over the crowd.

I appreciated those words more than I could say right now when inside I couldn't help feeling like I was always doing something wrong.

"Now we have our maiden home; it is an honor to restore this tradition to its true form," Auster announced, casting me a smile of acknowledgment.

People's eyes adored me like I was a goddess. I knew I was, but what I also wanted to tell them was that I was just like them as well. I bled like them, loved like them, and doubted myself like them. If I could get the celestials to see that, it was a step toward getting them to understand *they* were not much different from the fae, the humans, or even the vampires either. We were all people. One people. It was my destiny to show that.

I felt comfortable next to Zephyr. Aquilo and Notus couldn't help themselves with the occasional cold glare spared my way. Subtle enough that none of the onlookers would think anything of it.

Once I was guided over to the front of the tree by Zephyr, a line started forming down the aisle and my hands clammed up. Auster had told me before what I was expected to do. I would grant each person a tiny orb of light made of my magick, they would wish upon it, and it would be let go to attach to the tree like the ornaments. On Star-Maiden Day, it was tradition that I would gather them all back, and send their wishes to the stars.

It was all hope and superstition, but that was a beautiful thing.

The first in line was a child. She had long blond hair and bright blue eyes that peered up at me nervously. I crouched to her level.

"What's your name?" I asked.

It took a patient moment for her to push past her hesitation.

"Naya," she said.

"I have something for you, Naya."

In my open palm, I created the tiny warm glow. Naya's expression brightened, cupping her small hands together.

"It needs your wish before it can fly," I told her.

The light hovered in her hands and she was so taken by it that the sight was precious.

"I want mama to get her wings back so she can come home," Naya whispered to it.

My gut sank terribly. I wondered who her mother was. Had she been one of those saved from Alisus Keep?

Naya let her light go, and I stood to watch it fly high before settling on a branch as the first wish among hundreds that would adorn it by the end of the night.

How many of them would hold impossible dreams?

I forced a smile for Naya who launched forward to hug my legs quickly before skipping off happily, oblivious to how fragile her wish was. It was selfless, for her mother, and I couldn't make it come true.

"She's happy. Smiling. She has hope in her heart and that's all that matters," Zephyr said close by me.

"Everyone who was saved from the keep . . ."

"They got to come home and see their families again."

"Before they were forced away from them despite the horrors they'd faced." Zephyr's look was pained.

"Maiden," Auster said, drawing me back to the waiting line.

It was odd to hear him address me by that title, but it's what these people knew. Not Astraea, the person I am. But the star-maiden, the savior they needed me to be.

The night went on and I grew more exhausted hour by hour. The energy it took to create hundreds of small lights drained my magick slowly on top of the small conversations I had with people in between.

I enjoyed it, truly. It was easing my nerves to get to converse with people so personally and hear their wishes. It was touching to be part of this wonderful tradition.

When the last of the people left and the doors closed, I didn't care for poise and properness as I slumped down on the stairs before the tree. It was now a breathtaking beacon I couldn't stop staring proudly at. Glowing with my magick holding everyone's wishes for the new year to come.

"I'm proud of you," Zephyr said. Auster was chatting with some other celestials at the side of the hall.

I smiled with gratitude. "Were we . . . friends?"

He felt the most familiar out of the brothers.

"Yes," he said. "Good friends, actually."

Katerina had said so too, adding merit to his claim. He sat down with me and I took in his wears of silver and turquoise.

"Do all the houses have their own color?" I asked.

"Yes. Sapphire for Nova, turquoise for Luna, crimson for Sera, and gold for Aura. We each have our own constellation too," he said, tapping the eight points of a constellation made of brass on his jacket.

"I have my own?"

"Your color is violet, like your magick."

I was eager to learn more about the celestial houses, but right now all I wanted was sleep.

"You should stay the night in Althenia," he said. My fatigue must have been weighing on my face.

"I've been thinking so much about the war and needing to find my magick, but I miss books," I confessed. "Auster said we could visit the library but there hadn't been much time with all these festivities."

"I could take you tomorrow," he offered. "Show you more about the houses."

I thought about Nyte with a want to go back to him, but perhaps more I wanted to stay here a little while longer since I couldn't have both.

"Then I'll stay," I said.

Zephyr's smile was warm and genuine. His sight slipped to Auster as he finished speaking and headed to us.

"Trust yourself," Zephyr said. "You don't have to be compliant in all things."

He looked me over head to toe, like he knew I hated the bright white of the gown I wore.

Eltanin crept onto my lap. Instead of burrowing like he usually would for a sleep, his head canted curiously at Zephyr, feathers fluffing. I was beginning to learn a language from him from his quirks alone. I was sure he was trying to impress the High Celestial.

Zephyr chuckled, reaching out a hand, and the dragon was more than receptive to him, hopping from my lap to his.

"He seems to really like you," I mused.

With Auster, he was more subdued, uninterested. Unless food was involved, in which case he'd let an enemy be a friend for a while.

"He has good taste," Zephyr said. "A remarkable thing. I never thought I'd see a celestial dragon and I'm almost convinced he's some kind of illusion."

"He'll be aging up soon," I said sadly. "On Star-Maiden Day, I think, is when the full moon should be."

"Ahh, you're going to have your hands more full with him then."

I smiled fondly. Eltanin had become an unexpected pride and joy in my life. My attachment to him often reminded me of Nyte. He was a thread of my existence I couldn't live without now.

"Ready to go?" Auster asked.

I took his hand to reluctantly stand. All I wanted was to collapse onto a bed.

"I think I'll stay, if that's okay. It's very late now anyway."

Auster's whole demeanor relaxed to a pleased softness.

"I would love nothing more."

He regarded Zephyr with a single nod. The High Celestial placed Eltanin on my shoulder before he headed down the aisle.

"I hope to see you tomorrow, Astraea," he called.

I nodded, excited about spending more time with him and seeking out the library.

"I'd rather hoped we could spend the day together before you leave again," Auster said.

I couldn't place it, but it felt like he wasn't fond of Zephyr. Not like how he seemed closer to Aquilo and Notus.

"It will just be a few hours," I said.

Auster nodded but it was tight. He reached for me and I allowed him to pull us through the void until we were back in my rooms.

"If you need anything," Auster said, heading to leave.

"Thank you."

He looked like he wanted me to say something else, perhaps ask him to stay longer. I hoped he wouldn't ask again about my incomplete bond with Nyte. Auster left without another word and the moment I was alone it was like the weight of expectation I didn't know had been crushing me had lifted completely.

I climbed into bed, still dressed, only taking off the silver halo crown. My eyes weighed so heavy and Eltanin curled up comfortably with me.

Staring out at the sky I thought about the day's events, and drifted off with hope chasing away the ever-growing tension of war.

45

Nyte

Astraea didn't come back.

I watched the veil shimmering darkly in the distance, leaning in one of the archways of the bell tower.

How lonely the night was without her to find in the sky.

How silent the world was when I couldn't feel her within.

How tormenting my own vicious mind was, reeling from the thought that I was no longer her home.

It was just a matter of time before she realized that. Found better in the land of her people, and her other bonded who was everything she *should* want.

Everything I couldn't be for her.

It was real fucking ironic really—I was only truly heartless when I was without her. My miserable, cold heart always had been, and always would be, in her possession.

I took a drink of wine, sitting on the ledge and trying to stop my demons from surfacing. They wanted to tear down the veil to reach her. Kill everyone in my path to take her.

But love couldn't be selfish.

I existed for nearly one hundred years before her, but I only knew what it was to *live* after I'd met her.

PART
SIX

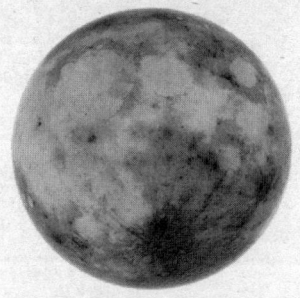

46

Nyte—Past

Drystan thought he was winning this game; Nyte kept his smugness from shattering that hope.

"You're losing your touch," Drystan smirked, playing his card. "Something on your mind, brother? A certain fallen star, perhaps?"

Nyte gave him no expression but that only widened Drystan's smile to a grin.

"Have you figured out anything from that diary yet?"

"This and that, nothing of significance yet. The language is over a thousand years old."

Nyte's brow lifted after playing his next card.

"Well enjoy translating fables," Nyte said.

"You're no fun," Drystan quipped. "I've taken it on as my personal side quest since you two keep me out of your main affairs."

"You've been with us plenty."

"*Plenty,*" he repeated with a disgruntled scoff. "Do you know how tedious it is to sit around the keep and listen to father rant to no end about how it's been years and you've still not brought him the star-maiden? Meanwhile I know you're out there discovering other interesting shit I'll never know about with her as ally-enemies."

"I tell you everything once I'm back."

"Do you though?"

"What's that supposed to mean?"

Drystan's chin tilted down in knowing accusation.

"You think I haven't noticed how you look at her now? How she often looks at you?"

Nyte's jaw tensed. "You don't want to go down there, brother. Forget whatever it is you *think* you observed because it's false."

Drystan never did shy away from provoking him. It was damn infuriating.

"She's it, isn't she?"

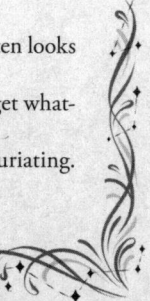

"Not another word."

"Denial doesn't erase a mating bond."

Nyte's rage flared at the term he spoke so casually. As if it was nothing. As if it wasn't an impossible, incredible, absolutely world-damning thing that should never be heard.

He took a few breaths to calm the fuck down.

"It changed nothing before. It changes nothing now." Nyte set down his cards, pinning Drystan with a look that made sure he knew he was serious. "Don't ever say that out loud again."

"Why? Don't you see what this could mean? Shit, unless father found out, he would force you to use it. You would gain her power and be able to wield the *key*—"

"Enough," he snapped.

Then everything quieted with a pull he felt within.

His senses homed in on it by instinct and a stilling calm overtook him. One of cold, terrible dread the likes he'd never felt before. Then he scented it. Blood. Not just any and his eyes snapped to the break in the wall before a nightmare he didn't know he'd harbored the terror of consumed him, watching her stumble into the archway.

Astraea.

Her silver hair was tangled and painted with streaks of red. She bore her weight against the stone; her hand clutched over her abdomen stained crimson. When her tired eyes lifted to find him with a silent plea for help, Nyte lost it.

His chair flew back with the force he stood with. "Everyone get the fuck out!" he roared.

Channeling through the void, Nyte caught her before she fell.

"What happened?" he demanded, overcome with a sensation that tightened his throat. Panic? It was so foreign he didn't know what to do with it.

"I didn't—I didn't know where else to go," she panted, face pinching in agony as bodies blurred around them to get through the exit, knowing Nyte was beyond sparing a life that didn't get out fast enough.

He scooped her up, and Drystan swiped his arm to scatter everything off the table Nyte laid her upon. Her breath came in short gasps, eyes flickering with terror. He cupped her cheek.

"You don't get to die on me," he said firmly, forcing her to meet his eyes. "You still have hell to give me."

Astraea tried to nod, but she didn't believe him. "I'm scared."

He slipped into her mind, trying to take some of her pain and terror, but what she was experiencing was like nothing he'd faced before.

"Nyte," Drystan said, in a tone hushed with dread.

When he followed Drystan's attention to the wound, Nyte almost fell to his fucking knees. It glowed faintly. A violet hue he knew the sight of.

"Where's your key, Starlight?" Nyte asked, as soft as he could for her when murderous rage was beginning to tremble his bones. "Who the fuck did this to you?"

"I don't know," she said weakly.

Nyte's chest never skipped such a hard beat as in that moment. She was fading fast. From a wound that would be fatal to her from her own weapon.

He met his brother's eyes and the grim look in them spoke what he could not, *would not,* accept.

She was dying, and there was no curing such a wound. Not even with his own blood.

But there was one way to save her.

Nyte wasn't thinking right. He wasn't thinking at all. Only desperation drove his actions.

"Get out of here," he said in a cold calm to Drystan.

"What are you going to do?"

Astraea's eyes slipped shut.

"Get out!"

Drystan backed a few paces as Nyte lifted Astraea into his arms. He didn't go far, lowering himself against the wall with her back against his front.

"There's no going back from this," Drystan said carefully, concluding what Nyte was planning to do.

Nyte expelled the noise Drystan added to the sirens already blaring in his mind to try to stop him.

"Leave, and don't speak a word of it to anyone."

With one last lingering look of concern and protest, Drystan nodded before he left.

"Stay with me," Nyte said, willing his heart to calm as he dragged his sharp teeth over his wrist, cutting his flesh. He brought it to her lips. "Please."

It was madness how much the value of something became abundantly clear the moment it came close to slipping out of his possession. He'd denied the depth of his caring for her all this time and now he would resent himself if he was to lose her.

The silence beat too heavily, his skin slicked all over with the adrenaline coursing through him. Astraea stirred at his blood flowing down her throat. Her small hands reached for his forearm, not to pull it away but in a weak attempt to take more from him.

His lips pressed to her head and Nyte's eyes closed for the only damned prayer he'd ever utter in his gods-forsaken life.

Astraea's hand fell away from him limply, and when he held her still form and looked upon the paleness of her face, it was like the world began to cleave beneath him.

He only had seconds to make this decision.

In her most desperate moment, for some reason he couldn't fathom but became utterly beholden to, she'd come to him. Not Auster.

"Gods of the Stars, the Mother, and Death, hear me." His chest rose and fell deeply with the deceleration that flared a life inside him. "She is mine. I claim her."

A tether within him reached for her as his mouth closed on her neck, puncturing her delicate flesh. The moment her blood entered him he became irretrievable.

He was hers.

Until his last breath he would be everything for her. Even if she woke and still declared him her enemy. He would find her in every darkness. Trek realms and defy time to reach her.

His soul snapped like rope that frayed with fragile threads, searching for the new and better half to forge something precious. A bond he would protect for the rest of his life. Nyte clutched her tighter, a desperation overcoming him that couldn't get enough of her. When their souls finished reforging, he drew back with shuddering breaths against her neck.

The weight of what he'd done started to bear down in fractions.

He'd Bonded his enemy.

The one person he was never supposed to have.

She might very well hate him for it. But at least she would be alive to do so.

Pulling back, Nyte examined her chest first. Her breathing was shallow, but coming back stronger like the beat of her heart. Her wound stopped bleeding.

Nyte couldn't move.

So he held her, letting her head rest tucked too perfectly against his shoulder as he slumped back.

"Stay with me," he whispered. Over and over. The same three words wouldn't stop repeating from his lips as if she could be standing in a void to make her choice right now and he needed her to know he *wanted* her to come back.

He took one moment to pretend things were different. That what he'd done . . . wasn't cause for the end of the world.

Nyte's eyes widened with the spark of her weak hand slipping over his.

He breathed for her soul now. Lived for her heart. He was bound to her eternally and had so much to prove to be what she needed.

"Nyte," she barely whispered.

Her voice he would run to. Every time she called.

"Starlight."

"What—what happened?"

Astraea started to come around. She peeled off him when he wanted to beg her for a moment more. For what he'd done was about to shatter this peace he'd never known could exist for someone so dark and wicked.

When she stood, he copied slowly. Waiting for her to realize. Her brow furrowed and it was like he could feel her reaching for fragments of memory as she looked around, then down at herself as her hand caressed over the tear in her leathers and her bloodstained hands. Then she examined him.

"You saved me . . ." she said, calculating. "How?"

"Why did you come to me?" he asked, almost a beg.

If she'd gone to Auster, he would have had no choice but to do the same. She would be Bonded to him instead.

"I—uh . . ." Astraea blinked, pacing away as she scrambled for the reasons, the event which led her here and Nyte's rage was trickling back dangerously to hear it. "I was ambushed. And I—there were three of them. One of them managed to get the key and when they struck—"

Astraea's hand covered her mouth and he ached to reach for her. He'd never wanted to comfort a thing in his life but he could hardly bear her terror and pain. Nyte strained with the new surge of need to take it all from her.

"How did you save me?"

His chest had never pounded so hard. Never in battle, nor while staring in the face of death. This fear that drummed in him now was so foreign he wanted to claw it from its cage.

"You should have gone to Auster," was all he said.

She didn't know they were mates. Perhaps if she had been aware of it she wouldn't have risked coming to him.

"I didn't know who I could trust there," she said. "So I didn't want to go back yet."

Astraea scanned him. Twice. Unease backed her a step away and he didn't know what she was seeing.

"What did you do?" she asked carefully.

"The only thing I could."

She shook her head. "Did your blood heal me?"

Astraea must be able to feel him, and this was her conclusion.

If only it had been that simple.

"That wouldn't have been enough," he said.

Then her hand lifted to her neck, to Nyte's mark that was both terrifying and absolutely stunning to see on her pale flesh. Astraea gasped; ice-blue eyes snapped to his in shock.

"What did you do?" she repeated with ghostly fear.

"I think you know what."

"That's not possible. You're not—I mean, we're not . . ." her words faltered as she seemed to feel the denial was wrong. "How can you be my Bonded when Auster is?"

Nyte ran a hand through his hair. Mostly to distract from the flash of murderous resentment at the mention of the High Celestial. She wasn't Auster's Bonded, not anymore. Only Nyte's.

"I thought you were tricking me at first," he confessed. "The first day I saw you, I felt it—this pull to you I could only conclude as a mating bond."

"Why the hell would I trick you with that?" she snapped.

His eyes sliced back to her. "To make me fall for you? To get close enough to attempt to kill me?"

She laughed bitterly. "I don't need a damn trick to do that."

"Oh, really?"

Nyte stalked to her and Astraea backed up slowly. Something simmered between them. It was wild and passionate and he was on the brink of detonating from it.

He asked, "Which part do you find easy? Making me fall for you, or killing me?"

She met the wall, never breaking Nyte's stare, with heated anger that he found tempting. To provoke, unleash, then devour.

"If I wanted you dead you would have been," she said.

"And if I wanted to love you? Would you have let me?"

"This isn't a fucking game, Nyte. You have no idea what you've done."

"Oh, my Starlight. I know exactly what I've done. You came to *me*. You gave *me* no choice."

"You could have let me die."

"No. You made yourself mine the moment you got yourself captured in Astrinus. Your life, your death, and everything that exists beyond. You can't escape me now. Try realms, try time, I'll come for you. Or better yet, I'll wait for you because you can't continue to deny that you've been drawn to me too."

"We had a common goal, that's all. There will be a way to break this bond, there has to be."

Nyte's jaw tightened. His fists clenched.

"Tell me you don't want it."

"*You* don't want it," she accused. "You can't want it."

"Because monsters can't feel?" he said. Astraea's hard frown faltered. Nyte should leave. Let her find a way to break the bond, and he would be rid of her. But he didn't. Instead he braced hands on the wall to cage her in, tormented with his thoughts. The only reprieve would be to let them free. Something he wasn't used to doing.

"I've never felt fear," he began, reflecting to himself as much as confessing to her. "Not like this. Like I had something to *lose*. When I was young I would fear my father's hand and his words. A bit older I feared his cruelty to Drystan. Now, I fear nothing at all. How can one fear when one cannot die? I've felt it many times, dying, but I don't fear the pain. Then just moments ago, there it was. You. This thing I never knew I wanted so much that saving your life wasn't a want, it was a desperate need. It threw out every caution, consequence, and reason. It was fear so all-consuming I had no choice."

The beat of silence kept his body tense.

"What are you saying?" she asked quietly. Like she knew but needed to hear it.

He pushed off the wall. "I'm saying that somewhere along a measure of time I forgot to keep counting, that I grew to want to love you more than I wanted you dead. Then perhaps I wanted you dead to *stop* fucking loving you. Because I can't stop. And I didn't realize it was a root taking hold of me all this time, growing deeper and deeper. It's terrible, and something I wish I could rip free, but in all my capabilities this isn't one of them. But *you* can. So tell me you don't want the bond. Rip yourself free from me, Astraea."

He counted her precious heartbeats in the silence as she contemplated his words. Each one of those beats he carried in his palm, protected with his soul. That heart was his even if she would never admit it.

"When I was hurt, I wasn't entirely thinking right. I only wished to be somewhere safe, to be with the person who would help me most. I didn't command a place, or a name, when I used the Starlight Void to get away. Only a feeling, and that brought me here."

Nyte couldn't stop the hand he raised, easing across her jaw. Their skin on skin sparked through him like they created their own energy. This was one touch—they could ignite the world if they gave in fully.

"You shouldn't find safety with your enemy," he said.

"I shouldn't fall for him either."

His walls had been crumbling around her, and the moment he collided his lips to hers in a needy, desperate kiss, they all came crashing down. There was no part of him that wasn't hers anymore.

She had the armor to bear his claws.

The light to shine in his darkness.

She had the wit to outsmart him and the passion to ignite him. The anger to break him and the smile to reforge him. Nyte didn't believe salvation existed for the realm's darkest creature.

Astraea—the Daughter of Dusk and Dawn, the star-maiden—became his new existence.

In the years that passed keeping their bond a secret hadn't been difficult. He didn't care what the world knew, only that Astraea knew she was his.

There was a time before Astraea that Nyte had been complete darkness. He pitied that existence now. All that he couldn't see in the dark. His fingers traced lightly over her bare shoulders, down her spine, and he basked in the bliss of her soft sounds.

Nyte found the vampires that attacked Astraea a while ago, but he didn't get to kill them. The one that struck her died from wielding the key; his two companions were already corpses by the time he hunted them down. It was a torment that still often stole his thoughts. It would be easy to assume it was just an attack on their greatest enemy, perhaps to claim reward from his father for killing her, but that just put Nyte more on edge. He didn't stop trying to discover if anyone else knew anything about it, and more importantly, if there could be an active plot to try again.

He needed a distraction right now from his simmering vengeful thoughts about it.

"It's coming up to Star-Maiden Day," he muttered.

They lay in nothing more than black sheets in the bell tower. Astraea watched the twilight while he watched her.

"Mmm, don't remind me," she said, eyes fluttering at his gentle caresses.

"You don't like to be celebrated?"

"They rejoice in the creation of a savior. I don't often feel like such."

His lips pressed to her shoulder, then her neck.

"The creation of *you* is something I'd kneel before the gods who despise me for. "

Astraea turned onto her back, looking over his face with thoughtful silver eyes while her hands—those *damned* blissful hands that soothed a century of pain—traced over his chest.

"What about you? When is your birthday?"

Nyte's brow furrowed.

"What?" she asked.

"No one's ever asked me that before," he said. Nyte took her hand, kissing her knuckles. "Truthfully, I don't know."

Astraea pushed herself up abruptly, face pinched in adorable accusation as Nyte lay back, hooking an arm behind himself.

"How can you not know?"

"Most of us don't have a whole realm reminding us every full circle of the sun."

"Your father must know," Astraea demanded, more passionate about the topic than he expected.

Nyte's hand caressed her arm propped beside him.

"I've never cared to ask him."

"Rainyte—"

"Shhh." He pulled her over him. Her skin against his was the single most rapturous feeling in the gods-forsaken world. "I don't want to talk about me. Certainly not about my father."

"This is important—"

His mouth claimed hers. "I can think of more important things," he said against her mouth.

"Nyte, you can't just—" this time she was cut off by her own squeal as he flipped the two of them over. She giggled as his mouth trailed down her neck. "Stop."

Her protest was a breathless sound, and contrary to the word, her hand slipped into his hair, tightening with the slow pass of his lips down her chest.

"Can I ask you something?" he murmured over her skin.

She gave something of a yes in a moan and he smiled with satisfaction.

"Why did you never bond with Auster?"

Astraea drew a long sigh. "You really know how to kill the mood."

He chuckled, kissing her once before settling beside her again.

"You don't have to tell me," he said. It may have been a burning wonder, if only to know why she'd reject someone who was far better for her than he.

"Auster wanted more than just a bond—for us to be romantic and intimate. Most pairings do. For the longest time I thought there had to be something wrong with me to not want it. Our match was favorable to the gods who created me, and of course to our people. Everyone told me I was just being stubborn and rebellious *not* to want him."

"You are stubborn and rebellious," he said, reaching to hook her glittering hair that fascinated him.

"Clearly, to be lying here with the enemy. The scandal that would erupt."

"I think it would incite far more than a scandal, Starlight."

He didn't care, but he was trying to be civil for her.

She sighed again, staring thoughtfully at the ceiling. "I tried to love him how he wanted. We tried intimacy and a relationship for all intents and purposes."

Nyte changed his fucking mind. He didn't want to know about her tie to Auster when the mere thought of him riled a possessive madness.

"He couldn't satisfy you," Nyte murmured.

"And you think you can?" she taunted.

His hand hooked under her knee, lifting slowly to act on the dare she was inciting in those seductive silver eyes. Discovering Astraea's incredible flexibility had him wondering how in all hells he came to be bonded to something so exquisite. Divinely perfect.

"I know I can," he said. When her leg lifted over his shoulder, Nyte eased his aching cock into her slowly, devouring the pinch of pleasure over her face. "You tell me in every sound you make. And how perfectly you take me into your body. Don't make me remind you because I won't return you tonight, perhaps not tomorrow, and it'll be your job to explain your absence."

"Arrogant of you," she breathed, slipping a hand around his nape for purchase.

Astraea cried out sweetly with his next sudden plunge deep into her.

"I have an ambition," he said, pained and losing himself in the heat of her. "That you're never going to remember another inside you but me. Or hands on you that aren't mine. It's only fair. When you've utterly ruined me."

"Best do better then, Nightsdeath."

He growled low, adjusting his position and wrapping a hand around her throat. He let that dark side of him surface, enough to shift his appearance. To frighten her. Yet Astraea only followed the dark vines growing across his skin, reaching her fingers to them, and her tight heat squeezed his cock tighter.

She was going to be the end of him.

"I don't think you're ready for me to ruin *you*," he said, voice thick with lust.

He thrust forward suddenly, earning a sweet cry from her that he craved more of, setting a pace that had them exerting themselves in their pleasure.

Nyte would never get enough of this. The endless ways he could fuck her, feel her. Every time felt like a gift he'd done nothing right in his life to deserve, but he would never let go of it now.

Shifting, he held himself over her, drinking in every crease of desire over her face before watching where they joined. He slowed his pace, basking in the delirious sight and envelope of heat each time he sank into her.

Astraea's hand reached between them, and Nyte fucking lost it watching her excel at her own pleasure.

"So fucking perfect," he growled, kissing her deeply.

"Don't stop," she rasped, focused on her climax. "Just like that."

"Give it to me. In my name. Let me feel you come around my cock."

It only took a couple more plunges before she gripped him like a vise and her other hand scored his back with the impact of her orgasm. He could watch this infinite times, and it would still feel like he was a nightmare mistakenly sent to a dream. When he wanted to be everything for her yet feared she would one day wake up and realize he was wrong for her.

But this felt so fucking right.

Nyte followed her, fucking them both through the tremors of ecstasy, and even though this wasn't the first time they'd become entangled and sweat-slicked tonight, it wouldn't be the last either.

"You are my ruination, Astraea," he said in a gravelly murmur.

"Then maybe I didn't fail in my task to end you after all."

Her fingers combed through his hair as he slipped out of her and kissed her chest.

"You win," he said. "I'm on my knees for you. I might never be the hero, but I am the villain for you."

"My villain," she mused with a pleased smile.

"Always."

An hour later they reclined in the bath together. Night had fallen and the full moon they watched was serene as they bathed in a silence without words, but there was more to be spoken in the touches they shared.

He didn't want to think of the daylight when she would leave him again when the first sun rays broke.

Every time they parted, the villainous side of him contemplating ways to end Auster, then take reign of Vesitire himself, but Astraea would never forgive him. He could be patient for her. Though he didn't know what for. How they would ever make this last and the perfect fantasy being in this tower had become would perhaps only make the shattering of it that much more devastating to face.

"Are you happy?" he asked.

She gave him a reason to find want in the things he'd once despised. The rise of a new dawn. The scent of honey and lavender. The sickly craving she had for things like a spice called cinnamon he'd never sampled before.

"Why wouldn't I be?"

"The lying, the secrecy. The fact that this would never be accepted."

"I'm happy in each moment I'm with you; that must count for something against all that's out there," she said. "Even before you bonded with me. The times we traveled. It was like freedom from a cage I never knew had been crafted around me."

"You're free with me. On my life." He leaned his mouth to her damp shoulder.

He didn't want to think about to what end. There was no end to this. She couldn't go anywhere he wouldn't follow her. There was no one he wouldn't kill to keep her. No realm he wouldn't break apart to find her.

Auster wasn't the biggest problem. Nor was it getting the people to accept them together. Nyte had been reeling in torment with the quakes growing worse. It affected solar magick, which meant it was harming *her*.

Their perfect pairing was a devastating existence.

"There's somewhere I have to go for a while," he murmured.

He didn't want to leave her, but he'd been putting it off too long. It was time for him to try to go back to where he came from and find a way to break this curse. Drystan was adamant that he join him on the journey. It had been his plan, in fact.

"Where?" Astraea pushed up, twisting to look at him in concern.

"I'm going to find a way to stop the quakes."

"I'll come with you."

"Not this time, love," he said gently, lifting a hand to her face.

"This is very *un*villainous of you, and it doesn't suit you."

His mouth curled tenderly. "I'm trying to be good for you."

"I don't like it."

"I think I'm a bad influence on you."

"Where are you going that I can't come with you?"

He tucked a wet strand of hair behind her ear.

"Somewhere very far from here, and I can't risk anything happening to you."

"I won't risk anything happening to you either."

Her stubborn defiance was one of his favorite things about her.

"Can you just trust me for once?"

"No."

Nyte chuckled. It was all he could do. The thought of leaving, not knowing how long it might take, and potentially coming back with no answers at all, it killed him in more ways than she'd know.

Drystan would be waiting for him at dawn. It was time to try.

Astraea's mouth leaned to his, coming shy of meeting . . .

Sudden distant screams tore her back, her head whipping around to the archway windows.

She didn't miss a beat in climbing out of the bath, slinging on a black silk robe and rushing to see what caused the distress.

"What is it?" Nyte asked, drying off and beginning to change.

"I don't know," she said vacantly. Then she spun, seeming to tunnel away in a focused calm as she changed.

Nyte's teeth ground. It better be something fucking catastrophic to have ended their final night far too soon. That might have been a villainous enough thought for her but she didn't appear receptive to humor right now. He admired her fierce will, her unhesitating response to any action. It also terrified the damned life out of him how unquestioningly she would run into the target of any threat or danger.

The thought of leaving now when something was wrong was unfathomable. Not if she could be in danger. He would follow her, just to be sure.

When they approached the archway Nyte pulled on her arm. He looked over every inch of her face; he'd done so a thousand times yet it was never enough. He took her in like each time could be the last—that's how fragile she made him. How precious time felt around her.

She waited for him to speak but words abandoned him in a need to kiss her, pull her tightly to him for one more heartbeat of pretend.

"It's you and me, Starlight. Nothing can change that."

47

Astraea

I found Nyte in the middle of a wide and empty expanse of land.

He stood in the center where it looked like a meteor had pummeled the ground and torched the surrounding radius.

I approached slowly. Something felt so ominous and tragic about this place. Nyte was the most unkempt I'd seen him—wearing his usual black pants and boots but only a tucked in shirt with rolled up sleeves. No jacket. No cloak. He had to feel the icy air billowing around. Closer, and I noticed his hair was disheveled like he'd run his hands through it many times.

"What are you doing here?" I asked gently.

He had to have sensed I was near but he didn't look at me. I stood right in front of him now and he only stared at the ground.

"I wanted to know if I could survive losing you again," he said at last. "If you never came back, or if you chose him."

Then it hit me. My vision swayed and I stumbled a step. Then I couldn't stop the anchor that sank me to my knees as my hand touched the ground.

The image that flooded my mind was the most haunting and dire scene but I closed my eyes and reached for more. I had to see it.

Nyte on his knees. Hugging my body like he could return the life to it. His tears . . . the absolute suffering pouring over his face broke a dry sob from me. Then his cry—like an agonizing call to the gods—cleaved through my soul. It blasted through the battlefield. Incinerating every body that had fallen and those who still stood fighting. The sound of his heart breaking and his soul shredding stole every breath from me.

I wanted to tell him it would be okay. That no matter what it took, I would find a way to come back to him.

Just wait for me.

Nyte's hands on my arms dragged me back to the present and I found his golden irises through blurry vision.

"I died here," I croaked.

Misery overcame his expression.

"I can't do it," he said, barely there. "It's you and me. Or you have to find a way to end me if you don't want that. Promise me."

"I want you," I said. It tightened in my chest like desperation. "I'll always want you."

Shuffling forward, I straddled his knees and locked my fingers in his hair.

"Through every realm. To the collapse of the stars in every one," I promised.

"You didn't come back. For a whole week. I was close to—shit, I don't know."

"As it turns out, the festivities in Althenia are far more elaborate than here. One event led to another and I couldn't let those hopeful people down. I wanted to come back every day but I was exhausted by the end of each one and they convinced me to rest the night. I have to keep my promise to go back for Star-Maiden Day. But until then, I'm yours. Only yours. Take me home, Nyte."

He slipped a hand over my jaw to kiss me fiercely and it erupted in my chest. The defiance of us poured out in passion as he crushed my body to his and took us through the void.

Next thing I knew my back was against the wall of the bell tower. Our place.

"There's just one thing," I rasped with his hungry mouth descending down my neck.

"You can tell me anything."

"I can't bond with you. Not until we find your father and kill him."

Nyte drew back, searching my face with confusion.

"When he got into the temple the gods told him how to kill you. Once we complete the bond, we become one, then my blood can do it. And he has it."

"Shit, of course," he said vacantly. "I don't know how I never considered it before. It's humorous, really. I've always thought you'd be the death of me."

I pushed him lightly but his smile was such a joy to see.

"This is serious."

Nyte merely leaned in again, kissing softly over my collar.

"We'll find him soon enough."

"You're not worried?"

"I promised you eternity. I can wait a little longer to reclaim our bond. For now, this is enough for me."

He kissed me hard, and I wanted to warm his body still chilled from outside; I didn't know how long he'd stood there before I arrived.

I reached down to untuck his shirt; shadow circled around me in place of his arm, holding me against him and the wall while he took off his shirt.

"Can you feel me through your magick?" I asked.

That arm of smoke wound around me again then up and around my throat. I gasped at the light pressure.

"Yes," he said, watching me wrapped in his darkness with a wild lust in his eyes.

Heat gathered between my legs with the sinful thoughts.

"Then I want you to feel all of me through it."

A primal growl rumbled in his throat as he leaned in to kiss me, planting his hands by my head while his shadows pulled me to his body. It was overwhelming in the most delightful way. As if there was more than one set of hands upon me but all I could feel was him. So much of him yet somehow still not enough.

His magick slipped under my layers and I moaned into his mouth with the featherlight caress of it over my skin. The clasp of my cloak came undone first, falling to the floor. He undressed me so slowly it was torture while our kiss turned deep and desperate. The contrast was driving me to madness.

I tried to reach between us but shadow wrapped my wrist, pinning it to the wall, and his real hand slipped over mine, interlocking our fingers.

"I need you," I said, pained with the desire rushing between my legs.

"For how long?"

"Forever."

"Good."

I clamped around him tighter with the pull of the void and my back met soft sheets.

Nyte gripped my waist as he straddled me on his knees and my back curved to his touch, wanting our bodies pressed together, but he kissed down my chest instead.

"Black suits you better," he said huskily, tearing the white corset at my bust.

He tore right through my chemise too; his teeth nipped at my peaked nipple that pushed into his assault for more. Giving the other the same attention, flicking with his tongue before sucking, his hands continued to tear down my skirt, exposing me to him swiftly and fully.

Nyte shifted and my legs fell open for him, knees bending. The air breezed across my center, slick with my heated arousal. I gasped when it felt like rope lassoed around my ankles. Then my wrists, pulling them together above my head before all the bonds tightened.

Nyte's lips had barely left my flesh; his hands explored every dip and curve of my body like he planned to leave no inch of me untouched by him tonight.

"I can't get enough of you," he growled. "I can feel every part of you with my own skin and my magick and still I'm starved for you."

My hips lifted, desperate for attention between my thighs.

Nyte's eyes flicked up to mine and he leaned down, circling a hand around my throat and barely grazing my lips with his.

"Please," I whispered, partially a whimper.

I drew a sharp breath with the sensation of a light touch crawling my thigh.

Nyte's hands remained, one by my head propping him above me, and the other caressing sensually along my throat.

Shadow touched my core and my brow pinched tightly with a silent moan. Nyte's gold eyes turned molten, watching my ever flicker of reaction while he planned to feel me through his magick first.

"So ready for me," he said in a husky taunt, planting soft kisses along my face.

Then that shadow dipped into me, and I did cry out then to the pleasantly strange sensation of it. He began thrusting into me, slow at first, and our eyes locked with a wild, daring passion.

"Fuck, you feel incredible this way."

The shadow expanded like adding a second finger and I strained with a moan against the shadow bonds that held me at his mercy.

"A little more?"

I felt so full but at the same time I wanted more. Every time he asked I thought I would always want more.

"Yes."

"Such a good girl," he said, devouring my next cry in a kiss as his shadow expanded inside me again. He fucked me slow and deep, drinking in my every moan and expression. The intensity in his eyes crept over my skin like a shallow rippling of flame.

Even restrained in submission to him he made me feel powerful. Worshipped. His acute attention to my desire gave me a euphoric sense of confidence.

Being fucked by his shadows was unlike anything I'd felt before. Like his fingers but with a new humming vibration that was tingling through me and racing me toward a climax faster. When another tendril snaked across my abdomen and targeted my sensitive apex my head threw back to the added burst of pleasure.

"Oh gods," I cried.

"Just me, starlight. I'm your god."

In this moment every part of me agreed.

"Deeper," I rasped, feeling so close my ankles pulled against the restraints and my thighs began to shake. "Please."

Nyte groaned, pushing his magick into me deeper than I'd ever felt anything before and when it curved, hitting a certain spot I didn't know existed to explode pleasure with every thrust—I couldn't tell when my orgasm began. Only that I was trembling with the utter ecstasy rocking through every internal piece of me. I cried his name and this euphoria stretched endlessly. His shadows kept fucking me through it so that I became dizzy, seeing stars, *becoming* stars. Pieces of me scattered far and fast only to snap back together as I came around in a gasping, trembling mess.

Shit. I didn't think there would be an end of new explorations and world-rocking orgasms with Nyte.

"You come so beautifully." Nyte's whispering breath caressed my ear. "You call for me so exquisitely."

His magick released me and my fingers threaded through his hair. The gold in his irises marched like flames for me. I pushed up and kissed him with everything I was, high from the release and overwhelmed with the need for more. To give him it all back.

"My turn," I said.

Hooking my leg around him, our gravity was flawless as our positions switched. I kissed down his neck, over his tattooed, scarred chest. My fingers undid the ties of his pants and he lifted his hips, helping me remove them.

Taking his hard cock in my hand, I flicked my sight up, relishing in his tight jaw and the way his fist clenched the sheets. Eyes locked on his, I slid my tongue along the thick vein of his shaft slowly before lapping over the tip.

"You're killing me," he rasped.

I smiled in satisfaction. "As I hear, it's my sworn duty."

Teasing him, I continued to flick my tongue over his head and lick down the length. There was a certain gratification when I didn't need his ability—to hear his thoughts—to know his flexing grip on the bed was how he was refraining from holding my head in place and fucking my throat raw.

I knew I would let him, but this was more fun. There was power in the control he gave me over his pleasure.

My cheeks hollowed as I sucked, past the point of teasing. I hummed around him, working my hand in tandem.

"Tighter," he ground out. "That's it, *fuck.*"

His hips started shallow thrusting into my mouth with my movements.

"If you don't want me to spill down your throat you better stop," he warned.

I only sucked harder, letting go with my hands to brace them on the bed and take him deeper.

"Fuuuck. Stay like that."

I hummed in answer, letting him thread his fingers into my braids and use my throat. He wasn't too rough, knowing the limit of how far I could take him. Then he came and I sucked again, pumping him until he was spent and his whole body tensed, fingers tightening to the sensitivity.

"I'm not done with you yet," he panted, coming around.

Releasing him, I peered up at his toned, sweat-slicked torso. A godly sight with the sunset spilling over his tanned skin.

"Bring those pretty thighs to me," he instructed.

I didn't really understand what he wanted, shuffling until I straddled his middle, but that didn't seem far enough for him. I squealed, reaching up to brace on the headboard when his hands curled my thighs and pulled me higher,

A blush fanned across my cheeks peering down at him under me.

"This is new," I muttered.

"It's not," he said, kissing the inside of my thigh. "My memory serves perfectly; this is a particular favorite position of yours. I'm sure it will come back to you in a second."

Nyte's tongue on me threw my head back with a shuddering cry.

"Lower your hips for me," he instructed. My thighs slipped further apart and he groaned in satisfaction, fingers digging into my flesh. "That's better."

Nyte unraveled me.

I couldn't help myself, slipping a hand through his hair and rocking my hips. It felt both obscene and incredible, fucking his face like I would his cock. His encouragement in the way he sucked and licked without mercy only made me more desperate in my chase.

"Oh, fuck," I rasped. The beginnings of an orgasm tingled my skin but I wanted his cock inside me before I came again.

Yet I couldn't stop . . . I was starved for this release and the way his tongue teased my opening, pulling me down more to dip his tongue deeper, alternating between sucking the sensitive bud that shattered stars behind my closed lids. I came undone with a cry of muffled sounds and maybe some words under shocking waves of bliss.

I was utterly spent. Panting hard and clutching the headboard to gather myself back together. Nyte was so tender and patient, kissing my thighs and waiting for me to climb off him.

It took a moment for my thighs to stop quivering.

"You were right," I panted. "Definitely a favorite."

Nyte gave a satisfied smile as I shuffled down carefully with the ache of my muscles from that position, but it had been worth it.

When my legs straddled his hips, I leaned in to kiss him deeply, moaning when I shifted myself to feel the hardness of him against me despite that near painful shock of over sensitivity.

"Is this you telling me you haven't had enough?" he murmured huskily.

"Better work harder," I teased.

My slickness coated him with my movements and I squealed when he hooked an arm around me and flipped us.

"Don't taunt me, Starlight; I'll fuck you so hard you won't be able to leave this tower for days."

My knees tightened on his hips, pulling him down closer.

"I don't plan to. So do your worst."

Nyte kissed me slowly. Searching and passionate.

"I will. After I feel every perfect inch of you and worship your body like the goddess you are before I destroy you."

His cock slid against me with his teasing thrusts, easing away the sensitivity to have me needy for him again. With his next draw back, he sank into me so slowly it was like he wanted me to feel how complete we were together.

He kissed me deeply, his hands explored me tenderly, he fucked me passionately.

"You're the only thing that makes me want to live, Astraea. Beyond being a weapon for someone to use, a cause for someone to gain. I want to be everything *you* need me to be."

"I don't want you to change. Not a single thing," I said, tracing the golden tattoos of his slick chest.

Nyte accepted that with the way he leaned in to kiss me, and the way we moved together was so tender and claiming. He made love to me now, like a promise, a defiance. It was us against the world.

I gasped when he moved us unexpectedly and my ass was set down upon something cold. Leaning back, my adrenaline surged peering over my shoulder at the expanse of the city behind me. My fingers curled over the ledge of the archway window and Nyte kneeled between my spread legs, his cock sliding across my core from the low perch.

"This is your world, love. I'm just your villain to take it back for you."

His cock entered me again and I moaned, head tipping back to feel the cool air whip through my hair.

Nyte's arm circled around my curved body, leaning in to press his lips to my chest. When I closed my eyes it was like we could be flying.

His pace picked up, and his magick snaked across me again before dipping between my thighs. My brow pinched tightly with the vibrations, and Nyte swore as I clenched around him, fucking me deeper with a precision that knew just how to send us both crashing to our finish together.

I turned utterly boneless, struggling to keep my elbows from buckling. Nyte thrust a few more times as he spilled himself, his whole body tensed, glorious with the growls of his release.

As we came down, neither of us could move. Nyte braced with one hand on the wall while the other held me around my back, as if he didn't trust I'd keep the ability to hold myself up. I didn't either, as tiredness swept me and my eyes fluttered.

Nyte lifted me, carrying me into the room before he laid me down on the bed.

"I got you something," he said tenderly.

"You did?"

The smile that curved his mouth was giddy—so rare. He pulled back, and I watched him circle around the bed before opening a drawer and pulling out something wrapped in brown paper.

He lay down beside me and I took it from his hands when he offered. It was heavier than I expected.

"What is it?"

"I wouldn't have gone to the trouble of concealing it just to tell you."

The paper was awkwardly folded and wrinkled, like he'd tried many times to get it right and given up trying to make it pretty. I bit my lip imagining his struggle and warmth pooled in my stomach.

"I love it," I said, admiring the misshapen package.

"You don't know what it is yet."

The effort of his humble wrapping felt like a gift itself. Anytime Goldfell had presented me with a wrapped present it was always perfect and proper, and what was underneath was always another measure of control. Something he could give me and inevitably take away.

I peeled the paper carefully and I knew what it was the moment I caught a glimpse. My eyes lit up at the globe I held. I shook it, and this one had to be enchanted as midnight flooded the glass inside for the stars to shine brighter as they danced around a small rendition of the bell tower from the outside.

"It's beautiful," I whispered. My throat tightened with emotion.

Nyte pressed his lips to my shoulder. "Happy birthday, love."

My fingers traced the engraving. "The brightest star needs the darkest night."

"You and I, we're inevitable. The gods want us to believe we're destruction, but I've come to think they fear what we could become if we defy."

I dropped my arms, the globe hugged to my bare chest.

I reached a hand to his face and his enclosed on it, his lips pressed to my palm.

"I want to bond with you," I said.

His eyes flickered a brighter shade of gold and I loved the language they could speak to me. Nyte guarded himself from the world but at the same time his feelings were right there. In passion his irises were bright, in anger dark. In jealousy they could appear more brown and in lust they were molten ore. Right now . . . they were *smiling*. A rare tone that never lasted long because the world threw so many obstacles in the way of our pursuit of happiness.

"I want that more than anything," he said, taking the globe from my hands and laying it on the large space beside him so he could hover over me.

"But we can't," I said.

"Why not?"

"You know why."

Yet even with the reason of my blood being a weapon that could kill him, he was making it difficult to resist. Nyte shifted, cupping my jaw and leaning his mouth to my neck.

"Everyone can die. They survive through a thousand ways to die every day. I can live with having to avoid one."

"No one has half a realm that actively wants them dead."

"Probably more than half."

"Nyte," I all but moaned his name when he was planting kisses down my neck, his body pressing into me more.

"Fine," he said and I shivered with the single note of it. "Though not because the strike of a weapon with your blood through my heart could kill me, but because one with mine is another thing that could kill *you*. And I'll comb through the minds of everyone to kill anyone who knows that and would think of using it."

I hadn't even thought of myself but of course . . . in binding our souls as one, that possibility existed.

Nyte lay beside me again, idly playing with my hair.

"Can you enjoy Star-Maiden Day while I'm gone? With your friends—for me."

"I don't have friends."

"Yes, you do. *We* do. Rose convinced Zath to come with us across the veil though I think he'd much rather stay here with you. But you have Elliot, Zeik, Sorleen, Kerrah, and Nadia. Pretending that you don't care about them is getting old like you."

"I'm old?"

"Ancient."

"Technically, so are you."

"Except I got three centuries of beauty slumber."

"How beautiful you were," he muttered bittersweetly. Tracing my silver markings, they glowed with a shimmer in reaction to him. "You shine as bright in the sky as you do right here."

I reached for the golden constellation on his neck among his markings. "I think you would burn through the skies."

Like a phoenix. It was the name of his constellation and I thought it fitting for his eyes of fire.

Pushing him, I hooked a leg over his waist as he lay back.

"I love you," I said.

Three words that felt like freedom and security as one. I wasn't afraid of it anymore and Cassia's words came back to me with a phantom three pulses in my chest.

If there's one thing you're not allowed to give up on, it's love, Astraea.

Nyte pushed up against the headboard, and to watch his surprise turn to rare joy was worth confessing those three words of delicate vulnerability.

I didn't know when I'd begun to fall for Nyte. I learned love was silent. It wasn't like being caught in a web, it was like we didn't know we'd crafted one together. Slowly, because precious things took time. Until it became a home I wanted to protect with everything I was, and stay here with him for eternity.

"I love every version of the night you are," I whispered when he didn't speak, only marveled over my face as if he was repeating my words in his mind to believe them.

"Say that again," he said, so softly it fluttered in my stomach.

"I love you."

His head tipped back against the headboard and his eyes closed. Then I watched a peaceful smile break on him.

"One hundred and nine thousand, five hundred, and seventy-three days," he said quietly. His eyes opened and fell to me; his hand cupped my cheek. "It was worth every second of misery in them to hear that again. I haven't stopped being completely, madly, irretrievably in love with you. Whether you rule the sky or the land, I *live* for you, Astraea."

His palm slipped around my nape, bringing my mouth to his and I kissed him with more need than ever before with my feelings fully free.

Nyte waited despite the fact that we were destruction and our love was chaos. That hadn't changed.

It didn't matter. I loved him. I couldn't stop loving him any more than I could reverse the flow of water. I was his and he was mine eternally.

My darkness.

My nightmare.

My night.

He slowed our kiss until he pulled back enough to search my eyes. "But love also isn't enough to describe it. Your heart, it beats in my chest, just as mine has beat in yours. I'm not capable of returning it, nor letting it go, even when your body was gone and I was forced to stay. Thank you, Astraea. For I don't know what would have become of me in your absence if you hadn't given me this part of you to keep safe."

48

Nyte

The sun set on Star-Maiden Day and I watched it from a rooftop, imagining how exquisite Astraea would look for the ball across the veil.

"Pining doesn't suit you," Elliot commented.

The break of my peace wasn't unwelcome; I needed the distraction from the next twelve hours or more that Astraea would be away from me.

Turning, Zeik wiggled a bottle of wine at me. Celestial wine, from the blue tint through the glass, and I didn't want to know how they acquired it. They were all here. Sorleen even seemed relaxed and I wondered how much they'd had to drink before seeking me out.

I took the bottle, drinking it hard and fast to take the edge off my emotions.

"What are your plans for tonight?" I asked them.

"*Our* plans are that we are getting the fuck out of this cold and *that* is merely a sample of what we'll consume," Zeik said.

"Not getting out of our company this year," Kerrah said, pushing into my side.

For once, I didn't harbor an inkling of ire toward the jesting. My mood was often sour in reception, I couldn't help it, but they were never deterred and I couldn't fathom why.

From the high of the four full nights I'd spent alone with Astraea in the tower, I had her to thank for this *want* to enjoy this day.

For Astraea, I would pretend today that I was nothing more than a fae, and that those around me . . . perhaps I could regard them in my chest as friends for tonight.

"Happy Winter Solstice," Elliot cheered, clinking another bottle against mine. "Or should we be calling it Star-Maiden Day now too?"

As the generations cycled by and the star-maiden became a myth in the minds of men this side of the veil, they celebrated it here as the Winter Solstice for a long time. I knew it wouldn't happen in a year, but I was looking forward to the world remembering her.

"Either way . . ." Zeik drawled as Kerrah squealed when he hooked an arm around her and pulled out a stem of mistletoe, holding it between them.

"Ugh," Nadia said, swiping the bottle from me. "Will we be suffering their flirtations all night?"

We all looked away as they kissed. Usually I would spend today in solitude in the bell tower.

"Probably," Elliot said, and I didn't miss the glance he spared at Sorleen and the way it pulled a timid smile from her.

I was glad they were finding comfort in each other. In this world of war and after all they'd lost, they deserved to reach for their feelings unapologetically.

"There's games of knife-throwing downstairs," Nadia said to me. "Winner gets to drive a blade through Drystan's chest?"

I cast her a warning look to which she merely shrugged.

"Worth a try," she said, taking another long drink.

"We're onto human wine and piss water now," Zeik said, leading Kerrah inside the establishment.

From Nadia's comment, I was stuck on the thought of my brother, wondering where he was and what he was doing. Was he alone?

"No pining and no sulking until dawn," Zeik said, clapping a hand on my shoulder.

I didn't know what gave them the brazenness to be so bold toward me. Part of me flared with the need to defend myself, make them fear me, until I wondered why. I'd spent so long under my father's iron fist, then smothered by my own dark torment, that this kind of attitude around people was foreign, but I wanted to try find it comfortable. Natural.

So I decided to try tonight. To be . . . *free*.

Once, only Astraea had the ability to make me lose track of time under something other than misery. Yet tonight, I was in no hurry to be anywhere. I was enjoying myself like this was an old pastime. The only twinge that wouldn't allow the past to leave me completely was reflecting that there was another time I'd felt like this: with my brother. When we would escape to plan travels we would never see in an empty abandoned hut, or gamble for fun.

Nadia cheered after her win at knife throwing against Zeik. She was beginning to ease in with them in a way that I felt familiar with as I studied her. Present for the most part, sometimes letting loose, but eventually the walls would come back up around her, and the armor against feeling would be put back on.

"The two champs are up," Zeik grumbled, patting my shoulder as he sat down beside me.

Kerrah beat Sorleen, Elliot beat Kerrah, I beat Elliot, Nadia beat Zeik, so now it was Nadia against me to crown the overall champion.

"This is pointless," I grumbled, finishing my drink.

"Scared to be humiliated in front of your little cadre?" Nadia taunted, flipping her knife.

I almost rolled my eyes. Pushing up, I swiped the five small knives from the table.

"You first, Nightmare," she quipped.

"I didn't know you'd become that fond of me to give me a term of endearment, little rogue."

"Only seems fair."

Flipping the first blade, I threw it in the same breath. We were all so competent at this that hitting the markers for points wouldn't be a challenge. So instead our game leaned on luck. There were ten tankards across the two shelves that had different numbers in them, and the order was shuffled each play; the one with the highest score won.

My first tankard knocked sideward and I caught a glimpse of the *thirteen* underneath.

"Have you stopped wasting energy on your futile quest?" I asked casually.

Nadia threw her blade. "I'm still blood bonded to him, so no."

"He's up to something with the Elder Vampires. If you're really a woman of loyalty instead of a pest that keeps appearing in my path, you could be a great spy for me."

She regarded me curiously. "You made it perfectly clear you wouldn't let me kill him."

"I'll help you find another way to break the bond."

Nadia huffed. "Spare your breath."

I shrugged, throwing my second knife and watching the tankard fall.

"If you got what you wanted—to be free from him—what would you do next?"

It wasn't often I cared to know about people's personal affairs, but I couldn't deny my curiosity about the lone wanderer that had bravely, boldly, approached me and somehow made herself seem like she'd been one of the Guard all along.

"Are you saying I'm out of the Band of Nightmares?"

"Since you've officially named us, that would be a shame."

Nadia threw her knife, then I followed, until we both had one left.

"Is there anything Astraea could do that you wouldn't forgive her for?" Nadia asked.

I didn't like the question. It turned my whole body still and my mind racing when it wasn't something I'd ever considered truly. My instinct was to say no—but that was only because my trust wanted to believe she wasn't capable of doing anything not worth forgiving.

"I don't think so," I answered.

Nadia threw her knife and eyed me carefully. "If she turned on you?"

"She should have a long time ago."

"If she chose Auster?"

"A better choice, for all intents and purposes."

"If she turned into your villain?"

I threw my blade, seeing the number inside; I'd won by three points.

Turning to Nadia, this stem of conversation was starting to crawl with the bitterness I was trying to keep subdued for the night.

My villain. Acting against me. I couldn't fathom what would make her do that unless she finally saw sense and tried to kill me for real.

"I've long come to terms with that possibility," I said. "Maybe I'm even still rooting for it."

Nadia didn't hold my stare; her thoughts traveled and I wanted to hear them. But one rule was absolute to me—I never used my invasive ability to reach into minds on any of the Guard. Once that trust was breached, it would never fully return.

"You said you had no one to go to. What happened to your family?" I asked.

"I never really had one," she said coldly. Lifting her green eyes, I knew the mask all too well. The shield she raised against the hurt. "I mean it when I say vampirism has its perks. Perhaps the wicked were destined for such a fate. When I got out of the mountain, I tracked down my father and two brothers. I killed them."

I didn't flinch. It wasn't surprise that flickered through me, but rage. Because whatever they'd done to earn death from their own blood had to be something of the worst evils. Nadia carried herself well, too well sometimes, so that anyone else might believe she didn't need reason to kill. That she was like me, a merciless monster.

"Good," I said.

Her expression relaxed. Then she huffed a laugh. "I haven't told many people that, but you're certainly the first to be pleased by it. I guess I shouldn't be surprised."

"Killing is something of a sport to me."

"Are all the heinous things they say about you true?"

"I couldn't say. I don't think I've heard half of them."

We all drank for a while longer before we left the establishment.

"The night is still young!" Zeik exclaimed. By the way Kerrah had to aid his walking, I figured that wasn't accurate for him, at least.

"I have to go somewhere," I announced.

"Oh no you don't. Astraea would have our asses if we let you—"

Zeik didn't get to finish as I stepped through the void and came out atop a small mountain clearing surrounded by forest. I kept walking toward the abandoned cabin until I pushed the door open. The creaking hinges cut through the whistling wind and the floorboards groaned at every step I took within. It was far more neglected than the last time I'd been here.

Thoughts of Drystan from earlier had brought me here. I didn't expect to find him, but I felt the presence of him in these decrepit walls regardless. Despite the decades he'd watched me waste away behind a veil, no matter what he could do to me now, he was still my brother.

Stopping in front of the mantle, I realized there was another reason I was compelled here from something Astraea had thought so loudly I couldn't avoid hearing it. I reached for the wooden carving, not just a bird, but a phoenix.

She knew it was the constellation I wore. A mockery, really.

As I twisted the base of the carving, the wings splayed out and the body glowed golden. My heart pounded, waiting for the voice with a tightening grip that almost slammed it shut. Then it came, in whispering gentle notes I would never forget.

Nothing can betray you more than your own heart, my son. No matter what you do, you must never give it away, and never let the light go out of it completely.

I snapped the wings back together and my grip trembled against the impulse to crush the figurine.

It was my mother's voice.

I'd failed both her warnings by giving my heart to my truest enemy long ago, and when Astraea died, only pure darkness resided in my chest.

I was trying to prove her wrong. Giving Astraea my heart wasn't my weakness, it was my greatest strength.

Hearing the Guard outside, I supposed Elliot would have been the one to guess where I was. So I calmed, setting the figure back on the mantel for however many years it might still stand.

Heading out of the cabin, I intended to meet my *friends*—a term that would take time to get used to—and let them disperse the ever-hanging cloud of sorrow for a while longer.

The night had been . . . good.

Too good.

That I should have known—me of all fucking people should have seen that happiness was a trick into complacency.

When the ambush came, we weren't prepared.

The first scream came from Nadia and my sight targeted her. To my relief it wasn't pain but rather her battle cry as she had her legs hooked around a nightcrawler's shoulders, snapping his neck before they both fell. She was moving again in a heartbeat and then so was I.

Nightcrawlers and the more savage of the transitioned vampire line flooded into the clearing.

"Kill every single one of them," I said, my voice echoing with Nightsdeath, who pushed to the surface.

I didn't wait to see the Guard act, I was lost in my own movements. The quickest way to incapacitate a nightcrawler was by the wings. I threw my dagger from my side into the spine of one before I grabbed another that had made the mistake of sprinting toward me. I tore his wing with my bare hands and tossed him aside to bleed out painfully.

Blinking through shadow, I pulled my blade free from the other night-crawler's back and it drowned in dark blood from his neck a heartbeat later.

When I fell into this state of numb, mindless killing, bodies fell faster than I could care to count and blood coated my hands.

I didn't know how many I got through before I heard the first whistle of an arrow. Spinning, I caught it a second before it could plunge through my chest. Seething at the arrow tip, the dark pull was familiar.

I'd only encountered it one other time—crafted specifically to incapacitate fae.

My sight snapped up with livid fury, searching for wings of silver feathers instead of the leathery texture of nightcrawlers, but I found none. No celestials but this material I'd only seen in their possession. In my moment of distraction, searching for Auster in particular as the leading culprit I suspected, another of those arrows soared and I wasn't fast enough this time. It struck my back.

My teeth gritted with the searing explosion of pain but Nightsdeath helped push through it. Sheer rage and adrenaline made me pull the arrow free and focus back on the threats I could chase on the ground while extending my senses for more arrows.

"Nyte!" Sorleen called. I'd never heard that panic in her quiet voice.

When I found her, the chaos became silent to me. So still and deadly silent. They were all compromised. Elliot, Nadia, Zeik, Kerrah, and Sorleen. Held by nightcrawlers.

Who stood behind them . . .

"You finally came out of your cowardly hiding to face me, father?"

His face alone made me want to plummet the world into darkness to be rid of the sight. He wore a hood and merely smiled.

I tested the minds of the nightcrawlers on instinct but to my growing fury I couldn't penetrate them so easily. It wasn't beyond my capabilities but it was a huge gamble as to whether I could break through to shatter all their minds before they tore the hearts of the Guard from their chests.

"What do you want?" I asked, shaking with the restraint it took to not rip through anything that moved.

"Your surrender, Nightsdeath," my father said.

I chuckled darkly. "I could kill you with a single thought."

"Then they will die too."

"You're a fool to think I care that much for them."

Father gave a cruel, mocking smile, stalking between the Guard littered through the clearing. Then all it took was a look from him.

Less than a second.

For the first nightcrawler to act, still clutching Sorleen's heart as her body fell.

White rage flashed my vision and I had to close my eyes for a fucking breath before I turned this mountain to ash.

Kerrah whimpered and the beast inside me was pacing, ready for retribution to spill so much blood I might very well drown in it this time.

"Harm another one of them," I said, my tone unrecognizable with the chilling echo of Nightsdeath. "You'll be nothing but smoke and ash when I'm finished."

All personal feelings had to leave me now. I couldn't look at Sorleen's body and allow the distraction of how she'd finally looked like she was learning to *live* again tonight. Now she never would again. I couldn't feel anything watching Zeik reach for Kerrah's hand, like that small comfort with each other braced them in the face of death. Nor could I feel for the devastation of Elliot's struggle as if he thought he could reach Sorleen's lifeless form that painted the snow crimson and fit her heart back where it belonged.

"I only came to have this first leg of victory myself before the rest unfolds. You thought yourself cunning, dangerous. You've never been anything more than a weak, useless talent the Dark God never should have blessed."

That word was like a lashing. *Blessing,* until I stared my father in his cold eyes and realized he was right . . . for what lurked beneath my skin will be the thing to eradicate the poison he was once and for all.

"Behind you, Nyte!" Nadia yelled.

I pivoted to catch the arrow flying for my back and redirected it to pierce through the eye of the male holding Nadia. I caught another and once again became distracted by the sickening *wrongness* radiating from the material Auster had armed himself with and gloated about possessing at the guardian temple.

My sight of lethal rage flicked from the arrow tip to my father. A fae. So why would he have such a thing to incapacitate his kind?

There wasn't time to calculate that.

Where was that fucking archer?

Another arrow whistled and I narrowly missed the strike. Catching it, I sent the two I held hurtling for my father with the same velocity as a bow.

They . . . struck.

Right into his neck, and it had been too easy.

Too fucking easy.

I blinked through the void, catching him by the folds of his coat before he could fall. The hood came down, and that's when the glamor released. Some kind of magick that shifted the brown eyes I knew too well into a darker shade. The aged wrinkles of his skin smoothed out with youth.

He hadn't been here at all.

The mockery blinded me but all I could do was let the body in my grasp fall. With that diversion of my attention . . . it cost me.

Somehow, I knew to meet eyes with Zeik, and the haunted goodbye in them would linger in me until the darkness finally claimed me for good. Hand clasped with Kerrah's, they both fell. Hearts torn from their chests.

And then . . . *Nightsdeath.*

Darkness rolled out of me in a way I'd only lost control of once before. When I'd held Astraea's lifeless form and it settled that she wasn't coming back. This magick didn't know friend from foe. It was pure, undiluted *death.*

In this moment I was the villain the world whispered I was. Unapologetic. Merciless. Not who I wanted to be but what I needed to be.

The only thing that reached me in this place of unending darkness was the last thread of humanity that lived within me. *Her.* Thoughts of her. Feelings of her. Everything I wanted to *be* for her. Astraea was the only reason I managed to keep anchor to the world before I tore it apart in my anguish.

The power that was blasting out of me started to ease. I knelt in the snow quickly melting and flurrying away as the world reformed around me. It resumed in a sight of wreckage and chaos. Many broken and shattered trees in the blast radius and the cabin . . . it ceased to exist and that only weighed on my despair.

There were only three bodies left beside me when everyone else had turned to ash and bone. The one at my feet that had impersonated my father, and I didn't know how I'd done it, nor been aware, but the protective sphere around Nadia and Elliot blew away on the next gust of winter wind.

I couldn't move. Could only stare at them somewhat stunned they were still alive. Nadia held Elliot's head in her lap, and when he coughed, spitting blood, I moved.

He'd been seconds from having his heart torn out too.

"The little rogue saved me," he rasped.

"Never speak of it," she whispered.

I'd never seen Nadia so ghostly. In shock.

"Get him somewhere warm. Find a healer," I said.

I couldn't feel much. All I knew was that I was still vibrating with rage and my vengeance wasn't sated. It was only just awakened.

I'd tried.

To be good. To be better.

I'd tried for her but now . . . now I could see it was all wasted breath.

I am the villain my father made me. That the world condemned me to be. I am Auster's enemy, and he'd called for me. I couldn't stop thinking about the arrows and even if he had nothing to do with this, I knew where to find him faster than I could find my father.

"Once you are gone," the male choked on the arrows in his throat. Still. Fucking. Alive. "She will be next."

The next blood-gurgling breath he took was his last, then I stood, gripping him with shadows that flooded in every entrance to his body and set him on fire from the inside out.

His parting words felt like a countdown had been struck, and I wouldn't be too late to save her again.

"Where are you going?" Nadia called.

I didn't answer. She was nothing to me. *They* were nothing to me. If Nadia and Elliot had any sense of self-preservation they would stay the fuck away from me.

49

Astraea

I stood on the balcony overlooking a courtyard flooded with more people than I'd even seen together before. They had come to see the star-maiden—dressed in a silver and white gown that fanned around me like I'd drowned in starlight.

"You are magnificent," Auster said, coming up beside me.

The crowd responded adoringly to his wave and his arm snaked around my waist.

This construct would be easy for the people here. A High Celestial and the star-maiden. In the eyes of society we were a perfect pair for power and peace.

Only my heart refused to agree.

It might have been wrong of me to imagine Nyte by my side instead. To think of us ruling side by side and having the people accept us—*adore* our match—like they did now for Auster and me.

When my moment of pretending was over, my chest filled with sorrow for a reality that would never be. I looked sideways toward the veil, thinking of Nyte and what he might be doing tonight. If he'd taken my pestering and pleading seriously, he would be enjoying himself with Elliot and the others.

The precious caw of Eltanin caught my attention. He was majestic flying down as the sun set. I looked past him, up to the blazing sky, and my chest swelled in bittersweet pride as he was about to greet his second full moon and would no longer fit in my arms like he did now as he landed.

I giggled at his small snaps revealing juvenile teeth; finding it hard to imagine them being capable of tearing through anything soon. His violet eyes wouldn't look too big for his head anymore. Patting the feathers crowning his head, I kissed them too.

Eltanin didn't speak our language, but we were beginning to communicate easily. We shared a goodbye for these moments but I was thrilled to watch him grow.

His feathered wings shimmied out, bracing to fly and night fell. He was restless, ready.

I let him go.

"What a gift our people get to witness. Both in you, and this," Auster said.

We watched him together and the crowed hushed too, knowing Eltanin was about to become a spectacle.

He flew higher and higher, chasing the moon.

Then he burst into a flare of light so bright we had to shield our eyes as everyone gushed and awed. I had to see him, blinking through the sting in my eyes to watch the stars rain with Eltanin's first cycle of youth, and he was absolutely breathtaking as he soared like a dark, glittering firework.

He was still small compared to what he would grow to in full size, but he wouldn't fit through most doors anymore.

"Beautiful," I whispered.

"Very," Auster agreed.

He squeezed my waist and though I didn't want to go inside, there was a ballroom full of people below waiting for us.

Rose and Zath were behind us and my heart tumbled just like the first time I saw them dressed in their finery earlier tonight. I'd never seen Zath look so proper—no tie for his dark blond hair but it was slicked back and he was so beautiful in his deep blue formal wears. Rose was in a navy gown that glittered like the night sky and I envied their dark colors.

Apparently it was custom for me to always wear white and silver. I had asked about another color, but the handmaidens who helped me dress were insistent and I didn't want to upset anyone at my first event.

Rose and Zath wore simple masks that matched their gowns. I was the only one who wasn't to wear one. Instead my face was painted with beautiful streaks of silver and glittering dust. Rose had called me a snow queen when she'd seen me. We'd laughed about it.

"Look at you," Zath said. Was he choking up?

"It's just an extravagant party," I mused, picking at the crystals on my bodice.

He shook his head. "You've come so far, Stray."

"And you're only just getting started, I think," Rose added.

Now I was tearing up, and I was sure to be reprimanded by Westeria, the artist of my face, if I ruined her work.

"As long as I have you two by my side, I'm ready," I said, taking their hands.

It wasn't enough, and Rose broke first to pull me into an unexpected hug.

"She's watching you always," Rose whispered. "And would be so proud."

My eyes closed as Rose brought Cassia here with us, as if she stood in this embrace too.

"Thank you."

"They're waiting for us," Auster informed us gently.

At the ballroom, Rose and Zath headed inside, leaving Auster and me alone in the grand hallway.

"How are you feeling?" he asked.

I took a deep inhale to push down more of my nerves.

"Fine," I said.

Auster took my hands, which I was trying to wring dry.

"You don't have to pretend," he said softly.

He always presented himself so elegantly. Proper and poised. Every depiction of celestial royalty. Tonight, I didn't know how he managed to appear even more breathtaking. Around his eyes and over his nose was covered in a white and violet mask like his attire. At least I wasn't the only one in the brightest shade of the spectrum.

Auster cupped my cheek and my chest pounded as he closed in, nearly pressing our bodies together.

Oh stars, was he going to kiss me?

Another fraction of distance closed and my hand reached up his chest to stop him.

"Auster." I said his name in a pained warning.

Now I was sweating more than before. Thinking he would be angry or upset and I had to go in there and dance with him to open this ball and he could barely stand to touch me.

To my surprise, Auster sighed, but then he smiled. Though it held a touch of sadness.

"I just need you to know that I wanted things to be different. I would have given you everything. We would have been conquerors together. But who am I to place myself where I don't belong in your heart."

"I'm sorry," I whispered.

He deserved more. Better than me. He would still have a chance at love, just not a bond but what did that matter truly? He was powerful on his own. A High Celestial who could have anyone he desired; I hoped he found happiness elsewhere.

"When you're ready, Your Majesty," a celestial said.

It was the first I'd heard him regarded with that title.

I looped my hand through his arm like we'd practiced.

"What title was I regarded with—before?"

"My Lady, of course."

That didn't feel right. Lower than his title when I was supposed to be the daughter of gods? My chest warmed as it did when I thought of Cassia, and her words filtered through my thoughts as the grand doors opened.

Do you want to know what I think could beat the King of the Gods?

The crowd gushed and parted as Auster led us to the center ballroom floor. We stopped, took a step back, and locked eyes in our bow.

The Queen of the Kings.

Auster placed a hand on my back and our hands clasped. He smiled, pleasantly as always, but this time I didn't pretend to feel it.

I threw all my unease and reservations into a vault in my mind to make it through this dance as the music started. Then to make it through the evening I knew would be long when already I was pining for Nyte.

Auster and I moved seamlessly. We'd practiced this dance before so I knew what I was doing, but it came to me like we'd done this countless times. Our eyes locked often and I couldn't explain why my unease grew and my body started to tense so much that I worried it would start to become noticeable.

I found Rose and Zath by the side of the hall, watching me like everyone else.

Our dance ended but to my surprise Auster pulled me close, flushing our bodies, and this hadn't been part of our rehearsal.

"You can't say I didn't try for you," he said, leaning close to my ear.

To everyone, it looked like an endearing moment. To me, I couldn't catch my breath with the warning that was seizing me still.

"Let me go," I said.

"Can you just answer me this?" he asked, pulling back to watch my expression. "What is it about him that I couldn't give you?"

My mouth floundered, trying to grasp some of the words that were floating through my mind, but nothing felt right as a satisfactory answer.

How could I tell him Nyte had managed to fill the empty cracks in me with himself? That he'd torn the heart from my chest centuries ago, but it was always safer with him anyway. How could I explain that it was inevitable for the brightest star to fall for the darkest night?

"Do I really have to choose?" I asked.

"He will always be the enemy of our people."

Because no one tried to see him as anything more. I could change that. I was *determined* to make the world see what I did someday and that meant I had to take my rightful place to govern again.

I said, "I don't want to lose you as a friend."

Auster huffed, a bitter sound that pinched in me with the disappointment shaking his head.

He schooled his expression. "Enjoy the night, Maiden."

The formality was a slap but I accepted it as his pain from the rejection, only hoping over time we could mend our friendship. He would come to understand and find his own happiness. I stared after him as he slipped through the crowd, heading toward the dais where his brothers stood, watching us intently. While Notus and Aquilo leaned in to talk to one another and judgment lined their faces, I was relieved that Zephyr cast me a small smile, dipping his head as if to say: *"relax."*

I shivered at the attention, making my way off the floor that started to flood with dancers to meet Rose and Zath.

"Everything okay?" Rose hedged.

"That last moment looked a little intense," Zath added.

"Everything's fine," I said. "I just need a drink."

"At your service," Zadkiel said from behind me.

My mouth watered at the cup he held. He wasn't lying—celestial wine was indeed light blue and even bubbly.

Taking a sip, my mouth exploded at the divine taste. My shoulders eased from their stiffness.

"Delicious, right?" he said with a grin.

Already my mood was brightening. I could do this. Get through this ball and head back to Vesitire at first light.

"We've been warned to take it easy," Rose complained. "Apparently human bodies don't burn this magickal wine so fast."

"I say that's all the more reason to indulge," Zath said, finishing off his cup and placing it on a tray.

He shifted his gaze around, appearing uneasy. It was his first time in Althenia and I supposed the new setting could be overwhelming. Things were more flamboyant, colorful. Wings and glittering wears. Fancy wines and food.

"You look like you could take the edge off," I mused to him.

"Just a lot of new wings around here," he muttered nervously.

I hoped he would come to like it here; it felt more like home with both of them with me.

Zath held out a hand to Rose. "Dance with me, Thorns."

"I don't dance," she said flatly.

"Sure you do," he said, plucking her cup from her and setting it down.

I giggled watching him drag her onto the dance floor. Rose's reluctance dissolved when Zath pulled her into a leading embrace, and I was as taken as she was by the look he doted on her.

It hit me clear as day and I wondered how long it had been going on and how I'd been so clueless; Zath was falling for her. Perhaps she was falling for him too, but Rose was harder to read. I knew my friend, and the fluttering in my heart over them dancing almost pricked my eyes.

"She's a special woman," Zadkiel commented fondly.

"Yes, she is."

They moved like the night sky spilled onto the dance floor and I could hardly tear my eyes from them even though I wanted to give them privacy.

"May I have this dance?" Zadkiel asked, holding his hand out to me.

A genuine smile bloomed on my face as I slipped my hand into his.

I laughed with Zadkiel. He had a natural ability to draw it from me and a light presence I felt comfortable in the arms of. The night was becoming enjoyable and I let the rocky start be forgotten under the new highs.

Hours could have passed for all I kept track but night had fallen fully when I was pulled onto the floor for another dance with Zath after we broke for more drinks and foods.

"So you and Rose?" I prompted, unable to keep my smirk down.

"She's not always so prickly, I suppose." He smiled, and I was so happy in that moment I couldn't explain it.

Rose might have thorns but Zath had the skin to bear the cuts, knowing a little blood was worth reaching the beauty for.

A loud rumble broke through the hall and I clutched Zath as the ground shook. My magick flared to the surface as people shrieked. Glasses toppled off the tables, causing upset through the cheerful hall.

When it stopped, I took a few breaths to calm and found the High Celestials talking intensely among themselves. Zephyr cast me a wary look and then I couldn't relax.

Zath squeezing my arms drew my attention back to him.

He wasn't looking at me but rather at something over my head. Before I could turn around, I was stunned by a phantom stroke up my spine. A presence that felt impossible but unmistakable.

Then his warmth enveloped me from behind. I almost passed it off as a convincing trick in my mind, until his fingers trailed down my arm and took my hand.

He turned me to him, and through the shadows of his mask, the dawn of his irises pulled within me.

"Nyte," I breathed, still uncertain when I thought of the veil that should have prevented him from coming to Althenia.

"Starlight," he said, a whispering breath across my cheek.

Something wasn't right. His arm slipped around my waist as the song changed and I didn't get a chance to voice what was crawling cold and dreadful over my skin.

"Will you dance with me? Just this once?" he asked.

I couldn't refuse. In his hold, he was the only person I'd wanted to dance with all night, and now that he was here, it was easy to forget everything else.

"Yes."

Nyte wore a simple black mask that covered half his face. So long as he didn't engage in eye contact, he blended in seamlessly and no one knew their one true enemy had breached their walls.

Pulled into his firm stance, I felt my stomach erupt in a flurry. Yet I couldn't place what was wrong. He stole me away into a plane of existence that only stood under two people in this entire hall, and the music only played for one couple. Us.

There was trouble in the golden eyes that guided me and anchored me. Icy detachment, but he was trying to let it subside for a while. Just for this dance.

Part of me was aware of our surroundings, wanting to check if anyone had noticed who he was yet. But this dance was too precious, and though it had only been a day, I'd missed him.

We stopped trying to follow steps. His head leaned down, cheek pressing to my temple like he savored my scent, our closeness. My hand was lying on his chest, finding his heart a far more exquisite sound than the music we swayed to.

Nyte took us through the void, away from the crowded hall. I didn't think about those who would have seen it, whether it might erupt alarm and send people searching for me. I didn't care.

He brought us under the stars, upon a rooftop, but it wasn't cold. In our minds, he made it appear like the clouds fell around us and we stood in the sky. Nyte changed our music to something that didn't feel like it was crafted for the world but just for us. The notes weaved like they were made from threads of us. Souls given song. I pressed into him tighter with the swelling in my chest.

I didn't know why my emotions started to choke me. Wanting to cling to this beautiful moment dancing with him but somehow I knew, right this moment, we were falling. That what we'd tried to be made us fools in love on borrowed time. Destiny had found us, and the pressure in its grasp was building so strong it was about to shatter the glass denial we'd crafted around ourselves.

"You said you couldn't pass the veil." I broke the delicate silence.

"I lied."

He spun me, my dress fanning around, entangling our legs and swirling the illusion of fallen clouds. He was masterful in his movements and guided us fluidly.

"Why?"

He dipped with me, bringing our faces close. "Because I'm selfish," he said, gently pulling me straight, and I followed his footing. "I can pass the veil . . . because I created it. The only consequence was that my passing through would destroy it. The day you died, the celestials would have been slaughtered. So I used your key, and I created the veil right before it shattered and scattered throughout Vesitire. As we were fully Bonded, what was yours was mine in power. Back then, I didn't care about the war anymore or who would be killed, but they were your people, and after I bargained with your parents for you to come back, you would need them."

"You . . . bargained with them?"

"Yes."

"A bargain has two sides. If I came back, what did you give?"

"My life. I've been dying since the moment you came back. We were doomed either way, my Starlight. And I chose to be selfish in being with you anyway for as long as I could. I wanted you to *want* me. Even if just for a while longer. I couldn't let you go so soon after having you."

"Your life?"

Dying?

No, that couldn't be true. He hadn't seemed weak at all. The opposite, in fact. Yet my chest was pounding faster.

"Our clashing existence. It grows the nights longer each year. I didn't know how many we'd have, but when night fell for good . . . so would I. Into an eternal sleep."

I stopped our dance, staring at him with incredulity.

"How could you?" I breathed, hardly able to draw air. Anger fueled by fear planted my hands to his chest and I *pushed*. "How could you bargain for me to come back when you were always going to *leave* me!"

My voice rose, my hands trembled. *Oh gods.* It was all starting to make sense and I didn't want it to.

"That's why you were going to leave the realm. To save yourself?"

"To find a way to break that curse. Then the one of our clashing existence. To come back to you. *Fuck,* Astraea . . . you must know there is no saving me without you."

My heart plummeted, my soul tore. How many other twists of fate could wind around each of us, pulling us in opposite directions?

With that thought I couldn't stand the distance I'd pushed between us. I stepped into him, grabbing fistfuls of his formal jacket. His hand smoothed over my hair.

"It's not by choice," he said quietly.

"We'll find another way to fight that too," I said, already trying to calculate.

"I'm not sure there is another way, love."

"Don't do that. Don't you dare say there isn't a way, not after all we've been through."

His expression softened at my anger, and he reached for a lock of my hair. I didn't know where we would find it, but they wouldn't get to take my memories and take him too. I despised the gods that had made me and didn't care if that damned my soul for eternity.

We shared threads of pain. Even in each other's arms, it was like we were being pulled apart. Nyte didn't answer me. I reached up for the tie of his mask and it fell away. My pulse started racing at the changing of his appearance like he'd been battling Nightsdeath right at the surface of taking over all this time.

"What happened?" I whispered in terrible growing dread.

"I'm sorry, Astraea. Sorry you have to witness the villain I am. I tried not to be . . . for you I wanted to keep trying, but it's not what I am. We were ambushed. Zeik, Kerrah, and Sorleen are dead. Elliot is fighting to survive, I don't know if he'll pull through."

My heart stopped.

"Dead?"

His lips firmed but his eyes were growing brighter, struggling with his wrath with the reminder.

"Nyte . . . I'm so sorry."

"Sorrows can't right wrongs. But I can."

"Who did it?"

"It was a nightcrawler attack. My father was there. But then someone was firing arrows. Those I've only ever seen before from Auster at the temple."

I shook my head, trying to make sense of it.

"Perhaps your father got a hold of some, or . . ." I knew my conclusion was a grasp in the dark. "Auster doesn't have leadership over the nightcrawlers. They hate the celestials."

Nyte didn't answer but I felt the flicker of disappointment that I would try to acquit Auster in his hard stare. It wasn't what I'd meant, but Nyte was beyond reasoning.

"I only wanted to have one moment of your day. To pretend we were something different. An ordinary pair dancing like ordinary people. All that mattered was that you were mine, and I was yours. Tell me you felt that."

"I did. I still do."

"Good." His lips brushed mine; I yearned for more because this was a goodbye.

"What are you going to do?" I asked desperately.

"I'm going to find Auster and kill him."

His decision was absolute but I was gripped by terror.

"You can't."

"It's too late."

"It's never too late, not to me. This world is trying to convince you there's no redemption for you, only this cycle of violence."

"You are my redemption. You are my everything. If all I have is those moments when you looked at me as if I was something other than a monster, that's enough. If you can never look at me like that after this night, then it was all borrowed time anyway."

His lips pressed to mine. So firm and with apology that I leaned into him, gripping the folds of his jacket like my urgency could change his mind.

I didn't know what it made me but I wasn't desperate for him to stop this course to save Auster. I was petrified of what his brothers and their armies would do to Nyte. He was powerful, but even he couldn't stand against all of them in the vicious war he would incite by killing Auster.

"I love you," he said against my lips. "Even if you hate me. Even if you find a way to end me. That will never change."

The declaration stunned me. It healed me and fractured me at the same time. I wanted to hear it again but not like this. Not like goodbye.

"Please. We can get vengeance together but not like this."

"There is only one way. He has to die. Your heart has always called to darkness but you don't get to become it. This is the only time I'll truly ask: let me go, Astraea. Condemn me, and reign like the stars eternal without me."

Nyte reached into the Starlight Void and the key glowed as he pulled it out. He held it to me, but didn't let go as my hand curled around it.

"Please," I whimpered.

"I clung to the hope that this time would be different. Yet it seems history was always destined to repeat no matter which path we took together."

It felt like he was declaring himself my enemy; my heart sped in denial.

"You look . . . there are not words enough to describe how you look tonight. Exquisitely powerful—like you never left at all."

I gasped at the tingling over my body, tearing from his sight only to watch the last of my gown turn to black battle leathers. And Nyte's finery was gone now too.

"I can't lose you," I said.

Nyte let go of the key only to slip that hand over my jaw and press his lips to my head.

"We are the stars and night itself. You could never lose me, nor I you. In our perfect world that would be a promise, but in this cursed one, it's a tragedy," he said, his final words wrapped in sorrow.

Then the screaming started.

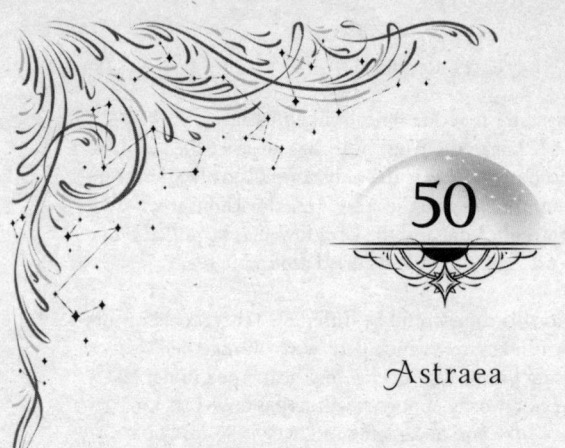

50

Astraea

I followed Nyte's trace when he disappeared through the Starlight Void. He stood in front of the Nova castle and the crowd outside ran from him in a chaos of screams and terror—because it was Nights-death who dominated the courtyard in a display of angry shadows that brewed a starless storm around him. I'd seen his dark side before . . . but not like this.

Nyte gave over so completely that I feared he was beyond reaching even by me. The black vines crawled over his jaw now, his eyes glowed the brightest I'd ever seen, and his skin inked around them. He stood there like the sun defying the night. Utterly breathtaking, but absolutely terrifying.

I tracked him carefully, trying to gauge what he was going to do, as the people cleared the courtyard. His focused sight targeted the castle and I antic-ipated his next move with seconds to spare.

As his hand lifted, I stepped through the void. Appearing in his path, I shifted my leg back, bracing for the impact of his dark magick that slammed into me as I angled the key to battle it. I cried out and gritted my teeth at the intensity of the power that awakened in me to contend with Nyte.

I am his bonded. His equal.

We'd been here before, and I had it in me to match his power even though my mind was chanting that he was too strong for me.

I am the star-maiden.

Nyte had shown me pieces of our past. He didn't withhold how much he believed in me then even as his enemy.

We are the stars and night itself.

My silver markings glowed and the world became so bright that I could feel the dark precisely. With a battle cry, I shifted stance, gripped Nyte's power with mine, and sent our anguish to the heavens.

The infusion of shadows and starlight became a beautifully devastating firework that could have taken out the entire island.

I heaved with exertion and stared off with the calm, simmering fury of Nightsdeath.

"Zath and Rose are in there," I yelled to him. He might not care for innocents with his mind given over to his dark side, but I hoped their names might bring *something* of him back.

"Do you think I care for you standing there? If you want your bones to become dust with his then so be it."

I didn't know if I was really thinking straight. No—only in desperation. Before Nyte could strike again, I channeled through the void, appearing in the ballroom that was still full.

"Astraea!" Rose called my name but I didn't have a spare second.

Nyte's magick vibrated through me, and the moment it collided into the building, mine surged out of me to flood light through the cracks the darkness made. My skin was slick and my arms trembled to hold this place from shattering.

"Everyone get out!" I screamed. *Shit,* my bones were aching. I didn't think I could hold it long.

To my relief people ran out of every exit they could. Many could leave through the balconies with their wings and yet I was panicking that not everyone would make it.

"What's happening?" Zath barked. He and Rose scrambled up to me.

"Please," I said through a labored breath. "I can't hold this long and you need to get out."

"We're not leaving you here," Rose said firmly.

"I'll be okay, I promise. But I can't protect you too."

"She's right," Zath said, his tone defeated, but I was so damn glad he didn't doubt and fight me right now. "You can use the void, right?"

"Exactly," I wheezed.

He nodded though it was stiff with reluctance. Rose took a bit of pulling to get her to leave with him but when they slipped out the door I closed my eyes.

Nyte's magick didn't battle me past the initial impact but I couldn't let go when he'd struck hard enough to collapse the castle. I breathed through the fire creeping up my throat to control this amount of power.

It's not him. It's not Nyte. His pain made him this and Nightsdeath had no family. No love. No mercy.

I couldn't hold on anymore, but I also didn't know how to retreat the power without it slamming back into me. It was out of my control now and I yielded, gasping with the implosion in me. Then I was falling as no more than a piece of stone or glass that was plummeting to the ground around me. All I could do was brace for the impact when I was out of time, and couldn't even feel for the void.

Arms wrapped me, a body shielded me, then a blast deafened me. But I was unharmed by the debris of the castle. I lied on the ground and managed to open my eyes, blinking to clear the blurriness. I stared up at the most hauntingly beautiful thing I'd ever seen.

Nyte had caught me and shielded us both from the wreckage he made. For a moment I thought I might reach him, pull him back from the course of vengeance that was unpredictable. Until he let me go. Nightsdeath stood, towering over me for a second with his anguish raging like the sun swirled around his irises. Then he walked a few paces away.

"Foolish Maiden," he snarled. The ominous echo in his voice sent a chill down my spine.

"You don't have to be this." I coughed with the dust choking my throat.

"Why should I be anything better to a world that spread my worst and hid my best?"

"Because I see you," I said, rolling onto my hands and knees. I took a moment to collect my breath, surveying the catastrophe of stone and glass with the air now infused with smoke and dust. "In all this destruction I see your pain, Nyte, and you're not alone."

His boots crunched over the debris toward me. Nyte kneeled, and his face was a heartbroken nightmare. The black vines crawled around his eyes, but he didn't attack.

"You are my only redemption," he said, searching me. "But you are such a small and breakable thing. If you were smart you would protect yourself from me."

"I'm never safer than with you."

"You're wrong."

"No, *you are.*"

Pushing to my feet, I stumbled over loose stone but I blazed at him.

"I was created by gods who wanted to control me too. I have a power people sought to *use* me for. Everyone looked at me as an example but no one *saw* me. Until you. I might not remember yet, but it's why the brightest star needs the darkest night."

"Then let's end this." Nightsdeath came closer. The darkness that wanted to shroud me not accept the light. His hand slipped over my jaw. "Together, my love."

"Not like this."

"What has the world ever done for us?"

"It gave us friends we care about."

"*People* that can be used against us."

"That's the sacrifice we choose for love. . . . Nyte." His name slipped out of me in a breath as I reached up to his face too, desperate to keep him from giving over to his darkness completely. "The world has always tried to paint you as a monster but you're hurting because you *loved* those who were taken from you. It's not weakness, it's your humanity."

"Humanity is weakness."

"Please," I said, pressing myself to him tighter. "You said my heart beats in your chest—feel me, and don't give up on yourself like they're trying to make you do. Fight for *you,* and for me. For our friends we still have to protect and a world I plan to stand by your side to restore. We are the night and the stars. The dark and the light. We will right everything together."

"You're so bright," he whispered, lips inching to mine.

I could have whimpered when those words meant something more to me. That he wasn't repelled by it so long as he accepted it. Craved it.

"Astraea!" Auster called.

It broke us apart suddenly, and I turned cold, cursing his interruption at the worst moment. I almost pulled him back, but now Nyte had found his target, and it was chilling to watch him stalk over glass and stone toward him. So frighteningly calm.

I gritted my teeth reaching down for the key staff; I used it to aid me walking to follow.

Auster stood with his three brothers, and I passed a look to Zephyr who was the only one who scanned *me* head to toe, brow furrowed assessing my state. I gave a small nod, though I was so tired I don't think it convinced him I was fine.

"All you do is kill and destroy," Auster spat. Nyte stopped far enough away that he had to raise his voice to be heard.

Amber from the fires around us glowed against the night.

"Then we're not so different after all," Nyte answered.

"You are an abomination on this land," Notus seethed.

Aquilo added, "A disgrace and monstrosity to the world."

Nyte paced sideways, stalking them. Every nerve cell in my body was sharp and on edge.

"You made me your villain only because you have always been mine. You condemned me by the color of my wings and the blood under my skin."

"We judged you by the blood *on* your skin. The blood you bathed in for centuries. Do you deny it?" Auster said.

"I deny nothing because your judgment is absolute by the scale of your own superiority. What would I care for the opinions of four privileged celestials that hide their worst, when your hands are just as crimson as mine."

Celestial soldiers started arriving around us. Screams and panic still echoed in the distance, picking up more, and it was an effort not to divert my attention to find out what was causing it if not Nyte himself. My strength was coming back enough to keep fighting.

"You cannot defeat all of us alone," Aquilo snarled.

"He's not alone," I said.

The four High Celestials targeted me. Even Nyte looked over his shoulder and thought his appearance was still changed, I thought he'd managed to push Nightsdeath back enough to not be so unfeeling. He wouldn't hurt me. I came up by his side.

"I do not want you, nor do I need you," he said, devoid of any emotion.

"I'll keep fighting you as Nightsdeath."

"I am one and the same," he snarled.

His hand lashed around my throat and the High Celestial's shifted. He didn't choke me but he trembled against the impulse to.

"Not to me."

My hands gripped his, Nyte hissed at the magick I burned him with, letting me go. I caught the key staff before it fell and took careful backward paces toward the celestials, keeping my daring stare locked on Nyte. I didn't go far, now standing as a barrier between the devastating forces that could erupt from both enemy sides.

"Look at what he's already done. You would turn on your people for him?" Notus yelled.

Nyte's jaw shifted, and maybe he believed this was me standing against him.

"They might be my people, but Nyte is my person. I wouldn't deserve the best of either if I didn't stand by the moments of their worst. That's humanity too. And I choose to turn on neither."

His gold eyes flexed at that but I turned around to meet the furious gaze of Auster. I could feel Nyte's magick more acutely if he decided to attack me and didn't fear giving him my back.

More distractingly than this volatile confrontation right now, the commotion through the towns was getting worse, growing louder.

"We're under attack!" someone yelled distantly.

The soldiers that had come to the aid of their High Celestials shifted, their focus turning toward the towns.

"He brought an army to slaughter your people," Auster spat. "That is the monster you love."

I had to look at Nyte then with a flash of horror.

"You brought an army with you?"

"I have no need for one. I only came for him."

Zadkiel came racing toward Auster. "Vampires. Too many of them have made it over the bridge and are attacking through the city. I don't know how they made it so far so fast without our detection."

My eyes caught on flickers of darkness in the sky. Nightcrawlers. The veil was gone—all that had stopped them from passing and savaging before. Nyte had destroyed it in passing through . . . but he was also the reason they had a century of peace before now.

In contrast to the dark night, a flare of light brought my sight back down to Auster. His brothers had already retreated to command forces against the vampire attack, but he stayed. I found the source of moving light in his hands. Lightning. Blue jagged strokes emitted around his hand of flesh. Of course . . . he had the power of *storm*. How could I not have realized sooner?

"You attacked us in the sky," I whispered. Not really looking for him to confirm that when it made sense now. That day, I'd finally found my wings, and Nyte was struck by lightning.

"It was intended only for him. I tried to give you a chance to choose right in this life, Astraea. But it's clear you will always be as much our enemy as he is in choosing him."

I braced with wide eyes when his lightning charged for me. Caught unawares that he would move to strike me, I didn't think I would avoid the impact of it.

A rolling wall of darkness surged up from the ground and I watched in stunned awe as the blue strokes broke over it. Nyte stood in front of me now.

"As if I needed any more motivation to end your spineless existence," Nyte said when the darkness cleared.

Then he attacked back.

The two of them quickly became a blur of lightning and darkness colliding. I was torn over what to do. The city was crying, innocents were being slaughtered, but Nyte and Auster had to be stopped before they wrecked the world in their wrath.

Zadkiel ran to me, looking just as flustered and terrified as I felt.

"What do we do?" he asked, and for a second I was confused why he came to me.

"How bad is the vampire threat?"

"*Bad*," he informed me. "Seems like a mixed bunch of them but the most brutal and merciless of all the vampire races. Do you think Nyte is responsible?"

"No." To anyone else it would be my pining heart that clouded my judgment of Nyte, but I knew him. It wouldn't make any sense for him to lead this kind of savagery. "He said he saw his father. I think he provoked Nyte to break the veil; it has to be him behind this."

I closed my eyes to think though it was agony to sway my focus from Nyte and Auster.

"We need to find the king to end this," I said.

"I'll gather a force," Zadkiel said.

He took my instruction like a soldier to a general and my shoulders squared at that.

I do not fear myself.
It's the greatest power I'll ever hold.

"No," I said before Zadkiel took off. "I want you to lead a force to defend the bridge against any more. The king is mine."

Wariness pinched his expression, but his moment of hesitation was gone in the dip of his head before he left, running into the thick of the soldiers.

Thunder boomed to shake through the ground. Auster's lightning broke the angry clouds that drowned us all in a heavy rainfall.

Releasing my wings, I shot to the sky, beating hard against the obstacle added by the rain. I didn't know how I would find the king, but I had to try if that could stop the vampires tearing through the city. The sight from above was even more devastating, displaying the shattered peace of this island of Althenia. What was once still and beautiful was now defiled in fire, blood, and ash.

Auster and Nyte had brought their battle to the skies too and I breathed through the tail blasts of their relentless attacks of magick. Right now, I had to leave them. Their war was personal but what raged below had been what everyone feared would come to pass.

I cut through the rain, trying to get a map on where the worst of the vampire forces were, but it was difficult with the focus of flying and distractions of terrorized people. Until my panic was heard as a familiar roar resounded over the screaming.

Eltanin appeared under me and I breathed in relief. He wasn't huge, but I felt his invitation that he was strong enough to carry me. Unglamouring my wings, I free fell, my stomach flipped, and I braced. Eltanin dipped to catch me gently with gravity. Adrenaline tingled through my body as I gripped his feathered mane. I might have to get riding equipment made.

Ember sparks glowed through his dark feathers but they didn't burn me. He was breathtaking. With the dragon taking control of our flight, I could focus myself. The skies were littered with nightcrawlers and my thighs clamped tightly around Eltanin's body. I shifted the key to a bow and conjured three light arrows.

I do not fear myself.

Releasing them, my aim focused on one but they were made of my magick, which broke them off to strike three nightcrawlers in close proximity. I yielded a smile of triumph, then conjured another. And another. Taking down as many as I could from the skies before they could rain their terror.

Just as I let my next arrow go I was slammed into from the side, throwing me off Eltanin. The bow slipped from my grasp and the sudden pummel left me floundering, gripped by a nightcrawler whose teeth snapped in my face as we fell.

All I knew was power, survival, and complete fucking *rage.*

I was not weak. I was not cowardly.

Hooking my leg around him, I cried out with the force I needed to twist our positions. With his back facing the direction of the ground we would soon shatter against, I thrust a hand to his chest, releasing a flare of light that tore right through him. He died instantly and I let him go.

I tried to scramble to release my wings but I didn't know if I could catch an updraft in time to save myself.

"Oomph!" I was caught before I had to.

By arms . . . but our position was too strange for it to be a celestial flying. Until I saw giant, leathery red wings out the corner of my eyes.

Stars above.

I pushed up, spinning to confirm it could only be one person. And one magnificent, huge beast.

"You're welcome," Drystan said.

I guess we had the same idea when I took in everything slowly in my shock. Drystan had a saddle made for the red dragon he'd found.

I didn't expect him to be here, but I became riddled with dreadful anxiety considering the secrets he forced me into a bargain to keep last I saw him. The secrets he forced me into a bargain to keep.

"What are you doing?" I asked, shifting around to sit behind him.

"Saving you, if that wasn't obvious."

"Are you with your father?"

I reached through the void, feeling for the key I'd dropped in my fall, but oddly . . . I couldn't find it. I had to give up when a nightcrawler dove for us and I gathered a ball of light to hit him with that sent him spiraling down.

"No. I don't know where he is but these vampires answer to him, that's for sure."

Then Drystan was only here for one reason.

"I can't do it."

"You have to. Don't go back on this now. You do it for him."

"If it doesn't work . . . it will break him instead."

Eltanin flew above us, and I was becoming overwhelmed with the chaos of events unfolding all at once. The vampires and the king. Auster and Nyte. Now this.

The red dragon was known for its breath of searing red flame. I clutched the back of the saddle tightly as it projected a blast through a mass of vampires before they could reach the bridge.

"Drystan—"

"Whatever you're going to say, save it for the other side."

"There might not be another side," I snapped. My grief made me sharp and my eyes began to prick.

"I don't want to hear it. Or I'll believe there isn't."

I let go of the saddle, circling my arms around him instead, and my cheek pressed to his back in the embrace. I wanted the memories of us so badly it hurt deeply, but this was enough. The feelings that broke through to assure me there was a time we were friends. Great friends.

"We need to distract my brother," Drystan said.

The dragon flew down and I clutched Drystan tighter with the rocky landing of the huge beast. It roared powerfully and Eltanin followed, landing in front of it. Drystan dismounted, using a rope to aid his way down, and I copied.

"Astraea!"

I couldn't believe the feminine voice that called out over the chaos. Spinning I found Davina atop a horse, galloping toward us. Behind her in the saddle was Lilith.

"What are you doing here?" I asked incredulously when they came to a stop.

"Aiding you, of course. This is what we've been preparing for," she said.

Davina didn't dismount. Behind her charged a fae army, now trapping the vampires between the celestials defending the island and the fae of the mainland.

"How did you know?"

Her sight flicked over my shoulder in answer. Drystan wasn't looking at us because Nadia had come too.

"Our resistance forces are fighting to prevent as many vampires on the king's side from making it this far as we can," Nadia informed on foot. Their forces were transitioned vampires that were loyal to Drystan, not his father, all this time. It's why he took on the position to oversee the creation of vampires from humans high in the mountains. He used his own blood when it could have been another shadowless far more ruthless and loyal to his father.

"Good, you should get out of here," Drystan said to her.

"I'm not going anywhere."

Nadia's desire to kill Drystan had been true, but they'd come to a resolution for now.

"I have to go lead my division," Davina said.

I nodded to her, and my pride swelled watching her take off with Lilith.

"About that distraction for my brother . . ." Drystan trailed.

When I turned back to him I gasped at the searing pain in my shoulder from the small blade Drystan lodged in it.

"No hard feelings," he said, ripping it free, and I hissed, clutching the wound.

There was no mistaking the presence of Nyte's shadows that surrounded us a heartbeat later. I glanced sideways to find him locked with a deadly stare on Drystan, which he diverted only for a few seconds to assess me.

"You have no reason for being here," Nyte snarled.

"Actually I do. We have unfinished business, brother."

"You've come to fight me?"

Drystan stalked around, closer to me, Eltanin gave an unexpected sound. A warning.

I watched Nyte's fingers flex, trying to subdue Nightsdeath.

Nightsdeath has no brother.

He'd told me that. If he lost the fight to keep him back he would never forgive himself if he accidentally killed Drystan.

My bones rattled at the high pitch of Drystan freeing his long steel blade. Drystan's gaze flicked to me, a muscle in his jaw working with impatience. I couldn't move but inside I was furiously shaking my head.

"I think this is long overdue," Drystan declared.

Nyte didn't need a weapon, but he pulled his obsidian blade from the void.

"I don't want to fight you," Nyte said. His tone was cold but something in me split to the misery underlying in it.

Drystan smiled, goading. "After all this time, you can't say you haven't wanted to have it out with me."

Nyte didn't lift his weapon. "Get out of here, Astraea."

I couldn't leave.

There was no more time to deliberate when Drystan struck first, and the two brothers fought as though centuries of anguish poured out of them. Wrongs against each other they had been tricked into. Torment they had lived through together. The blood of a father that wanted this—war not love. Soldiers not sons.

It tore me apart to witness this.

"You have to end it," Nadia said from behind me.

Her words trembled to my core. I turned from the brothers' feud to her with the eyes of a coward.

"I'm afraid," I said quietly.

The dragons were restless, but they didn't intervene. Eltanin watched Nyte, pacing in distress.

"I know," she said. "Me too."

51

Nyte

I couldn't fathom where the fuck Drystan had got a dragon from but that incredulity drowned under the unrelenting angst he expended on me through his sword.

Every clash of my blade against Drystan's was a fresh wound on my soul. Neither of us managed to strike, but Drystan was ruthless in his assault, far more experienced in combat since last we sparred centuries ago.

"Been training for this, have you?" I bit out, clashing left, right, left. Then spinning to his vertical swipe.

"I wanted to contend with you in some way, at least," he said through gritted teeth.

I could admit his skills were impressive, but he could never contend with me.

I didn't waver his confidence, humoring this dance for him to get it out of his damned system but the harder he came for me the more of a struggle it was to hold back Nightsdeath from ending this in a blink.

"You're angry with me for killing your mother, is that it?"

"I wasn't angry; I was in fucking *pain!*" That stunned me still. Drystan circled me, shoulders rising and falling with anguish. It touched a part of me I didn't know existed. "Come on, Nyte, you knew my mother wasn't all that close to me. Father certainly wasn't. I wasn't angry at you for killing her, I was devastated that you abandoned me. We were supposed to leave together, remember? Travel realms in search of your fucking cure. I waited for you and you never came. You chose her."

I hadn't expected his confession. All this time I'd thought his resentment toward me had been for killing his mother, but it was something worse . . . because this *was* something I'd chosen.

"She was in trouble," I reasoned.

"She would have worked it out. Instead you two stood defiant and that led to a battle I lost you both in."

Shit. I should have seen it sooner. Though he didn't show it, or perhaps I didn't care to see it, I knew he had to have mourned for Astraea too in their friendship.

In my grief I'd failed to consider his.

"I'm sorry," I breathed. Two words that choked out of my throat like knives.

How could I have been so oblivious to his pain? He'd always been the better part of me—I once believed his spirit unshakable but it wasn't. Not when I had been the one to shatter it.

"Me too, brother." I didn't like the way he said it. Like defeat. Goodbye.

His sight flicked sideways but I didn't get a chance to see what had caught his attention before a sheet of light acting as a barrier between Drystan and me had me shielding my eyes.

I knew what that was.

Astraea. Trying to stop this to save us both.

It didn't last long, but when the light fell, I saw I was wrong . . .

So hauntingly, devastatingly wrong.

There was a disconnected part of my mind that was drifting in an utter silent denial over what I saw.

The person I loved with every fiber of my being, taking the life of the first person to ever truly love *me*.

Astraea and Drystan stared into each other's wide eyes. Both their hands wrapped around the hilt of her stormstone blade in his heart.

How much of a fool I was to think I couldn't hurt like mortal men when right now I was ripped by agony so explosive it expelled from me.

I only realized magick had been rolling from me in powerful waves when the energy cut off as Drystan fell to his knees. I blinked through the void, catching him before his head could hit the ground.

Astraea stumbled back. I couldn't stand to look up at her right now or I feared what I might do.

"Nyte?"

"Yes, brother?"

Drystan's breaths labored. "What happened to us?"

I held him, trying to gather the strength to keep my composure.

"We were born into a cruel world and given to unforgiving hands," I said. "I was supposed to protect you, and failed you."

A pained huff escaped his lips upturning in a sorrowful smile.

"You-you didn't fail me," he stumbled. My heart was wrecked. "Thank you for everything. Despite what happened . . . I—I missed you. I wanted my best—my best friend back."

"I'm right here."

I hugged him. *Fuck* I should have done this more.

"It tore me apart," he said, faltering with each word now. "The resentment all these years. I wish I could have let it go but the pain was all I had when everyone was gone."

"I know," I said, splitting inside with grief. "You deserved so much better. You're going to *have* so much fucking better. So you're not going to die, do you hear me?"

"It's not her . . . it wasn't her . . ."

He could hardly form a sentence anymore and I fucking lost it.

Death doesn't get to win this one.

Through my pain and anguish I called to him. As the servant and the messenger he made of me. He *owed* me and I was going to collect, or I was going to raze the realm and rain down the stars.

The God of Dusk and Goddess of Dawn had answered my call for their daughter last I faced this, but Drystan and I were sons of Death.

Astraea kneeled, incredibly seeming to offer to take Drystan from my arms, but my cold eyes only targeted her with anger and heartache; I risked falling apart completely with her near.

"Let me," Nadia said, and though she wasn't much better, at least she'd never followed through on her threats about him.

Astraea . . . I couldn't comprehend this as reality yet the image of her with her blade in his chest scorched into my mind.

Nadia took my brother, cradling his head while the air began to stir until it was a violent hurricane we defied within its center. What stormed around us was made of wailing lost souls and endless black oblivion. No stars, only the dark at the end of everything.

Ravens, hundreds of ravens, beat furiously in the circle of claiming—they were his calling card.

Then out from the depths came a wraith of the night. Death itself.

He had no face, only a haunting void through the hood of his cloaked body that floated as if it was made of shadows—that was his gift.

Over his shoulders he had tall, obsidian feathered wings—that was his mark.

Though his form was huge, it was not as frightening as when I'd faced this primordial as a mere child.

In his hand was a glinting scythe with a missing chip on the underside of the lethal curving black blade.

"My son," Death spoke, a creepy admiration in his tone.

"Spare him," I demanded. "I have given you everything. Now spare him."

The primordial's hood tilted to my brother as if giving the request some deliberation.

"I will not."

"You can have me," I bargained.

"No!" Astraea cried. My fists tightened at her pain but I was fucking torn to shreds over her mere presence.

"I already have you, Rainyte Azrail Ashfyre."

Each one of those names shackled a claim on me. From birth, from His creation, and from a faraway lineage.

I despised them all.

"I will end this world and everyone in it. Only to travel to the next and end it too. There will be no realm for any god to feud for the souls they created upon it."

"Perhaps I crafted you too well, Nightsdeath. I will not release your brother for your soul which already serves me. But I will spare him . . . for hers."

He had no eyes to track but I knew his sight targeted Astraea and the rage of a thousand storms trembled through me.

"Not in any hell. Or any time," I growled.

I didn't think my world could shatter more than when Astraea answered for herself. "I'll do it."

My head snapped to her. No matter what, I couldn't stop loving her even when she wrecked my heart that she owned. She was my one true blessing, and my ultimate curse.

It all happened so fast I couldn't stop it.

So final I couldn't reverse it.

"Then it is done."

"No!" I yelled.

I tried to run for her but an arm of darkness slammed into me from the hurricane we were engulfed in. My soul cried.

On my knees, I was held from reaching her helplessly by death's shadows. Power I could not contend with. The fear in Astraea's eyes would haunt me in every hell I met.

Then her head threw back with a gasp as Death approached her.

"Stop!" I pleaded. "I'll give anything. Just not her."

Yet Astraea—my pure, stunning, and marvelous star—was the only thing of me he didn't have.

Until now.

Immobilized, I felt everything changing in her. The Dark God's claim.

The God of Death won in unleashing his own perfect weapon—me—to punish his rival gods of Dusk and Dawn. That wasn't enough, now he'd come to take their divine creation.

Astraea's body lifted as tendrils of starry smoke circled her body. I watched in horror as her silver wings were slowly engulfed by darkness—each pure feather changed to black.

Oh Starlight, what have you done?

Unlike me, her fingers bathed in silver, her silver markings shone, animated over her skin while harnessing this godly power. The iridescent strands of her hair glowed too. She was pure, magnificent starlight.

"This is what I have been waiting for." Death marveled at the making of her.

I was just the example. The test. Astraea had always been his greatest prize waiting for the perfect moment and I'd summoned him here. The impact of that killed me.

"You've made a fine servant, Nightsdeath. But her . . ."

Her tattoos glittered like she was made of a million stars. Her irises glowed white with so much magick I would have bowed to her in submission was I not already on my knees.

"Lightsdeath will drown this world in starlight."

52

Astraea

Being claimed by a new god was like I had bled the old blood inside me. My body was weightless, suspended in time and space. In a pure, dark oblivion while fire crept over my skin and boiled in my veins.

I didn't know how long the torture held me in its grasp, but I knew when it let me go, I would never be the same again.

My memories . . . they came crashing back. As if this was a gift the God of Death granted for my suffering to join him.

They drowned me. Images, feelings, thoughts. I was dying under the crushing weight of it all that was barreling into me relentlessly. Too much to consume at once that I couldn't sort reality from dream. Past from present.

Until the fire stopped devouring and my body came down in the ashes.

Floating.

Then falling.

And it wasn't anything physical that would shatter me because my heart was already obliterated.

Before I returned to my plane of existence, the God of Death uttered one final thing to me.

When this dawn ends, eternal night will fall.

I gasped, choking on ashy air and struggling to grapple a clear image when everything was so *bright*.

Then I remembered what happened to put me here.

Drystan.

My eyes snapped up. The sudden movement amplified my splitting headache and I whimpered.

I found him lying on the ground so still; his head was in Nadia's lap and I tried to crawl to him. I was too heavy. My whole body. I couldn't peel myself up.

Then I caught a flicker of my wings splayed limply on either side of me. They were *black*.

Death's mark, as Nyte had once called it.

There was no hiding what I'd done now. Who I'd sold my soul to.

"He's breathing," Nadia called to me.

The relief that weighed me down almost buckled my elbows, the only support against my cheek meeting the puddle of rain.

"What have you done, Starlight?" Nyte's voice was so quiet in agony.

What had I done?

My mind was a swirling pool of memory and I didn't know where to begin. Until only one dominated above all else and I couldn't believe it . . . all this time.

The heart-shattering revelation I only remembered now caused my silver markings to glow and my power felt world-ending. I didn't know what was happening to me. Color was stolen from my vision, I could only see dark and light. I pushed up, swaying into Nyte, who steadied me. His hands on my arms were so dark it was like he was made entirely of shadow and I was pure shimmering starlight.

"Lightsdeath," I whispered, both haunted and exhilarated by the prospect of this power I became.

"You're going to be okay," Nyte said, I'd never head him so fearful. Uncertain.

Blinking, I pushed back the growing power inside me to focus on his beautiful face. The light couldn't exist without the dark but Nyte was so much that I feared I could be repelled by him. As Nightsdeath and Lightsdeath . . . we would only want to end each other and that realization nearly buckled me.

I had to tame the power inside me.

So I thought only of the parts of us that were perfect for each other.

"Nyte," I whispered. "I watched you too. Every day."

He searched my eyes in confusion. Tears filled mine when his brow smoothed out as he understood what I meant.

"You remember?"

I nodded, choking a sob. "Not everything . . . but I think I will."

Utter misery split in his eyes, like he wished I hadn't seen him from the sky. So much had changed and yet it was like no time had passed at all. Only because no matter what, the one thing that remained absolute . . . was that I loved him. I loved him so much that it was pure, unending agony.

Before I could bask in any piece of blessing that I would get to remember what we had before and tie it with all we built in this life, I had to confront one devastating thing.

"The last memory you showed me wasn't the day I died, only the beginning of many battles between our sides. You didn't show me the day we fought. How I left you that final day and I went to him . . . didn't I?"

Nyte stiffened. He pulled back and contemplated his answer.

"You didn't want to hide us anymore and I didn't think it was safe for you to expose us. We argued about it that night, yes. We were at war, with battles raging near every day."

"I left to tell Auster anyway, thinking it might result in a ceasefire for a while."

"But you never made it to Althenia."

Pushing Nyte's chest, I could hardly grapple stability for the weight that gathered in my knees.

"Because he wasn't there."

Feeling into the void, I still couldn't find my key and that was the final snap of my control.

Fine. I didn't need it.

"Astraea, what are you—?"

Nyte didn't get to finish before I splayed my wings and shot to the sky. Wrath beat between my shoulder blades to numb the ache of my body. My mind swirled with a mess of thoughts and memories but I had to find Auster.

The city was burning so fiercely that not even the rainfall could smother the fires. I swept through the smoke-clogged air, following the tether inside me that would lead to him from being his Bonded despite the fact that I wanted to tear out all essence of him from my being.

"AUSTER!" I cried into the night of heartache and ruin.

I felt his lightning before I saw it, pivoting in time to miss it, and I cast out a gale of light in the direction it came from. The clouds were too thick to see through.

Now, I was fucking livid.

Stars, too many thoughts and emotions were coming back to me from the past in confusing flashes and waves. Nyte wasn't the only reason Dusk and Dawn took my memories.

I floated in the sky when I became overwhelmed by myself. All my emotions made me volatile and there was a new, endless power within me that threatened to change my vision again. I was glowing, and as I glanced through the angry gray clouds I gasped at the illusionary giant form it was like the clouds rolled and darkened to create—Death. The depthless black hood was a void that could swallow me whole. His scythe was a glinting black metal with a missing chip on the underside of the lethal curve. The legendary weapon could claim a thousand souls in one swipe.

"What do you want from me?" I asked, barely a haunted whisper.

"The end of Dusk and Dawn."

"I can't kill gods."

"They are your beginning, and you will be their end."

It didn't make sense, but the second I opened my mouth to speak again Death's form was cut through as he was made of nothing more than clouds and smoke. In my distraction, I didn't brace fast enough before Aquilo's wind slammed into me, knocking me out of flight.

I should have known. Auster never did fight his battles alone.

Coward.

Tucking my wings in, I turned to dive, but when I was met with Auster shooting up for me I tried to splay my wings to retreat.

I was too slow.

Once he touched me I was wrapped in the familiar pull of the void.

My body fell to stone next and I groaned with the pain shooting over my hip and shoulder.

Everything was so much quieter here that the sudden change was punishing to my head. Pushing up on my hands, I caught my breath and cast my furious stare up.

There was nothing kind or warm in Auster's brown eyes. He examined my black wings and disgust flexed over his expression.

I looked down at his metal left hand . . . which I hadn't remembered was his dominant side.

Despite my anger I was tormented, utterly broken.

He'd lost it in battle, that wasn't a lie.

Only he left out the grim, shocking truth about exactly *how.*

"It was you." I faced the truth. By far the very worst of every wicked memory to have come back to me from the past so far.

Getting to my knees, I couldn't look away from him. I stood, and then we faced off in the present but my memory flashed us to the devastating scene of our past.

From this still temple hall to a wailing, smoke-clogged battlefield.

Past to present. Past to present.

From this moment to the last moment he held me before I died.

"That's how you lost your arm," I said. My soul ached, like it knew all this time but had been so deeply buried in denial to protect itself. "It was you who used the key and killed me."

"Yes," he said, so matter-of-factly. Not an ounce of regret.

"It was *you?*" Nyte's snarl echoed with a glacial note of death.

I turned to watch Nightsdeath take over him in an instant and he launched toward us.

He couldn't reach me.

I winced at the high-pitched collision between him and the magick veil that kept him back. I only managed one step toward Nyte before I cried out at a searing wrap around my wrist, quickly followed by the same type of thick shackle being clamped around my other. It happened so fast and the Nebulora burned deeply.

With all he strength I had left, I glamoured my wings.

"Hide them for now," Auster taunted. "Before I rip out the abomination."

I breathed to calm myself. I knew how to push through the effects of Nebulora but Auster must have figured that out too when the flesh of my back was then scored by a blade and the poison quickly roared through my blood, bringing me to my knees.

"I'm going to make the rubble of your castle look like a fucking mercy," Nyte snarled.

"I'm okay," I said though it wasn't convincing with my labored breaths. I couldn't lift my eyes with the tiredness bearing down on me.

"I can't lose my arm twice," Auster said.

The clang of metal on metal chilled me to my core. I didn't have to look up to know what it was.

Auster had the key.

Forcing myself to see the fatal error on my part in having allowed him the opportunity to have seized it at some point in all the chaos, I watched in terror as he fit it into the hook of his thumb on his silver hand. As if he remembered the exact grip of the key to have had his hand crafted to hold it perfectly for this moment again. To repeat history.

Nyte paced in front of the veil like a caged beast, eyes blazing on Auster as if he could kill with that look alone. There had to be something blocking Auster's mind. The veil?

I couldn't think. The past was still filling my mind with confusion and I covered my ears, scrunching my eyes shut to try and get it to stop. Perhaps if it did I would find something to help us out of this.

"I'm right here with you," Nyte said in my mind. It was a reprieve in the storm that was gathering. *"Stay with me."*

"Please make it stop," I said. Too many things were clashing, making me a helpless mess in pain.

"I can't reach you, love."

A new searing sensation hit me but I quickly knew it was only an echo of something that hurt Nyte.

My eyes snapped up, horrified by the sight of the bloodied arrow tip through his shoulder.

He was on his knees in front of me now, so uncanny in light of how we'd met so many times during the Libertatem. Separated cruelly by a thin but powerful veil.

"Stop!" I yelled.

My palms raised to the veil; maybe if I could figure out how to use Lights-death at will I could break it, but as I did my chains were tugged harshly to rip my hands back.

"Your death will be so slow you'll forget time under your agony," Nyte seethed at Auster, every promise he delivered in ice. "Your hours will feel like weeks. Your weeks like years. Every day you'll beg for death, always on the cusp of it, before I bring you back to my hell."

"I don't think so," Auster said calmly. So sinister and triumphant. "Though for a moment, you're going to get what you both want. You're going to bond."

"No," I said venomously.

The chains attached to my wrists were pulled suddenly and forcefully. I yelped, slamming to the ground with no way to catch myself. My head ricocheted off the stone, blurring my consciousness but I fought with everything to stay present. It was only then I realized it was Aquilo who held the end of my leash made of iron. He gave a snicker at my pain. I never liked him in the past. Notus was near him, hands clasped behind himself and face completely emotionless. Zephyr wasn't here.

Nyte stood, tearing the arrow free from himself before he threw it with such force at the veil that it obliterated into splinters. Then all the shadows of the room flooded toward him and I braced myself against the velocity of magick he summoned.

He struck, palm cast out.

Waves and waves of raw, furious power rebounded off the veil. Every vampire that had filed in behind him screamed as their flesh melted off their bones from his world-ending power. It shook through the temple, splitting cracks in the ancient walls, and if he kept going he might bury us all in the debris.

I shuffled to my knees. He couldn't keep this up, but a small flicker of hope surfaced at the cracks forming in the veil.

He could do it. He could break it to reach me.

I gasped at the spear of energy that pressed against my spine.

The key.

"Break that veil, and I'll kill her before you can reach her," Auster warned.

I didn't know if Nyte could even hear him through the hurricane of dark power that blasted around his side of the veil. Nyte stood there like a god defiant. So still and unwavering in his focused, targeted fury.

The stone in the tip of the key crafted to a staff dug into my skin deeper and my teeth clenched with the added surge of power Auster pushed through it.

Nyte's magick stopped all at once and I whimpered, hanging my head in defeat.

"Just get out of here, Nyte," I projected loudly in my thoughts. *"Please."*

"Never," he growled.

"On your knees," Auster ordered him.

Nyte trembled with his rage. He didn't look at me, only Auster, as he calculated with simmering vengeance.

"How could you?" Nyte seethed at Auster. "All this time. She fucking *trusted* you."

"She betrayed me," Auster spat, digging the key against me again. "She betrayed all of us for *you*. A vile plague on our land. I did what I had to for my people, everyone she turned her back on."

"You despise me so much," Nyte said, so chillingly. "Only because you're looking in a fucking mirror. No less monstrous. No less villainous. But completely fucking spineless."

"I am the realm's savior," Auster spat.

I will not break.

I will not die today.

Nyte's fist clenched as he shifted a step. Anger flexed his jaw.

"Rejection really drove you to this kind of madness?" Nyte continued.

"I said on. Your. *Knees.*"

"You're a fucking coward. Hiding all this time."

"Biding time, in fact. When she came back I wanted her to choose me, and she might have if you'd stayed *away*. I found her first, you know? Except she'd awoken with her memories for a while and remembered what I'd done when she saw me in that temple. She managed to escape us and we lost track of her. I recently learned your brother was the next to find her running scared through the woods but he let her go. We tried to find her again. I sent out groups daily to scour the land for where Drystan had hid her. Did you know he had a protection charm on that manor? Inside, no celestial could see her."

I knew Drystan had found me, but not the extra measure.

"When I learned from Zadkiel that she seemed to not recognize him, nor herself, I thought perhaps there was a chance to right the wrong of the past. This was Dusk and Dawn's way of giving us a fresh start. To let me step in and save her from your corruption so she could be the Maiden she was supposed to be." Auster leaned down to me but I couldn't look at him. Not until he forced me by directing my chin with the tip of the key. "This could have all been avoided, but just like the past, every death and devastation is all your fault."

My lip wobbled.

It's not true.

"Your evil is not my fault," I said through my teeth.

A flash of fury twitched his expression, so different from the kindness I'd been lured into without my memories. He wasn't the friend I remembered from ages past. Even now my heart shattered at the moment of betrayal I never saw coming. Never would have believed he wanted me dead despite everything. I loved Nyte, but I didn't want to lose Auster, who I'd grown up with as a dear friend. My heartache turned to rage so fast I trembled with it.

"You just couldn't accept I didn't love you the way I do Nyte," I spat. You're right; my memories can be taken, our story can be rewritten, but come five years or five hundred I will always choose *him*."

I knew my words and defiance would enrage him but I didn't care. He wanted my fear and submission and if I was to die here, I would not feed his sick satisfaction.

The back of his hand connected with sharp force to my cheek, snapping my head to the side. Tears welled in my eyes but I gritted my teeth, taking deep breaths against the throbbing pain.

What concerned me more was how everything done to me inflicted worse in Nyte.

"I said, fucking *kneel,*" Auster roared to him.

Nyte's stare was nothing short of absolutely lethal. He lowered slowly, never taking that promise of death off Auster.

"You won't win," Nyte said with deceiving calm. "Even if you find a way to kill me, it will not be enough to stop me from coming for you."

"I have a way to kill you," Auster said with a beat of triumph.

"Thanks to me." A new voice spoke. I shuddered at the waking nightmare it had become.

The king walked out behind Nyte and the moment he saw his father he tried to lunge up. It might have been the whine of pain that slipped through my tight lips that stopped his advance. Auster was prodding me, taunting me with my weapon, and I was building in anger. *No.* It was hot livid fury I boiled with.

"I gave you everything, Rainyte. Now it's time I take it away when you've served as nothing more than my biggest disappointment," the king said.

I couldn't decide who I wanted to kill more. Nyte's father or Auster. Both. It was just a matter of who *first.*

More bodies flooded to Nyte's side and mine. We were completely outnumbered, but the power inside me didn't see odds, only survival.

"We can fight them," I said in my thoughts.

"No, Starlight."

My teeth ground in frustration. How could he back away from a fight now? It couldn't be over.

"Every weapon in this room has been coated in Astraea's blood. Once you're bonded, all it will take is the right strike to your heart," the king said. As if he'd already won.

No. That couldn't happen.

Nyte threatened to burn Auster's province but I didn't think I would stop until I stood in a world of ashes if they took him from me.

I hissed when Auster grabbed a fistful of my hair, forcing me to stand. I couldn't look at Nyte when I knew he would be shaking with his inability to do anything but watch.

Auster forced me to face him, and I wished he could turn to dust from the wrath of my stare. He pressed the key to my ribs.

"You might not believe me when I say I truly hoped I wouldn't have to do this again," Auster said chillingly.

"NO!" Nyte yelled.

But it was too late.

Nothing could have prepared me for the searing, all-consuming agony that began with the foreign body piercing through my chest before every part of me was torched by my own magick. My body seized so tightly that I couldn't even register the careless, rough push toward the veil when the key was ripped out of me. If it hurt to pass through, I couldn't feel it.

My hand clutched over the wound that flooded with hot and sticky blood. Nyte caught me, that's all I knew—his beautiful face and our shared panic.

We'd been here before.

Right here.

"I'm going to make it go away," he said, in a tone I only remembered from this moment in our past. "Stay with me."

Always. My mouth opened to say it but I couldn't choke it out.

"Time is running out, Rainyte," Auster taunted.

Nyte cupped my nape. "Keep looking at me."

I locked onto those golden eyes that were my orbit. Nyte took us away in our minds. Off the ground surrounded by our enemies. He changed the beige, cracked walls to the scene of the bell tower around us instead. A beautiful, peaceful fantasy.

Home. This was our small and precious home.

Pain still lanced through me like throbbing beats of a countdown. My eyes grew so heavy, but I wasn't bleeding in this dreamscape, only held tightly in Nyte's arms in an illusion that this wasn't forced upon us. Our bonding.

"You-you can't," I said. "They can kill you if you do."

"I don't care," he said gently, tucking my hair behind my ear.

His sharp teeth sliced his wrist and I tried to pull my head back. I couldn't let this happen and be the reason he died.

"Please," he said. "For me, please."

My eyes filled with tears. How did we end up here again? Would this always be our cruel destiny? No matter how many times we found each other? It was tragic and so heavy on my heart, but I also thought it was worth it. For every moment that wasn't about war, or conflict, or duty. For all the time we got to be just us, for us, nothing more or less.

Though Auster and the king thought this bond was their weapon—that this was their triumph—I wouldn't let them have that.

I wanted Nyte. Without a doubt I wanted to bind myself to him eternally.

So I nodded, and let him bring his blood to my mouth.

The taste of him took my pain away and I indulged in it. I would never get enough of how alive I felt being this close to him. To have the essence of him running through me, which no distance could take away.

Nyte kissed my forehead and my mouth unclamped from his wrist. I gasped for breath, drunk on the high of him.

"You are my brightest star, I will find you no matter where you shine. I love you. Now, then, and always."

He kissed my mouth and I reached for his face though my hand felt so heavy.

I wanted to repeat that promise.

Now, then, and always.

I love you.

The words were there in my mind and he deserved to hear them back. But I couldn't free them from the trap of my mouth. I was so terribly tired.

His forehead leaned to mine as he declared the bond. His claim on me. I couldn't hear his words anymore. I was drowning. Back in the lake the first time he'd saved me. No, not the first time.

The moment he'd come to me in this life I knew I wanted to *live*. I wanted the shadow he was to never stop following. He set me free.

Nyte's teeth sank into my neck but I could hardly feel it. All I could see was the blurry rise of a new dawn through the archway window over his shoulder as he held me tight. I thought of how peaceful it would be to die here. In the arms of the other half of my soul, in the one place we found peace together, with the hope of a new day like a promise that we'd always find our way back to each other.

My pain numbed before I could fall into the beckoning oblivion.

"Stay with me," he whispered.

His amber eyes glittered. I'd never seen them this way before. Threatening to spill his misery.

"Yes," I croaked.

Our tranquil illusion started to break piece by piece. The darkness returned with the golden dawn changing back to the beige stone caging us in. The air turned dusty and the atmosphere became frightening.

Nyte held me the same, our faces inches apart while we caught our breath. I didn't care for the return of the vicious audience and bleak surroundings when this new precious tie inside me made me clutch Nyte tighter.

Despite everything, I smiled. A beautiful, euphoric laugh escaped me and though his face was grief-stricken, Nyte found the will to smile too. We were delusional and in some ways tragic, but it didn't matter.

"Separate them," the king snapped.

Our happiness in spite of what they'd done infuriated them, and that made it all the more triumphant.

Nyte was gripped by two males and the chain on my shackles was pulled sharply.

"You're so brave, love," Nyte said to me within.

I was used to hearing Nyte in my thoughts but that was only through his ability. Now, with our Bond fully forged, the link that ran between us shared our thoughts so much clearer. I *felt* them more than just heard his words as though our essence shared in them too. There was no land that could stretch between us that could prevent me from always being with him.

Our moment of joy snuffed out like a candle as our living nightmare resumed. My eyes followed the intrusion on Nyte's side. To my never-ending horror, I found everyone I loved being dragged in through the side entrances.

Zath, Rose, Davina, and Lilith.

I was pulled back through the veil as our friends were all pushed to their knees behind Nyte. His fists trembled but he didn't turn around.

"What have you done?" I whispered to Auster.

"What I had to for my people. This world. You had to be stopped. Then and now. It takes the strongest wills to go against everything in the heart to make the hard choices."

"You have no heart," I spat. "Only a thirst for power."

"Someone has to be in power. You are too weak, too easily led."

"You allied with the enemy," I seethed.

"As did you, remember? We're not so different, Astraea."

It was *not* the same. Nyte was not his father.

"How do you think Nyte's father knew you would go to Alisus?" Auster said. "It was me who told him you would return. Me who planted the idea that he needed the key. At first I only wanted it to have against you should you need to be put down again. But he went to the temple with it bravely, and found there is in fact a way to kill what is already dead. So I told him where you'd go, hoping he'd threaten you well enough to bond with Nyte, but you're too fucking stubborn. So I tried to convince you myself but I know you—your insufferable savior complex that only arises when your monster is concerned. It didn't have to come to this but I'm glad it did. For now, everyone will believe it was Nyte who broke the veil and led an unprovoked attack on Althenia. That their precious *star-maiden* stood by his side while his forces slaughtered her people. You have no allies left. No people to back you. It's over, Astraea."

Every sinister root of his meticulous, evil plan ran through my blood hotter. My shock and fear didn't last long, not with the growing *rage* inside me that I could barely contain.

I said, cold and promising, "Mark my words, Auster Nova, this world will know exactly what you've done before I turn your existence to nothing."

"I admire your will, I always have."

My friends tried to suppress their fear with the threat of four blades poised against their throats to take their lives.

"Did you know of the vile half-blood by your side?" Auster asked.

I puzzled over that. Lilith? I knew her mother was human and she resembled her fae father more with her green hair and small horns, but what did it matter?

When Zath was pushed forward, landing with a painful grunt onto his shoulder, my world spun too fast.

"There's no place for filthy Nephilim in this realm," Auster spat.

The term repeated in my mind. *Nephilim.*

Half human, half celestial.

But Zathrian?

My eyes locked on Nyte as Zath pushed himself back onto his knees.

"It wasn't my secret to tell," Nyte said through our bond, a plea in his eyes. *"The celestials have always shunned the Nephilim. They use the nightcrawlers to hunt and kill them. He wasn't ready to tell you, but he would have."*

Stars above.

It changed nothing, but seemingly everything.

Auster spoke of it with such disgust and I couldn't understand why. He looked at my friend as if preparing to give his death sentence.

"Astraea—" Zath said.

"How dare you speak the name of a pure blood," Auster seethed.

The groaning of a bow string rang through my senses.

"Stop! Don't you dare hurt him," I yelled.

"Such a weak, pitiful heart," Auster said. "We'll fix that soon enough."

In this hall of judgment and sin, every second was precious.

It only took one for the arrow aimed at Zath to strike through his chest.

My mouth was wide but it was Rose's scream echoing through the cave, chilling me to my bones.

Zath's eyes were locked on me as he fell, but Rose caught his head before it could slam to the ground.

I could hardly breathe.

"It's weak, but his heart is still beating." Nyte tried to calm my senses through the bond. He tried to keep hold of all that was drifting away from me.

"He'll die," I said, completely in denial of it.

"The Nephilim heal far faster. Don't lose hope that he's strong enough."

Nyte was trying to keep me focused when the threat was far from over. Between Auster and the king, the execution rounds had just begun.

Rose's soft cries were ripping me apart.

Don't you dare die, Zath.

"Before I kill you, Rainyte, I plan to make my victory against you eternal," Auster said.

Every hair on my body stood. There was no end to this nightmare.

"Show us your abomination of wings," Auster ordered.

"No," I breathed, yanking on my chains.

Until I was once again pulled back by them. This time it wasn't a sharp tug that ended. I was strung up between two stone pillars. Aquilo approached me from behind, his disgusting fingers hooked into my collar and he *tore*. I knew then what was coming as my back became exposed.

"Or she bleeds until you do," Auster said.

A whip cracked off the ground. Then the next second my body lurched forward at the lash across my flesh. It was more agonizing with the Nebulora coating the leather, but I grappled all my resilience to make it through this torture.

"I'm so sorry," Nyte said to me within.

I wanted to keep being brave for him when witnessing the harm done to me would be inflicting worse punishment than his own physical pain.

Though I knew his eyes would be swimming in misery, I had to see him. Sickness clenched tightly in my abdomen as Nyte unglamoured his stunning dark wings.

"No!" I cried again, weeping and helpless now.

Another lash cracked down on my back and my wrists strained in their bonds with the pain that seized my body tightly.

"Stop fucking hurting her!" Nyte roared.

"My brother can get carried away," was all Auster said.

Four vampires came toward Nyte.

"Look away. Please," Nyte said to my thoughts.

I couldn't stop begging them to spare his beautiful wings. "Please! Auster, *please.*"

"Your pleas are pathetic," he said in disgust.

I didn't want to watch but I couldn't look away. I couldn't leave him alone in this. Nyte blocked his feelings from me and inside I became so numb.

"I'm right here with you," I said back to him in our bond. Tears spilled down my face.

Davina and Lilith wept too, holding each other's hands. Rose cradled Zath who was so motionless and still bleeding. Everyone watched Nyte for the absolute horror we were about to witness.

It took two vampires to tear one of his wings, and a piece of me died to witness the abhorrence. The absolute barbaric crime.

"Nyte," I whispered, but he didn't look up.

He fell forward, hand braced on the ground, trembling stiffly as he bled out from his back. They took hold of his other wing and my vision doubled. I could hardly stay conscious watching them defile him. The second wing didn't tear free as easy and I pinched my lips tight, forcing down the nausea as a third vampire joined their efforts.

"I'm with you," I said through our bond. *"Don't shut me out."*

"This is not your pain," he said back, barely there.

He was fading fast. If he fell under now they would deliver him to Death's realm for good this time with the weapons of my blood they had.

Strings groaned, too many arrows slick with crimson pointed at Nyte, and I couldn't reach him, not physically or by magick with the veil.

"Astraea, I'd tear apart the threads of the universe to find you again. Shine bright, and I'll meet you in the next darkness."

Those beautiful golden eyes flicked up to me.

"No," I whispered.

I wouldn't lose him when it was like we'd only just met again.

"We'll take care of your disgraceful wings too soon enough," Auster said, leaning close to my ear like an evil lover's promise.

The key was right there. *My* weapon.

I am the star-maiden.

All my past life people tried to tell me what that meant. I was a gift to the people and I should be compliant, their version of *good.*

I do not fear myself.

Even in the past I had doubted what my power should be used for. Two gods gave me it, but I created it.

I am . . . Lightsdeath.

It might take time to master what this new power was and I knew Death wasn't finished collecting his price for it. Right now I had to be reckless. So when Auster stood, about to signal the fire of a dozen lethal arrows to take Nyte from me, I . . . *became.*

The magick coursed through me, shooting up my arms to break the chains first. The world around me was shades of dark and light and I reached for the brightest thing that called to me.

Wrapping a hand around the key there was only one thing I could do, remembering Nyte's warning about it.

The key is an amplifier to you. To anyone else, it's a volatile devastation waiting to happen. It will corrupt the mind of anyone who tries to wield it when it was only intended for you. In turn, it weakens the magick you harbor in punishment for allowing it to slip out of your possession.

Then I remembered how the king had been granted the will to use the key by Dusk and Dawn without consequence. and I couldn't risk him getting a hold of it here. So I did the only thing I could in this moment.

I used my magick to *break* it.

That blast exploded through the temple, taking off the roof and splitting the stone walls. The sky spilled above us with the break of a new dawn and I stood defiant in a storm of starlight, watching five pieces of the key float in the air. It wailed at being broken; something inside me yearned to fix it. Raising a palm, I sent the pieces far and wide.

I couldn't explain how this power, *Lightsdeath,* made me both invincible and terrified. It pushed beyond my limits right now but I didn't care for what I needed to do. My steps felt like I was floating as I reached the veil, and touching it detonated a new collision of deadly magick.

The archers were the first to die even though they no longer poised their arrows. At risk of them scrambling up from the blasts that knocked everyone down, I had to end them. Every soul I took now passed through me with a new purpose. Not for the stars anymore; as Lightsdeath I delivered them to Death's realm.

Nyte was exactly where he'd been before I became this. A few others were untouched too as if I'd somehow spared them from my wrath. He still kneeled in agony, made of mostly shadows, but there was a light inside him too. A beating heart inside the darkness I yearned to protect. I couldn't recall the names of the others behind him; they were irrelevant to this power that consumed me, but a part of me knew they were important. Not my enemy.

No. My greatest enemies were behind me and I registered that so late in my moment of distraction by the beautiful darkness in pain that when an arrow pierced my back, I was immobilized.

"Astraea." A distant, desperate voice called within me, trying to get me to reach back.

Lightsdeath began to slumber under this agony. My vision blurred and when a sudden impact threw me off my feet I could hardly feel it.

All I knew next was muffled screams and air I choked on with every breath as I tried to grapple for consciousness.

"Astraea!" Nyte called my name though the bond with such desperation I couldn't bear it. *"Where are you!?"*

Where was I?

I didn't want to know. I wanted to sleep but for him I tried to pull myself out of that daunting state. Blinking, my horror worsened when all I could see was stone and darkness. I was buried under debris. I heard an unmistakable roar that was the only reprieve in my misery.

Drystan had come with his dragon.

He would get Nyte and the others away from here, that's all that mattered.

So I said back to him through the bond, hoping it reached him, *"Tell Drystan the key is with the dragons. He'll know what to do to get it back."*

Someone found me. I curled into myself with a helpless whimper as they began digging toward me and all I could think of was that Auster had come.

"I'm not leaving you here."

"Nyte . . ." I shielded my eyes as a large rock was pulled away and a streak of dawn hit my eyes. They were close to reaching me. *"I didn't fall for you twice because I never stopped loving you. Through everything that tried to separate us— forgotten memories, lost time—it's always been you."*

"Starlight . . ."

"She's alive!" a voice hissed.

It was familiar, and I couldn't decide if I should be just as terrified by who had found me instead of Auster.

Once they reached me I was taken into arms I couldn't fight and carried in a brisk pace until the commotion didn't vibrate so much around me.

"I need to get back to him . . ." I tried to say.

"We can't go back there," he answered firmly.

I looked up then, and through the dark passages he hurriedly carried me through, I could just about make out Zephyr's features. I was in no state to fight him as he took me farther away from Nyte and the scene of devastation I'd left him in.

My heart cleaved in two. My soul wailed in agony. But soon I was too numb to feel any of it anyway.

53

Nyte

I'd left her. I'd let Drystan take me away from the wreckage of the temple when I couldn't fight him in my state. Not even now did I have the strength to storm out of this tall wooden tower of a home somewhere surrounded by woodland to find Astraea. That's all I knew about where he'd taken me as I sat on the edge of a bed staring out the long window.

It had only been hours since that hell we escaped but they dragged like agonizing days when Astraea was not with me. The sun was setting now, and I couldn't be sure why it felt like my time was running out.

A healer had checked my bandages several times. Having my wings torn out was a pain incomparable to anything I'd felt before. The phantom claws of the initial resistance, the blunt force tear, seized me when I was touched anywhere near the raw scores of my flesh. It was the only reason I wasn't tearing through Althenia right now to reach Astraea.

If Auster had her . . . I could hardly contain my utter outrage that Drystan had taken me and left her. All I could think about was how my blood spilled over the stone, and if they managed to gather enough, they could kill Astraea with it now.

The door creaked open and my fist tightened in the sheets. I hadn't spoken to anyone in the few times I'd been conscious enough.

They'd all made it out. Zathrian, Rosalind, Davina, Lilith, Nadia, and Elliot were somewhere in this multi-story hut. Zath and Elliot were more incapacitated than me but I wondered if it was my sheer will and focus on Astraea that was pushing through the strong need for rest and recovery.

Drystan lingered behind me.

"Where the fuck did you get a dragon?" I asked, voice devoid of any emotion. I needed to gather shit so I knew where to start.

"Same place as you—an egg once upon a time."

I was so fucking far from tolerating any humor. My teeth clenched in ire as Drystan wandered to the window in front of me. Astraea's dragon wasn't mine.

Drystan expanded. "In the diary I found all that time ago, I figured it out. The dragons were hunted nearly to extinction a thousand years ago, until a group of mages and fae found a way to hide them."

He dipped into his pocket, unfolding a parchment. My lazy eyes dragged to the table he laid it on and I recognized the enchanted map immediately.

"They were cast into paintings," Drystan told me, reaching for something else that stoked another familiarity. A new overlay. No—not new, he'd found that in the diary of the library too all that time ago. "Constellation Draco. These are the locations. Outside each temple is a giant dragon painting no one would think was anything more. They kept one dragon alive that delivered an egg. Fesarah. It was said the dragon hatched from it would be the catalyst to releasing the others through its tears."

I might have found the story remarkable if I wasn't in such dark despair; it was hard to find light in anything without Astraea.

He added, "Truthfully, I thought you would have figured it out, or at least had some suspicion, when the circle rune at the Guardian Temple was empty."

"She knew all this time," I muttered.

"Since just before she visited the guardians, yes."

I had more questions about that, but my chest was aching so badly with the recollections of Astraea's last words to me.

"She broke and scattered the key, just like it broke after her death, and I thought—" *Fuck,* I could hardly breathe. She was still alive, I could feel it in our bond. Though it was now a weapon to kill me, I was grateful for it. "She said you would know how to find the pieces. That the key is with the dragons."

Drystan's expression lit up with that knowledge. Then he gave an incredulous sound, shaking his head. He fixed the overlay over the map, studying it with a small smile.

"She's so fucking brilliant," he muttered.

"I only saw five pieces."

"There's seventeen named stars in Draco. Seventeen temples, and I hope that means dragons too. Hard to know which will have key pieces or . . . perhaps they all do. It seems there may be one last Libertatem after all. One that spans the continent."

My fingers slipped through my hair as I held my head in my hands.

"That will take too long. I'm not leaving her there another moment past getting my strength back."

"So we retrieve Astraea first."

I wished it was that simple. Easy as he made it sound. I hoped it was.

Drystan sighed, heading back to the window and folding his arms.

"There was also another prophesy. I know you don't believe in them, but we had to try. I asked Astraea to keep the dragon a secret because you would have only seen me as some kind of threat with it. I didn't know if it would bond with me but it did. Her name is Athebyne, by the way. I'm sure Eltanin will be glad not to be alone anymore. But . . ."

Drystan paused, flicking his eyes to me with pained disturbance.

"What is it?"

"I think Auster might have Eltanin. We haven't seen him since the battle."

My eyes closed briefly. *Shit*. If Auster harmed the dragon, I didn't want to think what it would do to Astraea.

"We have to go get them back," I growled.

"Just wait, you impatient bastard. You're not saving anyone like this and getting yourself captured again would just cause more hell for everyone."

I loathed this state of weakness so much I thought my rage of adrenaline could see me through killing Auster at least. But then there were his brothers . . . my father . . . *FUCK*.

"Astraea couldn't yet explain to you why she trusted me—why I asked her to kill me," Drystan said.

It was the wrong thing to admit. My blaze turned scorching and I targeted that lethal stare on him. Drystan winced at it.

I could hardly grapple sanity from what I was hearing.

"You asked her to *what?*" I seethed through my teeth.

"Astraea had to become Lightsdeath—it's the only way we stand a chance of winning this. Of both of you surviving it and of stopping the quakes once and for all. You never would have agreed to her trying and we needed you to summon the God of Death to do it. I won't deny it was a risk; he could have refused, killed her, let me die, or asked for something else, but it's been a long three centuries, brother. All I had was time and I don't have your power but there is often more might in knowledge.

"I knew the gods had their own wars and Dusk and Dawn had long been regarded as superior. Death has tried before to meddle with their plans; creating you wreaked havoc in the world they'd set up to create so perfectly to their celestial order with their daughter. Your bond I think was unexpected and more to do with your heritage as star-gods. But then Astraea came back and they bargained her memories in the hopes their golden era could be restored and Death would lose. They told father how to kill you and also that he had to ally with Auster to do it. Auster has always had the favor of Dusk and Dawn, as do all the High Celestials divinely chosen by them. Death wants them gone. So we had to take a chance. In claiming Astraea it severed her ties as the Daughter of Dusk and Dawn and made her Death's creation like you. He did exactly what we hoped he would. Legends speak of a Godkiller . . . and as you know a god can only be killed by something it's made of."

Astraea was made of Dusk and Dawn.

My hand massaged my forehead as I tried to comprehend this plan—this foolishly desperate plan—they'd conjured between themselves.

Godkiller. Shit, the fable was as incredible as it was fascinating. Remembering how Astraea had looked, the power she harnessed so bright and glorious as Lightsdeath, I couldn't deny he might be right if such a legend was true.

"How is there a good end to any of this?" I snapped.

"Because your death is next."

I huffed a bitter laugh. "You're nicer to me when you're dying."

"Speaking of—that was a shit experience I hope to never revisit. Though my comeback was a one-trick act of desperation. I don't know how you've died so many times like it was nothing." He shuddered. "It took me a while to come around, and honestly I feared for a moment the little rogue might have changed her mind to make it permanent when I woke despite her bond to me being severed. She was in on it too. But if she'd have been the one to kill me you would have killed her without a thought. It had to be Astraea."

Their plan was suicidal. Reckless. Dangerous. Stupid.

And brilliant.

Fucking brilliant.

Drystan said, "But if I'd just pulled myself together faster . . . got to you faster . . . your wings . . ."

"It's not your fault," I said.

It kept me weak right now more than anything. It was hard to explain the emptiness I felt with them gone. The wounds would take a while to heal, I'd been informed, but it was inside that felt fractured.

"Too many had guarded minds. I didn't stand a chance of killing all I needed to and attempting to shatter the veil to reach Astraea and Auster had the key right. There. He could have killed her just to break me. If I hadn't surrendered, he would have whipped Astraea every time I resisted."

Losing my wings to spare her pain . . . it was worth it.

I leaned my forearms on my thighs, clamping my trembling fists from how explosive I became with every thought of him. I couldn't believe I'd missed it. That I hadn't considered Auster a culprit even once despite Astraea's bond with me. She trusted him. They'd grown up together . . . yet I'd failed her by not seeing that ultimate betrayal. Instead, I'd fucking *protected* him and his brothers behind that veil.

"That bastard is going to pay," Drystan said to himself in a dark promise I'd never heard from him before. "Both of them."

"I don't understand what Auster has to gain from father," I said.

"Nothing. Not anymore. Auster got the answer to kill you and orchestrated the attack on his own people with what's feebly left of father's army—true vampire rogues that still thought he would grant them the world someday. Auster simply saw a way to further frame you as the villain and condemn Astraea as the enemy too when they found out she was with you. As far as the story will go—it was you who attacked, and Astraea was compliant with it.

I imagine the lot of us will be fugitives with Auster taking over Solanis now. We'll have to be vigilant."

He took a deep inhale, turning to me with tired, pitying eyes. "Father has foolishly expired his use and I wouldn't be surprised if Auster kills him before we can unless he manages to wrangle some alliance. He's like a serpent with five heads that way."

There was no better way to put it when it felt like we cut one head off and he was still fucking here.

"We saw you with Tarran and other Elder Vampires," I said with careful suspicion.

"I know," he smirked. "You two should probably delegate the sleuthing to someone else next time."

"They're allied with father still? Did they lead the attack?"

"No. They're with us."

My head was beginning to throb too painfully to absorb what the fuck he was trying to explain. Nothing made sense anymore. Everything I thought I knew.

I didn't care.

About the war. The collapse of the stars.

I didn't *want* to care about anything but Astraea yet I knew everything was tied together in a nightmarish path to get to her anyway.

"You should rest. There's a lot you need to understand—"

"I need to get Astraea *back*," I snarled.

Pushing to my feet, my stability wavered so instantly that I reached clumsily for the desk, knocking things off. I hissed in frustration.

Drystan approached but I didn't look up. He thumped something in front of me and I almost snatched it to snap it in two.

"It's just until you get your strength back. Healer's orders, since we knew you'd be adamantly against lying down."

Everything in me despaired at the sight of the black wooden cane.

"How long?" I asked.

His hesitation of silence was enough to close my eyes, sinking my thoughts further.

"They don't know for sure. At least a few weeks from what they know of celestials losing their wings in the past. Your balance will come back steadily, you'll need to eat more, and your power . . . well only you can tell us if that's been affected and when it'll come back fully. You might find your mind blocks or limits access to it so your body can heal."

I knew celestials losing their wings had a long road to recovery, but somehow I thought I'd be different. That I could push through it faster, ignore the pain, and *keep. Going*.

"I know this is going to be hard for you, but we're not all resting. You have to have a bit of faith in the rest of us to carry out the work for once."

Drystan laid a hand on my shoulder and for a moment it stopped the pacing beast inside me. I never thought I'd feel his comfort again. Part of me was questioning if this was even real. He edged the cane closer and I had no choice but to accept it if I wanted to keep my balance when letting go of the dresser.

"I meant what I said," he spoke quietly, like the remaining shadows of his resentment wanted to keep it secret. "I might have wanted to keep you two apart in fear of this tragic, vicious cycle. I wanted Astraea to choose me in friendship and if she didn't fall for you again, you'd leave this realm and we'd restore this one. But I've come to realize I don't care about the past, how dark and selfish you became, we need you. Not because of your power . . . we just need you. Both of us. We all have wrongs we're not proud of and that lead us astray, but somehow, I think we'll always find our way back."

I nodded. Glad for once, through my cloud of misery, that I had my brother back at least. Though we had a long road of mending our broken relationship ahead of us.

"She's resilient and powerful. If she doesn't save herself first, we'll get her out," Drystan said.

All that anguished in me about it was how I couldn't save Astraea. Not like this.

I shuffled with the cane to the window. My body was too heavy yet also hollow, my mind was foggy. Snow covered the trees and hills surrounding this tall cabin.

"Where are we?" I asked.

"We're still in Vesitire. This place is the home of Nadir, the mage we visited. It's cloaked so that no one should see it if they wandered past, no one can use the void to find us, and anyone who passes the veil around the protection perimeter triggers an alarm. It's not over, Nyte. In fact, I think we've just entered the beginning of the end."

Drystan left, and in the solitude my helplessness bore down fractions heavier. I had to put my trust in others and that was something I wasn't sure how to do. Every tap of the cane against the wooden floor sank the reality of my situation in deeper.

The sun torched the trees with a golden hue and the snow sparkled beautifully. All I could think of was Astraea's hair with a deep yearning in my chest.

I'm coming for you. I tried to communicate that to her through our bond but that link between us felt blocked.

Tiredness weighed on me with the slow descent of the sun and my pulse picked up. I didn't know where the panic came from. Why I was desperate for once for the day to defy instead of the night to fall.

I leaned more on the cane as twilight descended. My mind chanted Astraea's name, desperate for her to hear me. For her to know I wasn't abandoning her, not by choice. Never.

My hand trembled on the cane with the weight I could hardly hold on my own anymore. My eyes struggled to stay open but I couldn't miss a flicker of this last sunset.

I couldn't stay here. She was out there. Closer than Althenia. I could *feel it*.

Our bond seemed so distant but she felt right within reach and I wondered if being in this house was dulling our connection from the protective shield I was within.

Astraea was Lightsdeath. Another creation of His.

Our existence before had been clashing. Now I feared it had reached its climax sooner than any of us predicted. Nothing given was without sacrifice, and with the rapidly descending sunlight, I finally understood.

54

Astraea

I sat on the edge of a small, humble bed, and for a while, it was like no time had passed at all. Like I'd never left.

Looking out the dainty balcony window, I couldn't see the outdoors. I was underground, and if I could have stood from my numb state I would have seen the expanse of a deep, colossal shaft.

Before getting my memories back, I had struggled to believe there was over a century missing in my mind. My time had paused while the world kept pressing forward for three more. Now time was racing with all I had to catch up on in the centuries I was gone.

Nyte had waited.

I'd known this, and yet it was a whole new ache in my soul to have the trickling images and emotions of the past bringing such clarity as to why. What I felt for him was as certain as time, as promising as life, and as inevitable as death. Above all that was coming back to me, Nyte was the only sure thing that kept me grounded.

I knew where I was. Only I couldn't fathom how big and busy this stronghold had become in my absence. It was overwhelming, and why I couldn't bring myself to step onto that small balcony and see it in full clarity for myself.

They'd left me in this room after I'd awoken, near frantic, terror-stricken, and unable to get my mind to *stop*. They had made me drink a tonic and I was glad, for it calmed my storm.

A presence crept in behind me, and I knew the time for dwelling was over. I couldn't stay idle anymore.

The gods that created me had wanted a perfect idol, but the god that made me *Lightsdeath* had broken those chains of obedience.

The Golden Age would come again—my way. It would take knocking down the pillars of superiority one by one.

"How are you feeling?"

I turned then, finding Zephyr standing patiently, hands clasped behind his back.

How was I feeling?

The were no words in my mind anymore, only pure rage-filled actions I wanted to take. I didn't want Auster to know in words, I wanted him to *feel* it when the sky fell down upon him.

"Like I want to tear the world apart," I said.

"I was rather hoping you would say that." Zephyr smiled. "Welcome back, Astraea."

At first the sight of him when I awoke had struck me with dread as much as it might have to see Auster standing over me. Until my memory of Zephyr filtered back.

He was my friend and I trusted him. I knew that now. All the plans we made, the suspicions we confided in each other long ago . . .

"None of them will forgive you," I said, giving him one last chance to back away. But this was something we'd started long ago, and like Nyte, he'd been waiting too.

"Then I hope you remain as confident as before that we'll emerge triumphant."

"I failed before. I could again."

"You didn't fail," he said, coming carefully closer. "You became everything you needed to be to take your rightful place once and for all."

I nodded, choosing to be grateful for the loyalty I didn't deserve.

Just then a head of blonde hair curved around the door, and I relaxed in relief seeing Katerina. Her exile had been a ruse Zephyr had no choice but to partake in to keep her safe and not risk a conflict with his brothers, and I was so glad.

Auster was a harsh and powerful dictator. His views were absolute to create a world where the weaker people would always be *lesser*. His other two brothers followed his iron fist, but not Zephyr . . . his heart was too kind to shun his own people. Even *half-bloods*.

This sanctuary was another rebellion. For the Nephilim and celestials who had lost their wings and had been exiled by order of the High Celestials.

What most didn't know was that corruption was a poison in the roots of even the fairest beings, and goodness was a light even among the most wickedly portrayed.

So this place had been created as a refuge on the Forgotten Isles, east of Althenia. For their safety, and one day an uprising for equality.

One Zephyr and I had only just begun before I was killed.

"You and Nyte . . . you're the bridge to our peace once and for all," Katerina said.

My eyes stung as I pushed up from the bed, turning away from them. For the first time we were regarded as something of *hope* not tragedy. I clung to that notion, because nothing felt more absolute, more inevitable, than him and I.

"Nyte isn't the savior you pray for. But he's the one you hope will answer anyway," I said, looking over the wide expanse of the stone perimeter with an aching heart.

"None of us would have seen that without you," Zephyr said. "Auster and the others have always tried to make you believe it was a crime against your people to accept there was good in Rainyte, but it's those who are quickest to condemn a monster that are harboring something more vicious of their own."

For Auster, Notus, and Aquilo, it was the beast of superiority. I couldn't believe how many exiled celestials, Nephilim, and even fae resided here after three hundred years. When last I saw this place . . . it had been empty. A mere dream. Yet as glad as I was to see we'd offered a home and safety for them, it was abhorrent to see these columns so full.

Thousands of outcasts.

I hovered toward the dainty balcony doors and pushed down on the handles.

"Are you sure you're ready?" Zephyr said worriedly.

"I have to be."

The sound of people was only a distant murmur from inside the room; as soon as I stepped out into the hollow column it became an overwhelming racket. There was anguish and rage and terror fighting through the crowd and when I peered over the stone rail I realized why with my own dousing horror.

"You captured Aquilo?" I said in shock, twisting back to Zephyr.

He stayed in the frame of the door. "I tried to tell them not to when we passed him unconscious, but the others with us didn't listen. We have to let him go; keeping him or killing him is an act against the gods. It wouldn't be Auster and Notus we'd fear most, though their vengeance would come down in force."

Aquilo was strung up below by his wrists between two pillars. Ironic really, when he'd laughed at me in such a helpless position and now a dark part of me looked down again and was pleased by the sorry sight of him. A few men and women acted as a firm barricade to him against a crowd that wanted to spill his blood.

I climbed onto the rail and a few looked up. The pit began to quieten but I couldn't pay them any attention. I rolled my shoulders back and thought that I probably shouldn't release my wings right now with the healing ache of my muscles. When I caught a flicker of the black feathers behind me I was reminded of who I was now. Death-touched.

The pit hushed all at once to the dark angel staring down at them.

"Astraea, what are you doing?" Zephyr asked, growing increasingly concerned.

"Exacting justice."

I stepped off, letting gravity take me down sharply before my wings splayed, catching the draft that softened my landing.

The people let me pass and my resentment grew with every step closer to Aquilo I got. Those guarding him looked up behind me but Zephyr didn't follow. He kept hidden. An inside spy for them into the High Celestial houses all this time.

The guards let me pass.

Aquilo kept his head hung but he was conscious, eyes fixed on the ground, jaw tight.

"You won't even look at me?" I said, not recognizing the ice in my tone.

"You're the devil's maiden now," he spat.

My smile felt vicious.

"I quite like that, actually."

Kneeling, I gripped a fistful of his dark hair, yanking his head back. Aquilo's brown eyes seethed at me.

"Doesn't feel so good, does it? To be bound and powerless."

Shouts started out from the onlookers.

"Kill him!"

"He made outcasts of us all!"

"Death to the High Celestials!"

"You'll risk the wrath of the gods if you kill him," Katerina warned behind me.

I looked over Aquilo's head into the shadows. I couldn't be sure if my visions of Death were just that as I could have sworn he watched me now. In a mundane size this time, still no face, only a depthless hood. Scythe in hand. Waiting.

"I am wrath," I said. "And I am a god."

Aquilo *screamed*. My touch began to inflict his torture, invisible to everyone. I wouldn't kill him this time; I had a message to deliver. To give a taste of the High Celestial's own iron fist.

His wings were glamoured but that didn't stop me reaching them. I would have liked it to have been a spectacle for all those here who had been shunned for losing theirs, but I didn't have the patience right now to get him to break and reveal them.

The people knew what was happening soon enough. Down his back two slanted lines scorched his flesh he bled through his jacket. I drowned out his screams of agony. Maybe I should have been repulsed by what I was doing, but right now all I felt was rage toward Auster for what he'd done to me—taken three hundred years of my life away. I was furious over the ruling of Althenia that had continued in my absence when I could have helped stop it sooner so this place wasn't so full. And I was livid at the gods who gave me life, only to control what that meant—make a puppet out of me abiding by *their* supreme ideals.

Not anymore.

When I was finished removing Aquilo's wings I let him go. He hung there limply, barely maintaining consciousness now.

I stood with no remorse. No feeling at all. Then I turned to Zephyr, cloaked in shadow at the entrance of a passage on this level now.

"You can take him back now," I said to no one in particular. "Let Auster and Notus know we won't be silent. We won't be compliant. We're fighting back."

Zephyr looked at me like he didn't know who he saw anymore. When I next looked in a mirror, I wasn't sure I would either.

The crowd broke into applause and vengeful cheers. I didn't bask in any of it. They praised me for what I'd done, but there was no glory to be had in this first act of war.

I walked away, glamouring my wings again to maneuver while there was little space here. The tight mob of people was beginning to suffocate me and my anger cooled again to remember more pressing things to me right now.

I had to make sure my friends and Nyte were okay. I missed him. So much that I rubbed my chest with the ache swelling in me as we wound through tight stone passages in this underground maze. I'd only just got my memories back and while I was still recalling things and threading fragments of the past together, it felt like I'd only just found him again before we were ripped apart.

He had let them tear his wings out for me . . .

"How long has passed since you saved me?" I asked Zephyr, who was following me.

"A few hours. It's sunset."

Sunset.

That knowledge was like a punch when I recalled what the God of Death had said:

When this dawn ends, eternal night will fall.

"Nyte," I breathed.

Then I was running.

Zephyr called my name but it was drowned under the drum of my pulse.

I knew how to get out of here. I'd designed the layout through the underground caves before I died. Hurtling up the spiral stairs my lungs began to burn from the exertion, but I couldn't travel through the void under here; it was enchanted for protection.

When I breached the surface the icy air speared my throat. I closed my eyes, trying desperately to feel for Nyte to channel through the void to him. The world felt too cold and vacant. I couldn't feel him.

Panic riddled my mind, my chest, my *soul.* I paced, trying again. When I still couldn't reach him I tried Zath, Rose, Davina . . . *anyone.*

Had something terrible happened to them?

Zephyr said he'd seen Drystan helping them all to safety on his dragon before he left with me.

I stepped through the void to Vesitire. The pedestrian traffic around me bustled past. So mundane. Oblivious. Their world was whole and normal while the ground crumbled beneath my feet and I scrambled like the streets were ablaze.

"Where are you?" I tried to call to Nyte through our bond but something was making it too distant and blurry.

I could still feel the essence of him entwined with me. It was the only thing that kept me from sinking to my knees in utter despair.

"I'm coming for you," I said, hoping in some way he would hear that, even if not in words.

Commotion sounded down the wide street and I dipped into a shadowed alley, watching the lines marching up.

Celestials.

Auster was wasting no time in staking his claim on Solanis. An acidic bitterness rose in me as I pressed my back to a wall for them to pass. Some stopped, hammering things intermittently on the walls of buildings.

When the celestial soldiers wearing Auster's color and seal passed, I slipped back out.

Curious, I gravitated toward what they were hanging. To my outrage and horror, it was posters of dangerous wanted persons.

The prices for each, dead or alive, climbed as I walked, examining the five variants they'd hung.

Davina and Lilith.

Zath and Rose.

Nadia and Drystan.

Nyte.

And me.

The reward money for capturing Nyte and myself alive was obscene. Enough to turn friend to foe to capture us. To make a criminal out of any saint.

"It's the star-maiden," someone whispered behind me.

"Are you sure?"

I spun, and the elderly human couple who'd spoken stared at me wide-eyed, but we'd attracted the interest of many others who were all examining the new posters plastered all the way down the street.

The elderly woman said, "Run, child."

I did.

As other people started to pique their interest, some advancing for me, I turned and raced down the alleys.

Voices grew at my back as though the city was coming alive fast and viciously for the chance to capture me, and I realized the gravity of what Auster had done.

Turned the whole city against us. Soon, the whole continent would see us at the enemy.

My eyes burned.

I had to find Nyte. We'd figure out what to do together.

Stepping into the void, I choked one sob in the silence of the bell tower.

I sank to my knees, not knowing where else to go.

The sun was setting too fast and if what the God of Death said was true; if this was the final glimpse of the day in consequence for what I'd become . . .

Nyte didn't have weeks or days or hours. He had minutes. My pulse had never raced so hopelessly as it did as I watched the fleeting rays.

"Please. I need you." I begged with everything I had through our bond.

Voices echoed behind me, and my heart leaped up my throat.

No. They couldn't know about this place.

How had they found me here?

I braced to stand and fight for our secret home above the world.

The soldiers didn't climb the tower.

I yelped, ducking at the loud *boom* that shook through the stone and into my bones.

Oh gods.

They were tearing it down.

Racing to the dresser, I snatched up the snow globe Nyte had gifted me, about to leave when the structure was blasted off balance.

I fell into the wall as everything in our once safe and sacred space was thrown and broken with me. The bed slammed into the stone, turning to wreckage. Everything was upturned and I watched as our home crumbled. Tears blurred the destruction around me. If I didn't get out I would be buried like our precious memories in here.

I stayed as long as I could in my desperate attachment.

Then I left through the void.

My knees sank into the snow with my cries as soon as I met the ground again. I clutched the snow globe as all I had left and I wished for him.

More than anything in the world all I wanted was to feel Nyte. He'd been through an unfathomable trauma, he'd done it for me, and I wasn't with him.

A pull within me silenced my cries. It could have been sheer desperation, but if there was a chance it was real . . .

Pushing to my feet, I scrambled through the darkening woodland, tripping over the unseen obstacles of branches under the snow. My palms were cut against the harsh bark I gripped to catch me several times and the few woodland claws that succeeded in pulling me to its ground but I didn't stop. I protected the globe with my body, not feeling pain right now anyway. Adrenaline pushed me on, keeping my skin numb, because time was too precious and I *had* to make it.

Breaking out of the tree line I came to a cliff's edge, then all it took was a sideways look to shatter me with delusional relief.

I cursed the snow for slowing my run, pushing with all I had toward Nyte, but he could hardly walk to meet me. The void wouldn't open here and my teeth gritted. *Don't. Stop.* I broke at the sight of the black cane he leaned on, as he clutched his abdomen and barely shuffled his steps.

"Nyte!" I called when he hadn't looked up yet.

When he did, the tired misery in his eyes cleaved my world in two.

Then he looked over the mountainside, as if he knew . . .

I sprinted with all my might through the thick snow, racing to beat the sunset.

He was right there.

Just a few more steps . . .

I never battled such an uncompromising force as time. Everything in me was screaming to make it *stop*. To let us defy just for a few more delicate minutes.

But as the last amber streak winked out across his face, the world rumbled with a violent quake, and Nyte's hold slipped on the cane. My knees plummeted into the snow, arms opening to catch him.

I cried out, taking the impact that sprawled us both from the weight of him. Pushing with everything I had, I managed to maneuver, hooking my arms under his and pulling myself up enough to hold his upper body in my lap.

The silence had never rung so loud. The darkness had never felt so haunting.

"Nyte." My hand slipped over his chest. His heartbeat was there but it was so terribly slow and shallow. I couldn't accept that Dusk and Dawn had won in inflicting their curse on him. "I need you."

He was so beautiful. So peaceful. Our bond turned distant but I wrapped my entire being around the eternal tie between us.

"I can't do this without you," I whispered.

I kissed him, smoothing away the sweat-slicked dark hair on his forehead. Despite his suffering, against what must have been strict orders to rest, he'd still come.

Somehow, he'd known this was his final dawn. And still he'd come for me.

The mountainside echoed with my pain and heartache. I held Nyte as I stared over the city of Vesitire, then beyond to Althenia. My tears fell but each forged my anguish, my determination, and my will.

The daylight might not rise again, but the brightest star thrives in the darkest night.

I was no longer the Daughter of Dusk and Dawn.

I was the Daughter of Death.

And this world would either bow, or watch the stars rain down upon it.

"I'll meet you in the darkness," I whispered, holding his head to my chest and keeping his body warm from the snow with the glow of my magick. "Now, then, and always."

PRONUNCIATION GUIDE

NAMES
- **Astraea:** ah-stray-ah
- **Nyte/Rainyte:** night/ray-night
- **Drystan:** dry-stan
- **Cassia:** ca-see-ah
- **Calix:** cal-ix
- **Zathrian:** zath-ree-an
- **Rosalind:** rose-ah-lind
- **Lilith:** lil-ith
- **Davina:** da-veen-ah
- **Auster:** au-ster
- **Nadia:** na-dee-ah
- **Zephyr:** zeh-fer
- **Aquilo:** Ah-quil-oh
- **Notus:** No-tus
- **Eltanin (Eli):** Elle-tan-in (eel-eye)
- **Athebyne:** Athe-bine
- **Tarran:** tar-an

PLACES
- **Solanis:** so-lan-is
- **Alisus:** ae-lis-us
- **Vesitire:** ves-eh-tier
- **Althenia:** al-then-ee-a
- **Pyxtia:** pix-tea-ah
- **Arania:** ah-ran-ee-a
- **Fesaris:** fe-sar-is
- **Astrinus:** as-stry-nus

OTHER
- **Crocotta:** crow-cot-ah
- **Hasseria:** has-er-ee-ah

ACKNOWLEDGMENTS

In the first installment of this trilogy I wrote in this space that one day I would move to a house with a garden for my dogs. We did it. So to you, my reader, thank you for picking up this story and traveling through the stars with me. There's so much about Astraea and her journey to believing in herself that is dear to me. Nyte is also a character I became deeply invested in because of the way he accepted his own path toward healing. I'm so excited to continue their story in the next book. In the meantime, if you're curious about where our gold-eyed tragic villain came from, with all the talk of "his realm," you might be interested in taking a trip to Ungardia by catching up with my other slow burn epic fantasy series, An Heir Comes to Rise.

To my dear friend Lyssa, you've been with me since the very beginning and have remained the biggest believer in me. Forever grateful for you; thank you for putting up with me.

To my agent, Jessica Watterson, I can't thank you enough for being the first to believe in me and my stories for this journey of publication, for championing this one and landing us in amazing publisher hands. I still have "pinch me" moments to remember this is real life and can't wait for a hopeful long future together.

To the rest of the team at Sandra Dijkstra Literacy—Andrea, Nick, Jennifer—thank you for being so prompt and wonderful.

To my editor Erika Tsang, it's been an absolute pleasure working with you on this book. Your support and excitement for this story has been invaluable and such a joy. I can't wait for the next!

To the rest of the team at Bramble, thank you for all the hard work and dedication to this book.

To Areen Ali and the team at Wildfire, thank you for believing in this story as passionately as you do. I'm so thrilled to have found an incredible home with you to bring these books to the UK and Commonwealth.

To Lila Raymond, as well as being a jaw-dropping designer, I value you as a great friend. Thank you for your stunning work on the cover and map yet again, and for being a wonderful human.

To my mum and Sean, thank you for picking up the phone for my every whim. Keep fighting, Mum, you have plenty more golden years to enjoy.

To my dad for buying every book of mine when they come out with no intention to ever read them; you're the real MVP.

To my dogs, Milo, Bonnie, and Minnie. We're going to enjoy this garden for a long time to come.

The story continues with *The Dark is Descending*,
the third and final installment of the epic *Nytefall* trilogy,
by *New York Times*-bestselling author
Chloe C. Peñaranda . . .

*'The blood that binds them,
may become the weapon to end them'*

Reeling from shocking betrayal, the Star Maiden Astraea must
now race against time to break the curse imprisoning her lover,
Nyte. She will have to decide if the hand of darkness, or that
of her enemy, is an alliance that could bring him back.

But with the loss of daylight and the realm on the brink of
ruin, Astraea and her companions must set off on their quests
to retrieve the Maiden's broken key, the only weapon that can
kill the wrathful gods determined to rule the mortal world.

Dragons will fly and their bonds may choose friend or foe.
Gods will face gods, fathers will face sons, and all will face
the end of the world. Because when the blood that binds
them becomes a weapon to end them, two star-crossed lovers
must yield to fate or pay their greatest sacrifice yet.